ISOBELLE

Also by Mary Lide

ANN OF CAMBRAY
GIFTS OF THE QUEEN
A ROYAL QUEST

Mary Lide

WARNER BOOKS

A Warner Communications Company

F
L7145

Warner Books, Inc., 666 Fifth Avenue, New York, NY 10103

W A Warner Communications Company

Printed in the United States of America
First Printing: May, 1988
10 9 8 7 6 5 4 3 2 1

Library of Congress Cataloging-in-Publication Data

Lide, Mary.
  Isobelle.

  I. Title.
PS3562.I344I86   1988   823'.914   87-21539
ISBN 0-446-51268-0

Designed by Giorgetta Bell McRee

Acknowledgments

The Atlas Mountains of North Africa and the Sahara desert have alternately fascinated and repelled Europeans, and the nineteenth century saw a new flurry of curiosity. Among the works of travelers and explorers of that time the following were useful in the writing of *Isobelle*:

R. Caillie, *Travels through Central Africa, Timbuctoo and Across the Great Desert to Morocco, Performed in the Years 1824–1826*; John Drummond Hay, *Western Barbary*, 1844; J. D. Hooker and John Ball, *Morocco and the Great Atlas*, 1878, and Joseph Thompson, *Travels in the Atlas and South Morocco*, 1889. I also found these books of special interest: General M.J.E. Daumas, *The Horses of the Sahara*, first published 1850; James Grey Jackson, *An Account of the Empire of Morocco*, 1968, and Ernest Gellner, *Arabs and Berbers*, 1972.

I should like to take this opportunity to thank my children and my friends for their loving support. My thanks, too, to the people who helped in the typing, especially Frances Eddy and Valerie Harris. And as ever, my gratitude to my friends and agents, Arnold and Elise Goodman, and my editor, Fredda Isaacson, Vice President of Warner Books, whose advice and encouragement have been of enormous help.

ISOBELLE

Prologue

When a storm threatens in the African desert, the sky darkens and its color turns to dull lead. The sun is veiled behind a great dust cloud and the air hums with a low muttering, as the wind mounts and fills the world. That wind strips away layer after layer of sand, like a pumice stone, moving mounds of it like chaff, throwing it up into new peaks, baring all the flotsam and jetsam of centuries, raising to the surface what has been long lost or forgotten and burying newer things as deeply. The next morning's calm reveals treasures that were old when the desert was young: coins, artifacts, pottery shards, even the ruins of old walls and forts. The storm that has shifted the sand has gone, the sun bores down; in a little while one cannot even remember how the landscape looked. And except for these mute, almost pitiful remains, mankind might never have existed here at all.

It was in the aftermath of such a storm, when the Arab boys came out to see what luck offered them, that a small leather bag was dug up. Half buried in the slope of a new sand hill, it lay as if it had been dropped there only hours before. It was not large but of a size to be carried in a pocket or a lady's old-fashioned reticule, nor was it old as the desert counts age, and the things it held within its inner knotted-silk lining were of little value, except in human terms. One of its contents was a locket, mounted in gold, holding the painting of a naked girl. She was Indian, wide mouthed, eyes partially downcast, her hair coiled freely about the nape of her neck, her loins bared in the style of an ancient temple frieze. The painting could have been copied from one of those statues of temple prostitutes except there was a look and feel to the way the mouth half smiled and the eyes gleamed that made her seem real. The little feet were turned invitingly; the long thin arms beckoned; no stone model this, but real flesh and blood. The date of the portrait was impossible to judge, in some ways it resembled a Persian miniature; but the gold filigree of the locket was certainly of European make, Venetian most likely, of the last century.

The second object was stranger still, a notebook, with marbleized paper and faintly ruled lines, the sort of notebook popular a hundred years ago, carefully clasped with a brass lock and key, the key still fitted neatly into place, as was the small brown pencil with which most of the early entries were composed. Inside, its pages were covered with beautifully formed writing in the style of the last century, or to be more precise, the first entries were, each one to a page, although in places there was only a line or two. Beneath them, in growing frequency as the diary progressed, longer passages had been added, presumably at a later date, to elaborate upon, explain, or give the truth to the original simple comment. The first entries were terse, often commonplace, the sort of daily log that travelers keep on a journey, to record events or hold on to reality. But as the story progressed, they came to resemble narratives or chronicles, long and complex. The first entries were clearly written; the rest, the later additions, were composed in quite a different style, crosshatched, written in microscopic letters, across the page and up and down, like a crossword puzzle without blanks or clues. A magnifying glass was needed to read them, the difficulty enhanced by the state of the paper, now dried out to brittleness but at one time having been blurred and stained with salt, sea water perhaps, or perhaps tears. Sometimes it seemed that the shorter the original section the longer and more intricate was the second and gradually, as each page was deciphered, a whole other world was revealed, intense, private, unfolding like some oriental paper flower, to display what its author may have meant to keep hidden, even from herself. The diary then, for such it was, was the property of a young woman of whom all that is known is her first name. To discover who she was and what she became, we have only her own words as our guide. *Rêves ou realité*, dreams or real, who can tell? These are two expressions she uses as she relates this story of adventure and love. It may be we are not meant to distinguish as perhaps she did not. Yet the original entry has a date, September 1870, when she seems to have left England for the first time. And we do know that in the autumn of that year, known for the severity of its storms, several ships were lost at sea along the North African coast, either steaming toward the newly opened Suez Canal or else taking the older, longer route around the Cape. Among those ships was one, brand new, which was called the *New Victoria*, presumably in honor of England's queen who by then had been reigning for thirty-three years. Victoria's husband, Prince Albert, had been dead for nine; the queen had not yet become Empress of India; the Franco-Prussian War was in full swing. Europe was rapidly moving into a period that we might recognize, mechanized, industrialized, modern. The Atlantic coast upon which those ships were wrecked and its hinterland were virtually unknown to the Europeans, except for a handful of French, who had been trying for some forty years to subdue the northeastern fringes of it. Even today that Atlantic coast is considered one of the most desolate places in the world, and its desert and its mountain ranges are still far from travelers' main routes, little frequented except by the tribal inhabitants. Even today there are places where few Europeans have ever gone, and in those high mountains it is rumored there are ruins of deserted forts, built out of the rocks like medieval castles, the brooding castles of Berber warlords who for many years resisted all attempts to bring them to heel. The names, the exploits, the wars of those lords are not always remembered, are lost to us, but within their secret lairs they once ruled as gods.

Two last asides, for what they are worth: One, in the nineteenth century, among English women of a certain type, the fascination for the Middle Eastern world became paramount. Their names are well known, Lady Hester Stanhope being one, and a Lady Isobelle, wife to Sir Richard Burton, the explorer of those parts, first white man to go to Mecca and survive. What fascination took these women so far from home and comforts is not clear, but fascination there was, and it, too, is recorded.

The second point is this: Just as before the eyes of a wanderer in the desert, mirages occur of water, trees, a whole fertile valley shimmering through the dust, so in the mind's eye can images form of themselves until a whole imaginary world rears up, peopled with dreams turned to flesh. They say that heat, monotony, loneliness contribute to this madness, if madness it is to find the means within oneself to slip so easily from a harsh world into a more pleasant one. But it is also known that such hallucinations are granted to holy men, to prophets, to visionaries, who search ever for a Paradise. Such visions also are granted to simple innocents whose needs are few, who want only to love and be loved. Substance is not what it seems, says one of the characters we shall meet; the tangible and intangible are never far apart. It would be charity to believe that what our Isobelle wrote was in the end reality for her.

CHAPTER 1

Entry One · September, Late, 1870

TODAY I write to record the loss of the New Victoria, sailing from England to the East. It was wrecked and abandoned upon a sandbar after a storm, but exactly where or how I cannot say. I alone am here, apparently the only survivor, although it may well be others have escaped somehow. This has been the saddest day of my life.

I wrote, as if putting down visible words would make the unbearable somehow less. What I wanted to do was shout my name, "Isobelle, Isobelle," to the vacant skies, the empty sand, the pitiless sea. "Here I am," I wanted to cry, and scream, and sometimes in those first lonely, terrifying hours I did, if only to make some sound to break the stillness and the emptiness. "Do not abandon me, find me, save me," until my throat ached and my voice cracked. There was no one to hear, nothing east or west, north or south, save sand and sun and those curling waves washing over the wreckage of the ship until only its masts showed. No one, nothing but death. If I wrote those words with any thought (if I were able to think at all in a state of shock so complete as to leave me numb), it was from a deep, primitive instinct to leave some mark somehow, somewhere so that I should not be lost and forgotten too. And when I tore off a page and wrote the date and fixed it to a rough cross fashioned from sticks, the message was meant to serve us all as a kind of epitaph, until the wind took the paper and blew it away.

I sat hunched under the flimsy shelter I had made, shaded by it from the sun, crouched, my head in my lap, hands covering my face, afraid to look up. That vast emptiness, that great stretch of sand terrified me as a starry sky sometimes does, myriads of stars, nothing between, nothing beyond. Sometimes I think I almost dreamt, convincing myself that in a moment I would awake to the sound of my dead mother's voice and her pleasant laugh. I could hear her and the woodland doves in the orchard and the cows coming through the manor fields toward the barn. One look around me, one look down at my torn and bedraggled skirts, my bruised and bleeding hands, immediately gave that illusion the lie. Apart from my crouching self, there was still nothing, no one, only heat and flies and all the debris of a shipwreck, scattered along the littoral, tossed about like children's blocks. I had not the energy to brush the insects away. Yet, as my clothes dried upon my back, and the cuts stiffened and burned, as I jerked awake from those seconds of sleep, already, despite myself, the instinct for survival was at work, the instinct Darwin has written about. I was not destined to die. *You are a survivor, Isobelle,* my friend, Colonel Edwards, had said (when was that, three days ago?) just before the storm struck. Had it lasted only three days, the storm that began with the wind coming up suddenly, "out of the calm," as the Colonel had said, in a spume of foam, driving the waves before it like a tidal bore? I might have been in another world, another life, a dream world, when I saw that foam and heard the officer on deck bellow his warning to the bridge. Certainly it seemed more than three days that we were tossed like driftwood, rudderless, the boiler room flooded, the fires out, driven southward by the powerful winds. The passengers kept to their rooms, then to their beds, the corridors so on slant, the ship so tossed that even walking below deck was dangerous, impossible without hanging on to the guiding lines. I do not remember if there was food; certainly the crew had little time to prepare it; even the stewards in their white jackets, who used to bow and smile, were red-eyed with fatigue, too weary to pretend that soon all would be well when it was already obvious that the ship remained afloat only by a miracle, this new and beautiful ship with its painted rooms, its elaborate engines, its brass rails. Simple acts such as lying down required effort; the ship rolled as if it were

being racked apart. Every timber seemed to stretch and groan; glass
smashed, doors swung off their hinges; and the trunks, which were
stuffed with my mourning clothes, broke from their fastenings and
tipped and crashed from side to side. I remember the noise of the
propellor, the thrash it made as it struck at air, and then its deep and
dreadful suck and roar as it was forced under the waves again. I
remember, too, my cousin Captain Lawson, calling through the open
door. He did not come in on this occasion, merely shouted to me,
his face stripped of its foppish grin and his pale eyes prominent with
fright. I had not the strength to answer him. Once in a lull I staggered into the corridor and, bracing myself against the door frame,
watched the sailors pass, grim and intent. They seemed like shadows,
about business of their own; worse than seeing no one. The walls
had buckled and heaved, and the effect of standing made me sick.
Then came one last grinding, splintering crash that tossed me headlong into a void.

That I also remember, nothing more.

When I regained consciousness, I was lying where I had been
thrown on the floor or the ceiling; I could not tell, tipped as I was at
such a peculiar slant. I could not move, arms, legs, hands numb and
hopelessly entangled in my skirts; my head was a blur of pain. But
after a while when sight cleared and I realized I was not really par-
alyzed, I discovered I was pinned beneath a steamer trunk, and the
faint light creeping through the steel hatch of what must be the port-
hole showed that outside day had come. Apart from my frightened
panting as I tried to catch my breath, there was no sound; and the
tossing and heaving of the storm was done except at intervals when
the ship gave a great shudder like a tormented beast, and a trickle of
sea water came curling along my spine, seeping under the door sill.
I did panic then, as I struggled to free myself, and for the first time
the silence began to appear, total and ominous, as no one answered,
no one came, and the cabin door continued to swing to and fro.

Fear gave me strength. I could feel the life come back into my
limbs and gradually I was able to wrench myself free. I had been
lying dressed most of the while, beside me, my mother's little reticule. I had packed it as we had been advised to do at the start of the
storm, with items, I fear, more socially proper than useful. Now I
caught it up and struggled across to the cabin door. Outside, the
corridor was aslant as well, the paneling broken and ripped as if by

a battering ram. The Turkey carpeting of which the ship owners had been so proud was already waterlogged, sodden as a moorland bog, its bright colors faded and blurred. Barefoot, my head still aching fit to blind, my legs trembling as if I had run a mile, I crawled up through the rubbish that had been tossed everywhere: abandoned boxes, torn clothes, even a spilled jewelry case, all the evidence of a sudden exodus. The first stairwell was blocked by a wooden hatch, forcing me to crawl on forward, or up; I was not sure at this point which was front, which back, or even if up and down were in the right place. I beat a second, greater panic back, one that makes me shiver still, that although free of my cabin I might yet be trapped below with every exit blocked. And all this while I saw no one, heard no one, felt only that deep shuddering in the depths of the ship.

The engines were dead, that was certain; and when at last I dragged up the last staircase (the one the crew used and which I, too, had frequented to gain private access to the decks), the open air, the sunlight struck me as painful, almost naked and raw. The decks themselves were in a greater state of confusion than the cabins below: a jumble of masts and shrouds, sagging bars and broken railings, timber, steel, rolled together like tangled wool. The ship lay, like a half-submerged whale, broadside across the sandbank that had breached its keel, and with each incoming wave, on the seaward side, the spray spumed over its stern, shifting it, turning it, pounding it as if it were made of matchwood. The crew, the passengers, my cousins, Captain Lawson and his righteous wife, who since my mother's death were made my unwilling guardians, the hard-drinking officers, the giddy ladies, the squalling children, all, all had disappeared. Only a mesh of ropes over the side was left, and the swinging davits, to show that the lifeboats had gone, washed overboard or lowered in haste. The ship lay abandoned and I with it. No one remained. I was alone. Except for Colonel Edwards.

Entry Two

I WISH TO make record here for everyone to read, that of all the people on this ship, only Colonel Edwards was my friend. He was a man I could have loved and who I think loved me. I was a comfort to him, and he saved me.

Colonel Edwards and I had met at the very start of the voyage. I never knew him by any other name; I never addressed him by any other, but he called me Isobelle. "Look over the side, Isobelle," he used to say, "there are porpoises following us today." "Look at the sky, Isobelle, and tell me what the weather will be." All those things he knew in his kindness would interest me. I had heard tales of him of course, before we left. "Fancy!" My cousin's wife had tapped the passenger list with her pointed nails and her eyebrows drew up in the frown that I had come to dread. "Read that. I thought he had disappeared years ago. You should complain. The ship's company should never have let him on board."

My cousin, a mere captain, Captain Percival Lawson of the Queen's Guards, had read the list as he was bid, with a frown of his own, followed by that sheepish grin he always wore when she harangued him. "Heard he was ill," he admitted, "they say, dying. That is why he is going back," he told her, tugging at the stiff collar of his shirt in the way he had. She retrieved the paper, snatched it, creasing the fold with determined hands. "Men like that never give up," she cried, "drummed out of his regiment. You'd think shame would have kept him low. And men like you aid and abet." She gave the children, who were whining around her knees, an impatient push. "Go with Isobelle," she told them, dismissing us, the conversation not fitting for younger ears. But I heard her say before we were out of earshot, "That girl's nothing but a country mouse. Even the children laugh at her. You should have left her to her rustic ways, not tried to make her useful. After all, that's why . . ." She did not quite dare say "that's why we brought her, to look after them." But she did say, "I warn you, Percival, I won't acknowledge that Colonel Edwards. Nor will any decent English person on this ship."

They talked of him, though, all of them, the ladies behind their hands and the other officers more openly. He seemed oblivious either to blame or praise, conversed with no one, I think, until one day he spoke to me.

I had come on deck early, before dawn, to lean against the rail and watch the day start over the sea. The decks were dripping wet where the bare-legged native boys had scrubbed them clean and on the railings moisture had condensed in great drops. It was already warm although the sun was not yet up. Soon it would glare down on us from a sky such as England had never seen, turning my little cabin into an oven (no "port side out, starboard home" for me, no POSH room to get the benefit of the afternoon shade). It would dazzle us, drenching us with sweat.

Each day since our departure I had come on deck at the same hour, glad for the respite from my sickly charges, those children my cousins thought I could not control, glad of a few moments peace. The ship, the pride of her line, spanking new from stern to prow, breasted the waves blithe as a bird, smoke from her new funnels streaming like a banner in the wind. I leaned on the rail and poked with my foot through the bars, so that the thick serge of my black dress, hung with crepe and already sticky with heat, surged out like a sail. I had not bothered to put my bonnet on but let the breeze lift through my hair, that unfashionable gold-brown hair my cousin's wife considered such a fright. Indeed there was not much about me that she liked. I poked with my toe again, perplexed, and more than a little alarmed, uncertain. It was not my cousin's wife who bothered me this time, nor her spoiled, cross children, but my cousin himself. Last night he had tapped at my door. Ready for bed, without even a wrapper on, I had foolishly opened the door, thinking it was one of the children. He had stood swaying in the doorway then moved into the cabin as if searching for something in the dim light. "Early to sleep, my dear," at last he had said, closing the door behind him, "the young officers were asking for you. They'll be desolate without your company." He had run his hand around his collar as if tugging at it to give him breath. He was wearing his regimentals this time, blue and gold, and I noticed how he kept patting himself under the stiff gold collar, down the frogged tight tunic, as if making sure all was buttoned and in place. I guessed at once this was an excuse. The young officers on board had little time for me, and if they had sent such a message they must have been drunk. However, the way it was delivered was certainly his. "You know," he continued in the special voice he kept for talking to his children and dogs, "if you need anything you have only to ask. I, we, are here to comfort you."

I could smell the whiskey on his breath as he lurched, or pretended to lurch, with the movement of the ship, spreading out his stubby fingers against the wall. His hand with its little ring of gold had trapped me too; his boots were now firmly planted on my nightgown; the ship had but to roll again, or he to pretend that it had rolled, and his knee would strike against my own, or at a higher, more tender place, of which the flimsy lace must have already given him a good view. His face was now close to my own as he tried a smile. "Can't be in mourning forever you know, and you are too pretty a little thing to mope." Now I may be young and innocent, a country mouse unused to city ways, but I know right from wrong. Before he could move, I did, ducking under his arm and getting behind him to open the door. "You are most kind, cousin," I had said, in my sweetest voice, "but I am used to caring for myself." Yet the incident now both vexed and worried me. He was my guardian, my only relative; I had looked to him to be an ally, a buffer between me and his wife since my mother's death had left me homeless, without friends, and certainly penniless. Suppose his wife should guess? She had taken me in because she hoped to use me on this long voyage to India. But I was expendable. She would be glad of an excuse to be rid of responsibility for me. And what if her husband were angered, or tried again? To whom could I turn if not to them? I was not suited for anything much except to be a country lady as my mother had been, to live a country life, marry, perhaps have children of my own. Now fate had cheated me and taken all those hopes away. I kicked at my skirts almost angrily, as if I were hacking at my cousin's shins. A sudden dry cough made me spin round, the sort of cough one makes to draw attention to oneself, and I looked at the man who was watching me.

I had seen Colonel Edwards before, although he kept to himself. He was not tall but thin, painfully thin, walking slowly with a cane, always to the same place, high up on this forward deck. His shoulders were set square, and his shock of gray-white hair and his long cavalry mustache, both in striking contrast to his sunburnt face, marked him clearly as a military man. He was reclining now in a chair, wrapped in a blanket despite the heat, a small black cigar between his lips. Perhaps he had spent the night on deck (and afterward I came to believe he did) but now he was observing me with a half smile on his face.

"That's better," he said, leaning back, coughing slightly; and drawing out his hand from beneath the blanket, he beckoned to me to approach.

I knew of course I should not. I should have turned aside, with a toss of my head and my lips pursed, so; that is what Mrs. Lawson would have done, pretending not to see him at all, yet by her walk, the swish of her new-bustled skirt, letting him know that she had, the proper way for a lady to "cut" a man she despised. But his commanding gesture drew me like a moth to a candle flame. Slowly, almost reluctantly, I left the railing and approached, not raising my eyes but always conscious of his gaze.

"That's better," he repeated. "I thought you were practicing how to kick a man overboard. Which one of the subalterns has been teasing you?"

I almost said, "Not a subaltern at all, rather, a captain," but bit back the words.

"Well, well," he said, coughing again and wiping his mouth slowly with a fresh handkerchief. "Well, well, the heat has got her tongue, but at least she still knows how to blush. I have been watching you, miss. There's a sensible soul, I told myself, come up on deck to see the dawn. Instead I find she's pining for company."

"No," I said, "I don't much like any of them." And at this indiscretion I blushed again.

He gave a sort of snort, half laugh, half cough. "That's honest," he said. "And you look better today."

"Better?" I asked.

"Less moping," he said, "angry. Fighting back. Besides"—he cocked his head to one side—"besides, I like you more without that bonnet on. It makes you look like a little old hen."

I had to laugh myself, although again I bit my lip. I had never met a man, old or young, who spoke so plainly.

But yet I insisted, anxious to make myself clear, "It's just, at home, I always used to get up with the sun. I'm not here to look for anyone."

"I'm glad to hear it," he said wryly, "although surprised. They call this 'the marriage run,' all the young girls angling for a husband and the young men trying to avoid becoming one." At my third blush in as many minutes, he said, suddenly hard, "Well, don't look for happiness in Eastern lands. If you want an English husband, and an English home and English children, stay in England where you belong. Take my advice and jump ship at the first port. You're not governess to those sour-faced brats?"

"No," I told him, "just a poor relative, filling in."

" 'A poor relative,' " he repeated solemnly, "that's worse. Not a fellow will dare look at you when he hears that. Men like a little inheritance to line their pockets, and if you've none, you're likely to get hurt, or forgotten when the voyage's done. Some women plan their life from the start and arrange matters to benefit themselves, but I don't see you doing that. You're too young and green." Then he leaned back and closed his eyes as if he had said his piece and was dismissing me.

I was suddenly furious. Since my dear Mama had died, nothing had gone right for me; there were too many people trying to tell me what to do, too many criticisms beginning to wear my patience thin. Besides, this arrogant man's scarcely veiled contempt flicked on some nerve.

"As for being young," I cried, blunt in turn, "age doesn't always make men wise. You must have been young once. And green. What took *you* from England in the first place?"

His eyes jerked open, looking at me almost startled, as if a kitten had snarled. He began to smile, the sort of smile I like, creeping from the corners out. I had not realized before how blue his eyes were, like pieces of sky. "By God," he said, "she does have a temper. Well, miss, you have made your point. Aye, I was young once, years before you were born, young enough to have survived the Indian Mutiny, and not many white men can say that. And death it was that brought me there, as it brings me back. And as I think it now has brought you." He nodded to my mourning clothes. "In my case, a father's death which gave an older brother rank and wealth and left me stranded, with not much else to do."

"There you are then," I argued again, greatly daring, "so it was with me. My mother's death. And nothing afterward." And saying it aloud suddenly made it seem both real and yet not so bad as I had thought.

That then was how we met. I found myself speaking to him that first time more openly of my grief, my fears, my distress, all my safe and happy childhood lost within a week, and he let me talk, words pouring out all the more eagerly because they had been so long pent up. I even told him of my cousin's advance but he laughed at me, pointing out the wife was too strict to ever let the husband get out of hand. And I told him what was said and done, all the talk of the ship, until I found I had also poured out all my distrust of the new life my cousins planned for me, in a fashionable India where there would be small place for me, perhaps none. The voyage over, what would prevent my cousin's wife supplanting me with a real servant at far less cost? But after that first day, mainly I listened.

We met each morning early, when there was small chance of us being seen, really none at all, as most of the passengers slept late. But I suppose, in time, we might have been discovered, and that gave a tinge of excitement that I admit I enjoyed. We never met by agreement, always as if it were by chance and never at any other time, although I sometimes saw the blue curl of smoke from his cheroot and knew he was in his private place. It was a strange relationship, I admit, doomed to end, with a man who, as he himself once pointed out, was old enough to have fathered me, and who in any case, as I could see for myself, was ill, perceptibly weakening, perhaps already counting the days to death. He never made a secret of the illness that wasted him, but having spoken of it passed on to other things that he thought important. And it was strange, too, that the first man I ever came to know and like was one the fashionable world rejected, as if that was a forecast of what was to come. And strange, too, I suppose, for him to find pleasure in my naïve company, as I believe he did. It was not that I could give him anything in return, not even the excuse of an audience, for he was neither vain nor selfish and did not need me for sustenance. We never touched, except one time; there was nothing of the body left for him to give, but of the will and spirit he gave generously, and I think he came to trust me as I trusted him.

I learned to listen then in those morning hours, perched at his feet like one of those young officers or a disciple listening to a teacher speak. I remember every word he said, although much of it was new to me, unsuited no doubt to a young girl's ears, opening up a way of life I would never have known had I remained at home. I suppose if the ladies on that ship had guessed at our conversations they would have been scandalized, seeing even in his memories things seductive, lewd. Well, words *can* seduce, and like a second Desdemona I drank in avidly what he said. But he told me of a world that was already past, gone, never to return, in which he had lived and been accepted. He told me stories of his soldier days, along the North West Frontier, by turns rough, cruel, and beautiful, when he had fought against the most cunning and brave men alive; he told me everything except his own personal life; that was left to the ladies of the ship, who hated him, not because he had lived like a man of the East but because he had married an Eastern woman and had had by her a child. And he spoke often of that Mutiny that had destroyed the old ways and bond, the blood and slaughter of the mutineers, the cruelty of the English in return. He did not tell me how his wife and child had died, killed by the British in revenge; my cousin's wife made that her task. Instead he spoke of men he had known, and places and friends. He gave me a hint, a vision, of a wider and more generous life, colorful, vibrant; and if he knew, as perhaps he did, that what he said would leave its mark on me, he may have given that to me as a gift, as his last will and testament. Or it may be I imagine this, and simply, knowing I had recently been bereaved, he found my familiarity with death comforting, as a parent may be comforted by a child.

And on the last day he had foretold the storm. He had the ability I think of presentiment, given sometimes to the very young and old, who live close to the edge of things, and often found among wise men of the East, who spend their lives searching for it. He had begun to talk of the desert that was unfolding on our left, just out of sight over the horizon, thirteen million square miles of it, changing and growing every year. He had waved his hand in its direction, south-east of us. "A lonely land," he had said, "where only the strong survive; vicious, cruel, yet having its own beauty if you hunt for it. Learn to survive, Isobelle. That does not mean taking the world and twisting it to your own ends. The tangible and intangible are never far apart. Beneath the outward and the obvious are layers of other realities, like dreams themselves. But tomorrow that desert will send us a storm. I can hear it already, singing through the sand. Look there." He had jerked with his cigar toward the layers of cloud through which the sun was just beginning to glare, like a red shuttered eye. "And there." He nodded upward to the funnel where today the smoke seemed to trail down in a cloud of limp soot. "No wind yet," he had said, "but it will come. We may not meet for a while, Isobelle, al-though if God so wills it we shall." He had smiled at me and for the first time I saw what he must have been when he was young. "I think," he said, "you will not forget me." I had smiled back and promised him, with all of youth's exuberance, that I would be there for him the next day, in the usual place. I should have known I tempted fate. For when I crawled on deck amid the wreckage of that storm, he was still there. And although he should have been dead he was still alive.

Of course he could not have remained on deck all this while, and yet, for one heart-stopping moment I thought he had, and he was lying there waiting for me. I expected to see the lazy coil of smoke, his thin hand's gesture, his blue gaze. But he did not move or speak, his face crumpled to gray, his lips stained too bright a red. I tried to run to him across the deck but the spray, the slippery wet, threw me off balance so I slid and fell and had to crawl again, pulling myself along however I could. And when I reached him I saw he, too, was caught, not as I had been by a mere trunk, but by a great beam that had cracked off somewhere overhead. Yet, such was my relief on finding him, the massive wooden stanchion seemed to me as unsubstantial as a twig or branch, and I pulled at it as if it would snap in two at a touch. And when I encountered its harsh immobility, I think I willed that it should move, that he should move and speak to me.

I tugged and ripped until my nails bled; I tried even to pry the wood away, finding strength I think that even a man would have marveled at, although the iron lever would have been too heavy to lift above my shoulder in normal times. And gradually like a drum-beat I began to recognize that all these efforts were in vain. I could not move the beam, I could not free him, I could not reach him. Yet, when at last realizing that, I cried out to him, he heard.

Somewhere he, too, found the will to open his eyes and speak. They were colorless, only a gray film left, and his voice was a husk of a whisper; but he summoned it up to order me. "Land," he panted, "food and water, go." And there was that harshness to his tone, a soldier's last command, that obediently I left him and scrambled toward the other side. And there stretched the shore, close, so close that had I been at home I might have swum to it, a pale, calm blue, like a lagoon, trapped behind the sandbar. That barrier of sand that had caused the wreck was now to offer me the means of escape.

I crawled back to where he lay, my mind suddenly clear to possibility. There was food; I could see crates and water casks, left behind or jettisoned because of haste, but haste would be needed for us too. Already I had glimpsed the first long ripple of a current surging round the edge of the ship. But I would not leave him as it appeared our companions had. I tried to get my hands beneath his shoulders, thin and fleshless as a ghost, and lay there to shield him from the spray. I do not know how long I stayed like that, clinging to him and trying to impart warmth to him, but at the end his hand moved once, slowly, toward the pocket of his coat. I felt in it for him and tried to press what was there into his palm, a small gold locket wrapped in silk. He seemed to recognize the feel of it, but left it in my grasp, his hand in mine against my breast. I do not think he knew any longer who he was or where, or who I was. I cannot say he spoke, but it seemed to me there were words, broken words, in a language I did not know and a smile that was for someone else. But to his last request, in English, I answered yes, kissing his damp cold cheeks, unfastening the bodice of my gown so that his face was against my warm and naked skin, trying to pour my youth and warmth into him, until after a long while I knew I could never give him warmth again. But he died content I believe, my friend, who had been seeking death for many years. I arranged my shawl about him; I said what prayers I could; I stayed with him until his gallant soul was gone. And when I came back, for I think I went some of the way with him, I realized that if I were not to die there, too, I must leave at once. As it was I slid over the ship's side into a deep and running sea and as the breakers began to roll the ship apart, rode with them, surrounded by a little flotilla of crates and casks across the widening lagoon.

So that is how I came to be lying on this hostile shore, alone, far from help, surrounded by a litter of shipwreck, with the sea creaming up now toward my feet. I cannot further mourn my friend, whose face in death was peaceful at last. Nor shall I forget the first man I embraced, already dead and my first love doomed, before it began. And when at last I fell asleep I dreamed of him, walking across a great plain, toward some woman who was waiting for him.

Entry Three

DETERMINED TO look for help, leaving the shelter I had built, I traveled inland, hoping to find some desert caravan.

In the morning when I awoke, stiff, aching in every bone, but clear-headed enough to take stock, I could admit that there was in all probability no hope of my being found. Even if the other passengers had survived, they must have thought me dead, and there would be no search party sent out by them. But, and this was the only "but" I could cling to, if no passengers were found, and the ship entirely disappeared, then perhaps some search might be forthcoming, either by sea or by land; and I should concentrate on that. So I worked away at little tasks, starting with simple things first so that the immensity of the whole would not overwhelm, and in this I think I was correct. And I also will admit that had I not been brought up in old-fashioned Georgian style, a country miss, used to farms and farming life, I might not even have survived the first few hours. All those traits of mine that my cousin had scorned: my broad hands, more used to tying stakes and pulling weeds than stitching samplers or arranging flowers, my sturdy feet (although no lady had feet or legs in those days), my good country walk, which had taken me for miles across the moors, and, last but not least, my common sense, which soon told me that if I did not rely upon myself there would be no one to rely upon—all these characteristics now helped me. I could not change my lack of years nor my innocence (which always looked for the best in everyone) nor my total inexperience of life, yet to counterbalance those I had youth's optimism, which can count almost as much. And so it was, remembering how the village boys used to build, I propped together a jumble of a hut, high up on the beach out of shelter of the wind. It concealed me from that long and raking littoral that stretched into infinity through a heat haze. And to the hut I rolled the water casks, and what food I could find. I felt myself to be a modern-day Crusoe in women's skirts. And I looped these up, thanking my stubbornness that mine was not one of the newer dresses with their fashionable bustles at the back that my cousin and her friends favored. Crinolines can be removed, and I had done that from the start. Yet although I meant to keep cheerful, singing to myself, there were times when I let myself sink beneath this crushing burden of solitude, for all that I tried to comfort myself with the thought that miracles were not achieved without some pain. If fate had kept me alive thus far, perhaps it would continue to do so. And I will say now I also believe that fate does not idly offer coincidence. If the Colonel and I had been left because we were both thought dead, perhaps his death was in itself an offering for my life. So I argued at least, and taking fresh courage in that belief, determined that, come the next day, I should clamber to the top of the sand dunes that edged the beach, there to spy out some track or trail or at least find out where I was (not knowing then of course, and happy in that ignorance, that a thousand miles of emptiness stretched ahead, a desert such as my friend had talked about, scoured by the wind, bare, inhabited by scorpions and snakes). And if, as the quick twilight came and the dark fell, hiding all but the incoming waves with their sullen roar, if then I lay shivering, prone to all the miseries I have described, may God have pity on all lost souls, and let me not remember those black hours.

I had made a simple innocent plan, not poorly conceived only impossible, to climb the nearest sand dunes, keeping the sea always in my view, to scout out the landward side. Taking two canvas water bags, which I had filled, and stuffing my diary in my inner pocket, I left at daybreak to avoid the worst of the heat. At the last moment, for company, I took the locket of the Indian girl. I had not realized I had brought her with me when I had left the wreck and regretted that I had not left her with the man who had cherished her, but afterward I thought perhaps it better so. He had no need of her and I did. For when I had opened the case I had sat and looked at her for a long while until her very nakedness became comforting, warm flesh to flesh, and her smile seemed to welcome me. I had begun to like the downward cast of her delicate eyelids, almost shy, if shyness could be found in such a pose, and the way her little bangled feet were planted firmly, slightly aslant, so that the sex was clearly visible. I had never looked at a naked body so openly, certainly not my own, and I kept hers close to me, strung round my neck as if a reflection of myself. And perhaps that was why she remained with me, a gift from her lover to me, that sometime I should learn what she had learned, that sometime I should know both her shyness and boldness.

I still wore my black dress, tight bodiced, hemmed with frills, black skirts frothing out into a lace of petticoats. I would not have needed to know how to swim; in truth those skirts bore me up like a bladder filled with air and in truth I clung to them as the last remnants of a real world, although I had no shoes or hat, and my hair had long lost its mandatory ringlets, and reverted to its own wild curls. Taking careful note of the direction of the sun and shore, carrying sticks with which I planned to mark my route, I began to climb, a Victorian miss on a Sunday walk. But the climb was not as easy as I had thought, although I was used to sand and rocks. I slid back as often as I advanced and the sand was coarse and gritty to my naked feet and already hot. By noontide, walking would be unbearable. The coolness of the night had gone, and at the first hill crest I stopped and tore another flounce from my underskirts to bind in strips about my soles. Even from that vantage point the way down to the little hut of sticks looked long and the sea and beach immense. But I turned my back and resolutely went on. And when I reached the top of the next ridge of dunes it seemed another ridge had slid between, followed by a third and fourth, each one veering at a slight angle from the last, each one divided from the next with a deep ravine down which I had to grope. In a very short while I had no idea in which direction I went, or worse, whence I had come, the sun already fixed burning in its midday place, the roar of the sea already dulled. The only clue then was the row of little stakes, and they were scarcely visible against the glare. Behind me, the line of my skirts left a pattern as if a snake had slithered sideways, but even as I watched the dry sand shifted and covered the footsteps where I stood. Soon there would be nothing of me left, not even tracks, yet resolutely I went on, hauling myself up along another ridge.

I do not really imagine how I thought I would see anything. But obstinacy can be as strong as courage and I could be obstinate. Somewhere I was sure there must be higher ground from which I could survey the route to the sea, and which would give a view inland. Perhaps at the back of my mind I was remembering a sandy beach I had known as a child where, starting from the rough dune grass, I had once followed a path to a fishing village nearby. So on I walked, into the midday heat, not knowing or not admitting that I was lost, sometimes sinking in the sand up to my knees, sometimes tripping over a dead root into a hidden hole, pausing when there was any hint of shade in the overhangs of the sand cliffs. I think determination must have deadened fear; certainly some sense of inevitability kept me going on as if I knew there could be no turning back, until at last, beyond exhaustion, I must have fallen and lain where I fell. The coolness of the setting sun revived me I suppose, and I suppose also I had collapsed upon the shadow-side of a hill else my story would have ended here. I was lying with my skirts pulled over my head in some instinctive gesture of protection and I had the distinct sensation of hearing running water close by. I struggled up, feeling for the water bags. They were still stoppered tight and I drank and drank, trying to slake the dryness from my throat which felt as if it were as cracked and peeling as my lips. But still the sound persisted, not coming closer, not yet receding, merely constant, a soft sifting sound that water makes running through sand.

I told myself at first that the noise was in my mind, the sort of noise exhaustion brings; then that it was the sea; perhaps the tide had swept inland, although I knew that impossible. But if I could hear the sea then I must be able to find it, before the sun set (not knowing then how fast desert dark came, not yet aware of the great peril I was in, or rather, although knowing it, like bearing pain or wounds, not admitting it so that the body can withstand the shock). But that slushing sound could not be denied, and in one last hope that I was near some sort of well I pulled myself up by strands of coarse grass to the top of the cliff.

Fate was kind again. A few moments more I should have been too late; a few moments earlier, and I would have been too soon, they and I as lost to each other as ships that cross each other's wake. I was standing on the crest of one sand dune that sloped down sharply into a deep divide. Upon the opposite crest, facing me, a line of figures shuffled along, filtering against the darkening sky. Too overwhelmed for joy or fear I began to shout, wave, tried to run, terrified they would pass me by, whatever men or beasts they were, terrified that they were a mirage of my own despair. The slithering of the camels' feet came to a halt. Across the valley I felt the men who rode them stare at me, silhouetted in equal amaze. And suddenly, like a trickle of the cold sea, a claw of fear came along my spine. This was different from fear of abstract things; this was real and present, so sudden that if death had offered an alternative I might willingly have embraced it. A primeval terror overwhelmed me and kept me rooted there, immobile, while every instinct screamed at me to hide. By the time I had forced my legs to move, it was too late. Already the camel drivers, with hoarse cries, were urging their beasts down the slope at a quick trot. Behind them the camel boys were racing fast, shouting with glee as they hopped along. It was too late to run, and nowhere to run to, so I waited for them. My limbs scarcely able to bear me up, I sat down, spread my skirts in a half-circle, and tucked my bare legs and feet underneath.

Entry Four

I STRUCK A bargain with the leader of the caravan and so went with them through the desert.

They came upon me in a rush, circling down the gully and around the side, wary I suppose or mystified, shouting to each other as they went, harsh guttural cries that resembled no language I had ever heard. A woman, white woman at that, sitting openly, must have seemed a trap, a decoy, to lead them into some villainy, and they unswung their rifles and cocked them, holding them by the barrel between forefinger and thumb, casually. Presently, assured that there was no ambushing force, no hidden troop, they came on again, circling closer now until one man, more venturesome, or more curious, rode up the slope. He was sitting on his camel's back, high in the air, with his bare feet planted on either side of its neck as he forced it to confront me. That tall creature, with its wagging neck, its yellow molars, green saliva frothing at the mouth, resembled some prehistoric beast and I must have screamed as I tried to push it away, making it snap its teeth at me. That scream gave them courage. The man began to laugh, a high-pitched laugh without mirth, and he shouted to his companions to follow him. Up they came, swiftly now, all cloaked, some black-turbaned, with the wide ends of scarfs tied about their mouths so that only their eyes showed, some in baggy trousers and striped shirts, all leaning forward on their saddles, all pointing and jibbering.

The man nearest me was small and dark with a shifty look about the eyes, bearded and long haired, looking and smelling like a goat, but I took him for a leader of some sort; and when I could control my voice and they had pointed long enough, I began to speak. I needed help, water, food, escort to a village or town, search parties for my shipwrecked friends. I listened to my own voice, almost surprised, as if it were a child's, echoing in an empty room. They paid no attention at all to what I said (which was not unexpected, since I addressed them in my own language not theirs) but continued to chatter among themselves as unconcerned as if they were bargaining at a fair. I had the strong impression that it was my fate they discussed; there was some altercation, some dispute, between the leader and the rest. I let them argue, sitting back as if I were not there at all, until one of the camel boys, greatly daring, slithered behind my back, and with his scrawny hand tugged at my skirt.

I beat him off as one would a fly but he or another came again, each one approaching closer than the last. Presently I saw their sharp knives glinting, half hidden, not held to stab or injure but to flick and cut so that within a short while the back of my dress, the sleeves, the demure white cuffs, were in shreds, ready to fall apart if I made a sudden move. Which I did, as did the men, whose arguments among themselves had not been so intense that they had not been watching out of the corner of their eyes. Now they dismounted eagerly, moving among the boys with blows and kicks, scattering them out of the way, advancing upon me in a group. I tried to scramble farther back, but I was already as close to the cliff wall as I could go and as I shifted the scraps of dress fell upon the sand in a shower of black until little remained except the bodice fastened with its tassels of jet and the under-petticoats.

The sight of my white linen and white legs excited them although I tried to pull the torn hem over my knees and knelt to shield myself. The boys were giggling now among themselves, darting in and out again like gadflies, one in particular goading me with the stick he limped upon, glad to find someone lower than himself to bait, his blind eye winking with the effort he made to peer under my skirts. But he kept a wary watch on the men all the while, and seeing them crowd up, backed off, not too far, close enough to witness what might happen next.

The leader, or so I name him, if he were such, was more interested in my hair and twined it round his fingers into curls, stroking it as one might stroke a dog, making me cry out as he pulled and tugged. As I cringed away he began to pull the harder, his stubby fingers reminding me of my cousin's hand. Frantically I tried to think what I could bribe him with, money, jewels. I had none, and it was clear to me what he wanted he would take. He was still holding his gun along the barrel but now he dropped it and with his free hand began to fumble beneath his robes, touching himself. I had never seen a man's nakedness and that goatlike protuberance emerging from a hairiness almost made me faint. He stood before me for a moment, legs apart, forcing my head back. Bent like a bow I thought I was about to vomit, the more so that he pressed himself upon me, grinning all the while. My fingers scrabbled in the sand, trying to find some leverage, and tightened convulsively upon the rifle stock. Before I could consider or he could push himself upon me again I seized the gun and thrust up with all my force between his legs.

He gave a strangled grunt much as a gelded bullock makes and let go, rolling on the ground. My fingers tightened almost of their own accord about the trigger and I held the barrel steady with my other hand, the sweat dripping down my cheeks and breasts. My eyes were watering, my breath came in great laboring gasps, yet surprisingly my hand did not shake.

"Now," I said, "behave properly."

He lay there groaning, hugging himself, whilst his companions jumped back, muttering. Clearly they could have as easily shot me long before I could have blown his head off, but as they did not do so at once, I had a chance to think. Never taking my eyes from them or from the moaning figure on the ground I tugged with one hand at the locket chain and threw it as far as I could, so that it lay glittering in the sand. "There is more where that comes from," I told them. "I will make it worth your while." I knew of course they did not understand, but sometimes gestures can speak as plain as words, and it was clear they were puzzled by me, uncertain what I might do next. No one dared touch the locket for a while but hovered indecisively between me and it, I still clinging resolutely to the gun, my would-be seducer still grunting and writhing on the sand, the other men watching me as if I were a snake.

At last one of the younger men spoke to me directly, the first attempt, at least on their part, to communicate. He talked in a mixture that was hard to place but eventually I made out some words of French.

"What would you of us?" He seemed to ask, "lady, what would you have us do? We are poor travelers, not wanting to do you harm." Or at least this is what I thought he said, it being to my mind more important that he said something to turn his thoughts from murder or rape.

"Help," I repeated now in French, "gold for help. My friends will reward you well."

My French is primitive but then so was his. And the word for gold was certainly familiar. Gingerly then, step by step, he advanced toward the locket, picking it up and turning it round and about before putting it between his strong white teeth. He, too, smelt like a goat and his face was disfigured with pockmarks, but at least he seemed to have more sense than the first man. And as he held the locket he must have released the clasp for he suddenly started, almost dropping it again, and invoking all his gods to protect him from some magical trick.

He examined it for a long while, dividing his attention between it and me, gesturing to the other men to come up, while their former leader, still holding himself, had no breath left to prevent them. I watched them almost calmly myself. I was aware that my future hung in the balance and that I could do little to change the outcome, except that I still held the rifle (which I did not even know how to shoot). Hindsight gives me right now to comment on my luck, not the least of it the portrait of that Indian girl, suggesting to them delights that their crude minds had not yet thought of. In the first place I think the caravan had already been looking for me, or not for me exactly but for any survivor, news of the wreck having been spread as news has a way of doing, by secret means along secret tracks. Had there been no wreck the caravan would not have come this way at all, far off-course from their usual line of march. And having found at least one survivor there is no doubt they meant to make the most of me. They would not damage merchandise of so much worth, although they might have had their amusements first; but, if they had to choose, my worth was more important than their sexual needs. Secondly, the thought of reward was an alluring thought too, something to play with as a second venture if the first should fail. Thirdly, the image of that naked girl roused in them not so much sexual fantasies of their own but ideas where such fantasies might be brought and sold. Finally, as I later found out, my discomfiture of their erstwhile leader was to my credit, many of the other men disliking him and glad to see him laid low. So in the end, common sense won, as it often does. I was not to be harmed or molested in any way, a camel was given me to ride, and a boy to lead it, and promises, for what they were worth, that "all would be arranged in time." The words for "gold" and "master" were mentioned frequently, both seeming to command equal awe, and I was "invited," for lack of better word, to accompany them. All this conversation, such as it was, was carried on in a splutter and froth of tongues so that half of the French was lost. But so it was arranged, although who the "master" was and what was his part were concepts too complicated to discuss at the time.

I will add one thing more. Weeping and tears, cries for pity, were things they were familiar with, expected of all women and taken in stride. My moment's quickness, my look of resolve (although God knows that did not last long), revealed me as a woman who was prepared to fight back, a new phenomenon and one to be treated with care. As I have said, it would have been easy to disarm me; and, in fact, after the first surprise, only a polite fiction kept me in charge of the gun, but the fiction continued so none of us had to lose face. As for the locket, having tested the gold, their new leader returned it, without damage too. I am sure they thought that if my friends should find me first, it would serve as proof they were not robbers nor meant me harm. All this I repeat is surmise. I did not then know their minds at all, and still do not know enough to follow all the twists and turns, but the truth lies somewhere midway between. In any case they had agreed to give me shelter for the time. And when this "master" arrived (for although he seemed to have many names this was the one they used most frequently), when this "master" came, then the charade could be played out to the full. Until then, we must wait and see, "as God wills."

But I digress. Albeit whatever the cause, the men backed away in respectful silence or facsimile of it. Kicking up one of the urchins, he of the blind eye and lame foot who had been most troublesome, they told him to lead my camel, which, after much kicking too, knelt, so I could scramble aboard. Up it surged, and back and forth, back and forth I rocked, as we set off. The rest of the caravan, which had been anxiously waiting on the other hill, prodded on their mounts and all began to move ahead. The ex-leader, still moaning mightily, was bodily lifted out of the way, and the new leader took his place. I kept my eye on the fallen one, sure he would do me some other mischief another time (as indeed he did) and clung to the saddle, praying I should not fall off as I trotted along in their wake. So, one misery was exchanged for another, but at least I was no longer alone. And where the caravan went and where they took me or what they planned, that, too, was in the hands of God.

CHAPTER 2

That first day, or rather night, for it was almost dark when we moved forward again, we went farther than was customary, for the stars were clear and the moon hung like a half-sickle in a clear cold sky. The caravan had dallied long off-course, scavenging about the shore, and in order to reach its usual watering place was forced to make up for lost time. A caravan on the march is a haphazard affair at best, its progression ambling and slow, its course a constant winding in and out, the company scattered over several miles as each camel and its driver look for a grazing place. But one thing motivates the whole: the search for water; that is a continual and relentless drive. For water is not easily found, not even by men who live in the desert and know its ways. Wells may be blocked by chance or by foes; frequent sandstorms obliterate the trails and change the landscape; sometimes the water holes dry up or become poisoned by their own minerals. On my own, I should surely have died within days; even Arabs can die yards away from the water they have been searching for. That first evening then there was an added sense of urgency to our group. They kept close together and with frantic cries prodded on their beasts.

Other camels bore the striped tents or *basoors*, where I learned the women were kept. These tentlike structures bounced and swayed precariously as their drivers forced the camels into a trot, whilst inside, the women wailed and squealed piteously. The hoarse cries of the drivers, their frequent shouts, the moaning of the camels themselves, made such a noise I thought I would be deafened, but when at last we reached the water hole (I could not tell if it was their usual one or one found by chance) the cries redoubled as men and beasts rushed to drink. Some of the camels lay down in the water, still drinking as they sank up to their necks, their bellies bloating like drums, while their riders, having drunk their fill, scooped handfuls up to splash their heads and necks. Water here must have been plentiful; on days afterward I saw them use camel's urine to wash. Presently, a line of little fires began to burn as the evening meal of millet and camel's milk was prepared. As for me, when my camel had been forced to kneel by the reluctant blind-eyed boy (who kept himself well out of reach at first, either because he thought I would repay his earlier mischievousness or more likely because he thought I truly was a witch), I fell to my knees where I was, too weary to do anything but sleep upon the ground, although even in sleep I kept the rifle well tucked in and ready against my side.

I awoke to all the confusion of a caravan preparing to leave. Men screamed and cursed, camels groaned and kicked, the chaos was indescribable. Some traders, more holy than the rest, bowed amid this noise, as peaceful as in a mosque, to say their prayers; some took the chance to pack and repack their loads of ivory and gum to make more room for those boxes and crates they had found upon the beach; others, seeming to be in no hurry at all, sat at their ease in the shade of the palm trees, smoking their pipes.

Despite the early hour there already was a haze of dust and heat and ahead of us stretched a wilderness similar to the one we had crossed the day before. I had slept like one dead, scarcely moving, and was so sore and stiff I could hardly stand. I was overwhelmed by various personal needs: hunger and thirst, a longing to wash the sand and sweat away, and a desperate want to relieve myself. Since there was nowhere I could go to command privacy, at last I did as the men did, squatted to the ground off at one side; but as no one paid me attention it was quickly done, and in time I learned to be as unobtrusive as they were. I supposed I could draw water from the well but when I saw it, green-scummed, festooned with camel dung, I resolved to make do with my two water bags, still partly full from the day before. I knew no way to ask for food, but at least I could endure hunger. After a while, however, the camel boy, who I feared might have slipped away in the night, came up with a handful of dates that he held at a distance, making it clear if I wanted to eat I must give something of worth in exchange. The hand that offered those dates was grimed with dirt, covered with sores, but the one eye was sharp and bright. I gritted my teeth and agreed, tearing off one of the remaining tassels that had ornamented my dress and that I could see he coveted. But I, too, had begun to learn and I gestured to make him understand that the tassel would be his only when he brought me a plate of food, and a long strip of cloth with which I could make a covering for my head and face.

I was permitted to ride, unusual, I think; the old she-camel looked as if she would bite and roared complaint at every step, although I believe she was really tamer than she seemed. Without the help of my camel boy I could never have managed, as he knew, for he grinned as he waited for me to clamber into the saddle, a complicated affair of wooden sticks lashed to form a triangle and tied with palm-tree rope. It had a pommel and back rest, and was not uncomfortable; the difficulty was climbing into it and remaining there, there being no way up or down unless the camel could be made to kneel. In the end I let the boy mount in front to guide it himself, which he did, using his crippled bare feet skillfully and prodding constantly with a stick. When the shout went up to depart we were already prepared, and so henceforth each day we rode, the boy and I, a strange pair. I never knew his name either but called him Mohamed, which seemed to fit; and he, although he served me well, never touched or came close to me again, except upon the camel's back, when he endured my proximity with proud disdain. But in time he became accustomed to me I think, and boasted of me to his companions as if I were a camel who showed her skill. In the end we became friends, but that was yet to come.

Thus began one of the most wearisome journeys I have ever endured, one that might make a strong man quail. I cannot say it was easily done, nor yet that I could have borne it long. The heat alone soon brought me begging for water of any kind, even that filthy water I had scorned. Despite the scarf my lips cracked, my skin peeled, my throat was parched. I thought constantly of water, dreamt of it when I was not thinking of food. The petticoats began to slip from my waist as I lost weight. For if water was scarce, a luxury, food was almost as scarce; dates do not sustain the body for long, and the millet we ate was unpalatable like lumps of congealed porridge. From time to time when we came across other caravans, traveling like us, although in the opposite direction, all would stop to pass the time of day, and after elaborate exchange of greetings extra food would be served; but mostly we lived on dates and milk. Once when we came to a village and set up tents, there was much excitement, kissing, and hugging around the neck, and a feast was prepared of tough goat meat, which by then I was hungry enough to eat, even quarreling with Mohamed over the bones. I was at a disadvantage having no man to fend for me, and, being a woman, not permitted to eat with men, but Mohamed soon warmed to my service as he was quick to see the advantages notoriety brings. He was always first in line for food, and was not averse to bringing strangers to look at me, displaying me as a keeper might some rare animal. At these times I often sensed that much of the discussion centered on me, and became used to the way the newcomers would stroll in my direction, not looking openly, but examining me from a distance, as they might a nervous horse. Often after such an encounter the name of that "master" or "lord" would be mentioned in hushed voices. At least once a day the French-speaking Arab patrolled the area where I was encamped, making sure I suppose that all was well with his prize, by now having convinced himself that whatever his companions thought, he would let this "lord" decide what to do with me.

I came to recognize that word for master or lord, although I could not pronounce it, and at first pretended he was no concern of mine. I presumed of course, on seeing me, whoever he was, he would be persuaded at once to send me back to the closest English settlement. I had no means of guessing that such a settlement, if it existed at all, was many hundreds of miles away, and each day's journey drew us farther into a wilderness. Nor could I know that whatever I may have planned, their "lord" had no intention of rescuing me, rather the contrary.

No doubt without Mohamed I might not have survived at all. He brought me food; he made the fire; he fetched me water, careful to dig a new pit beside the old so that the water would be filtered somewhat through the sand. When the nights grew cold, as they now did, for we were moving inland toward the mountain range, he found or stole dirty camel blankets for sleeping. And he revealed what was planned for me, although he did so out of pride rather than pity.

We had stopped at a miserable place, nothing but a few stunted trees and a water hole, and late at night when it was dark and most of the camp was certainly asleep, he brought me a heated pot of water, an unheard-of extravagance. Making gestures under his own greasy cap he showed he meant for me to wash my hair, repeating many times the word for gold. I was touched and surprised, but not much interested in complying. The heat, or bad water, had made me feverish, and all I wanted was to lie and sleep. But he insisted, for once pulling at my arm and jerking me awake, repeating even more earnestly that word for gold. Since my hair was almost as matted as his, full of grit, unkempt, I was startled, but after a while I agreed, more for quiet than for vanity, especially when he produced a soft clean rag to dry it with. I confess it was a relief to comb the clean strands with my fingers and to smell the wild thyme that he had thrown into the pot to mask the usual sulfur smell, and in the dark I took pains to wash myself. By now I had almost abandoned my own clothes and wore a mixture of Arab ones, which, with an adjustment of brooches and tapes, I had turned into a long white tunic.

Clean and dressed I summoned Mohamed to see the result. He appeared so rapidly I was sure he had been watching all the while but I let that pass. His pleasure was not feigned, and he capered around me with undeniable glee. "Gold," he said, but now he did not mean my hair, "*dhahab*, gold, much gold," and he mimed a pile of it, passing imaginary coins through his hands and pointing at me to ensure that I understood. Gold indeed, gold to buy and sell, and I the object to be bought.

I was scandalized. I had never thought of that. Who would dare, I thought, to sell or buy another human—but I knew it was done. There were slaves attached to the caravan, and although I had not "bought" Mohamed, he was a slave. And what else had they kept me for, and pampered me, except to sell at great price. And who to be the bidder for this prize? None other than this unknown "master," this "lord."

My indignation was followed by anger, so sharp and fierce it made Mohamed shrink back, his pleasure in serving a mistress of such worth somehow gone awry. I paced about, cradling the rifle in my hands. No man, I told myself, lord or not, shall buy me. Rather I would cover myself with dirt, stain my face with dye, cut off my hair, use any means to foil their plan. So I resolved and so the next day warned the French-speaking Arab. I felt sure he understood, for his pockmarked face darkened and he gnawed his lip, looking for a moment like one of his own camels. I pressed my advantage home. "Your reward will be greater," I told him, "if you let me go. The English have great lords too; they will pay well for me." Finally when he ducked and scraped and tried to smile, I thought he had agreed. In fact, my display of anger only strengthened his resolve to be rid of me as soon as he could, for I was too great a responsibility, and he hurried the caravan forward with increased speed, toward the rendezvous, meanwhile guarding me even more closely than before.

I had no alternative then but to go along. But my resentment festered and grew. I watched my captors as carefully as they watched me, gauging their haste and their underlying fear. For fear there was of these Berber warlords, as pungent as the camel smell of my captors. Well, then, I thought to myself, their fear at least shall be to their loss; as for that "gold" they anticipate with such avarice, I shall make sure they have none of it.

The wait was soon over. I had already noticed the excitement and alacrity with which all had mounted one morning; no one loitering today for prayers or talk, the former leader throwing his usual malevolent glances at me but with greater frequency than usual, as if realizing he had lost his chance. I had observed the day before that the sand dunes had seemed to flatten out, giving evidence of sparse vegetation that the camels eagerly plucked, chewing great strands of it as they moved along. The oasis we had stayed at was large and the water fresh. I might have guessed that we would find some permanent town close to so comparatively fertile a place. Yet, when we reached the red walls of the "town" it seemed only a scatter of houses bunched together in a mass, rising to a peak, surrounded by clay battlements with rounded gates cut in their sides.

We stopped outside the gates upon an open stretch of land, the camels glad to be unpacked so soon after such a short march. The drivers hastily sought shelter from the sun; the ladies, who seldom left their tents, ventured out curiously. But the town itself seemed deserted; no inhabitants appeared upon the walls, although the gates were thrown open and no guards kept them. From where I stood on the plain below the houses looked like doll houses without windows or doors, only blank walls and flat roofs, layered upon each other like slices of cake, so close together that it seemed one could have used them as stepping-stones. The roofs were deserted although one would have expected people to have crowded there to comment and stare. Nevertheless, I had the impression of many watching eyes; the closed box lids, the shuttered apertures seemed to conceal a frantic humming, a buzz of activity like that in a beehive where all the bees had been shut inside.

The rest of the caravan had obviously settled down to a wait. The sun was hot, the dust glittered, as did the walls; it was the hour for sleep. Restless myself, growing ever more apprehensive, conscious of that hidden hum and stir, I walked across the open place to peer inside the gates. Narrow streets ran uphill, choked with dirt, winding around in a spiral toward the hill crest, but they were empty too. They looked cool despite their litter and around each corner seemed to branch into a snarl of lanes. I thought suddenly, I could run up those. I could lose myself in that maze and before anyone would find me I could knock on a door and beg shelter. In a town this size there must be people to understand. Someone here would be bound to help.

Upon the thought came the deed. I snatched a quick look around. The square might have been filled with statues, all sunk upon their sleeping selves; the camels chewing contentedly, the boys playing some game against a wall. I did not even try to run at first, simply walked inside the gates and began to climb. At first, that is. I had scarcely gone a hundred steps when the hubbub broke out below, shouts, cries, a thud of feet. The men from the caravan burst through the gate, guns at the ready, clamoring for me to come back. I began to run in earnest then, as did they, pounding up the mud lanes, my breath coming in great heaves. I was in no state to run far or fast, although I had been nimble-footed on my own country moors, used to jumping over rocks. But the Arabs were no more used to running than I, and were less fleet of foot. Besides, they were angry and excited, alarmed that their "gold" might be lost, fearful, too, of what to say if they should be left empty-handed. They paused to fire warning shots, all at random and not dangerous; paused to run down side alleyways that a glance could have told them ended in a blank wall. Their lack of cohesion was my chance and I took it. I thought perhaps fate would smile on me again. But although I had time to knock on several doors, beating on the great brass hammers, and shouting in French, no one answered; even the humming seemed to have stopped as if everyone inside were holding his breath. And although I continued up the hill, girding up my white skirts to give me speed, I could not find any refuge or place to hide, nor anyone to offer help.

At the top, where I paused again, expecting the path to end at a village square or open place, as in most European towns, revenge caught up with me. Among my pursuers was the man I had felled the first day, a leader whose leadership I had destroyed. Now he stood and took open aim. The first bullet went wide; the second, ricocheting from a stone, sliced my leg, high on the thigh.

It had been fired to kill, and as I fell, a third bullet smacked against the wall above my head. The shock of the blow knocked me off my feet and sent me rolling down the slope; yet such was my impetus I actually staggered up and kept on, dragging my leg behind me. It felt numb, more like a weight, leaden and heavy as if something were tied to it. I think I did not even know I had been hit at first until, looking back, I was almost surprised to see the great red blotches left upon the dust.

Behind me, my pursuers, my captors, my vendors, swarmed. I heard the shout they raised when they scented blood. It steadied them. They did not mean to lose me and now they came on carefully, sure of me. But I did not intend to sit waiting for them this time. Knotting a scarf around my leg to stem that first rush of blood, I continued, weak with shock, along the alley I was in, roughly parallel to the way I had come up. Still no one came to give aid although I saw shutters move and knew there were watchers standing inside the doors, peering through the keyholes. Their silence angered me. I knew they must be afraid, and afterward I knew what they were afraid of. Such was the terror of a warlord's anger that they preferred to see me hunted down rather than raise a finger to help.

I was determined not to give in. With no thought now in mind except to keep moving, I staggered down, whilst on the other side my pursuers clambered up. But my strength was fading fast. Sometimes I simply let myself slide; sometimes I rolled over parapets, until at last I came to the end, unable to move another step, nowhere left to go, the open gateway in front, the open square, the open desert beyond.

I rested then; I cannot judge how long, perhaps only for a few seconds, perhaps for many. Time seemed to melt and run together and then flow past at such a rate it left me behind. Above me, I could hear the men, still tracking me. Sometimes one of them would give a shout at some clue: a thread of white cloth, a footprint, a splash of red, for the wound had begun to bleed, slowly again, despite the knotted scarf. But my pursuers, too, were out of breath, anxious, determined nothing now should go astray. They moved with extra care, searching every inch and corner, doubling back to dig at every hole, making sure they missed nothing. The end was certain but they meant to make it so, savoring perhaps the moment of recapture that would truly make me what I should always have been, their prisoner and their slave. Knowing that, biding my time, I waited until they were almost upon me. And when there was no point any longer in trying to hide, I stood up and openly walked out through the gateway as openly as I had walked in.

They were close enough behind to have cut me down, more than close enough to shoot, yet they held their fire. And as I crossed between the gates I could see why. Outside, the sun still beat down in red-hot waves, and against the red mud walls the sand seemed the more brilliantly white by contrast. I turned to face the caravan, but it was gone. Gone was the bustle, the confusion of pack animals and men, as in a dream, vanished. I knew my mistake at once. In coming down the hill I had unwittingly followed a path to another gate; this was not the gate where I had entered; this was not the place where we had halted. And these men waiting outside the walls were not part of the caravan.

They were standing at the far end of the open space, a line of black-robed figures in the sun, their horses fidgeting behind them, pawing the dust. The light caught at their long curved swords, thrust without scabbards into their belts, and their soft boots scuffed the dirt. As I emerged from the shadow of the gateway I felt, rather than heard, a whisper run across their ranks, like a breath of wind through cypress trees.

Behind me came my pursuers, running fast, bursting through the gate. Seeing what lay ahead they also came to a halt, huddling together under the arch, arguing furiously among themselves. I knew before they stopped what caused their fear, but it could not stop me.

Dragging my leg, my white robe unbound, I began to cross the square. I did not hurry, indeed I could not, and even the effort of moving made my head swim. I could see the waiting horsemen clearly now, black-robed, their heads and faces wound in long black scarfs, their eyes glinting through the slits.

The sun was in my eyes as well, but I would not look down. At a halfway point I paused, the throbbing in my leg like a constant stab, my lips caked and my throat on fire.

"Bastards," I shouted to the skies, "bastards, to chase a woman like a hare. Am I an animal to be hunted for sport?"

The horsemen did not reply, did not move, but their horses did, sliding away uneasily, shying perhaps at the scent of blood. Then one reared and plunged to the front. It was a great black beast with high curved neck and tail, and seeing me it thrust with its forefeet scattering the dust in white spurts. Its rider was tall, black like his horse, horse and man seeming one. They blocked the sun, advancing ominously, the falcon on the man's arm spreading its wings.

"Bastards," I cried for a third time, this time in French, some unknown energy giving me words I did not know I knew, "cowards, to chase someone weaker than you. I match you wits for wits if not with strength. Do not think to buy or sell me. I am no man's slave."

I tried to move again; my legs would not obey me. I wanted suddenly to lie and fall asleep; I wanted sleep to engulf and shelter me. I wanted to lie in shadow away from the sun. And it seemed each time I moved, each time I breathed, pain stabbed like a knife.

I thought the black figure leaned forward in his saddle observing me. I thought his dark eyes behind their scarfs stared at me as a hawk stares. "What else should men chase," I thought he asked, and I thought he smiled, "but women, and who else should women flee but men?"

I wanted to say, "Pursue all you will, you will never catch me." Perhaps I did. The words seemed to grow too large to fit my tongue. I tried to move my wounded leg; the blood gushed forth and puddled on the thirsty sand. My white robes were blotched with it, saturated with it, and I heard a gasp, was it his gasp or mine? A darkness shadowed me, the dark eyes glinted, the talons stretched, the softness of feathers encompassed me. I fell into darkness and became part of it.

•   •   •

I woke to such a contrast I thought I must have passed to paradise and closed my eyes in case it should be true. But when I opened them again, several hours having already intervened, I knew it must be night and I was still firmly on this earth, as the cool air, the shadows from the oil lamps, the smell of hot candle wax testified. A rush of homesickness overcame me at those familiar things; the damp whitewash on the walls, the garden herbs, and the white-coated fig-ure beside the bed, hunched forward as my mother used to do when she read to herself.

The voice that spoke was French, a doctor's voice, and the drink offered me was dark and bitter, biting at the edges of the tongue. I drank, slept again, and, with daybreak, was sufficiently restored to know I must be in one of those village houses and that the man beside me indeed was French. He stood at the bedside, giving his medical credentials with military precision, as strictly professional as if he were in a Paris hospital, explaining what had to be done, what had not been done, all in rapid quick-fire style, which slid uselessly over my head. But he persisted, obstinate as was his way as I was to find out, his round face with its pointed beard growing red in an effort to make me appreciate the miracles of science he had performed, he, Antoine Legros, once a military doctor, now reduced to caring for the poor in this humble town. When I did not respond as he would have liked he shrugged and ordered me to swallow. Whatever that bitter draught was, some plant, some Eastern drug, it dulled the pain, making it seem disembodied so that I could view it dispassionately as belonging to someone else. And so I slept again. When I awoke it was the second day; the doctor was still there but drunk as a lord.

My waking was more natural this time, and for a while I could forget my wound. The light filtered through a kind of screen; the tiled floors were damp and cool; the sun glanced off the bottles by the bed; and sprawled in a chair, his head upright, where I presume he had passed the night, his hands crossed tightly on his chest, the little doctor dozed, from whose mouth, slightly agape, a belch of brandy fumes emerged. But when he stirred and saw me watching him he was not so drunk that he could not stagger to his feet, feel my pulse, examine eyes and skin, test the bandaging on my leg.

"Good, good," he hiccuped at last, "good, good," dragging out the long "o"s lugubriously, "if you had died on me, *mon dieu*," and he made a graphic gesture of cutting his own throat. When I failed to understand, for it seemed more like bad luck for me, "That black infidel," he hissed, "that Berber baron, plucking me from this quiet village like an egg, twenty horsemen clattering through to root me out, battering on the doors to break them down. '*Sortez sortez*,' they roared as if I were an insect to be stamped upon. Out I came. *Bien*, a doctor is a man of good repute, not to be bellowed at by cattle thieves. Their leader did not even have the grace to dismount. 'Hold out *votre main*,' he tells me, leaning on the pommel of his saddle, thus." The little man stretched his hand to show me what he meant. It shook and shivered to the fingertips so that he was forced to shut it up tight. "But then," he explained, proud as a peacock, "I matched my hand with his. Oh, his was larger perhaps, he being tall and powerful, but as his hand did not tremble neither did mine. 'I am a surgeon,' I told him to his face, 'I have as steady a hand for my business as you yours.' I meant of course he uses his hands to hack and maim, I to cure. He took my wrist between forefinger and thumb, as if it were a bone to snap. 'Sew me up a wound,' says he, 'without a scar. Have it healed in three days time, *trois jours*, or else use that skill you boast about to sew your own head on.' "

He sighed again. "*Moi, je suis médecin*, a doctor, trained in Paris, and for my sins sent to labor among these heathen, who prefer to heal themselves with sticks and potions, *les pauvres. Sacré bleu,* I do not need to be frightened out of my wits by a madman who expects even sickness to obey his will. 'I'll do what I can,' says I, to his back, for he was already riding off, leaving his men to pack and bundle all I required. For when I protested I needed this and that, 'Take him and his hospital,' he said, and so was it done. Well, you were in a sad state I admit, artery gone, and the tourniquet pulled so tight I wonder gangrene had not set in."

The thought of those black-robed figures, or their leader, working over me was more bothersome than I liked to admit, that while I was unconscious he should have lifted and touched me, moved my clothes, bared my skin. I felt myself grow hot at the possibilities, but the little man was continuing. (He spoke always in French you understand, I write but a literal translation as my memory serves.) "Three days then, *trois jours*, that's all he gave; that's how much he thinks of my skill, although I stitched you up as delicately as a Breton lacemaker. And he watched me all the while like that hawk of his, contrary to the laws of propriety, although I grant that he is cleaner than his men. I suppose he meant to make sure I made no mistake. '*Moi, je suis médecin*,' I told him. 'I claim the right to look after my patient as I think fit. I have cared for soldiers, it is true, who would make slight of such a wound, but even they could not walk on it. *You* might, I suppose,' I told him, 'but not a young and tender girl, *pas une jeune fille comme elle.*' "

Whether in truth the doctor had said all this, a trifle overfierce for his own meek self, I cannot say, but what he next said certainly rang true. "I could not make him change his mind for all I begged. '*Trois jours,*' that was the reply he gave, holding up three fingers as if I could not count. He gave me everything else; drugs, this house (its occupants forced unceremoniously into the street), this bed, all that was required in fact to set up a surgery. But if you are not on your feet tomorrow morning he'll have my head."

Tears of fright or drunkenness rolled down his cheeks, and he almost wrung his hands. And I will say this of him in retrospect, whatever ill-fate had left him, stranded here, an exile, I suppose for some crime, drunkenness may well have been the main cause and his weakness might have been well known. But, apart from drunkenness, he was a careful doctor as he claimed, a kindly man. And as I was to learn, in many ways a good one, although, as in most people I have known, fear or prejudice robbed him of the ability to think.

Meanwhile I lay and tried to make sense of what he had said. At last, "But why three days?" I asked, since that seemed to be his main concern. My puzzlement made him more nervous than before and fear suddenly became articulate. "*Trois jours*," he shouted. "*Parcequ'il a dit, trois jours*. He said so. What more reason do you want? And three, because that is all the time he has. And when he goes, you go with him."

He began to babble then, trying to explain, now in Latin, what damage the rifle shot had caused, and what greater damage if I moved too soon, but what finally emerged was this. "He gives the orders; this town is his. Why should he search me out in it, although I was minding my own affairs? Why else is he called 'master' by these miserable fools, who cringe at his name? Look. *Regardez cette maison*." He beat on the house wall. "This bed"—he beat on it too, so that its brass railing shook. "The best in the village; do you think their owners had much choice? Nor the caravan, whose goods he has seized for their pains; nor yet the man who shot at you, beheaded on the spot? If he orders you to walk or ride or crawl, you will."

His reply horrified me. I had no reason to wish a man's death nor to be in any way responsible for it. I had no wish to disrupt the lives of people who had already shown their disdain for me. You can imagine what I felt, exposed to such notoriety; every ladylike instinct quailed. But this was only the beginning. I was to know much worse.

"Where does he go?" I asked when I could speak.

The little man shrugged. "Question the Arabs," he said. "They will tell you beyond the east wind, where the falcons breed, if that makes sense. *Moi, je dis*, I tell you; outside the law. He is the law where he comes from. He makes or breaks it as he pleases."

"And you will permit that," I cried, "you, a gentleman, will let him take me there?"

He wept again and did wring his hands. "I have no choice either," he sobbed. "God knows I wish no ill to anyone. *Je suis médecin, pas soldat.* I cannot fight a hundred men." He added after a while, trying a smile, "I do not think he would harm you though. Besides," truth now coming unashamedly, "besides, they say he does not much care for European women, for all that his mother was one."

I let him weep, and afterward when he slept exhausted by his outburst, I lay back through the growing heat of the day and tried to conquer my fear. I would not have you think this was as easy as I may make it seem. I was not a heroine; merely a simple country girl, innocent of men, but resolute. We grow flowers in my country home, so insignificant you have to search for the petals beneath the leaves, yet they can withstand the fiercest gales and their roots are tenacious, clinging deep into the granite soil. Country people are like that, I think. And as I have said before I have a good feel for common sense. Whether the doctor in his drunkenness exaggerated, as indeed he might, it was clear this lord and his men were dangerous. It also was clear that in this case the patient must protect the doctor, rather than the other way round. So, taking the substance of his remarks rather than the particular, I resolved that if all depended on my walking, walk I should. And under cover of the blankets I began to flex my toes, shift my knees, each movement bringing tears to my eyes. I also realized to my discomfort that my clothes were gone. Well, I suppose that was reasonable, mine being in no fit state, but I suddenly saw the significance of the little doctor's remark, and thought of those hawklike eyes watching as I lay naked and unaware. Where I came from if a woman felt sick she pointed to the painful place on a doll made to resemble her, but that, too, was a nicety that could wait. Now I concentrated on making myself mobile again.

The morning of the next day, the third day, found Dr. Antoine Legros restored to his full self. He was standing by the window, looking out when I awoke, crestfallen, contrite, but in his way also resolute. He had no need to tell me what I could hear, the bustle of departure, less disorganized in fact than a caravan, but there was no way to disguise the sound of men, of horses, of movements in the square outside the walls. He looked at me, and I at him. There was no need either for us to say anything. Neither he nor I could "fight a hundred men." He was pale, but not without courage of his own, revealing for the first, although not last, time some of the splendid inconsistencies of his nature. "*Je vous quitte,* I leave you now," he said, back ramrod straight, as if about to face a firing squad (which in all honesty I think he believed he might need to do). "I tell you to lie still and not excite yourself." What he meant was clear, that he would confront the leader on his own and would accept the consequences. I could not let him do that for me.

"Come on," I said. I struggled to sit up although the covers kept slipping from my naked breasts, not much of them, almost like a boy's. "Find me some clothes. He shall not have it all his own way."

Those were brave words, too, I suppose, at least I meant them bravely, a female David to fight against Goliath, in a shift. But fair seems fair; the least I could do was give support. When Dr. Legros realized that I was obdurate he had the frightened woman of the house bring a tunic, of soft linen, too long, but I managed to tie it up. I tried to smile at her but she would not look at me, crept in and out, sliding away much as Mohamed had done. And when I was ready, as ready as I could ever be, I told them to open the door.

I had realized by now the house was on the lowest tier beside the gate, the closest building I suppose to where I had originally collapsed, so I had not far to go. He helped me at first, the little doctor, whose head scarcely reached mine, althought I am not tall myself, the little man taking most of the weight and fretting continuously beneath his breath about all the medical things that would go wrong. Outside, I halted for a moment to let a morning breeze blow through my hair. It was early still, with that gray-blue mist that I had come to like although it was a mist of heat not rain. Pain made me feel sick, and I had to keep swallowing as if I needed air. I could feel the sweat already running between my shoulder blades. On the far side of the square, where they had been waiting the other day, the horsemen in truth were preparing to leave. Bridles glittered; stirrups clanged; the men, who had not yet put on their black headdresses nor their cartridge belts, were throwing saddles over the backs of their mounts. Even I could tell what splendid horses they rode, fine-headed, with long manes and tails, and slender legs meant for traveling fast. But not through the desert sands. Where then?

We made a little crowd, I suppose, as I paused there to catch my breath and to attract attention intentionally. Soon all the men were watching us. Some, leaving their horses to the care of grooms, came strolling up. Close to I could see their faces clearly now, and many of them were young and clean shaven. The older men were bearded, but all had long black hair, thin features, their skin blackened by sun and wind. Most of all I noticed their eyes, dark, fierce, as unblinking as a hawk's. There would be no pity there.

I pushed the doctor aside, shook off his arm and stood alone. Forget the pain, I told myself, concentrate on something else. I fixed my eyes on the ground, at each shuffling step searching for a sort of mark to aim for, a piece of straw, a pebble, a scuff line; I used each as a kind of goal, holding my hands slightly raised in front of me to balance myself. The sandy soil felt like wool my feet sank through; sometimes the step I took shrank to the size of my own foot, sometimes the distance I struggled to cross seemed to gape as wide as the whole empty place, and after the first moment I could feel the red-hot lance that transfixed all my right side. But still I shuffled on, sweat running now across my face and stinging my eyes.

A shadow fell across my path, blocking the way. I looked up. There stood a man in black, tall and powerful. *He held three fingers up.* I held three up myself, although the effort made them tremble like a leaf. "Three days," I said, "this is the third."

He never answered, but, matching me, step for laborious step, drew back so that I was following him. I did not look down again, only at him. I could not see his face, overshadowed by that thick headdress, and the glittering on his belt and sword blinded me; the black cape flared as he moved and his hand, a strong hand with a thin wrist and long slender fingers, seemed to draw me on as if a rope was attached from it to me. Once when I faltered I thought that hand twitched from the place on the sword belt as if to touch mine, but that may have been only a flicker of the light. Step by step I took then, to match with his, until we had drawn level in the center of the square. And behind me, like a ripple I heard a hum, the sort of sound men make among themselves when approving.

I could go no farther, my strength was suddenly done, drained out like water from a sieve. The ground buckled and heaved as it had on board the ship and I scarcely had the mind to say one last piece, what I had been saving myself for. "You bid me walk," I croaked. "As if you were God, I suppose. But so I have. Now let me go."

Instead he caught me as I fell. I had the impression, distant but clear, of the hard feel of his belt, his arms, contrasting with soft folds of cloth, and a weightlessness, as he held me off the ground. When I could see again I seemed to be lying on a pile of cloaks; the little doctor was patting my hand although keeping all his attention riveted upon the other's back. And the "Master," having turned to his men, seemed to be ordering them. When he turned 'round again and stood looking down at me, I felt a coldness, as if indeed he was of a size to block the sun. He did not speak at first, merely fingered his belt where the long and wicked sword was thrust.

"So," he said and his voice seemed silky smooth, no anger, no surprise, a bland statement of facts, "you took me at my word. So shall I you yours. 'God,' you said. Then I think you do not challenge God. Twice have you challenged me. What else would you want that a God could give?"

I tried to answer, the words seemed lost, my head ached, my body ached, I felt as insubstantial as a breath of wind. Yet I would not be silenced. Right is right, and fair is fair, not to be trifled with. "Justice," I said to him, but so low he almost had to stoop for it. "Let the caravan depart, without further harm. Let the doctor go free as well, and my little camel boy. But reward them first as they deserve."

"And in return for all of this?" His voice was as low as mine; I could almost feel his breath upon my cheek, and yet it seemed to me I still could not see his face, overshadowed by that long scarf. I felt, I cannot explain it otherwise, a great longing to lift it up and see what lay beneath. I felt, I cannot explain otherwise, that, despite myself, here was the way my journey must go on. Whatever else I meant to say, or should have said, or afterward might wish I had, hung there in the balance on my next words. They came out slowly, dragged out, against my will perhaps, and yet, I think now they were what I willed or what were willed on me to say. "Their freedom," I insisted, "in return for mine. Only then will I come with you, of my own accord."

Not until long afterward, after many hours of sickness and fever's pain, did I realize whatever I had said had been said in vain. For we were moving forward now, I could tell it, slowly, so as not to jar me, and there was a shuffle of feet beside the litter where men guided the pack mules to avoid the ruts. Beside the litter on one side I saw the little figure of the doctor stumbling resolutely along, whilst on the other Mohamed held a leading rope and grinned at me. Ahead of us and behind, I could hear the horses of the guard, but where the leader was I could not say. The road was hard, upward, over flint rock; we were journeying then, all of us, away from the plain toward the range of foothills that came thrusting out like claws. And one last thing. When I thought back over these events, these confrontations when we had met and clashed, these times when we had exchanged words, when what we said was itself like a sword flick before a real conflict begins, I could not afterward recall in what language we had spoken. Or even, such was the effect he had had on me, if we had really spoken at all.

CHAPTER 3

Now followed the strangest part of the journey, undertaken by an even stranger company. Sometimes I wondered at our companionship, composed as it was of so many diverse parts: two Christians neither of whom spoke the same language or had the same background, an Arab slave, six guards, whose Berber tongue no one knew at all at first, and a handful of muleteers, as stubborn as their mules and, like them, prone to falling asleep. Yet as we lurched across a landscape as barren as the moon, it seemed a friendship was formed, made up as much of things unalike as like. We seemed set apart, alone, awash upon a lunar sea that slid deep inland, cutting around the outcrop of cliffs. As I look back now to that time, when, like a child, I lay cocooned within the litter walls, listening to the shift of stone and grit, letting myself drift, I realize that in myself then there flourished a desire to make all things familiar and safe and a longing for a gentle journey after so much pain. Perhaps I even wished the journey into a pastoral interlude, in which my fellow travelers appeared like shepherds in some Arcadia.

Such imaginings are doomed to fail. And I knew this in my heart although I could not admit it at first. Yet for a while that fellowship did exist and those who were part of it were to cherish it. And I will confess that when coherent thought returned, as it did eventually, in a rush, I felt more distress for my two friends than for myself. That they had become prisoners as I was meant our fates were joined, and I felt responsibility for them strung round my neck like an albatross. Mohamed tried to soothe my fears. "I asked to come," he told me one day when, by fits and starts, I had begun to pick out words and phrases in his tongue, and he, quicker in this than I, had begun to pick up ours, like a chicken pecking at corn. He had even learned to communicate with our guards (although their language seemed to come more easily to him as in later time I was to find out why). He sat perched on the litter shafts like a fresh-plumaged bird, in his new shirt and blue burnoose, his lame foot tucked underneath and his lank hair trimmed. Sitting sideways like that, idly poking at the mule as he used to do with his camel stick, his blind eye turned away, his profile had a sharpness that in another race would have been termed beautiful. I felt a rush of exasperation mixed with solicitude. He seemed so young, scarcely older than those fretful children I had been assigned to watch, yet at the same time worldly-wise, in a way they would never be, even full-grown.

"I told them," he said, pointing to the guards, "that you needed me. In the desert did not I serve you well? But I also told them that they needed me more." He grinned showing the white teeth of which he was inordinately proud. "How else, I asked them, will her tent be pitched at the day's end, how will her fire be lit or her food prepared, if I do not take care of her? For they are devout men, not used to dealing with Infidels. At first they laughed." He bunched his robes against his scrawny ribs to mimic them. "But after a while what I said made sense, they being soldiers, not accustomed to guarding females. They told me to clean off my camel stink and if I could keep up with them I was welcome to try." He looked from me to them and a suspicion of a wink crossed his good eye. "Besides," and all the cunning of the East was in that word, "besides, they know how hard their work is. Their horses must be fed and watered and washed in the evening when we camp. Their bridles and saddles must be polished and their weapons cleaned. They soon realized that my two hands would be of use to them even if my lame foot was not. And when I have taught these noble lords how indispensable I am, then they will show me what I really want, which is to ride and fight as they do." He cried passionately, "Is not the horse the most noble beast in the world? Oh, I know the camel is beloved of God, the wisest animal. It remembers all God's many names, even to the hundredth unknown to man. But compare a camel to a horse! One is ugly as I am, the other is a god itself."

Of course he did not confide all this at once but spun his story out, Arab style, to pass the miles. I did not have the heart to argue with him (although I thought his hopes most unlikely ones), especially when the doctor confided a third secret, which Mohamed kept hidden from everyone. "He believes, *il croit*, poor sot," the good doctor said, toiling away beside us in the sun, for he scorned to beg a ride like a camel boy, "that if he clings close to us, to you in particular, his lameness will be cured. He saw you shot, he saw you lamed. *Voilá*, such is his superstition that he thinks he saw magic when you walked. Moreover, did not you claim to have been hunted, or not hunted, I forget which, like a hare? That is a sacred animal in his world. Perhaps he imagines you are a holy woman who can perform miracles." He shrugged, that French shrug that says much more than words. "So he intends to stay with you, hoping your magical qualities will rub off on him, to say nothing of my more mundane medical skills."

This last was spoken dryly, without a smile. "But if I had seen him at birth," he burst out suddenly, "I could have saved him. Waste, waste. Ignorance and disease and dirt go hand in hand. There are a thousand unfortunates such as he, a hundred thousand, in this land, so backward and miserable. He may have volunteered to come," the little man went on, "but I did not. Who argues with a gun? Especially one held by a Berber man. Although since the Berbers spared my life I suppose they think I owe them gratitude. And their lord, at least, paid attention to me in the end. For I told him that, having seen you walk once, he should not expect another such miracle. 'She'll not hike up a mountain peak,' I said, and to my surprise, he agreed. He gave us this escort for our use and told them to go as slowly as I thought wise. And so they do," he added with a touch of pride. "For once they listen to my advice."

I tried to express my thanks, but the doctor waved away my gratitude. "Am I the man to leave a patient who needs me?" he cried (and I should pause to confirm that no woman could have tended me with more care and delicacy in those first days; no doctor could have been more devoted to my recovery). "Besides," and now, as Mohamed had, he revealed secrets of his own, "besides, for a long time I have wanted to come into this mountain wilderness. It is a place where few Europeans have ever been. I have heard of only one who dared, a German, and he traveled in disguise, for fear of being caught. But, under the protection of this Berber tribe, we can journey openly and see what no one has seen before. If I survive to write down what I find, in time my notes may make me into an explorer of great repute. And thus my fame will spread, and I shall be allowed to end my exile and go home."

He spoke self-disparagingly, as was his style, but I sensed a thread of hope warming his usual pessimism, albeit it did not last long. Gradually on this ride I came to understand part of the complexities of his nature. It was true he possessed a genuine wish to help the sick and a burning desire to alleviate the miseries he saw. Counterbalancing these good qualities were ones less admirable. Unbridled curiosity for one (which may have made him a doctor in the first place), quick temper another, contempt for all things "uncivilized," and, most disturbing of all, a kind of resentment and self-distrust that caused him to act irrationally. Added to these were the effects of heat and thirst, especially for the brandy which his system craved; no wonder he often appeared cantankerous. But inconsistency was in his nature, as well as innate goodness of heart, and I began to realize that he never felt satisfied, would never truly feel at home even in his place of birth, no matter how much he claimed to long for it. All this I learned in time. I only thought then, as I watched him trudge along, how incongruous he looked—his frock coat stained with dust, his black hat blotched with it, his black umbrella unfurled against the heat, his little feet cramped into their cracked leather boots—as incongruous as one of those black-robed horsemen galloping down the Champs Elysées. I did not then suspect what an explosive mixture was fermenting in him, to ruin us. Yet for a while he seemed content, and once convinced that I was on the mend, he kept himself occupied with taking notes in his neat scientific style, and he never sighted a village without insisting we approach, although the guards would have prevented him. Arriving there, he would stamp off with his medical bag to round up the sick among the helpless villagers. "All it takes is tact," he used to say, this most tactless of men, polishing the sweat off his face with his red handkerchief as if he were polishing his spectacles. "And when we see the 'Master' again, as we must when we reach his mountain fort, I shall demand he change the way his people live. *Il faut changer.*" I let him chatter on, not taking him seriously, as I should have done, not yet aware of how dangerous his actions were, not yet knowing the nature of those dangers.

One night an incident with the guards gave a foretaste of things to come. Six guards accompanied us, all young, even their captain.

It was his first command, a strange one I suppose for him, to ride as nursemaid to a sick girl, a mad doctor, and a slave. I never knew his name or that of his companions, nor why this duty had fallen on them (although perhaps their very youth made them more tolerant); and as they never looked at me or spoke to me but merely stared over my head as if I did not exist, I cannot describe them accurately. What I learned about them came from Mohamed who, worming his way into their confidence, acted as our go-between (although in the beginning I am sure he invented most of their conversation, understanding probably one word in ten). Beneath their stern outward expression I think at heart they were simple men, fond of joking and argument, fond of horses, fond of all women who were not Infidels. To pass the time they liked to dispute among themselves, and they had a childish love of gifts (which bothered me as I had nothing to give them). One evening then, when we had settled for the night, they began to exercise their horses for sport, showing off their skill. From the shelter of our little camp site I watched them eagerly while Mohamed, wild with excitement, explained, for the twentieth time, the habits of their Barbary steeds, the qualities of endurance and speed, the mating patterns, the names of dams and sires, tumbling out information, as if a horse could be as much a person as a man. The youngest guard, the dandy of the group, proud of his shirt and new shoes, was learning from his captain how to lift a handkerchief from the ground with his sword while leaning over the horse's side. The captain had him practice this maneuver repeatedly, at one point demonstrating it himself, with a sudden burst of speed, a graceful swerve, and a triumphant shout as he swept past, the scrap of silk firmly skewered on the sword point. The noise made the doctor look up. He gave a snort of derision, and when I paid him no heed added angrily in a loud voice, "Barbarians, war-crazed. I told you so. That is all they know about, how to practice for war and death. *La guerre, toujours la guerre,* war first and foremost at all times. War is the only thing these Berbers understand."

Although I do not think the guards could have heard him, Mohamed seemed to sense the meaning behind the words. He bristled, much as the doctor might have done himself. "You are not right to call the Berbers war-crazed," he cried, in that mixture of languages that we had grown accustomed to. "Since he inherited, the Master has kept peace among the tribes as his father did in his time. I tell you, without him and his men these mountain folk would be in a sad state. He alone, in a single fight, overthrew the man who had usurped his father's power, and united all the tribesmen again. He . . ."

"*Bien sûr*," the doctor snapped. "Just so. Single combat, between robber barons, who live as we did centuries ago. Berber, barbarian: that is where the word comes from; that is how the Romans coined its use. For forty years we have been trying to cure them of that barbarism along the Mediterranean coast where once I lived. And to my mind it will take another forty years before we begin to see improvement. I know what sort of 'peace' your master keeps; I know what his men bring back each night. Money! Squeezed out from poor villages like the ones we pass. Blood-tax. Blood-tax, so that they will be spared from the war he would otherwise unleash on them. And they, poor fools, have not the sense or means to resist. *Quelle justice-ça!*"

By "we" of course he meant "we French," and by "barbarians" I suspect everyone else. Although his vehemence seemed to swell him up like a balloon full of air, and although at any other time I might have been amused at his Gallic excess of spleen, I was suddenly afraid. It was as if I felt the cold wind of presentiment. That night, after Mohamed had retired in a huff and after the horsemen had drawn back to their fire and squatted around it without speaking, their behavior different from their usual joking and singing, I thought, He has given offense to men upon whose goodwill we must rely and who have power over us. For the first time it occurred to me that we were alone with them, dependent upon them, far from any other help. I thought, It is not wise to find fault with such men. But the offense had been given, and there was no way to unsay it. And whether he meant to or not, next day the doctor was to offend again.

I think only one thing was in our favor at that time, one quality in those guards that even Dr. Legros could not despise. It lay behind every word they said, every move they made, every thought. And that was their loyalty to their lord. Their bond with him was as strong as that of any medieval knight; they would live or die for him as he commanded them. And because he had told them to, they would live or die for us. Even though the doctor had insulted them, they would not fail us when we needed them. Yet that loyalty was the very thing I faulted them for.

I have said I had felt compelled to make this journey, I do not know why. Perhaps it was fate, that Eastern fate in which I was coming to believe. I still felt the compulsion, as strong as before, but in addition I now felt anger, flaring hot, at the recollection of how I had been deceived. If consciousness of the Master lay behind everything those guards did and said, so it hung, like a shadow, over me. I confess freely now, that if my first thought had been concern for my friends, the second was most un-Christian anger that I had been made to look a fool. What use were all my fine heroics, I thought; what benefit had I gained? My friends had been made prisoners like myself (even if they professed not to mind). I might have saved my breath. And to be put in bondage to a lord who had failed to keep his word, what an anticlimax that was! I had once believed that any man, especially a gentleman, was bound by his oath. A promise was a promise, and an oral agreement should be as binding as a written one. I had offered myself as prisoner in return for my friends' liberty, and I thought he had agreed to my terms. (At least I convinced myself he had. To believe otherwise would have made me seem even more foolish.) That these young guards should show such loyalty to a faithless man bothered me, almost as much as the original treachery. I told myself that I was no ignorant Berber girl, easy victim to a man's trickery, and that when I had regained my strength, when I had caught up with him (for I learned that he and his men rode ahead to meet with the other tribes along the way), when I saw him next, I should tell him what I thought of him. I realized of course I had no hope of outwitting him unless I could face him directly, and that I meant to do at a time that suited me. I ignored Mohamed's protest that I had small chance of ever seeing him at all. In the midst of all these tribal affairs, the complaints of a mere woman would merit no consideration. Well, righteous anger does some good, acting as a goad, pricking up the will to succeed. So I, too, nursed a secret grudge, although I had the sense not to voice it aloud. And, like the doctor, I did not accept the fact that fate has a way of twisting things, so that when they happen they are not as was meant at all. As the next day proved.

We had stopped that noon beneath the walls of a small village that nestled at the end of a valley, like an unexpected mushroom growth, pale pink in color and frilled with turrets and battlements. The valley floor where it stood had widened here; there were traces of small fields and orchards, and a half-dry riverbed, along whose edges white salt flats spread out like sheets drying in the sun. In spring, they said, the river ran in flood and the bare sticks of trees burst into leaf. It seemed a pleasant little place, no different from many others we had seen, except that above its rose crenellations a round white dome glistened, looking rather like an onion flower. It was a mosque, dedicated to the Prophet's name, occupied by a sect of holy men, sacred to the devout, and forbidden to any Infidel.

By now I had grown used to the pattern of our days. The morning start with its hint of cold, the noonday halt out of the sun, the evening camp had all become familiar and routine. Our companionship seemed almost commonplace, and, except for last night's unpleasantness, on the surface everything appeared tranquil. I might almost claim to have felt happiness. Perhaps I even believed, had I thought at all, that in the end all would be well, and I would find friends waiting to rescue me. I cannot tell you if what now took place was simply by ill-chance, or if the gods willed it so, as punishment for complacency, a warning, such as this land inflicts upon those who think to alter its ways. Countless times since I have returned in memory to those peaceful moments and wondered what we should have done to prevent them lurching on into the chaos that was to follow.

Countless times in memory I recall those warning signs and curse my own shortsightedness.

Mohamed and I had wandered down to the riverbed where the village girls were drawing water from its reed-fringed pools. By then my health had so much improved that I was able to limp about, leaning upon Mohamed's arm, and he, although anxious to be used as a walking stick, would dart behind me when I paused, to press his withered foot firmly into my tracks, seeking the cure that superstition promised (although by now I had already begun to sense in myself that hesitation in my gait that was long to remain with me, that unexpected spasm of muscles locking into place, which suddenly rendered me immobile, as stiff as a piece of wood).

What happened next seems to jar apart the peaceful scene, as a picture is shattered into fragments. I remember the girls. I remember how they smiled and giggled behind their hands at our guards, who like us had come down to the water holes. I liked those Berber girls. They were tall, unveiled. Beneath their silver headbands, their sun-brown faces and serious eyes reminded me of girls at home, seeming more familiar to me than the ladies of my cousin's world. Country people where I was born stare in the same way. And young girls everywhere laugh at handsome soldiers who flirt with them. I remember thinking that, compared to these girls, Mrs. Lawson and her companions on the ship had seemed the strangers—as alien as the concealed women of the caravan—their malice and hypocrisy as blinding as the Arab's veils. I remember, too, watching the way our men dismounted, sliding one leg over the saddle easily. I liked to see them with their horses, busily passing the leather buckets, shouting to Mohamed to make haste and help, and was amused by the way he left me to scuttle forward, falling over himself to serve these new masters he idolized. "Paradise," I heard him cry to the girls, as the young men told him what to say, priding himself on his new-found ability to act as interpreter, "paradise lies in three things: a jug of wine, a good book, and women's thighs." These three things he had never known himself, but his words were enough to make the girls blush and laugh again, louder than before. They flicked their hair, moved on, pretending anger that they did not feel, and the guards, as young men will, pretended to follow them. Into this pleasant company Dr. Legros burst, as if all the devils of hell were after him.

I cannot judge if the guards were to blame, becoming careless, letting him wander so freely. I do not know if it was my fault, for not paying enough attention to what he did. I know even less what had soured his mood that day, rendering him irritable, restless, dissatisfied. I can tell you only that when we had stopped outside the village, he had stalked off alone, as was his way, without a word, and had deliberately gone inside the walls, making for the holy shrine.

Afterward, I wondered if it was the heat, the flies, the dust, that had dulled his sensibilities. As an explorer he had never showed much respect for this strange land he was to explore. Or it may have been that his obsession for details made him careless of consequence. I can tell you only that when he returned, amid a shower of well-hurled stones, most of the village came hot-foot after him, cursing him, berating him for sacrilege, howling threats at him for having defiled their mosque.

"Make haste, make haste *allez, dépêchez-vous*," Dr. Legros shouted as the stones fell among us with skillful aim. He tried to run over the riverbed, pushing the girls aside. "Mount quickly, *vite, vite, vite.* These fools have mistaken my intent." What the "intent" was he did not say, but the villagers did, accusing him of trespass of the gravest kind, of confrontation with their holy men, and, worse, of argument with the head priest of the sanctuary. Even so, we might have made good our escape, for despite their numbers, the villagers were simple people and were not armed. But we hesitated too long, arguing among ourselves what to do, until behind them, crowding down from the winding alleyways, the first white-cloaked men began to appear, arms folded like judges, silent and ominous.

Noticing them, our guards suddenly began to see this village uproar in a different light. Muttering among themselves, stern-lipped, they urged their horses forward, dragging at the litter shafts, trying to kick up the muleteers, asleep on the riverbank. In the equally sudden silence that fell upon the villagers, we tried to form a ragged line. It was Mohamed, ever bearer of news, who was the first to break that quiet as we started to edge along. "This is a sacred place," he whispered, almost too frightened to speak. "And those holy men are powerful warriors as well as priests. Their leader is a *Marabout*, descendant of the Prophet Himself. To go into such a shrine is bad enough; to enter wearing shoes, an insult that must be repaid in blood. But to dispute with the Marabout, push past him in his own mosque, turn your back on him, Allah be merciful, who knows the punishment for that profanity."

Antoine Legros had the grace to look abashed. A religious man himself, I do not think he would willingly have offended any Christian alive, but perhaps the Islamic religion did not seem real to him. Mohamed's admonition had touched a nerve. He may well have thought that no one would have noticed him, and the villagers' reactions had frightened him; most probably the frustrations of the day made him splutter into rage as he had before, but what he said infuriated our men. "Holy place," he cried, "cess-pit I say. And those 'holy men' are criminals. Consider what they do in the name of religion, what cruel tricks they play, what liberties they take with simple folk. As for their miracles, do you know what they are? *Une bonne femme*, a fishwife, knows more of medicine and healing."

As an explanation of an error on his part, even if unintentional (which I began to doubt), this speech was a disaster. I suspected the guards guessed some of the doctor's discourse, and I thought they would unsheathe their swords on us. Mohamed opened and shut his mouth like a fish. But the effect upon the muleteers was to cause mutiny. They threw down their bundles, loosened their animals' reins, and made every sign of abandoning us. Some even started back through the rank shrub and grass while others sat upon the ground as if determined to go to sleep, obliging the guards to haul them up again.

We had come only a short way from the river course and once more had begun to climb. A curve in the path had hidden the village and its inhabitants; but although we could no longer see the pink walls we could sense the anger rising up to us in waves, or at least I could. Ahead of us the granite cliffs shimmered in the heat, a curtain of madder and gold, made all the more vivid by the white glare of more salt flats. Suddenly the little valley, previously so quiet, began to seem like a trap. This was obviously not the place to be caught by an angry mob, and no one realized this better than our guards.

Although the doctor's comments had angered them, and his contempt for them was clear, they swallowed their anger, cursing vigorously, making certain we knew in turn of their contempt for us. But despite all their efforts to chivy us along we seemed to lose momentum at every step, and they cast nervous glances over their backs, as if expecting pursuit.

It is said in this arid land where heat can dry the air like fire, where the mind can be burned free of dross until only pure sense is left, that there are men who have the gift of foretelling calamity before it strikes. I cannot tell you when I myself became aware of it, like the mutterings of a storm before a thundercloud. It was not a thing to hear at first, not even something to touch or smell, yet it made the hairs rise on the back of my neck. Mohamed felt it when I did. He dropped his stick and began to slither like a snake toward those cracked salt flats, seeking safety where a horseman could not ride. "Run," he screamed, "run." And those muleteers who were left with us began to run as well, in their panic trying to push each other from the path.

The doctor and I looked at each other, he too plump to run anywhere and I too lame to try, and in any case not sure what we were running from nor in what direction we should go. And all the while the sound, the thrum, like a heartbeat, throbbed toward us, rising along the valley like those waves of hate that I had sensed before.

Our guards had heard it, too. They were forced to give up their attempt to control the baggage train, left us to our panic, and swept their horses round to face the way we had come. I could make out the sound now for myself, the noise horses make, many horses galloping fast over dry and stony ground. *Those holy men are warriors.* Now we were to see that for ourselves.

Now whatever else I have told or written about our guards I have not stressed sufficiently their courage and their steadfastness. There would have been plenty of time for escape; their horses could outrun the wind and perhaps no one would have faulted them for abandoning Infidels who deserved to be punished for their sacrilege. Even so, our six guards never faltered for an instant, never broke out of line, never let their horses move out of step. Spurring on with hard raking sweeps, using their spurs as they never do unless at a charge or in a danger so imminent that they have no chance, they rode back down the path, two by two, swords drawn, to defend us from an enemy our own stupidity had made.

That enemy charged toward us, a great sweep of them, so great that although they were on the downward slope they broke through our men, meeting them and dividing around them on either side as a wave bypasses a rock, and like a wave sweeping back again. Our men did not give way or run, but waited calmly in a circle, facing defeat. Outnumbered, caught off-guard in a place almost impossible to defend, caught by our stupidity, and encumbered with us who were their responsibility, they never uttered one word of complaint, simply did their duty as they had been ordered. And like the brave men they were, they fought at first on horseback, then on foot, against holy warriors who were determined to kill.

Death comes quickly in this harsh land that has no time for pity and no place for mistake. How long does it take to transform laughter and pleasure into grief? How long can happiness withstand pain? How long? As long as is needed for six men to withstand a score. Even some of the horses were killed and horse-killing in this land is counted more a crime than murdering men. The doctor and I were forced to watch, helplessly, as those young men whose names we did not know, those laughing lads the girls had flirted with, sank beneath the bloodstained swords until only one man was left—their captain. Before he fell, pierced by a lance, he screamed the same word at us, "Run." Midbreath he died. And then it was over and done, finished, this brief moment of conflict as if it had never taken place; and so were vanquished our little dreams of content, our little hopes of security. And so were ended our captain's first and last captaincy, he and his men all crumpled like dirty rags. And of our fellowship only the doctor and I left alive.

"Guard them" their lord had said, and guard us they did. Bitter must have been the doctor's thoughts when he realized what his blundering had caused. And I felt bitterness that I had been unable to prevent the violence. Yet neither bitterness nor grief had place then. Death had struck abruptly into our midst, now it was to reach for us.

The doctor was stunned. He had no strength left to speak aloud. And I was speechless, overwhelmed by the casualness of our defeat, by its ease, its speed. Already our attackers were cantering toward us along the track. One was beginning to search through the pockets of a coat whose wearer, this very day, had boasted of its embroidery. Another held the rein of the captain's brown stallion that would not eat unless he hand-fed it barley and milk. Another wiped his sword on his white cloak, making me flinch. Most passed us as if contemptuous, searching out the muleteers, who, scattering like chaff, tried to outrun the enemy. That enemy played with them for sport, as our men had done once with scarfs. I wanted to block out the screams, prayed that Mohamed's hiding place would be spared; surely he had had time to hide beneath the cliffs, surely his cunning would keep him safe. I shall never block out all the sounds; they haunt me still in the dark night. Nor can I block out the sight of the remainder of the group surrounding us. They leaned upon their saddles watching us, white-robed and still, although their horses stamped and blew. We might have been a pair of goats, rounded up for sacrifice. But all these memories pale before the appearance of their leader, when he shouldered his way through.

He was white-robed, like his men, blood-splattered, a holy man, avenging a sacrilege. And when he came to a halt and looked at us, I saw a face that stopped my breath, it was so cruel, fleshy with age and license, the nose long and thin, the mouth etched with disdain and brutality, the eyes glittering and pouched with hate. This was the face of the Marabout, a man of God. He had watched us leave, had gathered up his men and mounted them, following us with one purpose: to avenge himself on these unclean Christians, lower than stray dogs.

Seeing him the doctor turned milk-white and began to pray, beneath his breath, crossing himself incessantly. In the circumstances this was the worst thing he could have done, for here even crossed hands seem a display of faith to people who only cross their legs to sit. "*Mon dieu, mon dieu,* spare us," the poor man moaned, gripping my hand as if it were a martyr's bone. "I have seen such fanatics before. When they swept down out of the hills, they murdered old men, women, children, for spite. Better to have died in their first assault than have lived as hostage to their cruelty. We killed our wounded rather than let them be taken alive. I escaped them once; I ran from them. Now they have caught up with me again." A blow to his mouth silenced him. The old man crowded his horse against us, words of command trembling on his lips. I saw his mouth open upon our death; I almost felt the sword fall.

Then his expression changed. A smile came creeping, gone in an instant, not a smile for remembering. We were Christians, I repeat, in a land where few Christians had ever come. I often had heard the whisperings behind my back. Not even death would come easily. Whatever courage I had left quailed before that old man's smile. Neither greed nor gold nor lust would tempt him from his determined course; certainly not cries for mercy or restraint. Rather, he would welcome them to sweeten the moment of revenge. Thus it was not a command for immediate death that old voice spat out, but rather "Spare," and after a moment's pause, "until we think of a fitting end." And again a look passed over his face, in which triumph and calculation shared equally.

What point was there now to debate the reasons that prompted the attack: the doctor's actions in the mosque, our own unpreparedness, even possibly some long-nurtured tribal enmity between these men and ours that fate had now unexpectedly given them to use? The truth may never be fully revealed, for who lived to question or respond? But one thing was clear, even while they bound our arms and feet, blindfolded and gagged us then threw us over the spare horses, having us as prisoners was worth more to them than not having us, and whatever the real motives had been, our capture more than served as recompense.

I do not believe that being a foreigner, a Christian, in the Islamic world of that time was of itself an offense. Other Europeans had survived; some had openly displayed their faith. But others had been killed, usually for some trespass into a holy place; ignorance is easily mistaken for contempt. But for this holy man, the wars of long ago, the Crusades, were still in force, and he felt himself the chosen leader of his faith. As victor, he had the right to dispose of us, not just our bodies, but our souls. So not only revenge motivated him but righteousness that would condemn us to a death we dared not even contemplate. And it was that self-righteousness that made the old man smile as he anticipated the satisfaction soon to come.

Bound then, face down, we were hung over the backs of horses which now were spurred on past those cliffs and salt flats where I believed that Mohamed, at least, still lay concealed. We could not see the dead or the mutilated, left sprawled like litter on a shore. Nothing moved or breathed, except perhaps the scavenging birds already beginning to wheel high above our heads. And as we climbed, higher still into the hills, along a trail that seemed scratched from rock, the riverbed we could not see must have stretched beneath us like a scar, with its rose-colored fort and the dome of its sacred shrine. I felt empty, lost, racked with a sense of guilt, as if we had betrayed friends who had not abandoned us. I will add only one thing more. I have never known, or hope to know again, such discomfort as through that hot afternoon. The thongs were so tight they bit into flesh; our eyes and mouths were bound with filthy cloth so we could hardly breathe. Jostled unmercifully with each step, I think we might have welcomed death. Behind me, at every stride, I could hear the doctor's gasps. I had no idea where we went, nor for how long, except that we rode much faster than usual, and when at last we did slow down so that the horses could strain upward, I judged from their gait and their labored breath that we must now be near the highest point of the pass. With more resignation than despair, I thought, No one will ever find us here. No one will follow us. Yet such is the determination of life, such its tenacity, that when at last our captors drew rein and pitched us off, we were still alive and conscious of where they had brought us.

They left us as we fell, removing only the gags and blindfolds, more I suppose to ensure that we did not choke than to allow us speech; more to let sight torment us than to give us a last look upon the world. We had come into a kind of plateau, or canyon might be a better name, a wide-open place, hollowed out between granite cliffs as if by hand. The pass up was tortuous and steep and the entrance was narrow, between two cliffs that opened on either side and curved around to join again at the other end in a shape like an egg. We lay on the eastern side, at the widest part, beneath a cliff so high and

sheer it looked as if it were one solid rock. Down its sides little
threads of silver marked the path of waterfalls that tumbled into a
series of small pools at its foot. The western cliff, facing us, was not
so steep, in parts covered with a great scree of stones. Small bushes
and scrub grass grew there, and trails, like goat trails, wound in and
out, up to the crest, where the sun still burned, red and gold, outlining the edges like jagged teeth.

We lay in the shadows where we had been tossed, our faces
half buried in the short dry grass, listening to the sound of those
waterfalls. We could taste the sound; feel it upon our burning skin;
sense its coolness on our cuts, as with careful maliciousness our captors paraded their horses past, throwing water on their backs, letting
it fall in great shining drops, letting their horses drink their fill from
those small deep pools, and drinking deep themselves. *"Mon dieu,
pitié,"* I heard the poor doctor moan, "pity us." The sky was pitiless,
and so was the red granite rock above our heads, like polished glass,
and so were the western sun-tipped slopes, with their little aimless
trails, leading nowhere among the rocks. And pitiless were the men
who squatted at their ease beside the closed-in valley end, away from
its mouth, planning what to do with us.

We lay and waited. Hours or minutes passed, flowed into each
other, became part of centuries. When I moved, I remember how the
dry plant pods rustled, sending black seeds flying. I remember how
the dry grass pricked. Twisting on my back, I stared up at the western cliff, trying to imagine what I could see there, from the top. I
tried to recall what once had been a friendly argument between Mohamed and Dr. Legros. Yes, paradise, paradise was what they had
been talking of, not joking about it as the Berber guards had, but
debating seriously whose idea of heaven was better, that of the East
or West. If Mohamed were here now, I thought, both he and the
doctor would be proved wrong. In spring, this valley could be a
paradise; in spring, there would be flowers and grass, a pale blue sky
and little pools, deep enough for swimming. Yet now today, it will
become a hell for us. So much for argument, I thought. I remember
even beginning to smile as if my thoughts were amusing me, as if I
had forgotten where we were. I remember feeling surprise on jerking
awake from brief moments of sleep to find nothing changed. Once,
heaven forgive, I almost imagined I were safe at home, and accepted
this valley as the meadow where I used to run as a child. I could

smell real spring grass there, feel it soft between my toes; and when I ran, as in those days I always did, skirts aswirl, the wildflowers sent up their smell of clover and mint, and green and fat grasshoppers bounced ahead on springs. For a second's beat, that dream seemed real.

By now the sun had almost gone. Only a faint glow hung about those rough crests where, like shadows on a dome of glass, dark flecks dipped and swung—birds of prey tracking us, circling round, waiting. I remember staring toward the canyon's mouth, where the pass curled out of sight. I remember looking back where our captors lounged. Hands washed, prayers said, devout men all, they lay around their fires, feasting on spitted meat and barley bread, deep in talk. They kept no guards, they felt so secure, and their guns and swords were stacked as hay is stacked, in ricks, whilst, no doubt, they earnestly discussed what death would fit us best—to be plunged headfirst to drown in one of those pools, or to be tied out on the plain, to go mad with sun, or to be dismembered, joint by joint—pictures rose like shards to stick in my mind. Yet as I lay and watched, a kind of peace came over me. To see your death, or rather the means of it, walking, praying, jesting, in the shape of your fellow men, and to know you can neither change their minds nor prevent their exercising their will upon you, is a dreadful thing, so full of horror it blurs the sense, and so God in His mercy intends. After a while fear becomes so great there is nothing left to fear. I lay and waited patiently. And as I listened to those flutes of waterfalls, that raucous laughter, the doctor's constant prayers, it seemed to me there came another sound, a shiver of noise like the one I had heard earlier. It seemed to fill the air, a pulse beating in the head, like blood, like sap rising in trees.

Heat and fever can distort sounds as well as shapes. I thought it was only the pounding of my brain. But when I pressed my ear to the ground I heard it stronger, far away, yet every moment growing closer, until the earth seemed to shake. For the second time that day I sensed danger, approaching fast. Unable to move myself, I shouted to the doctor so loudly that, half asleep, he began to roll, pushing me beside him, over and over, through the dust, until we were pressed hard against the side of the cliff. Those frantic movements saved our lives.

Our captors had heard the sound as well. They left their food, ducked under the horses' hobbles to cut them loose, and snatched for their guns. Black wafts of smoke flared up as the cooking spits were upturned. I looked at my companion and he at me, as in both our eyes was mirrored the same thought. It had a name, *rescue*, even though we admitted that the hope was small. Twenty of our enemies, mounted, alert, already riding together toward the canyon's mouth, could hold it against a multitude. A pass that twisted and turned toward a narrow entrance could easily be defended by men inside. It would not be easy for men outside to break through. And in any event, we were not likely to survive, small chance of that, I thought, since we were still bound, and were still within our enemies' reach, at their mercy if they should decide to shoot.

Along the valley that enemy spurred, those twenty men whose fanaticism gave each the strength of ten. We were half blinded by the acrid smoke of their musket fire, and deafened as much by their shouts as by the hail of spent cartridges that now clattered against the cliff face. There was no need for them to ride fast; the valley floor was not overlong, and the narrow entrance was their best defense. Seeing how many they were, I tell you, and how they grinned among themselves (for there was light enough to show their righteousness triumphant), I shuddered and closed my eyes at the thought of a second massacre I knew must come. The little doctor thought so too, shivering beside me in his heavy coat, his round face drenched in sweat as if he felt cold and hot in the same degree. We could not stand, rolled up like rugs; we had only mouths to give each other human sympathy, as we clung together, whispering private prayers. The drumming rose to a steady beat, horses, again approaching fast, and our captors raised their rifles to shoot.

They were stationed, almost at random, at the canyon's entrance, scorning the shelter of the rocks on the western cliff, thinking themselves invulnerable. What happened next was as astonishing to them as to us. Instead of the horsemen they expected, a mass of riderless horses burst out of the gap, like a battering ram, a ram that moved and twisted and re-formed, driven from the rear, stampeding out of control and running wild. Those horses surged into the entrance, pushing everything in front of them, breaking through the startled men, scattering them, as straw is swept. We saw several riders lose control and roll beneath those pounding hooves; others, trying to hold back their own mounts, were caught up in the forward thrust and swept along with it, churning within inches of where we lay. To and fro those wild horses beat, and to and fro went those with riders, until at the valley end, where the herd came against the closed-in walls, we heard the frantic neighs and shouts of animals and men forced against a natural barricade. The dust spurted in clouds. Round and round the mass swirled. Curses and sporadic gunfire added to the confusion, amid which the doctor and I lay like ones dead. And there, within three feet of us, a rider sprawled upon his back, brains smashed against the cliff, his sword still gripped in his hand.

It took us but a second to recognize the significance of that sword. At once we began to roll toward it much as we dreaded being trampled by a stray horse galloping past. Awkwardly I gripped the hilt between my knees whilst the doctor sawed with his hands across the blade. But our fear gave us strength. And once he was freed, it took but another moment for the doctor to cut me loose, and as long to start upright, almost as painful as being bound, when blood began to flow through cramped veins. And now, wiping the dirt from our eyes, trying to peer through the haze of dust, we became aware of a second phenomenon, almost as strange as those riderless horses: the arrival of the men who should have been riding them. Hitherto our efforts had obsessed us, and our enemies were still too engrossed to think of anything else except controlling the herd or trying to pen it in. Horses were too valuable to let run free. I could hear their leader's raucous voice, raised, not in prayer, but in ordering his men to turn this way or that, to catch hold of them. And what we saw was this, a mirage I thought, a trick of light, to make the western cliff seem to come alive: a wall of men.

The day had indeed dimmed in the canyon itself, but beyond it night had not yet come. The sky still held faint traces of blue, and although the western cliff was in shadow as I looked up at it, along the goat trails, between the shrub grass, shapes were moving, dropping down from ledge to ledge, almost as if they were goats. Some were on foot; some led their horses across the scree, the horses scrabbling along like cats. Showers of small grit and stones followed them, as if the whole cliff face were moving in a miniature avalanche.

Dr. Legros recognized what it was before I did. "Quick," he hissed at me, "*courez*, run." He rubbed the circulation back into my ankle bones, rubbed his own, and, taking careful measure of the distance between us and the canyon's end and of the space between east and west cliff, he began to trot across. As I have explained there was no shelter on our side, only bare, straight rock; our only hope lay on the western side with our friends. I never thought to hear the doctor use that word to describe barbarians he had said he despised, but there our friends were, a cliff of them, and there safety lay in their midst (although no Berber I have ever heard of would go into battle without a horse and how the cliffs had been climbed was hard to imagine for anyone, let alone men not used to walking).

I began to limp toward those friends, trailing my wounded leg. A stab of pain, where strained muscles gave way, left me marooned in the middle of the open floor, in plain view of everyone.

By now our enemies had begun to reorganize. Some of the more cautious must have been keeping watch, suspecting another trick, the trap that they had thought to set now sprang shut with themselves inside. A fresh outbreak of yelling set all those who survived swinging round, their leader's white cloak conspicuous in their midst. Back they came, firing wildly as was their style, making for me in a rush. It took them a moment too long to make their move; those single riders who came hurtling on ahead were easy marks and were shot off their horses by our men on the cliff. But I still could not move; my muscles were locked in place, and I had nowhere to hide, nowhere to go. I stood there, mesmerized.

Fear drained me of thought. I can record only what happened next as if it had happened to someone else, frame by frame, like one of those daguerreotypes, moved by hand. The doctor had come stumbling to the foot of the cliffs, where already a few of our men had installed themselves behind the boulders that fringed its edge. Wordlessly he turned to shout, arms going round like windmills; wordlessly he started to stumble back. A man mounted on a black horse took the last incline in a bound, swept past the doctor, and galloped forward in a spray of stones. I knew the horse, even though its rider was hidden, stooped over the horse's side, head down, his cloak spiraling like wings. I knew the rider's style, as he bent to pick me up, plucked me from his path like one of those silk handkerchiefs, and swung back toward the cliff, veering at the last moment to avoid it. He leapt to the ground to take my weight, dragging me after him, just as the first bullets began to slam into the rock on either side. Headfirst I pitched into a crack, and headfirst he came upon my heels, his long legs curled up like a cat's, tugging at his gun to free it from the folds of cloth and aiming it into the air. And with a shout, a battle shout, his men above him prepared to shoot.

I reconstruct what happened next. I saw little, heard little, I confess, face half buried in the shale. Each time I tried to rise, a hand or foot upon my back thrust me hard down again. I know there was a regular volley of rifle shots, as our captors, now captured themselves, tried to break out toward the pass, and a lull each time they were driven away. The man beside me had been kneeling to fire over the rock, which was scarcely high enough to shelter him. Now, in the long last pause when our enemies withdrew to the valley end, he slid down and began to reload, his rifle barrel red hot. Slowly and stiffly I started to shift to face him. I heard the bolt jerk home as he handled it in a deft and quick way. I knew him, I say, stretched out beside me in the semidark, almost at ease, like a cat new-fed, as alert as one, his eyes glinting catlike above his scarfs. Then he turned away, head bent again, as he struggled to tear a piece of cloth, holding one end with his teeth whilst he wrapped the other about his arm, equally practiced in this, swift, as if he were still handling a gun. He watched me as I continued to crawl, insectlike, on all fours, my body so bruised it felt on fire like the barrel of that gun. I was so out of breath I did not have the ability to say anything. This was not the meeting I had meant to hold, and this was not the best place. Certainly I had not intended to fall to my knees, whilst he remained nonchalant, at ease, cool, even in the midst of battle's heat.

He heaved himself upon his feet, hands on his ribs as if they pained him, too, still wiping the trickle of blood from his arm. "So," I thought he said in that soft Arabic I was beginning to understand, "still alive. That at least is good news, enough trouble as it is, a battlefield no place for a woman running loose."

Something about his tone of voice, its slow cadence, its insolence, set my nerves on edge. I tried to sit up straight, dragging up the remnants of my pride. Anger made me taut, as did fear, my throat too dry, my lips too dry to speak in any but the most blunt terms. "I did not ask to be caught up in a Berber charge," I croaked at him. "They attacked us, not we them."

For a moment I thought those eyes narrowed as if to dispute with me. Then I caught the glimpse of a smile, almost a genuine one. It said, louder than words, "You think these are true Berbers. They are only scum, not worth the effort of following them."

I forced myself to remain calm and to give my voice a touch of disdain, matching coolness with coolness, arrogance with arrogance. "Why then did you?"

He was on his feet, beckoning. His men above him on the cliffs were sliding down beside him, those on horseback, his household guard, vaulting over the lowest ledges to the valley floor. On the edge of the rock he looked back at me. "How else," I thought he said, "should I use you to bargain with?" Then briskly, no mistake this last, "A Berber charge. Here is a real one." And he, too, vaulted over the rock.

Single-handed he fought. I think he could, without waiting for his men. I suppose he felt so confident that they would follow him that he strode alone to his horse, which had been standing patiently. (Most horses I know would have run away.) He sprang into the saddle, leaned and spoke into his horse's ear. As if it understood, it uncoiled like a spring and leapt ahead. Behind him, a step behind, his loyal guardsmen followed him, filling the valley with their long black line.

Have you ever seen a Berber charge? They ride at top speed, hanging over their saddles to swerve and twist, firing their guns indiscriminately to frighten an enemy. In a charge all their marvels of horsemanship are brought into play, and the skill with which their mounts are taught to charge and wheel and charge again, the un-canny rapport between horse and man, for which they are famed. But most of all, their courage is shown, as fierce and indomitable as their will.

Down swept the line, their lord at its head, in a tangle of hooves and steel; no need to press horses whose intent was so in tune with their own. Swords were drawn, razor sharp, to cut through flesh as butter is cut. Over and through that line swept, and over again, treading down all that stood in its path. I watched them from the shelter of the rock where I had hauled myself upright, straining to see through the growing dark, where the evening shadows were fast lengthening. Yet even so there was enough light to see a man cut in two; to see a severed arm fall wide and the almost startled look on the victim's face. And light enough to see an old white-cloaked man force his stallion upon a black one. I knew what words stained those bitter lips, "Kill, kill," even as he himself was killed, a sword driven under the heart, as he raised his own sword to strike back. I saw the stain blood makes on white robes, spilled as carelessly as water is spilled. And even when I closed my eyes I could not block out the sounds, the great grunts of breath, the groans that men make when they strain themselves to the uttermost. And when, after a while, silence came, it was almost as loud as sound.

I stayed where I was, too weary for thought, too heartsick. It was the little doctor, crawling painfully among the rocks, calling me by name, who discovered me. Behind him, like the miracle I had been praying for, came Mohamed, full of smiles, seeming none the worse for wear. He carried a water bag almost as large as himself. Whilst we drank and washed our cuts, and soaked our wrists to numb the weals, he congratulated us upon our escape and crowed in excitement at his own—almost, it seemed to me, forgetting his dead companions in his eagerness to prove how brave he was. "I heard those men coming," he told us, complacently. "Why did you not run as I did? I know our horses too well to mistake those others for ours; their hooves are not shod alike for one thing. I hid among the crevices above the salt flats until you were gone, and I waited for our lord's return. I knew he would not leave us behind."

They helped me out, the little doctor fussing like a hen, his own arms raw, his face bruised, but his spirits much revived. I think he had almost forgotten the initial cause of the attack; certainly he acknowledged no blame for it. Now that there was real work for him, he reverted to his brisk professional self, anxious to see to the wounded without delay. Leaving me to Mohamed's care he scuttled off, shouting for stretchers and bandages, services; I thought grimly that he was not likely to be well received. Men who bind their own wounds with the help of their teeth are not inclined to look for, or need, other help.

Squatting down beside me, Mohamed was full of a tale that read like a storybook; first, boasting of his own escape, he described it again and again; then telling of the lord's return and his rage at finding his men slain, his anger, hard, ice-cold like a granite slab. Next followed the resolve to rescue us. A story interminable finally ensued; how men, who loved their horses like their children, willingly offered them as bait, unsaddling them and driving them toward the pass, a maneuver that our captors' carelessness had made easy since they had made no attempt to hide their tracks nor set watchmen on the rocks. Last came the climb up the western cliff, step by step, although Mohamed had not attempted it and had come himself with the horse herders, carried by one of them. "But mountain men are used to hills," he boasted once again. "And those who gave up their horses were as willing to climb as anyone. Only the lord and his personal guard kept their stallions with them, leading them as if they were dogs, so they could make the final charge." He clapped his hands, faltering into silence, the savage gleam in his one good eye dimming at my noticeable lack of enthusiasm. But he could not resist one last boast. "And how he rescued you," he cried, clapping his hands once more. "No other man rides that well."

He clapped his hands as he used to do when our guards had achieved as much at their evening sports. Yet today had not been for sport, and had the attempt failed I certainly would not be alive to hear Mohamed's praise. Sick at heart I say, saddened by such violence, revenge as heavy as prison bars, I felt for the first time the weight of gratitude. I had not even given a word of thanks to the man who had saved my life, but merely had added another complaint to the many I harbored against him secretly. I had not even expressed regret for what was, after all, our fault. For the first time in my life I learned that regret as well as gratitude demands a price. And so, sitting there with my friends, whose lives had been saved, as mine had been, by a man I professed to despise, I forced myself to see things as they truly were, to admit responsibility and to accept that the future might not be as simple or as pleasant as I had come to hope. Nor was there any point in finding fault if I were at fault myself.

Night by now had fully come. It hid the fearful activity of a battle's end, the sorting of the dead, the dying, the wounded, the friend from foe, no prisoners taken among fighting men as none had been made the earlier time. And when it was finished, I thought, little fires would begin to flare as the soldiers lit them, one by one; horses would be rounded up, hobbled tightly; the valley would revert to calm. Mohamed would set up my tent from whatever place he had rescued it, and there I should go to sleep, if I could lie down without fear of never getting up again. Beside our fire, low-spirited that his help had been so little in demand (amulets and charms, even red-hot irons clapped on open wounds, seeming more effective than his French medicines), Dr. Legros would take up his usual place. Wrapped in blankets, for decency (for unlike the rest of us, who slept in our clothes, he placed his beneath a stone, to keep them pressed, after carefully brushing off the dirt), he would bend over his notebooks as if he were culling through the day's work, at the end of surgery hours. What would men make of those notes, I thought, for whom even writing is unknown, suspect, threatening to endanger their very selves? And what would become of Mohamed, the would-be great warrior, who had fled at the first hint of danger? And what will become of me, the Englishwoman, set down in a land that has not proved as familiar as I had hoped? I reached about my neck for the gold locket I still wore and flicked it open. How had she managed, that little girl, that girl wife, married to a man whose world she had never known? And, trapped in his turn by violence and its aftermath, what had her husband felt? What had Colonel Edwards said? His voice seemed to fill my thoughts as if he sat beside me once more; I could almost smell the tobacco smoke. *Do not twist the world to your own ends. Accept things as they are.* That was good advice, I thought, and yet, at the first test, I had forgotten it.

The valley was quiet now. I could hear the fret of the waterfalls. The pools were lined with men, washing, drinking, watering their horses, talking softly, as men who grieve. There would be at least six missing friends tonight, perhaps more; there would be empty spaces among the camp fires and wounded to nurse. And at the far end of the valley against the cliff, the lord's tent stood with its double walls and high roof, its black pennons, slashed with red, fluttering in the breeze.

I stared at it. More than ever I sensed a mystery, stronger than before. What it was I did not know, almost did not care, although it frightened me. I tried to tell myself that this man who rode and fought like a medieval knight of storybooks was not an English officer, and all the wishing in the world would not make him one. Underneath those robes, those scarfs, I thought, is a face, a man I have never seen, and perhaps do not want to know. And for a moment, like a nightmare, flashed the image of that old cruel, self-righteous smile. The Master had cheated me, had lied, deceived. He had some plan or else he would not have rescued me. Did not he speak of "bargaining"? I thought, I do not know what that means. I owe it to my companions, to myself, to find out. For a long while I have been promising myself to meet with him; now the time has come.

But I also thought this. I owe it to the dead men, those dead friends, to make him understand all the things I have begun to admire in this land (although I have come late to understand them, and admit them reluctantly). Yet have not I been admitting them all along, the beauty that I find in every turn, in flinty soil and granite rocks, in naked hills spread out like finger bones, grasping among these arid plains? Like someone hitherto deprived of sight and smell, I have learned to recognize what I have never known before: the icy tang of early light; the noonday dust, ripe and hot; the bitter smoke from these torn bush fires. And most of all, I have come to appreciate the endurance of men who are as spare and indomitable as the lands they live upon. I owe it to them, to myself, and to him, to tell him so. And in this way the debt of gratitude and regret will be paid.

CHAPTER 4

I did not allow myself time to think. Taking Mohamed by the arm and forcing him to accompany me, he bleating like a goat, I limped toward that black tent, my spine ramrod straight, as Colonel Edwards would have approved. Closer to the tent I became aware of flickering lights, voices, movements back and forth, shadows of men against the black walls, giants bestriding the world. They made Mohamed shrink away. "Those will be his officers," he squeaked, "you'd never thrust yourself upon them. Allah be merciful, they'd believe you mad." He obviously considered me so himself, all his illusions of my saint-hood gone, and he tried to wriggle free, anticipating a new scandal worse than the last. I let him go, then squatted down as he would have done and waited, alone in the dark. This was the other side of the beauty of this land, the one I did not want to know, the side of violence and sudden death, of cruel revenge and wild extravagance in victory. This was what Colonel Edwards had been forced to deal with when his countrymen avenged a revolt from which his wife had tried to rescue him. I began to sense the difficulties I would have to face. After all, I had no idea how this dark lord might react when he had had time to mull over events. He might well know anger of his own. As I waited huddled the wind, spiraling down from the high wastes to the north, set the flags crackling in stiff folds, as if to test my will.

That I have a stubborn streak must be apparent by now. It had already stood me in good stead; I thought it might again. I tried to convince myself that since I had dared to come, I should wait. But the longer I waited (until the night grew old, until the lights were dimmed, until by groups, by threes and fours, the companions bid their lord farewell and returned to their own bivouacs; until I was sure he was alone), the weaker my resolve grew and I was almost ready to run. I think I would have, had not the guards ringing his tent seen and beckoned to me to approach. And when I did not move they came toward where I crouched, startling me to my feet. I told myself it was my air of resolve, my high-mindedness, that had impressed them. Now I realize they were merely puzzled, wondering why I had hesitated so long. A Berber lord might well expect some pleasure at a victory feast, and, left on a battlefield, most women would not have waited at all; most would have come fawning at once, flattered perhaps, and glad to please. Such ideas did not occur to me then; that they do so now proves how much my life has changed. Then, seeing no way to avoid the inevitable, I merely took a deep breath of air filled with the familiar smell of stable and camp and forced myself to follow those guards as they pushed back the heavy tent flaps and stood aside. Why did I go with them? What did I truly want? Who knows, or who can say why I made myself enter in. Perhaps some desire to set things right, some ingrained pride, some feeling that, as I owed him explanation so he owed me one. Were these my motives? Perhaps I tried to argue that what was fair for him was also fair for me, and I deserved to make myself be heard. Perhaps, most of all, I needed to satisfy my own curiosity. But I repeat, I do not know. I can say only that what I expected in no way resembled what I obtained, was so far removed from it that I might even have thought what happened next was not real and I had dreamt it all.

Within the tent all was dark except for one single lamp. During that long wait I had had time to imagine many things. Unchecked imagination runs riot sometimes. I had pictured rich furnishings, down-filled fringed cushions, silk rugs—not likely on a battlefield! I was sure that there, amid Eastern opulence, like Bluebeard, the lord would lounge among the wreckage of his feast. By rights, I thought, there should have been torches dripping wax, and rose petals on the floor, and dancing girls. Most of all I was prepared to be offended by those dancing girls, swaying their glistening bodies to the sound of tambourines. What met my eyes was a space stark and bare, a typical soldier's tent with only an empty tray, a bowl or two, nothing to show there had even been feasting. The floor was spread with a rug, but no one lounged there with face at last revealed, pouched and satiated with desire. Except for a curtained recess to the rear and a stack of weapons by the door, all was emptiness. Only two things stirred: a pair of falcons in one dim corner and a young man, almost asleep, on guard.

He started up as I came in, half guiltily. He had been sprawled in unmilitary fashion, at ease, upon a chair, his booted feet propped nonchalantly on a kind of campaign desk among a litter of what looked like maps. I caught a glimpse of dark-shadowed eyes rimmed with fatigue, a white shirt, European style, open at the neck, European riding breeches, before those leather boots thudded to the floor in a shower of paper like snowflakes.

"Where is your master?" I tried to make my voice as severe as that of my cousin's wife, questioning one of her husband's young officers, although I could never sustain her coldness long, and I stared at him curiously as he steadied the lamp with one hand, making ineffectual attempts to rearrange the maps, as flustered, I thought, as any subaltern caught in a doze. He stared back at me as Mohamed had, as if in truth I were mad. It occurred to me for the first time that there might be men in the camp who had never heard of me, although I had never assumed my presence had been kept secret. But if he did not know who I was, so much the better, I thought. Any Berber masquerading in European dress (a strange choice in any case) might have European sympathies and might be willing to offer help. I rephrased the question a second time, more loudly, in my simple French, hoping to make him understand. "Tell your master here is the English gentlewoman whom he will escort back to her wealthy relatives. Tell him the Lady Isobelle would speak with him."

My new title, Mohamed's invention, pleased me so much I repeated it. "Even if he is asleep behind that curtain there, wake him up. What the Lady Isobelle has to say is most important."

I pointed to the recess behind his back. The man, certainly young enough to have a shock of hair that stood on end and nervous enough to tug at his collar and shirtsleeves, still seemed too bemused to comment, and merely jerked the curtain aside. Its brass rings rattled noisily, setting the falcons flaring awake as it swung back, revealing an inner room, made for sleeping in but as empty as the outer one.

My resolve weakened. This was certainly not what I had planned. And to have braved so far for nothing was disheartening. I had watched the Master's companions leave. I could have sworn he had not passed without my seeing him. So what was I to do? Summoning up my courage and my limited knowledge of army men and recollecting too late that I did not have to justify myself to a sleepy guard, who was possibly half-drunk himself, "Slunk off then, to carouse," I said, trying to console myself, "drinking somewhere to excess with his officers. Or perhaps" (thinking of those dancing girls) "up to even worse things." And when the young man still did not reply, again half to myself, in my own tongue, "Why don't you speak? Are you afraid to talk?"

The young officer had regained his poise. He sank back into his chair, buttoning his sleeves with one hand whilst he shouted for a slave to bring a second chair for me. I was surprised. Most Arab men I knew preferred sitting on the ground. And when he did speak he surprised me anew for his French was more correct than my own, and it was pure French too, not governess-taught, halting and inadequate.

"Give me chance, mademoiselle," he said, which made me suspect he knew my language as well, although henceforth we talked in French. "What do you want?"

I suppose his question was overblunt for an underling, yet underling or not, he, like those other men, was loyal to his absent lord. For he was continuing, his tone mild, "Drinking is forbidden to the Muslim world. Nor do I think any lord has to answer to you for his goings-out and comings-in. And what worse sin would you wish on him?" And I swear he grinned, as if visions of those dancing girls had also flashed through his mind. "But if you mean that he and his men were drunk on victory, better victory than defeat. After all, it was you and your friend whom he was rescuing."

He spoke without emphasis, but I flushed. What he said was fair and for a moment left me, too, without reply. I closed my mouth with a snap that must have been audible. First blood to him. It did not help to tell myself that I *had* come, in part, to thank his lord, nor that I need explain nothing to this young man. I owed *him* no thanks. I considered him. He seemed too young, I thought, too suave, too . . . ineffectual (was that it?), or too "civilized" in his European dress to have ridden in such a charge. But I had many concerns, too many, to take time to dispute with him. And in his lord's absence he would have to serve as audience for what I was about to say, since I sensed the opportunity would never come for a second attempt.

"My friends and I," I emphasized the words, "have endured

enough. Look." I stretched out my wrists to reveal the marks, and would have hoisted my tunic to show my ankles had not modesty prevailed. "My companions and I were taken prisoners, bound, carried off to be killed. Our guards were slain. What else have I known except misfortune since misfortune tossed me on your shore? So, I have some right to ask, what does your master plan for me?"

For a moment he looked at my hands, and I thought his own tightened with sympathy. It was too dark to see his face. (I should explain that since I had come into his tent he had moved the lamp so that its light fell on me, not him. I began to think this was a Berber trait, this concealment of oneself, almost second nature, among men more than women, it appeared.) But his answer was not especially sympathetic. "Rumor gives a different version of events," he said. "It is said that you, or rather your friend, abused the laws of sanctity. That does not excuse the attack, yet gives a reason for it. But be comforted. There were those who suffered worse."

Again an argument that was hard to refute. I bit my lip, uncertain how to proceed, at each attempt seeming to run against a wall of logic that left me floundering, at each attempt seeming to be proved in the wrong. "Tell your master," at last I said, "I am aware of that. I deeply regret the wrong done and the consequence, but it was a mistake to have brought us here, and I should never have agreed to come. I beg you to ask him to take us back to the coast."

I had the feeling he was watching me intently. I tried a smile. "You speak French well," I said, trying to make him understand, hoping to harness that flicker of sympathy. "Surely you have traveled abroad. You must know how Europeans act. No civilized gentleman would hold a lady against her will."

Better I had left those last sentences unsaid. He drew back; his voice grew cold. "I have traveled. I have learned French in France. I know the Europe you speak about. As does our lord. Let me remind you of something." And now there was no doubt of the irony. "When the first Arab leader broke into these plains and reached the sea, he rode his horse into the waves to prove there were no more lands to take. Yet eventually his descendants crossed that sea and invaded Spain. Four hundred years afterward, another conqueror, a Berber one, followed them. When London was a mere jumble of huts about an open sewer (which to my mind it still is), those Berbers inherited cities, gardens, palaces that are the wonder of the world. It is said a

Spanish king once swore he would rather die a slave in the kitchen of the Moors than live a prince in Christendom. Before you mouth words like *civilization* and *gentleman*, remember him."

His rebuke was just and I felt it so. "I beg your pardon," I said, almost abashed. "I know nothing of history. I am not speaking of a thousand years ago. I speak of today, and it is my future and that of my friends that I care about."

"Then"—he was coolly insolent—"you are worse educated than I thought. Are all English ladies of rank so ignorant?"

"And who are you?" Provoked, I rounded on him. "You speak out of place. Are you your master's mouthpiece?" I thought, A guard in my cousin's regiment would be flogged for such impertinence, but I choked the words down. Instead I tried to reason with him. "Suppose that soon, very soon, those Europeans you despise reverse the process and invade *you?* To the north, France already has. How will you deal with them? As your master has dealt with us?"

For a moment I thought I had gone too far. I could sense the anger still running hot. But when he replied he spoke evenly. "First you tell me to talk, then to be silent. These are things best not discussed. I cannot speak for a master in everything."

"Does he mean to use me as a trading piece in some bargain?" I cried, my suspicions aroused. "Is that his plan? I would never agree to that. I would . . ."

"Our master believes," he said, cutting across my protests, "as do all thinking men, that one day, when the Europeans have exhausted the other lands they have conquered, they will try to conquer ours. We live on the edge of a vast continent whose resources are not known even to ourselves; certainly it is a temptation to men who hope to rule the world. But we may resist them longer than they think. And since I hear they are now at war among themselves, you may grow old before anyone tries to barter for you. However, there is one question I would like to ask."

And now he leaned back, as if at ease, tipping the chair on its legs, his voice almost as nonchalant as his master's own, yet having the same rapier thrust. "In your country, what is said of a lady who visits a man's quarters alone, without a chaperone, at night? Here she would risk her good name."

There was no doubt of the sarcasm. I felt myself flush. I tried to argue, lost the thread of my argument, fumbled to a silence.

"Or is it"—and again I had the feeling he was observing me

narrowly—"that for an English lady of rank, such normal standards of propriety do not apply? But our lord has not taken advantage of you, as far as I know. Did not he arrange for your comfort, order a doctor to attend you, supply you with guards, allow you to travel at your own speed? Did not he risk his life for you? Has he asked payment in return?"

The desert world loves dispute, but this was too close to the bone. I began to suspect I should not bandy words with this haughty young man, and yet some last flicker of pride made me determined not to give in to him. "What do you mean by 'payment'?" I asked. "Is not gratitude enough? I offer gratitude willingly. What other sort of payment would he want?"

He shrugged, his face a blur, his white shirt a blur, only his voice precise and clear. "Well," he said, "if not a rich ransom that a lady's worth might bring, perhaps you might offer him something only you could give to please him. He might take that as fair, seeing the trouble you have caused."

In the pause that lengthened I felt myself blush again. Once more, unbidden, came thoughts of what might please a lord. I pictured again those dancing girls. I saw them, half naked, in their silks, come out from behind that curtain, drawing it aside with their thin arms. I saw the way their feet turned out, and how their dark eyes peeped from their veils. In the hot lamplight their bodies, heavy with oil, would gleam, and their scent would drench the air. And behind their slight presence, there would be a great dark weight, a dark shadow, in its black cloak.

The young man stirred uneasily. Could he have guessed my thoughts? Such things are possible. Or perhaps he had visions of his own to dry the mouth and set the pulses beating fast. I heard him swallow hard.

"Your master," I found myself whispering, "what is he truly like? How old is he? Is he kind?" Questions I did not know I longed to ask came tumbling out; I almost think they were what I had meant to find out all along. "Or is he like that old man out there, that old dead man?" And I shut my eyes on the memory of that coarse face with its cruel lines.

If my spate of questions surprised me, how much more did they the young man? But he recovered fast. Afterward I wondered that he had replied at all. Suppose his lord had returned and found us discussing him? But the answers were always diplomatic, if that is the correct word. Only afterward did I begin to realize that most of the time his replies revealed little, being at best half-truths.

"What is he like?" He repeated the question as if he had not heard me correctly. "My master is not old, nor yet so young that he cannot distinguish truth from falsehood. He is a just man and, I think, generous. What he owns he holds, be it lands or men. If he desired a thing he would take it if he could; nothing would make him change his mind if he thought he was right. Some may call him obstinate or think him hard. And if he is suspicious of foreign meddling, it is with good cause, because he has seen it at close hand and because he himself covets no man or his lands. If that is kindness, then call him kind. But what is his own, he keeps."

"Is that why his men honor him?" I swallowed again. Almost unbidden the thought flashed through my mind, Then what do his women think? Does he own many of them?

He gave me another appraising look; then, almost as if I had spoken aloud, "If he *owned* a woman," he said, "he would own her for his use, as he owns his guns, his hawks." He pointed to the corner where the falcons, as if they guessed he spoke of them, sidled nervously again and beat their wings. "But if he *wanted* a woman, and she him, do you think there would be talk of payment or grati-tude?" He did not look at me afterward but I sensed the distinction he made and the rebuke he implied. It made me pause and gave an unpleasant sense of how I might appear to him: a thin girl, not over-clean, lame, an Infidel, not very alert, not even built to pleasure a man, not knowing what those pleasures might be. For the fourth time I felt my cheeks grow warm, as if his opinion mattered to me. Some desire to mollify, some unsatisfied feeling that I was not mak-ing headway with him, a growing uneasiness made me persist.

"Is he married? Does he have scores of wives, a harem?"

"The law allows him but four wives. Myself, I think one would be enough for any man. So thinks he, since he is not wed. But in his fortress there are many rooms, and old; who knows who lives in any of them? And since he is young it is not likely he has lived alone. However, *harem* is an Arab word, not a Berber one. Have you seen our women veiled? I do not think he needs to lock his women in a harem. Most of them come willingly."

Most of them. "But what if they resist?" Again I found myself whispering as curiosity got the better of me.

"Why should they?" He sounded genuinely puzzled. "Is that not what women do best, pleasing men? Why should they want to escape what also is pleasing to them? As for numbers"—he shrugged—"he bids us round them up at the season's end, like sheep, and, when he has made a choice, the residue he gives to us, as you call us, his officers."

It took me a moment to penetrate the dry tone. Then I thought, indignantly, how dare he jest! Is it possible he is teasing me? I tried to draw myself up stiffly as my cousin's wife would have done. "You must be proud," I began to say, in just her tone of voice, "to serve such a model of depravity and lust."

But I knew I could not best him. Like his master he would be too quick. I could almost hear his reply. "Depravity is something I know little about. I am not privy to what a lord's mistresses say of him. As for lust, I did not think you European ladies knew the word. Love you certainly talk about, and marriage vows, not quite the same, although you seem to think they are." What he did in fact say, his voice so cool I could not tell if he joked or not, was equally impertinent. "Is it correct, mademoiselle, that you have little knowledge of the world, or of men? My master could make allowance for inexperience. He does not dislike young girls, providing they do not talk too much. What he does dislike is meddling incompetence. And lies."

Now he had said too much himself. Conscious of my dignity I rose to leave, so quickly that my leg buckled under me and I had to sit. My voice went quavering out of control, although I tried to match his coolness. Aware that I had allowed the conversation to spin too far, "Tell your master," I said, "he has no right to bring me here. Tell him to let me go. Tell him I am not afraid of him."

"You should be." It was his turn to sound stern. "I told you he was just, not merciful. He will not welcome troublemakers in his camp. Nor spies. You can tell your doctor that. Nor would he like to hear how you have tried to win me to your side. Even I, who know him well, what did you call me, 'his mouthpiece,' would not dare befriend you unless he approved. My life would not be worth the air I breathe. Would you want to see me crucified, spread-eagled in the sun? Would you want your little body smeared with honey for the ants? That is the law here; death for unfaithfulness in women as well as in men."

He frightened me, turning my little boasts to absurdities. Mention of those punishments, reflecting the ones I had been imagining just hours ago, made me pale, made my heart beat so I could not speak. I thought, Dear God, is there no end to cruelty? As we began, so must we end? I heard him asking, soft-voiced himself, "What is the matter?" while a second time I struggled to my feet.

"No, no." My voice hardly seemed my own. "I have already admitted responsibility. I do not wish to harm anyone further; enough hurt has already been caused by us. I asked you to help only because..." But I did not know how to finish without offense. "Because you *look* as if you might; because you seem younger and less alien."

He said unexpectedly, "You have a gentle heart, rare in women anywhere and seldom found in Europeans, especially foreign women who are a misery, like all foreign things in a land not meant for them. But it is not written that gentleness in women is worth more than gold? I am well used to looking after myself. It is you who are vulnerable. Tell no one you have spoken with me, except your friends, and those you should warn. What I can I will try to do. Not because of your asking me to, nor because of European ways, but because of your own goodwill."

He snapped his fingers, a sudden hard, imperious sound. The guards drew back the tent flaps and motioned me to leave. I limped out as painfully as I had come in. But one last thing. Before I left he took my hand and bowed over it. His own hand was large and closed on mine with unexpected firmness. It reminded me of something, someone, that disturbed me, until long afterward I remembered the long fingers and strong grip of Colonel Edwards when he had comforted me.

•　　　•　　　•

I found Mohamed waiting after all, crouched like one of those hares he believed so magical. The guards saluted us and let us through. Together we scurried back to our own camp fire. But no longer did it seem safe. I felt the eye of the Master on us, just but not merciful. I began to sense the underlying terror of which Dr. Legros had warned and which, despite those warnings, I had never really appreciated. *He makes the law, outside the law. Spread-eagled in the sun.* New terrors I had never thought on before, fresh barbarities, burnt in my brain. Yet in England, within living memory if not within my own lifetime, a child could be hanged for stealing bread; a man transported for killing the sheep that fed his starving family. I was not so ignorant that I had not heard of America's recent war against slavery; I knew of the new type of slavery, said to exist in our new industrial towns. We, too, had our share of cruelties. They had never troubled me before as they began to do, now that there was something to contrast them with.

I studied my two friends. Beside the embers of the camp fire Mohamed huddled, gnawing on a crust of bread, his expression full of reproach. What do we gain, that look said, to brave the anger of a lord who has full power over us, if you forget to mention our plight? Did you ask what we should do next, without guards, or mules, or muleteers? I think suddenly he began to understand the extent of the misfortune that had befallen us; he suddenly became aware of what the loss of those six men, those six friends, meant. Meanwhile, the doctor persisted tranquilly in his scribblings, using the final flickers of firelight. He might not have stirred from where I had last seen him, and even when I went up and stood by him, it was long before he recognized my presence.

"Put those writings away," I cried, "before they destroy us, and you."

The little man, startled by my harshness, began to argue, but I talked him down. "Think what happened today," I said. "What made those men come after us? Think how you spoke of our guards who saved our lives. You will be our death as you were theirs."

He jumped up in a tumble of rugs, looking harassed, looking more than ever like a frightened sheep in his woolen underdrawers. He rushed to where his clothes lay weighted with stones and began to scrabble in his pockets, pulling scraps of paper out, until as in a farmyard he was smothered in a cloud of white, like goose down. "Mother of God," the poor man cried, "what earthly harm is there in these?" He held them up by fistfuls, his precious notes, consisting of sketches, drawings, maps, all thumbnail size. But on their backs, crisscrossed, as since I have learned to do, in a maze of spidery French, were all the details, observations, records, that a military mind would make, for an invading army's use.

They steeled my resolve. "What plan did you have for these?" I asked and asked again, refusing to be deterred by his reasoning, which he turned full force on me, although he had little ground for maneuvering and he himself was not at his most dignified. At last he admitted more of the truth than I wanted to hear. His eyes grew cunning and blinked rapidly behind his steel spectacle frames. His face grew red. "Why do you persecute me?" he whined. "I am here only because of you. *C'est votre faute.* Must I forever do penance for a mistake of my youth, when I now have a chance to clear myself? As you know very well, these maps and notes will prove invaluable to people who are not familiar with this land. They are my passport to escape." In the end he confessed what I had suspected. "My superiors will pay me well for them," he cried. "And when we come, as come we shall, we shall need maps like these, notes like these, to mark the route. And like that German, my name will go down in history."

By "we" he meant again "we French" and by "when we come," that invasion that "all thinking men" expected. Except me. I pitied him, to be sure, but I was adamant. *Our lord does not welcome spies.* I did not mean for my friends to suffer "just" punishment. I asked Mohamed to help me round up the pieces and consign them to the fire. As they flared up their author sagged in sodden misery. "There," I told him, panting after our efforts, "the evidence is burned that would have risked your skin. He guesses what you are up to; do you want the blame for everything? Henceforth keep quiet; do not practice medicine on unwilling patients and hide your ideas in your head."

But when the charred flakes had shifted to ash, and I told him of the new friend I had made, neither he nor Mohamed appeared as pleased as I had hoped; quite the reverse. Fear seemed to diminish them; they shrank back as if to avoid contact with me and for a while refused to speak. Mohamed eventually summed up their feelings. "Allah be merciful, that was no Berber you met. Who ever saw a Berber horseman in leather boots? They are known by their shin calluses. That man was a *jini,* come to trick you." In the same breath, the doctor, leaving off his private lamentations, berated me as harshly as I had him. "No lord," he pronounced, "least of all this one, would entrust such a man, a younger man, with affairs of state, to say nothing about the charge of womenfolk. It is you, Miss Isobelle, who have endangered us with your foolhardiness, far worse than anything you say I have done. Such a man, in the lord's tent, alone, in his absence, can be no ordinary guard. No magician either, but some close friend, or relation, *oui, un frère,* a half-brother perhaps, although I have never heard of one. Male relatives do not usually last long in this world; they are either killed at birth or murdered when a son inherits, to avoid conflict of claim. Perhaps this brother plans some coup of his own and will make use of us, instead of our using him. You have played into his hands."

"A half-relative," Mohamed said moodily, suddenly knowledge-able about state matters. "Then he will be a gelding, a eunuch, the worst kind, none their like for malice and spite. God knows what such a one might have in mind. But in any case we cannot go back, as you have asked. Think what those ambushers would have done to you and how much worse to me, a Muslim renegade who serves Infidels." He lapsed into gloom, not lightened by the doctor's tart query as to where his courage had gone. In vain I tried to reason with them and tried to persuade them that the young man had not appeared treacherous to me, although I also had to admit, to myself at least, that I was finding it difficult to crystallize exactly what my opinion of him had been. He seemed both so mild and yet so hard, so suave and yet so rapier-quick, so young and yet so self-assured. But I put thoughts of him aside. We were in a sad state ourselves, each blaming the other, each casting fault. I crawled into my little tent, full of regret. My wounds ached; my spirit ached; nothing had gone according to plan, and all seemed confused and dark. And outside on either side of the fire, my two companions tossed as restlessly.

That night I had a dream. Part of it I had dreamt earlier in the day; it was as if this new dream began where the other had left off. I was at home. The sensation was again so vivid that I could hear the sound of finches twittering in the hawthorn trees and feel, as before, the freshness of the grass where my old white mare plucked it up in mouthfuls by the fence. But now I went along that fence through the meadow to a place where I could see the house. Its bricks were warm in the afternoon sun, and the windows were open wide. On the gravel walk my mother and her friends were strolling up and down. I could see the gentlemen's black coats and hear the ladies' tea gowns rustle as they stopped and turned. I came toward them eagerly, expecting them to call my name. "Isobelle," they would cry, "welcome home." The air between us seemed to harden and congeal, until, like a real wall, it separated us, a wall of glass through which I could see in but through which they could not see or hear me. I was dead to them and their world. And when their faces turned, I realized they were not even people that I knew. My mother was dead, I was dead, and these were strangers who had never heard of us. And I knew I would never return to see my home again.

And, with the morning, this other world, where also I did not belong, this Berber camp, swirled about us with the noise and energy that is the pattern when its men prepare to ride. First comes the call to prayers, thin and high, spiraling into the cold clear air, reminding the devout to kneel. They face the rising sun and bow their heads. What thoughts run in their minds, what peace fills them afterward? Servants bring them water to brew the hot sweet tea they like. They throw blankets over their chargers' backs, cinch on the high ornate saddles with their silver ornaments, adjust the wide stirrups. The horses blow gently through their nostrils, toss their fine small heads, their long manes and flowing tails so unlike those of our horses at home, which are clipped and bobbed. What was it Mohamed had said of them, of all the animals in the world these are the most beautiful; of all the riders these are the most brave? God spoke to the south wind, he said, bid it reveal itself, and from its essence created the Barbary horse. God said, Let it run. And from the fire He made the men to ride.

Now, by ones and twos, the riders were beginning to form a line, not as in my cousin's regiment, in strict array, stiff in their uniforms; but almost lounging in the saddle as in an easy chair, so much at home it was clear they must have been riding all their lives, so nonchalant, that it seemed impossible that in an instant, they could be transferred to cord and steel, ready to follow their master, their lord. Over them he holds the power of life and death for he can order a man killed, as casually as he might call off a hunt or summon his favorite dog.

The pools that yesterday had maddened with their sound were covered with a film of ice, but I went toward them, longing to plunge myself in despite the cold. We were still skirting the edge of the foothills, but behind us, thrusting up from this valley like a great dark weight, the mountain mass began to rear, high above us, its snow-covered peaks running north and east. I counted the days, the weeks (was it that long?) since shipwreck had changed my life. When I stooped to cup a handful of water, my reflection, like that Indian girl's set in an oval frame, stared back from the still surface. I almost would not have known myself. Where was the Miss Isobelle, the English miss that Colonel Edwards had mocked? Where were my mourning dress, my ringlets, my black crepe? I saw a face, browner than it had ever been, thinner, with eyes too large, a face whose planes and angles had accentuated themselves, topped by a mop of hair streaked with gold, like the rising sun. Not a face my English friends would know, not one to inspire a man. *I like you better fighting back*, Colonel Edwards had said. Today I did not even know what to fight against.

Behind me there was a stir. Slowly the ranks were on the move. Their riders would be winding their scarfs about their cheeks, for cover against the heat, for protection against the dust and wind? Or for hiding behind, a mask, to frighten and confuse? Where was my young officer? I could search for him in vain, I thought, lost somewhere in the crowd, in the rear perhaps with the younger men. But I did not believe he would betray us; I did not believe him marked for death. I did not mean to betray him.

Now they would be moving into a trot, the horses breaking out of line, as if the exertions of the day before had but increased their liveliness. The sun's rays, already mounting above the cliff, would catch at their accoutrements, setting the silver agleam. When they had gone there would be nothing left, bodies already tipped away, ground swept clean, only the white scars upon the reddish rocks where bullets had scraped. If we did not leave with them we, too, would be tossed away like chaff. I willed myself not to look, not even when the line ground to a halt, and I heard one horse wheel aside and come toward me, its hooves thrusting through the dry grass.

But I did look, heart beating fast, in expectation, or fear, I am not sure which. But it was not the Master, arrogant on his black horse, nor yet his young aide-de-camp. An older man, betwixt age and youth, with grizzled hair and beard, his face stamped with the marks of loss and pain, was watching me, leaning on the saddle of his stallion, arms crossed. He did not say anything for a while, merely watched. There was something nerve-racking about his stare, something familiar, and yet I returned it boldly. He was not a man I knew, but his thickset figure and square jaw had the look of authority, and when he spoke, it was in his lord's name. Afterward I came to know him well. He was the second-in-command, the chief adviser, or Vizier, brother to the former lord, and of all the men in this camp, the one most hostile to our presence there. But then I only sensed in him some enmity, some old hate concealed for the present, but deep felt.

He spoke. "My lord, Lord of the High Atlas, Master of many men, Beloved of God"—the list of titles stretched as bright as those silver coins about the horse's neck—"the Lord of the High Tigran, bids you ride with him. He can no longer wait for you, nor allow you to dawdle as you have become accustomed to. Winter sends its first warnings and the passes will close. He orders you keep up with him."

My mouth was dry as if I had not drunk my fill, as if I had kept it open to let the cold air in. "And if we do not," I said, "if it proves too difficult?"

"Then leave," he said, tonelessly. "The way back is open to you."

"Leave." I repeated the word beneath my breath and Mohamed, who, unseen, had come bustling up, moaned it aloud. "But that is tantamount to death."

I recovered myself to come closer. The horse, like its rider, battle-scarred and venerable, showing signs of many wars, began to sidestep wickedly. "We would not last a day alone," I told him. "Without supplies, fresh horses, guards, we would not have a chance and so your lord knows. Moreover we should need proof of a safe conduct, which so far has not been much in evidence."

The man let his horse fret and stamp, and rubbed his grizzled beard. I was shocked to see his hands, the backs of them twisted as if the flesh had been stripped from the bones. "You ask overmuch," he said, "from a lord who hitherto has been indulgent. No one makes demands of him."

That galled me. Suddenly I felt forced to say what was on my mind, not wise I knew, but better than meek subservience. "*Indulgence* is a word overworked. Nor has it achieved anything so far." I pointed toward the disappearing line, almost lost in its own trail of dust. "Why should I trust a man who does not dare speak to me himself? Faithless was he to me once, and faithless may be yet again."

The older man began to splutter with rage. Foam appeared around the edges of his beard, just as it did on his horse's bit. I thought he would gnaw his lips apart. "No man," he managed finally to jerk out, "much less a female Infidel, would dare challenge the honor of a Berber lord. I was in the square that day. I heard your shameless words. I heard what was offered on your part, and what silence my lord observed, promising you nothing in return. You wag your tongue overlong and loud. Were my master not a kindly man he would have had it cut off. Before you prate of dishonor beware the consequences."

Too late I began to regret my rash words. I felt cold run along my spine. But I could not prevent myself. "Why should you doubt a lady's word?" I said. "I am a lady of means and rank. I speak for my companions and myself. All I ask is, what does he plan for us?"

He had swallowed his anger and now was steadying his horse, patting it with one of his maimed hands, whilst with the other he felt along his sword belt, in which his curved dagger was thrust. I felt he was of two minds, either to let his horse trample me to bits, or draw his dagger and skewer me on the spot. His amber-brown eyes ringed like a hawk's stared down at me dispassionately. He must have known the effect he would make; he must have relished the chance I had just given him, yet not even triumph showed.

"There were survivors from that ship," he said. "Most of them reached land in small boats farther north. The dangers of that coast are well known for many ships have foundered there. So is the greed of the Arab caravans known. The Sultan's foreign advisers"—he sneered the words—"the Sultan's pet foreigners, to protect their own kind, have ordered that records of lost ships be kept, naming the Europeans on board. Among the list of passengers from the *New Victoria* there was no mention of a Lady Isobelle. And among those missing and presumed dead, only two English persons were named, a colonel of an Indian regiment and a governess. Since you cannot be the first," his voice smooth like cream, malice-smooth, "you must perforce be the second. A lady, I think, you said you were, and so we took you at your word. But among our people, ladies of rank do not do menial work. We leave that to slaves. Nor will there be a ransom for one already believed dead."

I was silenced, the heart knocked out of me. Not so much at being caught in my stupid lie as hearing a truth. "My cousin would never do me such a wrong," I wanted to scream. But I knew he might. Or rather, his wife might, for economy, for spite, for being rid of a duty she had never wanted from the start. And she would force my cousin to agree. The captain would run his finger beneath his collar as if to jerk it loose, as if to relieve a strain, and in the end he would obey. All these thoughts flashed through my mind, like things I had always known, and were gone like sparks flying up from the fire. I have never felt so bereft as at that moment, my last hope gone and all faith in English honor lost.

He was repeating, with a hint of relish now, savoring his triumph after all (was that also his master's wish?), "No ransom, no rich friends, never a title to bargain with. And in our world, no bargain ever possible between a woman and a man, certainly never between a lord and slave."

He kneed his horse on, passing so close that the gravel from its hooves spattered on my clothes. But after a few paces he reined back fiercely, bringing it almost to its haunches as he shouted over his shoulder his master's command, however reluctantly. "My master, in his mercy, gives you one more chance. You and your companions are to follow him. And if you have any sense, keep them in place else I myself will string them up by the thumbs, as you see once was done to me."

•　　•　　•

Although I tried to be brave and resourceful, most of the time I felt I simply blundered from one crisis to the next, thankful just to remain alive. Fears assailed me like those bullets raining down upon the rocks. One moment I felt we had no choice but to journey on; the next, we should go back, whatever the consequences. Among my companions morale was low, Dr. Legros having sunk into his former pessimism. (And I will repeat, whatever crime had sent him into exile, made him a wanderer with no home, as his words seemed to confirm, cruel indeed was the punishment—to offer him the chance of escape and then remove the means.) Mohamed refused to speak. Having believed me a princess of the blood at least, he had so lost face to hear me reduced to a slave, not much better than himself, that he seemed to have given up all will to live. As for my young officer, his importance paled in comparison with that of the older man, that Vizier. Antoine Legros confirmed what I had thought, that this Vizier was as powerful as he had seemed, being also that most rare of things, a younger brother who had remained alive and loyal. "Without his help," the doctor insisted, "his nephew, this present lord, might never have inherited. They say, in his youth the Vizier suffered fearful imprisonment for some crime but never faltered in his loyalty. He certainly speaks for his lord. And any younger man, learning what he has just told you, will have the sense to lie low himself. You'll not find help again anywhere in this camp, Miss Isobelle. Accept your fate, as now I must accept mine."

Ours was a grim partnership as we rode on. And yet, it still was a partnership, as shall be revealed in time, although for the moment strained to the uttermost. Meanwhile we had another hard ride ahead, the last of our journeying. We traveled fast. By that I mean, once mounted we never altered pace, nor stopped, nor strayed, but kept up the same speed, hour after hour. There were no more leisurely starts or noontide halts, and at the day's end we fell and slept almost where we were, too tired to make a fire or raise a tent. Thrust back among the grooms and slaves, we were obliged to forage for ourselves as in the caravan; there were no friendly guards to arrange for us, no friendly villagers to harbor us. On the march, if a man had personal needs he merely turned aside for a moment, off the track; he even let his horse stale under him; he had no time to feed or water it, and certainly no time for us. Thus we began to climb, deep into that mountain hinterland.

We ourselves rode mules, horses not considered safe, and no doubt too valuable. The mules were hard-mouthed and obstinate, as is their nature, but sure-footed on the steep paths. After a while, even safety seemed of little account, of as little consequence as hunger or weariness. All that mattered was moving up and up into the mountains that now enfolded us in their shroud of mist. When we awoke every morning, wrapped in blankets because of the cold, we saw how the men seemed to sniff the air and their horses stretch their nostrils out, as animals do, searching for the approaching blizzards that would bury us. I could not have lasted many days on such a ride. Even on a mule the saddle was too hard, the stirrups too long, and although my wound was healed, the constant weight on the muscles seemed to pull them out of place. Mohamed was as miserable, gritting his teeth and clinging on grimly. Mountain heights terrified him, and he swore that if he were once restored to earth, he would never willingly mount an animal again, for all that God had blessed it. But the doctor, the most unathletic of men, showed unusual fortitude. Once in the saddle he stayed there, although he heaved himself up with the grace of a sack of wheat. At times he displayed a surprising knowledge of strategy, a stock of almost military lore, which made me believe my suspicions of his army past were correct. I began to think perhaps he had served in that French desert-army, the Legion, about which he now spoke, in his turn, often telling tales to pass the miles. But mostly we simply hunched forward, gave the mules their heads, and endured; where before we had been like to die of heat now certain we were to die of cold. I never saw the young officer along the way, nor the Vizier nor their lord. I never . . .

But I lie. And I have resolved to tell the truth as far as rests within my power. I saw the Master one more time. I never spoke to him, nor he to me, except two sentences, one at the start, one at the end. This was not the meeting I had hoped to have, but it was one I cannot forget.

It was the third day of our ride, the last, as later we found out. Well, that itself was a thing to rejoice about. We had bivouacked the night before in a pass strewn with rocks, where the wind blew with such force it tore at the ropes holding the tents as if to send them swinging into space. We had crouched together to keep warm, but the cold was so intense that sleep became impossible; even I could smell snow singing in the air. Before daybreak most of the camp was already astir, beginning to edge toward the head of the pass in the hope of finding shelter on the other side. I had wrapped a blanket about my head and was trying to pull myself and my mule along a track that would have made a muleteer blink. It hung above a drop so steep that I was glad clouds hid its depth. I was on foot, and my mule, in its obstinacy, had turned its head toward the cliff and refused to budge. Behind and in front, men were crowding in a mass, all in search of somewhere to make a fire, shouting to friends, trying to prod on their own animals. This pass was notorious, once a whole caravan had perished there (but that was three hundred years ago, although they spoke of it as if it had happened yesterday). My mule blocked the path; the more I pulled, the more obstinately it stood; we were locked in a battle that I was bound to lose. The shouts behind me intensified. Any moment now someone would use a whip, if not on me certainly on the mule.

I guessed who was coming before I saw him, on foot, like the rest of us, he and his guards, heads down, wrapped in their cloaks, to keep off the wind. Perhaps it was the hush as men let him by that alerted me; perhaps it was the crowd who followed him, eager to see what would happen next, anticipation of the encounter warming their blood like food or drink. "You," he said, his voice like that lash I had been expecting, "force that animal along the path, or I boot you both off myself." It was plain that he did not recognize me in my heavy wrappings. But I knew him.

I had dropped the bridle completely now, my fingers frozen by the leather, slippery with wet, and when I turned, instinctively, I suppose, I put my hands up, palms out, as one does to block a blow. He was on foot, I repeat, the officers of his guard behind him, each of them wearily plodding along with his horse in tow. They were in no mood to be stopped by an ineffectual rider and his mount. But as I turned he realized who I was. There could be no other in his camp who moved so lamely and who did not know how to control his mount. He let out a curse, one of those Berber oaths wicked enough to make a mule blush, and strode up to me. I could not sense his mood, but his men did. They backed away, suddenly their eagerness diminishing, as he planted himself in front of me, hands on hips, looking at me, as if he had never seen a thing so feeble or disheveled. Well, I did not like being lame, I who had never known a day's illness before. It offended me. If I had ever thought of complaint, pride alone would have kept me quiet. And I hated that mule. Yet standing there before him, feeling the sudden spasm in my leg as it locked into place, I knew I could not move and would rather die than tell him so.

I felt his will clash with mine. They say there is a thing, like a spark, like the charge that powers a thunderbolt or makes lightning flash. If it has a name I do not know, but I felt it between him and me, that thing without a name, strong enough to make the blood run, to melt the bones. And I put up my hands again.

Before I could utter a word of protest he had picked me up, both hands clasped about my waist. He might have been removing an obstacle. Beneath the blanket he must have felt my body shivering with cold, fingers numb and face blue with it, leg frozen into place like a block of ice. He never spoke, simply shifted his hold and carried me on up the pass until it widened out. He had carried me once before, but I had no conscious memory of that time. Now I could not escape what I felt, the broad shoulders, the active stride; this was no old man, certainly not a man who did not know women. At the head of the track he paused to catch his breath, cleared a patch of ice with his foot, threw down the blanket that I had worn, and dropped me on it like a sack. Before I realized what he was intending or could stop him, a thing so immodest I am reluctant to speak of it, he rolled up the side of the long tunic I wore, baring the scar along my leg. He stooped down, gripping with fingers so hard that he brought tears to my eyes. The pressure was intense at first along the muscle line, the pain almost obscuring the indelicacy of being tossed on my back like a slut, legs apart, skirts rucked up. But it is also true he behaved as if what he did was not to me and as if my leg, bared to the thigh, was not an appendage of mine as he massaged me with deliberate skill. I felt the pain begin to roll away, and the cramp lessened, disappeared. Almost sobbing with relief I lay on my back and closed my eyes, release overwhelming the shame.

He straightened up and drew the blanket over me. I sensed a laugh, soft, indulgent, the sort of laugh men give when faced with a difficulty at once insignificant and easily solved. "Be comforted," he said, a phrase his young officer had used. "I would have done as much for my horse were he lame." And *that*, certainly, no one had ever said before. He pushed my feet together with his own, turned his back, shrugged his cloak on top of me, strode to where his men had waited in a knot. They crowded around him; he waved them on, mounted, and rode ahead. I lay there on the ice, covered with his cloak, and let the tears roll down my face for embarrassment, for relief, for that other thing that has no name. Presently one of his captains came back, had me ride with him, and so I did for the rest of that long, cold day. But one other thing I will admit, although it shames me to the core. While I lay naked to his touch and his hands were closed about me, hard and skilled, I never took my gaze from his, never for a moment looked down or averted my eyes, as in all modesty I should. And he, although his features were as ever hid in the wrappings of his scarfs, he never took his gaze from me.

And that truthfully was the last encounter that we had before we reached this strange journey's end.

CHAPTER 5

We arrived at our destination as dusk fell. All day, the snow that had been threatening drifted in a fine gray mist, settling on the animals' coats and powdering our hair and woolen cloaks like ash. But once the pass was crossed a fertile valley stretched below us, forested with juniper and cedar, its sides terraced with fields of almond trees. At every crossing on the downward track, little groups of men came to pay their respects, crowding round to embrace and to be embraced, local dignitaries I presumed, solemn in their white robes, the dramatic effect spoiled only by the noise of sheep and goats brought forward as tribute for a celebration feast. But where we rode, at the back of the line, I heard the doctor whisper that there were fewer tribesmen than was usual and they were not overwelcoming, although superficially they made a display of loyalty. I cannot judge the rights and wrongs of this myself (although later events were to prove rumor right). I can only say no emperor could have responded more proudly than that proud man on his black stallion, making it prance as if it trod on the rose petals of a victory. Yet when we entered between the castle gates, huge, iron-tipped, meant to withstand a siege, the crowds that lined the narrow streets, the brightly dressed women who hung from balcony and tower, gave proof this was no tyrant's return. And the guards, those great warriors, were transformed, in an instant, to ordinary men as they waved back, shouting up lewd invitations to the girls, embracing them when they could reach. They reminded me of our six friends and made me realize that this was their home. Here was where they were changed into husbands, fathers, lovers. Here was where they came when their work was done.

We had ridden, I repeat, at the end of the cavalcade, the doctor, Mohamed, and I. Perched behind my taciturn captain, I had come right under the walls before noticing that they were man-made. From a distance, the lines of turrets, redoubts, and battlements looked as if they had been sculpted out of rock, dark brown against the gray of the sky. Yet the entrance of the citadel (I call it that, but it was more like a walled city than a simple fort) might have led into a town from the Crusaders' time, who knows how old, built perhaps in the period of the first Berber conquerors. And when we reached the main courtyard and my rider set me down, we ourselves looked as out of place as if we had strayed back into the twelfth century.

The cobblestones where we stood were worn and grooved, littered with the straw and refuse of the stables. Behind our backs reared the great mass of the main castle, tunneled underneath into a warren of dark passageways. Before us, in the open square, children ran and squealed under the horses' legs; women, those women of the balconies, resplendent in their lime-green and turquoise wools, hung on their husbands', lovers', arms, like fluttering birds. The lord and his entourage had disappeared, presumably into one of those inner halls with which the castle was laced like a honeycomb. We could hear sounds of talk and laughter; servants ran back and forth with trays of food. Strangely enough, or perhaps not so strange, these sights and sounds made us feel more alone, as if we were cut off from everyone.

All day long thoughts of what would happen when we arrived here had obsessed me, as they had the doctor. (Mohamed, conversely, relieved to be on firm ground, had professed delight at everything.) It had begun to dawn on me that once we were here, we truly were in a Bluebeard's grasp. I worried away at the idea of what a slave could be forced to do, a female slave, who could not be sold or traded off. I could think of nothing suitable for an English girl, lady or not, certainly nothing that a well-bred Christian should ever contemplate. Yet think of it I did, with apprehension. And such is the inconsistency of our human frailty that I felt resentment at now being ignored; to be left cooling our heels whilst our master dined was not what I had in mind. But if I confess that strange ideas occurred to me as we stood or sat or shifted uneasily from foot to foot on the edges of that huge yard: visions of torture perhaps, in those lower undercrofts, or wild orgy in the rooms above (neither of which I saw in detail, only in vague outline) I hope I am not misunderstood when I say it is not the most comfortable feeling in the world to wait upon the fringes of other people's happiness, anticipating dishonor for oneself. But fate still had some surprises in store. All that was needed was the time to unravel them.

We waited. We waited. We waited, my companions as restless as I was. The voice of the slave who brought a message made us jump. He had glided from one of those dark subterranean passages like a ghost, his face gray-white, and had obviously learned his lines by heart. "Your friend," he began, "the officer of the guard you met, bids you follow me. He and our lord," he choked over the word, so great his terror I supposed, "must ride out again, tonight, and they wish to see you housed in safety before they leave."

This news was better than I had expected, but my two companions were not convinced. "Who would leave here on such a night?" the doctor cried, whilst Mohamed, with his customary shrewdness, asked what we all feared. "Who is this officer who values secrecy? We know nothing about him, not even who he is."

The slave paled even more, if that was possible, choked down a reply. "Hurry hurry," was all he would say, constantly glancing behind his back as if he suspected that people were watching him. On one level his behavior made sense, especially if the young officer felt endangered by helping us. But I had begun to be suspicious too. "What of the Lord Vizier," I asked, "does he approve of this message?" The effect was even more dramatic: I thought these questions would demoralize our messenger and make him bolt. But he clung desperately to the same theme, that we were to trust him and hurry, hurry, without delay.

"If"—the doctor spoke cautiously—"if that young officer acts *without* his lord's command, which is possible, he endangers us as well. If he acts *with* the contrivance of his lord, this may be as close as we shall ever come to apology, or blame, for the way we have been treated these past few days. *Moi, je pense . . .*"

What he was to think was never known and his logic was lost. With a strangled cry of alarm the slave turned and disappeared, not running so much as sinking into the earth, down one of the long tunnels. And now from another one, we saw the castle guards, in their red-and-white uniforms, advancing toward us out of the gloom. They were tall, their red turbans lending them height, and against the darkness their black faces seemed to render them invisible, only the white of their voluminous trousers and the red of their tunics standing out in sharp relief. Some of them seized my companions and hurried them off. I could hear their shouts long after they had disappeared behind the gates where the horses were stabled. The remaining Negroes encircled me and seemed to be waiting for orders to proceed. These were given (completely unexpectedly) by an old veiled woman. Deftly throwing her veil around my head to gag my cries, she beckoned to the men to lead me away. I cannot tell you where we went, through a network of corridors, up steps of stone and wood, along underground burrows that led suddenly into the cold night air. I think now the route was deliberately lengthened to confuse, and perhaps we came back close to where we had started from. But when I had recovered sufficiently from shock to shout, twisting and turning to break the hold, kicking, scratching where I could reach, I do remember my disbelief that in all this vast and teeming place, not one person heard the noise we made. Unless, and this was a thought to chill, no one *dared* to hear. *There are many rooms and so old, who knows who lives in them.* I did not mean to be buried in some forgotten room. But the more I struggled, the tighter my captors held, and the louder I shouted, the further the silence seemed to spread.

Finally the old woman ordered the guards to set me down in front of a heavy wooden door. She beat upon it three times. It was opened; I was thrust within and she, close behind, pushed the door shut and locked it with a great heavy key. She gave the key in turn to an old watchman who shuffled forward and pocketed it somewhere beneath his flowing robes, then squatted down again, a self-satisfied look upon his dark face, as if capturing guests was an everyday affair. The old woman, with a sigh, as if relieved at work well done, retrieved her veil before I tore it apart, and rearranged her robes, disheveled in our rapid transit. Beckoning to me imperiously with her thick fingers ringed with gold, she waddled through the archway into an inner room. Since there was no way out, and all the screaming in the world seemed useless within these walls so thick they absorbed sound like wool, I obeyed. And that is how I came into the harem of the Lord of the High Tigran. And this is what I learned there.

I had never seriously considered what a harem might be like. The young officer in the tent had led me to believe I would not find one in the home of his lord. Although, on looking back, I had to admit that there had been no definite denial of its existence; the man had merely answered my question with one of his own. And to be fair, I should explain that I do not now think the present lord had ever been inside it or called it by that name. Yet once it had been so. I cannot judge if it was similar to others in this land, or if what I found there was unusual, or if its inhabitants seemed strange. I only know that in the way fate has of twisting things, nothing was as I might have expected.

The place was dilapidated, forlorn, as even a casual glance revealed, sinking into shabbiness, like a run-down boardinghouse. Whatever garden of delight had flourished here had gone to seed long ago, all its luxury and vice reverting to dust like a country graveyard. Three women only were left to wallow in its emptiness. (I exclude the old watchman who, surrounded by the fumes of his pipe, stayed on guard as if protecting a thousand concubines.) I came to know those three women well, too well for comfort or safety.

First there was the old one. That she was old was proved by her wrinkled skin, her gray-black hair twisted into a nest of plaits, by her huge distorted body, layered with fat like a pickled egg. But her eyes were bright; her hands were strong, although dimpled with flesh; everything about her bespoke strength, and when she wanted she could move her swollen feet as quickly as a younger woman. Denuded of its veils, her face might have startled anyone. Dark-skinned, almost black, her cheeks were stained red, with a deep blue line painted from her lips to chin, turning the color purplish. Whatever her status (and Mohamed had once explained that most Negroes were slaves, brought to this country from its southern borderlands and often in time achieving great rank and power) and whatever her age, there was no doubt of her authority. Most of all, it was the size, the sheer bulk of her, that dominated. (And perhaps I should add that one of her most offensive traits was her appetite. She ate continuously, meals of such elaborate food that to one like me, so recently starved, both they and she appeared obscene. To her mind beauty meant flesh and she tried to fatten me with fennel seeds, as if I were some goose to be force-fed into suitable plumpness—efforts that failed, since the taste sickened me and had the reverse effect!)

When she clapped her hands two other women appeared. One was obviously a servant, a small halfwit girl, carrying a tray loaded with plates. She stared at me with open mouth, as if I were as much a freak. The other was such that, if looks were anything to judge by, she should have been the mistress here. She was a Berber. Tall, much taller than I was and still young, she had the bearing of a duchess. In European clothes men would have turned to watch her pass. I say "European" clothes for emphasis. In her own, in long white gown of silk bound with its colorful overwrap or *haik* arranged in artistic folds, her neck loaded with chains of coral and amber, she towered over us, and when she walked her ankles and wrists shimmered and rippled under the layers of gold. But she wore these ornaments and moved her body as if careless of the effect; and this lack of personal pride, if I can call it that, this gracefulness, made her hauteur all the more pronounced. It gave a special distinction to her arrogant face with its long nose and fine-shaped eyes. It gave her a kind of freedom that I admired. But there were two other things that were to mar this first impression of her and make me wary of her from the start. These were her jealousy and her malice. And so strong was her personality she made both clear.

"So." She walked around me, much like a farmer surveying a calf for sale. "This is the Christian." She spat the word. "You will have your work cut out, my dear Safyia, to make her presentable. Look at those clothes, in rags; look at the dirt ingrained in the skin. That yellow hair, like straw, how will you get it to lie flat? And nothing, nothing, will disguise those big European hands and feet." She gestured with her delicate fingers, so thin the amethyst rings slipped around them. She spoke in Arabic, most of which I understood, listing labors for a Hercules. But she could not resist one last insult. "And all before our lord returns; impossible! For shame," she hissed at me, anger getting the better of her. "He and his *harla* must ride out again, as soon as they have ridden in, and all because of you." She took a step toward me, so full of menace that I felt myself cringe away. "She does not even know what a *harla* is," she cried. "A war party, a battle horde, that is what our lord leads. And you and your friends are the cause. Have not his allies complained of you? Have not many defected from his alliance because of what you Infidels did and the bloodshed that ensued? Will not you be to blame for fresh bloodshed?"

This was information not made to soothe the nerves, although it gave substance to the message that the officer had sent. Nor was the method of its giving calculated to make me feel welcome. The older woman, Old Safyia, paid scant heed, merely went on gulping tea from a small glass and fingering the honey cakes that she called "gazelle hooves," because of their shape, not even bothering to wipe the drips from her chin. She reminded me of one of our village worthies taking tea in imitation of the fashion of Queen Victoria's court, except she wolfed it down with even less manners than a villager. The ensuing silence unnerved me. I began to feel afraid again, fear tingling against my spine even as I fought it down, even as I tried to resist. "Take me back," I began, bravely enough. "Where are my companions? Who are you to keep me here? We were meant to go somewhere else."

Both women pretended not to understand, only grinned when I spoke of "somewhere else." I say "pretend" because they could understand when they wished and when they spoke I understood them, although their Arabic was thick and slurred, obviously not their native speech. After a while Safyia removed a cake from her mouth. "No, no," she said through the crumbs, shaking her head, making the elaborate braids wag out of place. "This is where women must live. These are the rooms of women who serve our lord."

This reply did not please the Berber woman. She frowned. "Women of the lord," she repeated as if the words stung her lips. "That title has to be earned. And our lord has to bestow it himself. He has bestowed it upon me. As his wife I take precedence. I say she will not do. To begin with she is too small and frail, to say nothing of her stupidity."

The older woman ignored her again and continued chewing, observing me placidly. Then she smiled as at a wayward child. "There was no marriage," she said, speaking to me and, through me, at her accomplice. "Show me the books. There is a blank against her name. I keep the records and I know. I remember"—and now her voice, too, grew loud, tight with anger held in check—"I remember, as she does not, when these rooms were crowded with girls, waiting to become a 'chosen' one. That was in the days of my former lord. When did he not return from his wars with someone for me to teach? She thinks me old perhaps, past my prime. But I am not so old that I do not know the rules. I made them. I mean to keep them. I remember other concubines who played the game their own way and lost. She believes those days are gone. But I am not gone. Nor am I so old that things can be done here without my saying so. I, too, was once a favorite. I, too, played for control. And as you see, I won. No one questions my authority and even our present lord leaves me alone."

"Perhaps." The Berber woman allowed another sly grin to cross her face, as if she saw her chance. "But that Frenchwoman whom you swear you hate, did not she marry the former lord? Did not she steal him away?"

Mention of a rival, even one of long ago, made the older woman shake. "She did not last," she cried. "Before and after her I still had slaves to do my will; a hundred eunuchs were at my command. I have seen beautiful women come and go." Now she addressed the younger woman openly, becoming sly herself, tormenting in turn. "They let men enjoy their beauty as bees the flowers. Beauty soon fades. Power, brains, skill, those are the things that last. And so my former master knew. When that French whore sent all the other women away, he did not permit her to get rid of me. And after she left I still remained. When his son, our present master, marries, I shall rule over his household as before."

It was the turn of the younger woman to give way. She sank to her knees in a sign of respect, touching her lips to the old woman's feet in their yellow heelless slippers. Beneath her veil of hair her eyes glittered out at me unrepentant and full of spite.

After a while Safyia allowed her voice to soften into calm. "All in its place. When the moment comes we shall both present her as was done in olden times. But she is young, untried. They say she has a temper and our lord will not have her tamed. We shall both be called upon to make her worthy of him. But there is no rush. When our lord returns, then will be the time."

And that is how I learned what I was wanted for, and why the younger woman came to be jealous of me, and why the Master had kept me safe.

Well, I suppose I should have guessed before; what else should female slaves be good for? And no doubt I sound ridiculous, coming upon the idea so late. For my part I think it remarkable that I thought of it at all. I had few illusions about myself, and the hardships of the past weeks could not have enhanced my physical charms. I had never had a suitor nor thought of one. To imagine I was to be prepared to be the lover of a man I did not even know both shocked and scandalized me. Remember, I had kissed only one man and that was after he was dead. Had I lived out my life where I was born, and where perhaps God had once meant for me to remain, perhaps I should have thought of marriage in time, and made a match with a man of my own class, and I suppose I might have found happiness with him. But I had good country sense. I guessed enough of marriage bliss to suspect that love scarcely entered in, provided there were lands and wealth (which, since my mother's death, I lacked). And I guessed that lovemaking was a duty to be got through somehow. If pressed, I might have admitted that to my mind women of my age and class had few rights, few hopes, few desires. *European ladies do not know the word for lust. Lust is not marriage or love.* But, I thought, if marriage and love are the things that lust is *not*, what is it then, this thing called lust, that everyone talks about? Here in the ruins of a place once given to its sole pursuit I was to find a version of it.

Old Safyia had set herself that chore. She saw in me the obvious means of restoring her former powers and planned from the start to use me as a pawn to that end. But she was lazy. While she sat and dreamt the hours away, or, more like, ate through them, her companion, equally resolute and more alert, determined to wreck her plans and made my life a misery. At first I did not dislike this younger woman, despite her jealousy. Her name was Rashmana. I write it as it sounds; I cannot reproduce the harshness of the first consonant nor the rasping of the vowels. Rashmana might have been pitied I think. I might have come to enjoy her sudden bouts of vivacity when she would dance and sing, or tell tall tales of her life with her father's men. At those times her eyes would glow, her proud resentment would soften, and she could coax even the watchman to do as she willed. Her tall body with its firm back and breasts would seem transported from these walls, back into the mountains where she belonged and where I wished, more for her sake than mine, that she could go free. But her moments of frivolity were few, and even then she could not forget her dislike of me. Jealousy festered in her like an open wound. And, although God knows I never meant to give offense, every word I spoke, every look, only offended more.

In the beginning I thought her spite was fed by boredom, of the sort that set her squabbling with the servant girl (and she, poor soul, not understanding half that was done to her). She started, as most bullies do, with small things. Sensing at once my need for privacy, which like all ladies of my time I clung to, she took pleasure in breaking it, even pulling her sleeping couch close to mine so that all night I would have to listen to her muttered dreams. Realizing her manners irritated, she found delight in spitting on the floor at my feet, or belching or scratching or other unpleasantness. When I tried to hide my nakedness she would pull aside the loose smock I wore to comment loudly upon the smallness of my breasts, the thinness of my waist, the unseemliness of my scarred leg, meanwhile flaunting her graceful body unashamedly. I tried to ignore such pettiness as best I could, tried to take no notice of her, until one day she forced me into protest.

I had found a small gray cat, which had crept out, half starved, to eat the food that I did not want. I had begun to make a pet of it and, seeing my pleasure in its company, she in turn began to tease until I drove it away myself to prevent its being hurt. Provoked, she laughed, and behind my back she pretended to limp as I did, at the same time touching one finger to her head as if to indicate my mental deficiencies, causing the poor halfwit to giggle with merriment. I rounded on her then. "If your master's orders brought me here, on his return he will expect to find me well-treated," I said. "Your sort of welcome will not please him." I lied of course, for I was still not certain in my mind whose orders had separated me from my friends, sometimes I thought it more like the Vizier's work, and sheltering behind the Master was an irony of which I was not unaware. Mention of him spilled Rashmana's resentment into rage.

We had been sitting in a sort of anteroom, huddled about a small charcoal fire for warmth. Old Safyia and the servant girl were dozing in a drug-induced sleep, for like the watchman they both smoked a herb called *kief.* Rashmana started up, her body rigid with hate, her face dark with it, dark and dangerous. Before I could protest she had seized me by the arm and forced me through the archway past an empty courtyard once full of flowers, into that labyrinth of inner rooms. "Telltale," she hissed, "sneak, spy. Come here to ruin all I care for. Do you think to take my place?" She struck at the marble pillars passionately as I tried to struggle free. The fretted carvings crumbled about us in small white shards. "See this," she cried, "and this and this." She stamped upon the cracked paving stones and tore at the tattered silks until the curtain rings rattled hollowly. "All gone. Vanished, Old Safyia's world. Here was where her women waited, each hoping to become a chosen one; some waited all their lives. So you want to be one of them? Then look at this."

She reached down and from beneath a stone bench dragged out a fistful of scrolls, unwinding them in yellowing heaps upon the floor.

The rows of Arabic script ran in blurred lines before my eyes. "Here are the record books she boasts about with the list of names she says she keeps. She never spoke of the second list, the list of children, of sons—the dates of their births, the dates of their deaths, and the same." She kicked the scrolls aside contemptuously. "Life and death," she repeated. "That is what true power is. That is how a chief wife put an end to all the little hopes and little plans. That is what happened to those who tried to supplant her."

She suddenly leered at me, her face a mask. Animosity leapt out at me like flame, all the more frightening that she fed it with her own pent-up resentment. "Now you know what the stakes were," she said. "Now you know the games we play."

She was watching me intently. I could not take my gaze from her eyes, their pupils narrowed like a cat's, unblinking, unwavering. "But there are other ways," she said after a while, and now she was whispering. Her whispers, too, seemed to echo hollowly. "See here." She thrust me against a wall and kept me pinned whilst she fumbled with the heavy bars that held an iron shutter in place. It swung open with a bang, and a slash of light leapt in at us through the window space. Behind its oblong shape the outside wall dipped down into shadow like the opening to a well. "Once," she hissed, and her voice had dropped, it fell like water dripping onto stone, "once there was a girl brought here, like you. She was a virgin, small and pale, colorless like a ghost. She claimed to be a princess in her land and refused to be made a chosen one. Nothing would convince her to be prepared; she swore that even as a prisoner no man should dishonor her. When the time came she ran through these rooms setting the curtains fluttering like birds' wings. She stood where you are standing and gazed out of this window just as you are doing now." Her words were falling like water, softly, persistently. "It is not so very far," she was whispering. The wind took her whispers and drew them up into the air. "You could float down upon that wind. It would catch you up and carry you away as if you were falling into sleep." And for a moment it seemed the pressure of her hands was lifted as I took a step forward and my head bent of its own will toward that nothingness.

But I resisted. I resisted the whispers. I forced myself to look down, deliberately, into that darkness where the layers of shadow deepened against the cliff and the rocks at the foot sprang up like fangs. I forced myself to turn away, summoning up all my strength to push past her away from the wall. My own heart was beating so loudly I felt I had to shout to drown the sound it made. "No," I said. "No," I cried. I made myself laugh although the laughter rang false. "Who had the right to force her? Who has the right to force me? And who, dear God, who gives a man such authority? Does anyone 'prepare' him? Does anyone ensure he pleases first?"

I hurled these questions at her like pistol shots, surprising her, surprising myself. She could not have understood, for I shouted out in English but she understood my resistance and was bemused by it. Like all bullies she had thought me incapable of defense. She hesitated, biting her lip, her handsome face twisted indecisively. She hesitated too long. Before she could make up her mind or take another threatening step, Old Safyia came waddling through the archway, roused I suppose by our absence, or perhaps by the noise we made. Shaking off the effect of the *kief*, she advanced purposefully herself. Rashmana tried to laugh her suspicions away. "Your new protégée will never succeed," she sneered. "She does not know what a man's body is nor what his private parts are for. I am sure she has never seen a naked man, since she does not even like her own nakedness." She grinned, showing all her splendid teeth. "Europeans only know one way for sex and that so dull even our servant girl would grow bored. This one," she waved at me, "is no different from the rest."

I let her talk and made good my escape. Afterward I made light of the incident and never talked of it, keeping my thoughts to myself. I tried to pretend that nothing very much had happened, but I took good care never to be alone with Rashmana again and stayed close to Old Safyia's side. And, I think, for a moment Rashmana was not sure what to make of me and made no open move. But sometimes in the night, when the oil lamp swung on its chain and cast a patch of light across my face, I would wake from troubled sleep, starting up, throat dry, to remember and to see the glitter of her eyes as she watched me.

Now followed a new sort of danger. Freed for the while from one trap I came into the second. Avoiding Rashmana, I was forced into Safyia's company. I cannot say hers was any better than Rashmana's, only different. For having sensed the hatred the younger woman bore me, suspicious of and perhaps knowing her, Safyia, alert to any crisis, finally roused herself to take interest in me, as she had said she meant to do. Her tactics were quite the opposite of the ones Rashmana had used. She began with compliments, wooing with lavish praise, exclaiming over the whiteness of my skin, the unusual color of my eyes, the texture of my hair, which she liked to brush and comb while Rashmana scowled. Her old fingers were surprisingly gentle as if to seduce me into compliance; but although I let her do as she wished and pretended to accept her fondling, in reality I withdrew from her as well, putting a barrier between us. Behind that barrier I let myself remember happier times with my friends and, although uncertain of their fate, would try to picture meeting them again. I would remember the young officer and tell myself that he at least would find out where I was; had not his servant been a witness to our capture? And sometimes I even thought of the Master and wondered what had happened to him. Perhaps he never would return either, a war party sounded dangerous; perhaps he would be killed. But if he were killed then I would truly be in the grasp of these women. There was no way out for me and so I was obliged to humor them.

Rashmana dismissed Safyia's efforts scornfully. She had learned another way to taunt me now, with my ignorance. While Safyia tried to teach me how to dance, bending my body between her hands, making it sway and dip as if to music in her own head, the younger woman would grin as my very bones seemed to stiffen in protest. "At her first time a man will rip her apart," she said, "she will so hinder him. Or he will fall asleep, weary of finding his way in."

Old Safyia countered this lewdness with stories of her own, how in her youth she had been a favorite and had brought delight to her master's bed. In response Rashmana would grow even more lewd, describing how she had first been deflowered, with a detail that shame should have kept concealed. I covered my ears and refused to listen to them, pretending that brutality had nothing to do with me. And Safyia would cackle at my reticence. "Take no notice," she would say, slipping another sweetmeat into her mouth and trying to force one into mine. "That Rashmana would couch with anyone when her desires are upon her, even with the doorkeeper. And he gelded as well as old." And she would cackle again. "That is one of the reasons she lost favor with our lord," she whispered in my ear. "Were he his father she would be dead. But you," she stroked my hair, "if you will let me I will show you how to approach a man, how to reveal yourself to him to make him more desirous of you. I will show you which perfumes to use, and where, to rouse his lusts." And she would glare at Rashmana, making her retreat.

"And I will teach you all the positions of congress, until you become an expert. There are as many ways of love as phases of the moon. Each has an advantage you should learn. I will show you how to lie like the lotus flower, or how to perform the act of the mare; I will show you how to stimulate desire and create it in yourself. And I will show you how to hold a man's penis so that his semen flows into your womb." All these and other things too explicit to relate she tried to explain, her flow of lascivious detail as distasteful to me as Rashmana's hate. Yet, despite my noticeable lack of interest, Safyia never relented in her efforts. She tested the sweetness of my breath and my urine; she inquired into my body secrets, even the monthly times, which since my hardships I no longer had. The very paring of my nails or strands of hair did not escape her curious eyes, nor the softness of my skin where the sun had not reached.

She would repeat the words for lustful acts in her own tongue, until I recoiled from her, as from a snake, lying in the dark. Openly now she would try to span my waist as if measuring it, or feel my breasts as if weighing fruit or try to flex the stiffness of my leg until I felt like a horse being groomed. And when eventually, as I knew it must, news of the Master's return reached her ears, she moved swiftly into action like a general on a battlefield, waiting for a signal to begin. Sex was the battle and the field the Master's bed. And I was to be made ready to meet defeat.

They say that many books have been written about the Victorian world, and women's place in it. Perhaps, as is claimed, English women have lost their rights and have been tamed by their men into timidity, have been taught by them to ask no questions and expect no pleasures in their sexual lives. I can only repeat I was a child of those times. But that did not mean I could not change. The question was whether I wanted to. And this I think a basic conflict between my life and theirs; what they would do by rote, because they must, I might come to, by instinct, of my own free will, in time. I did not expect them to understand the difference; I did not understand it myself at first, but because of that difference our greatest conflict occurred. And all because of one man.

I was roused from a sound sleep by a kick. Rashmana stood

over me in that small stuffy room where we three slept although she was usually the last awake. "Get up," she screeched at me, no sign of hauteur left, her large mouth turned down petulantly. "Lie-abed, lazy slut." She tore at the bedclothes, making sure her long painted nails scratched my sides where the marks would not show. Behind her Safyia panted, pushing the little slave girl along, weighed down with jars and bowls. Caught by surprise, I did not understand their need for haste, but whether in fact the Master had returned or was simply expected back, the old woman had resolved to waste no time. Equally she was determined that I should do her justice, her "novice," her "bait" to lure her lord into restoring her to power. Meanwhile Rashmana was equally determined that I, the rival who supplanted her, should not succeed. Between the two, no wonder I was as bewildered as a sheep at dipping time, pushed this way by one, pulled that way by the other, as both quarreled over me as over a favorite scarf both claimed. In the end Old Safyia prevailed. She had decided that the time was come, and all was to go forward as planned whether anyone wished it to or not.

Rashmana would have preferred to see my throat cut. "Shall that hussy have it all?" was the least of her complaints. She pouted and sulked, like a fractious child herself, as bolts of silks were unrolled, as cases of jewels were displayed, as perfumes were unstoppered and rejected as too strong, or too faint, as buckets of water were poured, enough to wash an ox. (All this was done without explanation, with myself as unwilling centerpiece, holding on to my make-do shift with both hands, refusing to cooperate.)

"She'll not have my goods," Rashmana screamed again, losing control. "That necklace is mine, part of my dower."

Safyia seized the casket from her, tipping its contents out upon the bed. "There can be no dower without matrimony," she cried. She rounded on the younger woman with a catlike pounce that sent my own little cat scuttling out of sight. "Ever since you came here you harp on that. But my lord never wished to marry you, and you, you threw yourself at him, whore that you are. He has often asked you to leave. It is you who have refused to go. Now, like other former favorites, it is your turn to make way for a new girl. Refusal to help a novice is punishable by death. And I will punish you if our lord does not."

Into the silence that followed these threats, this talk of death and punishment, I dropped my own thunderbolt. "Let her take my place," I cried. "I do not accept it. No need to open that record book for me. If she wants him I willingly give him up."

If I had flung cold water on them both I could not have achieved a faster effect. They both forgot their quarrel and swung back to me, Safyia incoherent with thwarted rage, Rashmana in fury that I seemed to be mocking her. Their anger almost united them. But Rashmana recovered first, suddenly realizing what my offer meant. "Let her be," I heard her say. "I know how to please, as she never will."

This open rebellion ripped aside all pretense of calm. Screams, succeeded by hysterics, by threats and counterthreats, followed with such rapidity I lost the thread of their arguments. But the old woman now showed the ferocity that old age had not yet blunted. One blow from that thick arm sent the servant girl reeling among a cascade of falling pots; another hand entwined itself in Rashmana's braids, forcing her to her knees. As for myself, Safyia caught me by the waist, tore off the flimsy nightgown, and dragged me across the floor. "Obey," she cried, thrusting my head down toward the water in its wooden bucket, and such was the power in her voice, such my cowardice, that I did.

She bathed me herself, scraping off the body hair with a pumice stone and powdering my skin afterward. She herself prepared the henna for my hands and feet, and the dye to tip my breasts vermilion. Equally subdued, Rashmana gathered up the disputed jewels and let the older woman rummage through, arranging them in heaps. She chose a great chain of silver, shot with amber and coral beads, and weighed it round my neck between my breasts, where it hung almost as large as they. She cut and reshaped my hair, wielding a pair of scissors as long and pointed as a knife, threatening to stab if I moved. And all the while she poured out a stream of advice, instructions, commands that I could not have remembered if I had wanted to, how to approach a man, how to serve him with wine, how to move seductively, making him look at me; I was not to speak, merely interpret his looks and signs. Once it might have made me smile to see her force her body to remember all these moves, trapped as it was in its rolls of fat. But when she came to specifics, specific acts, specific deeds, I covered my ears. Waves of embarrassment swept over me. I think it was not until then that I understood that this was no game, that it was meant for real, and this was what I, the "novice," was being prepared to do.

"How shy she is," Rashmana sniffed, "a stupid fool. My lord will never be satisfied. When he saw me in my father's camp passion swept him like a flame. Back he came that night. My father heard him in my tent and threatened to carve him apart. 'Step out,' my father screamed, his sword drawn, 'or I neuter you.' And out he came, naked as the day he was born. 'Try to neuter me,' he said, walking up to my father, speaking to him face to face, 'I give your head to the Jews to salt above my gates.' And he laughed. How would this weak lily flower," (she used worse term) "this orphaned waif without family or dower, react to such a man? Faint dead away." And she shot me a look of contempt to make sure I noted the difference between being raped with a father's contrivance, and not having a father to contrive.

I do not know if the story was true, but it might have been. That black-cloaked man might easily have acted in that way, spoken like that. I suddenly saw him in the flesh, as I had tried not to do, tall, lithe, broad-shouldered. I heard his sardonic, mocking voice. And I remembered, without meaning to, the hairy nakedness of the first Arab man. Fear rose in my throat. Surely that was not an attribute shared by both? Surely that was not the fate meant for me?

But Safyia had no time for talk. Grunting ominously she began to get down on her knees in front of me, pushing me none too gently back on the bed. "Sit there," she cried. She waved to the servant girl to bring a jar of oil, unstoppered it, and began to smear it on her arms, trying meanwhile to pull my knees apart. "It must be done," she cried, lathering her hands and wrists. "Open your legs." I saw the sly understanding in the servant's eyes; even Rashmana left off her sulking and peered forward, as intent. The older woman frowned to herself, concentration creasing her face in lines. She lumbered down, still lathering oil upon her hands and wrists, determination stiffening her body like a battering ram. "It must be done," she repeated almost to herself. "How else in an untried girl is the passage opened to let the male member penetrate? And it is always done, in any case, for measurement." And she tried to force her hands between my thighs.

I fought her then with all my strength, kicking at her hard so that she fell backward, spilling the vial of oil. Her hands were too slippery to catch hold of me although she tried and I slid easily past her outstretched arms, snatching for my discarded shift. Rashmana, rushing forward, slipped also upon the spilled oil, and the little servant maid, terrified, clutched a length of cloth to hide behind. Sprawled on her backside the old woman let out a shout like to split the air, whilst Rashmana, equally distraught, began to scream. Into this confusion the old black eunuch came shuffling. It was a scene that would have seemed more fitting for a slaughterhouse, or an animal escaping from its pen; the tiled floors awash in red dye, mixed with water and oil, the three women mouthing air, whilst I, poised for escape, confronted them like a goaded beast.

"Come back, come back," the old woman cried between shout and groan. "Shameless thing. Do you want me to ask him to help?" She pointed to the eunuch, who was advancing rapidly. He was heavy, old, half asleep, but he was strong. Between them, he and Old Safyia could have done as they pleased. Desperation gave me second sense. I stepped back cautiously, feeling my way, careful not to come within their reach, careful not to let them come behind my back, feeling for a weapon. And when I had it in my grasp I showed them it. It was the pair of scissors that she had used, knife sharp. "Now keep back yourselves," I cried. "Else I will use it on you, or on myself." And I stabbed at them with all the determination I was capable of.

The watchman certainly believed me more than able to attack. He withdrew, leaving the way open toward the outer hall, and pulled the others out of my path. I ran toward that anteroom, as fast as my leg would allow, and as quickly they ran behind, even the servant girl. I suppose she had never seen such sights. Step by step they tracked me, as wary as if I were a wild animal, as I went headlong through the colonnades with their marble arches, across the little courtyard with its barren soil, into the hall where the outer door was still locked.

I fumbled for the bolt, back to the door, one hand behind me, the other still holding the scissors in front like a dagger. And remembered, too late, the key that the watchman had hidden in his robes. He remembered it at the same time, and a smile of triumph lit up his watery eyes. He motioned to the others to keep a safe distance, wrapped a spare piece of cloth around one arm to serve as a shield or net to throw over me, and began to circle, preparatory to closing in. I feinted with the scissors, cutting at air, but I knew I could not continue to stand at bay, and my strength was fading. His longer reach, his experience, would overcome me in the end when I tired, or when I made a mistake and let him under my guard. I leaned against the door, almost sobbing for breath, trying to concentrate, trying to decide what was best: to run at him and stab him first, to bypass him and try to stab at one of the women, or, disdaining them, stab myself before they seized me. But I swear that the thought of giving up never crossed my mind, as they say it sometimes does when one is faced with an extremity.

But as I leaned against the door, I began to hear a commotion in the corridor, a thud of feet. The door began to shift, as someone on the outside tackled the lock with another key. I could feel the wood move against my back. Turning in time, I leapt aside, just as the door was thrust open. I caught a glimpse of startled men, some of them the castle guard, dressed like the captors who had brought us here; some of them the lord's own guard, returned I supposed, and in their midst a figure who shouldered his way past. With the remaining strength I had, I leapt toward the open door and slashed down with all my might at the man who now came in. And saw and heard, as if from a long way off, the gasp of my tormentors, and their silence, as that man took the blow upon his wrist.

Instinctively he had raised his arm to fend me off, and that quick movement saved his life, part of the material of his cloak blocking the blow. But I saw the line of blood along the gash, staining the white shirtsleeve; I heard the horrified gasp as the women recognized what I had done and put the blame on me. And I saw the startled look of my young officer as I stabbed at him.

CHAPTER 6

I will say this for him. He gave no sign of surprise, except that first startled look and that first involuntary grunt of pain. He took in the situation at a glance; myself, the cowering eunuch, the slave girl frightening herself into hiccups, the two women scuttling backward, hurling abuse and blame over their shoulders at an Infidel, who had betrayed their law of hospitality; a thief, stealing their jewels; a spy; whatever quick lies they could invent. Nor did I give him time to ask or question, merely clung to him; wrapped myself round him as if to create a shield—although, with good reason, it could be argued he needed rather a shield from me! I know there was blood, smeared on my naked skin; I know he held me in his sound arm, trying to stem the flow from the other one. Across the babble of voices I heard his own rasp out, so like his master's that I think it must have startled them as much as me. They subsided into a silence, whilst the other men who had been standing in the corridor now came storming in themselves, although Old Safyia screamed sacrilege, to enter in the lord's harem.

The men's averted looks, the sudden recollection of how I must look myself, and the realization of what I had done brought my senses back. What man, especially a young officer, would care to admit he had been stabbed by a woman, with a woman's weapon, in full view of everyone, however unintentionally? I tried to wrap my smock over my head, but the great silver necklace hindered me. I tried to pull the young man outside, all the while holding on to the scissors with grim intent, in case a second attack was made. The little golden locket that I had stuffed into an inner sleeve clattered to the ground, but I let it lie. For it had dawned on me, even more vividly, that in intervening so openly on my behalf, my friend had given his interest in me away, and worse, had revealed who he was to the people here. His own comrades might be persuaded into silence. But never those womenfolk. At first breath they would run to his lord to tell all they knew and invent the rest. Perhaps the same thought occurred to him. For catching me to him, so that my face was half buried against his chest, he scooped up his cloak and threw it over us both, as a disguise. Then, part leading, part carrying, he took me out, along the corridor, his boots grating on the stones, where, in long blotches of red, our progress was marked for all to see.

We did not go far (which later made me realize how contrived my first capture had been, an exercise meant to terrify). He thrust open a second door, slammed it shut, deposited me upon my feet, and with a half-muttered oath, began to examine his wound, flexing his arm. The cut ran down it and across the back of his hand, but although it bled freely he could bend and move his wrist. When I looked up again (for first I had tried to tidy myself, under the folds of his cloak, my smock so torn and crumpled as to be virtually use-less), he had ripped off a piece of cloth from the tattered shirt cuff and was preoccupied with knotting one end, holding the other be-tween his teeth, just as his lord had done. I was shivering with cold and fright. I had never stabbed a man before, and memory of how that sharp point had slid into his flesh so easily made me sick. But worst of all was the recurring thought of how I had endangered him; how, even as we stood here, vengeance might be hunting him. That possibility dimmed all the other questions that crowded into my mind and stifled them.

As if he guessed what I was thinking he turned around. And for the first time I saw his face, clearly, as clearly as those other women must have done. In this room there was no dim light for him to hide behind. And the face I saw was different from anything I had ex-pected. I knew the hair was dark of course, beaded now with sweat, tousled and thick, needing cutting, curling a little about the nape of the neck. I knew the eyes were dark and large. But not eyes like these, flecked with green and gold, long lashed, dark certainly, but in this brighter daylight changing color as does a faceted stone. I had not imagined the forehead with its thoughtful breadth under the rough crest of hair, to make him older than he had seemed; nor the aquiline nose and firm chin, as haughty as one of his master's hawks; nor yet the mouth, wide and generous, made to smile in a mocking way. As now it did. Look all you want, that smile said, I cannot help what you see. And I thought, not even meaning to, almost angrily, Dear God, where did he get such a face, like a coin from the time of Alexander the Great? And having seen it, who could forget it? I shall not.

I said, almost incoherently, "He will hear of this. What will he say when he learns you took me from that place?"

He finished knotting up the cloth with his firm white teeth before reply. (And it is strange, until that moment I had never thought of him as being capable of men's work, such as men did; nor of suffering men's wounds, as his master obviously had. I noticed for the first time the lines of fatigue shadowing the eyes, the faint growth of beard on the clean-shaven jaw, the mud on boots and shirt, all signs of hard riding. And I had thought him too young, what was the word I had used? too "civilized" for soldiering!)

He had ripped off another strip of shirt to wipe the blood away, with a gesture so similar to his master's that for a moment I almost commented upon it, had not there been more important things to take our time. And, fool that I was, I had not even offered to help, although I still held the scissors, so tightly gripped, that when I tried to drop them, with a shudder of disgust, they clung to my hand, sticky, too, with blood.

As if noticing my undressed state (although he must have done so earlier), he went to a large carved chest of sandalwood, and, throwing up the lid, beckoned to me to take a robe from the pile inside. He was still fighting for breath; I could see the way his chest heaved. He had been running before he broke in through the door and I might be heavier than I looked. Or perhaps his wound pained him more than he liked to admit, or I had struck deeper than he realized. But when I had struggled into the first robe I could find, too big, until I hitched it up around my waist with a cord, he merely asked, still absentmindedly wiping at the blood, "How came you here?" in his beautifully modulated Parisian French, whilst I, remembering my missing friends, cried at the same time, "Where are they, what have you done with them?"

He ran his unwounded hand through his hair, making it stand on end in the way I remembered him. But when I told him all I could recollect—the sudden capture in the darkness of that first night seeming now more sinister in the open daylight, he pursed his lips, as if in disbelief, and began to pace up and down, as if only in movement could he collect his thoughts, as if trying to work out something in his mind.

"That old woman," he finally burst out, "Safyia, has lived here too long, a spider beneath an untouched stone. God knows what webs she weaves in her fantasies." Now followed the slight hesitation that I had come to recognize preceded a reconstruction of facts, presumably to spare my sensibilities. "She was installed here in my lord's grandfather's time, a mere slave girl then, and she has long influenced the lords of this citadel, and their wives. Had she had a child of her own, without doubt she would have had him succeed, and neither my lord's father nor my lord would have inherited. But barren or not, she held control for many years, when there was a harem to control, as no doubt she has boasted to you."

"And Rashmana, who claims to be the present lord's wife, or more accurately, his betrothed?" When he seemed to hesitate again, I said, "If he brought her here, as she claims, he should marry her, not send her off in disgrace. He should honor his promise to her. And what about his promise to us? Did he arrange to imprison us despite his message of goodwill? Or was that what he meant by 'keeping us safe'? Why did he have to leave at all? Why did you?"

My accusations came rippling out with more force than I meant. "Who is responsible for mistreating us? How are we to survive?"

He interrupted my spate of questions coolly. "As for what a lord may do, or not do, with his women, you are not his conscience. Although I have heard that Rashmana pursued him rather than he her. But in his youth a man may make a mistake; he does not have to pay for it all his life. As for leaving, do you think anyone wanted to leave that night, unless it were a matter of life and death?"

He must have seen me pale. "Not yours," he said, "ours." He sounded more gentle now. I had the feeling he really wanted to ask, "Why do you always believe the worst of us? Why do you not accept things as they are; why do you question us?" More than ever, behind his expression, guarded and watchful, like one of those hawks, I sensed the uneasiness that I had felt at our first meeting; as if he wanted to say other things, as if he wanted to repudiate what I had said, as if, given time, he would have explanations that would reveal the truth. What he actually said was prosaic and just. "If I were to tell you all, I do not think it would interest or comfort you. Let me say simply a message was sent and arrived too late, or you were too slow to respond to it." (A shrewd guess.) "But since it was sent, why accuse my lord of treachery? If your companions are imprisoned, that does not mean they were harmed, and I myself would prefer the word 'detained,' meaning, to keep them out of harm's way. Nor were you hurt, I think?"

When I did not reply, more forcefully, "That old woman, she did not molest you in any form?"

There was a directness about this last question that made me wonder if he knew what the old woman had planned. I did not elaborate, trying to hide the embarrassment that stained my cheeks.

"But why do you always have to speak for your lord?" I cried, still not satisfied. "Is he afraid? Or does he not always know what you say in his name?"

He leaned back against the wall, nursing his wounded arm. He suddenly seemed very tired. He spoke slowly, as if trying to make me understand. "We have just returned today. Our mission was successful. It was also as necessary as wearisome. Of course, we did not plan to leave that night! Men are not always able to *plan* their lives with such exactitude as you seem to expect. Certainly, any sensible man, I myself, would have preferred not to have had to ride out into a blizzard. But perhaps there are some things you do not know. One"—he held up one finger, as his lord was once reputed to have done—"one, since our lord inherited leadership of this tribe, his aim has been to restore a Berber fellowship, started in his father's time. Two, on the night of our return, many of his so-called allies were full of complaint, despite their show of friendship, lukewarm at best, while others, refusing to honor their pledge to meet with him, made the same excuse: the presence of two Infidels whom they accused of causing bloodshed and unrest between members of our brotherhood. I do not say this to cast blame," he added, seeing the effect on me, a reiteration of that accusation that Rashmana had made. "I repeat, it was used as excuse by malcontents, who wanted to defect. Third, our remaining friends urged our lord to strike against these defectors before their example spread. And since a show of force, direct and fast, serves better than a long drawn-out threat, so my master did. With good effect. But fourth: it is not to create an empire for himself that my master formed this league, in spite of what his enemies may claim. Rather he sees it as a means of defense. Disunited, we Berbers stand no chance against the foreign invasion of which even you have warned. United, we may hold it off, if only we can bury our own differences."

It was the longest speech I had heard him make, certainly the most serious. It reminded me of other occasions when he had defended his master, this time I admitted with better cause. But he still was not done.

"Fifth," he said, and now he held up five fingers, a handful, his sound hand, "in his absence my master left his Vizier in charge. You have met him, you know who he is. Then you also know that he, my lord's uncle, has reasons for disliking foreigners. I told you they were not loved in our tribe. My lord's mother must bear the blame. When she fled from here, ran off, like a thief, in the night, because she could not endure our ways, she left behind the wreckage of two lives. My lord's father was old, in his dotage. He swore he could not live without her and he sent his younger brother to bring her back. That young man, tempted by her I suppose, perhaps seduced by her, helped her escape instead. He, too, paid dearly for a mistake that almost cost him his life. For he made a second mistake by coming back.

"In those days, death for a traitor was harsh, flaying alive, tearing off the skin from bone. And such was ordered for him when he returned. But the older brother had loved him well, sons of one mother, once dearest friends. In his desolation the older man could not bear to see someone else he had loved be put to death. The order was revoked, transmuted into imprisonment. And so the younger man lived. Later, in exile, shunned by his own tribe, he nursed his wounds (for the punishment had been begun), until the time came for the heir to inherit.

"The older brother, worn out by grief, shut himself up in his castle until he died; he let his tribal leadership fall into other hands; he let the alliance he had built decay. You might suppose the younger brother, who had been imprisoned, maimed, forced to live as an outcast, would seize this chance to right his own wrongs; instead, he preferred to repay what he saw as a debt of honor. Without his help the heir would never have inherited, or won back what was lost."

The young officer let the weight of that story sink in, so full of old bitterness and dread that I felt it like a knife blow. "You must accept then," he was continuing, "the Vizier's fears that the past may repeat itself; you must accept his lord's toleration of a man he reveres above all men. Time will be needed to release your companions, but it can be done. Nor would the Vizier have placed you in Safyia's charge had he known how crazed she had become."

A second time I thought, as apology it must suffice. But I still feared for my friends.

"They are not spies," I told him, "nor am I."

"But you are." The reply was bleak. "Anyone who lives here, carries off information about our habits, our thoughts, our hopes, that robs us a hundred times. Even without meaning it, you all are spies, you Europeans, trying to learn our ways." There was that fleck of pent-up anger I remembered from the other time. And what, I thought, did it mean? Now we were here, would none of us ever be allowed to leave? I said, partly angry myself, "I would not give your secrets away. But you, you have challenged the Vizier. What will your master say when he hears that, what will he do to you, now that you have compromised yourself?"

To my chagrin, and, I admit, growing annoyance, he began to laugh. "I never thought to hear an English lady use that word," he said. "A girl might be compromised, in a sexual sense, as you might be, here alone, with me. I never thought to hear it spoken of a man, certainly not myself."

The teasing note was back. It irked me that, like his master, he could joke in the midst of impending calamity. I thought, He'll not laugh when his master flays his skin. Yet, against my will, I seemed to hear my cousin's wife, her voice raised in shocked reproach. Here I was, unchaperoned, half clad, in a lonely room, with a man whose reputation I wished to protect more than my own. I admit I saw the humor but I refused to smile.

"Well then," I said, stiff-tongued, "if you feel safe, I have no regrets. But what will he do to me?"

That stopped his laughter. He ran his good hand through his hair, as if perplexed, giving him the boyish look I had surprised in him, half asleep, in his master's tent. I had never considered before how he had got there that night. Had he come scrabbling down the cliff, on foot, like the rest of the men, dragging his horse? Had he ridden in the charge? Perhaps in this also I had misjudged him; perhaps he was as good a fighter as his master was. That might explain why he had been so tired that night. I thought, It may explain his air of weariness today. I looked at him carefully. There was a tightness beneath the skin, as if his strength was drained. I thought he should not be on his feet like this, but, as if to prove I was wrong, he started up, beckoning me to follow him. For the first time I began to think of some of the similarities between the two men, although hitherto I had only thought of the differences. I let him lead the way through a series of small rooms into a walled-in garden, large and luxurious. Behind his back I could measure the width of his shoulders, the length of his legs. I tried to imagine what he would look like on a horse, holding a gun, whistling through his teeth as he fired. I tried to imagine how it would feel to be carried by him, really carried, up a cliff pass, or on a horse, plucked from the ground like a strip of cloth. Somehow the two images blurred, then jarred apart. There were some likenesses, it is true, enough to give credence to the doctor's suspicion of blood kin, but it seemed to me the likeness was not in acts or deeds so much as in voice and manner of speech, in things a younger man might learn or copy from an older one. Nor was he as sardonic as his master, but appeared more gentle, vulnerable. I would trust him as I could not that other man. But ... the thought slipped away out of my grasp, like a nagging memory, and afterward I could not remember even what I had been searching for.

We had come to the end of a gravel walk, at the far side of the garden, where high walls met in a peak. A stand of overgrown shrubs hung like a curtain against the wall. He brushed the branches aside to reveal a door set underneath, a stout door of heavy wood, green with age. Its brass locks and hinges had been recently oiled, and when he gave me the key, stored in a niche beside the door, it turned easily. We stood looking out over a long portico, set at right angles to the garden, more like a wide covered terrace, hung in space. The back of it was sheltered with a tiled roof, under which were stored chairs, tables, dead plants in great urns, discarded gardening tools, all the evidence of abandonment and neglect. But on the open side, one could gaze down from a balustrade that stretched into air, across the valley to the mountains, white with snow. That sight took my breath away.

He let me stare for a while, then touched my shoulder slightly to indicate what I really should be looking at, the door at the far end, similar to the one we had just opened, locked too, for the key was in the door, and above it hung a medieval bell on a thick chain.

"If you want," he said, "in need, ring that bell, and turn the key. You would find me; or someone would, in the guardroom beyond."

He glanced sideways with that half smile that I had always suspected and never been able to see. You have the key to your door,
that smile said. You see how the other door is opened. If you want
to open it, the choice is yours.

That was a smile to ignore, suggestive of too many things, all
ambiguous. Whilst he locked our door again I looked around carefully. The garden and the terrace beyond intrigued me as much as
did the inside rooms, which were faintly reminiscent of a past decade,
not quite of this land, not quite of somewhere else, a mixture of two
worlds. And the gravel walks, the strips of grass, the pale blue sheet
of water in a rectangular pool in their midst, reflecting the winter sky,
all gave this place more of the air of a pleasure garden than that drab
courtyard had in the former harem.

"Yes," he said, as if answering a question I had not asked, "my
master's father built it for his French wife. And when she left, he
closed it too, to go to ruin."

I thought of that poor French lady, hated by everyone except
the husband she had destroyed. Perhaps he guessed that thought
as well.

"I told you you have a kind heart," he said. "But before you
pity her, think how long it took for her lord to forget her. Think of
her son."

I had the clear image of a small, dark-haired boy, sitting here
on the grass, waiting, and I shivered. I looked at the man beside me.
How did he know all these sad details? What was this story to him?
Was it true he was part of the family; was he so related to his master
that he truly knew his mind? Was he surrounded by friends and
influence like some heir himself? I thought, Of all the people I have
met in these past weeks, it is a fact he is the only one I have *talked*
with, I might almost say the first since Colonel Edwards died, and
that means ever in my life. I thought, I do not want to be left alone
again. Meanwhile he was explaining other things, practical things—
how guards were to be set, led by the captain who had ridden with
me on his horse, all loyal men I could trust. Mohamed would be sent
to serve. (Mohamed, what a name for a slave. Surely, he almost
laughed, you must have given him that name; one no true Muslim
would ever give himself, for common use, that is.) And if there was
anything I needed I had but to ask; maids would be found to bring
our food—"Who are you?" I suddenly interrupted him. "I still do
not know *your* name."

"Have you not spoken of me to everyone?"

"Of course not, as you asked. Only to my friends."

"And what did they say?"

I smiled. "Mohamed thinks you a *jini*, up to tricks, and the doctor feels you may be a scoundrel, using us to feather your own nest."

"And you?"

I shot a sidelong look at him myself. I said simply, "I think I could trust you. No one has been as kind as you seem. If I could, I would ask you outright for help to leave."

He said as slowly, "My master twice gave you a chance to go. He believes you made a choice and you chose to stay."

I started to argue, but the arguments made no sense. Instead I said what I was to regret afterward, words somehow forced out of me without forethought. "Take me away. Ask your master for safe conduct to the coast. Tell him I am your mistress. You said he only likes young virgins. Tell him I am none; that I am your woman, not available to him." Out poured a plan that would have made a Safyia weep for its naïveté. How could I think his lord would agree? I knew he was sufficiently possessive to covet even a hound if someone wanted it. And so the young man explained, although at first I think he was startled a second time. His tone was expressionless; he might have been talking over a business arrangement, pointing out its flaws. "You are asking me to become your lover to spare you from my master's rape? Or are you really asking me to act as if I were, if and when such a rape should be contemplated? And after this alleged lovemaking, am I to understand that you expect me to take you away? And am I to inform my lord what I have done, or rather what I have not done, in expectation he will then give us a full escort to the coast? And after reaching there, what sort of reward am I expected to tell him I have had, or not had, I am not sure which, and . . . ?"

Well, I give you but a glimpse of how he tore my little plan to shreds. Open laughter would have been better, easier to live with. I looked at the ground, looked away, looked anywhere other than at him.

"One last thing." His voice was hard. I had forgotten that personal loyalty that I had admired. "You speak often of the Master with distaste. Does he truly horrify you? Do you consider him—what were your words—a monster of depravity and lust? As far as I know he never has raped anyone, not even an Infidel, despite Old

Safyia's claims." (Which confirmed one suspicion I had had, that he must have guessed the nature of her schemes.)

"So tell me this. Would it offend you to see him again?"

I cannot say what I should have answered, I was so confused. His plain speaking had unnerved me, as he meant it to, and I could not think. I wanted to say, Of course it would offend, if he has such thoughts in mind, but the words would not form. I wanted to say, I know *he* expects to make me his concubine, but instead the thought turned and became, *I* expect him to, not the same thing at all. I wanted to say, How can I believe what you say of him, or trust him? He is like a will-o'-the-wisp, here one moment, gone the next, always catching me off-guard, always leaving me discomforted. As ever, when I thought of him, that current, which has no name, sent its shivers along my spine, and I said nothing at all.

I stood there in the neglected garden made for a foreign woman who had not appreciated it and felt my silent thoughts fly out to the Master and felt his young officer respond. At least the young man answered as if he had guessed what I was thinking and how his lord would speak were he there.

Soft-voiced he suddenly asked me, "What are you frightened of?" And when I began to protest, he reached out his unwounded hand and put a finger on my lips. "Hush," he said. "My master would know what lie it was if I said you wanted me. And, to use words that you would understand, you cannot be 'in love' with two men at once. If you must choose, let the choice be for delight, not fear." And he kissed me before striding away. I heard his boots cross the gravel strip, and he disappeared. And presently from the corridor beyond came the sound of other men, clattering to attention before the door. I stood where he had left me, appalled.

As kisses go, his had been chaste, a whisper against the cheek. But I felt my body flare with it. What impudence, I thought. What did he mean? Because he has risked a kiss, or stolen it, how dare he believe he has the right to lecture me? How dare he tell me what I think, as if it were true it is his master I am waiting for; that whatever I feel when his master comes close, when he carries me away, when his hard hand grips my leg, is *that*, which no girl thinks of. All these half thoughts, half fears, these vague suppressed longings, swirled about me in a storm, as if a whirlwind had come into the garden, picking up dead leaves and plants, stirring up old memories. As before, I realized the young man was much more clever than I was. I had asked him questions that he had never answered, or at best, replied to with more ambiguities than I could assimilate. I still did not know who he was, and he had tricked me into revealing shameful things that as an unmarried woman I should not even know about. And worse, he had refused without even a show of emotion or gratitude. Sometimes, I thought, it seems that when I am with these men, I not only forget the manners that I have been taught, I even lose the sense that I was born with. I did not thank the master who rescued me; I did not apologize for stabbing his young aide-de-camp. I have forgotten every maidenly precept, every sense of pride. But I thought, suddenly defiant, as if he challenged me, I do not "love" anyone; certainly not an illiterate robber baron who has captured me, even less a callow youth who speaks out of turn, thinking a handsome face pardons all liberties, having visions, no doubt, of grandeur above his place. But I feel caught by them, like a trout on a fishing line. The more I whip my anger up, the more I feel a fool; the more I feel foolish, the more my anger grows. I am confused by them, provoked into revealing more of myself than I care to show the world, trapped into letting defenses down.

Mohamed's arrival served as an excuse to put these disquieting thoughts aside. He came through the door in a rush, the guards throwing his bundles after him. Out of breath, he sat down on the threshold, pent-up anxiety taking him to the verge of tears whilst I put my arms about him. But it was soon apparent I was more pleased to see him than he was me. Nor was it lack of luxury that distressed him, rather its reverse, as he looked around him distastefully. "They put us in a barrack room," he said, "with the guards." Once that would have been his dream, not so in reality, it seemed. "It was a large room," he admitted when I questioned him, "and the honorable doctor and I stayed there. Three meals a day, and water to wash twice." He made a face. "I have never slept indoors before," he cried, "nor used a bed. I could not breathe. If that is how horsemen live when at home I pity them. I have never been so uncomfortable in my life." There was a sort of horror in his voice. "And now they have sent me here to serve you, I am back in prison again."

It was useless to show him the French furnishings, the fruitwood tables and chairs, the long gilded mirrors, popular thirty years ago, the garden walks. All he saw were walls and roofs holding him captive. "I came from the desert to wait on you," he said at last, in an unusual outburst of honesty. "I served you faithfully as I did my desert masters. But I was not born a slave." And now what he said came from the heart, something long dreamt of, something that had supported his frail hopes for many years. "I remember the day I was sold," he said. "Men stood me on a block of wood, peered at my teeth, felt my withered leg. They ordered me to hold their hands. I thought it was to show they cared for me, but that was my childish fantasy. Yet I was free-born, a mountain man, perhaps of Berber stock. Ill-chance sold me too young into slavery, as ill-chance sold you. I did not expect to end my days in service of an Infidel." He did not add what he also thought, "I meant to be a fighter, as I was born to be, before fate made me blind and lame. What will become of me if your powers do not heal? What shall I do, who am afraid—afraid of horses and fighting, afraid of guns. Afraid of sleeping in a bed."

He crouched there, part man, part child, lost in misery too great for ordinary comfort. The last thing he wanted was my sympathy. But I felt that, despite his present grief, despite his deformed body, there was a spirit in him that would revive. And true enough, in time, he became more cheerful, telling me what schemes the doctor still formulated to lead a crusade against disease, telling me my new-found status would enable me to quash the rumors of my low birth. He became friendly with the guards, who endured him as they might a puppy set in their midst. But they would not let him out, nor anyone in (save the women who brought our food, the women so shy and scared that they crept to and fro like wraiths).

Most of the time Mohamed spent in sleep, rolled up like a ball as if to hide his disappointment, as if in dreams he could find again those hopes that had shaped his life, although by now he must have felt his birthright lost. Sleep is the opiate of despair. But sometimes in the night, when I heard his dragging step pad back and forth like a caged animal's, I felt his failure goad him with longing.

One day a veiled girl thrust a tray into my hands. It held a small box that contained my golden locket, retrieved I supposed from where I had let it fall. I stored it away with the great silver chain, which by contrast could only be called vulgar. Another day, another girl, equally veiled, handed me the gray cat that I had made a friend of, or it me. It settled quickly into its new home and followed me everywhere. I never knew who sent these gifts, nor why; never thought who brought them. I took the bringing and the gifts as simple kindnesses meant to please. I was wrong in this as in other things. But when the cat and I would play together or in the afternoons stroll in the garden in the milk-warm sun, the high walls that kept out the cold seemed also to shelter us from harm. And when Mohamed slept off the effects of his midday meal, I would dip my feet into the little pool, while the cat batted wildly with its paws at the small shoals of red-gold fish. They darted to and fro like specks of light, and I would lean over the edge to watch and admire. Soon I began to bathe there every day as I had longed to do in the mountain pools, first clad in my old smock, then without it, as I grew secure in the seclusion of those tall garden walls. And when I pulled aside the weeds that fringed the pool, the naked shapes that were depicted underneath seemed as natural there as I was, although I knew the Muslim world shuns the human form in art.

I would begin to think about the harem and all that had happened there, and about the strange arrival of the young officer. And I remembered the Master. With a feeling akin to curiosity, laced with fear, I thought of him and of his dark presence brooding over us. And I would wonder what I should do, seeming trapped between both men, not free of either, not knowing what either wanted of me, not knowing what I wanted of myself. Sometimes I tried to imagine what it would be like if I went to that hidden garden door and rang the heavy bell on the other side. What should I find? What would the young officer think or say? What would his master do? What would happen afterward? And sometimes I would think about my life in the harem and what I was supposed to have learnt there. And half-shamedly, I would consider this thing called lust, which the women there had surrounded with deceit and artifice. I came to realize that whatever brutality or cruelty they both had known, whatever cause both women had to rail against men and masculine selfishness, however much their years of training and their culture had sapped their ability to complain, it was not their loneliness or idleness that bothered them as much as lack of those same men. It was thoughts of them that filled their dreams and made them toss as restlessly as did poor Mohamed here; it was wishing for the Master's favor that caused Rashmana's jealousy. And I, who had blocked out from my mind what they had tried to teach, despite myself had begun to feel its fascination and its pull, although I had not yet the words to name it.

And sometimes in the night when I lay sleepless, too, I thought I heard, like an echo, the sound of the Frenchwoman's feet, her silken slippers beating up and down, wearing a path among her French furnishings, which were themselves a symbol of her predicament, and mine, not quite of this land but each lost to her own. She appeared to me then like a prisoner, as much a prisoner as Mohamed felt he was, in a place where no prison was meant. I seemed to see her piquant face with its delicate skin, frowning as she tried to compromise; I seemed to see her prettiness fade in a world that was about to close around like a vise. And when in my dreams she ran across the dew-wet grass, I stood by that garden door and watched her open it. At the other end of the long terrace a dark-robed figure waited for her. Did he hold out his arms in silence? Did she cry, "Let me go home"? I only know I woke with her cry in my ears, his silence in my heart.

•   •   •

I do not know what took me into the garden the next day, or caused me to go there so dressed, nor even what prevented me from stepping into the water as I always did. I only tell what happened; I do not try to explain. I had found a piece of clothing in one of the small inner rooms. When I raised the cloth to look at it, the cat had arched its back and spat, as if the sight disturbed it, although perhaps it was just a coldness in the room where the dust seemed to distill a strange arid perfume. It was not exactly a dress, the thing I found—more like a length of silk, transparent as a spider web. I slipped out of my clothing and into the wispy garment. It was held at the waist and hem with bands of gold, with a bodice of gold caught beneath the breastbone, and wide golden undertrousers attached by a side seam. When I moved quickly they flared over my white legs, and a wave of the same perfume filled the air, like a sigh, full of pity, full of pain. On an impulse that also I cannot explain, I outlined my eyes with kohl, found henna for my hands and feet, and uptipped the many little pots and jars searching for the rouge to rub upon my breasts to make them stand out red. When I was done I seemed as Eastern as the little girl, the little bride of my golden locket. Yet something was still missing, something still did not seem right. Like the cat I felt unease claw at my skin as if that old unhappiness was touching me. I felt myself shivering, the sort of shiver that they say means someone has walked upon your grave; it made me run outside looking for the sun. I snatched up the cat for company, but it struggled from my arms and stalked aside. I lay down on the grass, hands beneath my head, and tried to think as that Eastern girl would have done. What had been the secret for her and her man? They had both come from different worlds, they ... A little cat cry behind me startled me into reality.

The cat, persistently hopeful in its fishing, had dipped its paws into the water, then leapt aside, with a cry that I was ever after to recall. It had crouched, in the manner of its kind, claws spread, licking between them, as if it had been pricked by a thorn; and thinking this myself, I ran forward to pick it up. Some instinct made me glance into the water first. Its color seemed unchanged, clear blue against the tiles, but around the edge there was a brown tinge, and at one end, like small leaves, the bodies of the fish floated, their reds and golds already blurred.

I stepped back quickly, placing my feet with care. I watched the cat lick its paw, stiffen, roll as if convulsed. And along the grass verge a dark stain spread.

I remember thinking stupidly, What is wrong? Then more coherently, But who would poison a cat? There are guards, the door is closed; no one enters except the women with food. Suddenly, deathly afraid, I thought of Mohamed, curled up upon the cushions in his room. When I had come out he was certainly asleep, certainly alive, for I had heard him breathing heavily, although he did not twist and turn as he normally did. They had not put poison in the food then, but in the water, where I used to swim. Someone has been watching me, I thought, to know when and how; someone has been spying on all I do here. And if the little cat had not licked its fur, who would have guessed how I had died, drowned perhaps or suicide, the rectangular form of the pool already shaped to be a grave. Or who would have cared? And if not this time, I thought, then another, a second attempt, not poison, but a knife, in the dark. It is a dreadful thing to watch your enemies arrange your death, but, equally so, it is to know your murderers spy on you and plot in secret, treacherously.

Before I knew what my feet had planned, I was running across the garden to the hidden door. I pushed aside the screen of leaves and felt for the key. It was not there, and the shining new locks were crammed with earth. Careful, I told myself, holding to the branches for support, wait, be still. The garden was empty, tranquil. Nothing moved in the sun; nothing seemed out of place except the limp gray heap of fur. But someone had come in, someone had come to watch and spy, someone had come to kill. Careful, I told myself, think.

Few things have been so difficult. Each time I breathed my heart thudded so loudly I heard it beating against the wall, as if my spine were a sounding board. My arms and legs were trembling so that the leaves shook. But when I had controlled myself, what use to faint I thought, fight back, I knew only one person would have such a desire or the means to achieve it. And when I shut my eyes, in the dark I seemed to see the glitter of hers as she used to watch me, unwaveringly.

Thought of her malice was like a spur. I knew I could not fight her alone. I must find help; but how, but where? I knew I must not wait. She would not hesitate. Foiled once more of her prey she would be compelled to strike again. Mohamed would be helpless; perhaps his deep sleep was drug-induced, like that sleep of Old Safyia's. The doctor was still a prisoner. I could not reach my young officer in his guardroom behind the door. The guards who watched the outer door were supposed to be loyal, *men you can trust,* but if even one were treacherous, I could not trust any of them. I made myself list the opportunities for escape, logically and coolly. And I resolved that if I could not get to the guardroom by this private route then I must get to it by some other means, past the guards, along the corridor.

I closed my eyes again to visualize the way we had come when we had left the harem. I had not seen much, my head hidden, a cloak over me. I remembered more clearly how the blood had splashed upon the stones. I had seen even less the first time, only enough to realize that the fortress was a maze, rooms fitted into each other like a set of tinderboxes. But since garden and terrace faced an outside wall, any corridor following the same direction on an inside one must lead to the same place. But how to get past the guards?

If it had been hard to watch and wait, it was harder still to leave the shelter of the trees and cross the open garden. I felt my muscles tense, any moment expecting a hand or a knife at my back. My shadow stretched before me over the grass. I dared not look up for fear of seeing other shadows where there should be none. Mohamed still lay asleep, and could not be roused. Pausing only long enough to wind a long shawl around myself, and snatching up a ball the cat played with, I ran to the heavy outer door.

I felt better waiting there. I could hear men outside, shuffling their feet, murmuring, laughing. They did not sound like murderers, but one was, perhaps more, and one had certainly let in a murderer. Since only women servants were permitted to enter perhaps they had been the instruments. But when the door opened again to let them clear away the remains of our meal, I meant to go out instead.

If I had known how tall those guards were, three of them, in line like a picket fence, black-robed, their wicked swords unsheathed, I might not have dared. Three men to guard one door, a prize within; no one suspicious could have approached that door from the outside. But they did not expect someone to come out at them, head down, like a goat, and when the door first opened to let in the servant girl I threw the little ball so that it bounced between her skirts. Her screams attracted their attention as I hoped and gave me the chance of surprise that was all I asked. Butting my way through I began to run. Behind me I could hear the screams turn to shouts as the guards realized the trick that had been played on them.

I fled down the corridor, skimming over the uneven stones. I might have been surprised that I could run at all; certainly I had not run like this since I had been wounded, but fear gave me wings. And in my own home I had been used to running over the rough moors. Behind me I could hear the panting of the guards. Their soft shoes made little sound but their accoutrements jangled enough to waken the dead. If they thought of anything they must have presumed I was cowering in proper maidenly seclusion. To be duped by a foreign female was more than their pride could endure. Yet although their curses followed me, they did not run as fast as I thought they might, and when I came to a corner I saw why.

The corridor I had been running along was narrow, rough-paved, more like a tunnel than a corridor, without windows or lights. It had gone in the direction I hoped it would and at the corner turned at right angles, as again I hoped. This second passage was equally badly paved and dark, but halfway along it, just where I thought it must, stood a heavy door, the guardroom door. What I had not expected were the men on duty there.

This new set of guards was more numerous than the ones I had left behind, and, if truth be told, more alert, in that most of them stood at silent attention on either side of the door, as if glued to the wall. They scarcely bothered to turn their heads but allowed the nearest men to detach themselves and begin to stroll forward. Meanwhile my first pursuers had reached the corner, too, and, seeing how

I was trapped, had slowed to a walk, starting to laugh among themselves, as at a joke. By then I had begun to tire and my leg to ache. I had guessed correctly where the guardroom was, but being right would do me little good if I could not get close enough to find the help I was looking for. And who in any case would put such a guard upon the guards' own room? So while the men behind me gestured in mockery and those in front came toward them, I made myself continue on as before. And when both groups had almost met I threw myself upon the floor, rolling like that ball beneath their feet, making them stumble against each other awkwardly. And I began to scream.

What did I scream? I do not remember the words, but they were in every language I could think of, until the echoes rang and the lamps in their sconces beside the door seemed to splutter in outrage.

This was the last thing the men had expected, either the falling down or the screaming. They did not like to grasp for me so I went on slithering with that snakelike motion that Mohamed had demonstrated on the salt flats. They had bunched together in a knot, lifting their feet to avoid tramping on me, whilst those who had remained on guard forgot themselves sufficiently to lean forward on their swords to give advice, most of it contradictory. And seeing I could come no closer I shouted at last the only word that perhaps would make sense out of this confusion, the only word that someone should recognize, "Isobelle," as I had once shouted it to the wind and sea. And I thought, now, this time, someone must hear me, someone must come.

• • •

Someone did. There was an answering shout inside the door, the guardroom collectively, responding to alarm. Out they poured, the household guards in their red and white, the lord's bodyguards, black-robed, all looking for a revolt to subdue. I wound myself up into a ball and waited for them to stop their stamping back and forth, waited for someone to tell me what to do. By then they had begun to realize what was the cause, merely guardsmen running after a foolish girl, who had made them look as foolish themselves. They drew themselves upright, not overpleased you may be sure at being set in a panic whilst my guards—I suppose I may call them mine—conferred hastily apart. I recognized one of them as that same taciturn captain who had carried me through the pass. He was not so taciturn today, arguing vehemently, looking at me as if he wished he were still horsed and could give a good whack to set us on the homeward path. Then I saw his expression change. He snapped out an order; his men clashed to arms; so did the others, backs stiff against the wall, as their leader came out after them.

He strode forward, black-robed, armed himself, booted and spurred, as if he had just come riding in, or was about to ride out. Behind him, in the room, there was a hush. I was conscious of many men, dignitaries, councillors, turning to stare or listen curiously. I thought, suddenly ill at ease, with a strange quickening, That is no guardroom, or, at best, it is a room men *guard*, not where they live. But if *he* lives there then I have made a dreadful mistake. I sat on the floor, legs tucked underneath, head held down, and saw the last man on earth I wanted to see come toward me, his spurs grating over the stones. Concentrate on those spurs, I told myself, one long bar, not like European ones. Look at the boots, at my eye level; they are European boots, like ones I have seen before, scuffed a bit about heels and toes, in need of polishing. *No Berber horseman wears boots.* Then the long black tunic, the black cloak, the leather belts, the curved naked sword, all these were familiar also, and yet seemed out of place. My first thought was, Why is the Master here; my second was, I have been misled. My third—but I give you leave to guess the third. For I was looking now at the hand held out to help me rise. It, too, was a hand I knew, a long hand, fine-wristed and strong. And there across the back of it was the gash that I myself had put there. I did not take that hand, sat as if turned to stone, until with another softspoken curse he put aside his head scarfs. I was looking up at a face I knew, the black tousled hair, the flecked dark eyes, the half smile. Certainly it was a face I knew, not hidden now. Only it was on the wrong man.

CHAPTER 7

I sat on the ground and stared. Having seen him revealed for who he was, I had nothing to say. I stared at nothing at all, and his voice questioning me, shouting at me, might well have been a nothing too, as inconsequential as a wind blowing through the trees. "Why, wherefore, what?" I gave no reply. I felt I had sunk into silence caused by this mirror-change which, having shown me two people at once, showed me also that what I thought I knew I knew not at all. Both men were different, both were the same. And in my mind, like waves booming into surf, came my own questions: "Why, wherefore, what? Why have you cheated me; wherefore have you lied? What was your purpose in deceiving me?"

But "Why?" he kept on insisting. "Why have you come like this?" The young mouth above its lean shaven jaw was not smiling now; it was hard, angry, tight-lipped, rasping commands from the side as soldiers do. With my eyes shut I would have known that voice as the Master's in full power. It caused his men to run at his command. Some of them had already reversed their steps and had gone back to the rooms and garden; others, grim-faced themselves, had begun to fan out, searching, I suppose, for clues or traces that a criminal might have left. I sat on the ground, legs curled underneath me, waiting, as the Master did, for his men's report. And before him, my three guards waited also, their faces chalk-white, not speaking either, not looking at anyone, their eyes flickering shut, their mouths opening upon their prayers.

I suppose eventually someone returned with news, or perhaps in the end I said something, enough to give suspicion some shape.

His hands clamped about my waist, pulling me upright, thrusting beneath the delicate silks, hard hands, hard mouth. "Did it touch you?" His fingers were rough along the skin, feeling beneath the bodice curve. "Did that water spill anywhere?" His hands burnt as the poison might, as I tried weakly to break his hold, as I refused to look into his eyes. And I heard his shout for his battle sword, his weapon of authority, as if he, too, had gone a long way off, having no connection with me, nor with anyone who was there. It was only when I recognized the sound those guards made, a collective sigh, so slight it might have been lost amid the other sounds, that I had the sense to think what these things meant: that sigh, that order, that battle sword.

They had fallen to their knees, my three guards, as men do who face death. The sound was an intake of breath, such as men take when all hope is lost: an involuntary swallowing to compensate for a dryness in their throats, to hide a sudden gush of fright. I recognized the sound at once; had not I just experienced that last, overwhelming rush of fear myself, more than once? And I realized exactly what was planned for them.

Then I did begin to think, gathering up thoughts, and holding them close as a man might gather up his clothes to dress himself. My voice had no life in it I know, and I might have been an automaton speaking by rote. But I knew I had to speak, and fast. "No," I said. "No," I told him. "They are not at fault. You are, I am. I, for coming; you, for bringing. I have no place in this world, and that is the cause of everything."

The silence that followed my little speech reverberated along the dim corridors like an echo of some other time. I thought, This is not the first occasion when such words have been said; it may not be the last. But I'll not have men's blood upon my conscience. I could still sense the efforts of those men, on their knees, attempting to control their panting; they were trying to remain calm, like men who look over a precipice and see the rocks upon which their fall will break. And I felt his efforts too; the trembling of his right hand as it reached for his sword to swing it above his head, to sweep it down upon theirs. I forced myself to move, almost stumbling, legs like straws, as I stood in front of those three men, the fringes of my shawl brushing their bowed heads, interposing myself between them and their lord, who had the power of life and death over them. "No," I repeated a third denial. "They are not to blame. Search through your women's quarters first. There find your culprits." And so we waited for him to decide, not moving, not breathing, frozen into place. And when he finally lowered the blade it grated on the real paving stones with a raw and jagged edge.

He made a gesture for everyone to leave, including my guards. Like men who have looked into the depths of a ravine, they pulled themselves up, edging away from that precipice, wiping the sweat from their faces as if it had rained. Only their captain, that silent man, spun round and dropped to his knees once more. Without a word he touched the hem of my golden undergarment, as a suppliant, as someone whose life has been spared and who swears allegiance to his rescuer. And behind him, his lord, his master, watched, and ground his teeth with suppressed rage.

But he curbed his rage. The fit soon passed. Although having witnessed it, that anger men spoke about, I never forgot it. Calm-voiced by contrast I heard him order the search. Word was sent swift-footed throughout the citadel, to bar the gates, to hunt out anyone suspicious, and to take prisoners. I heard him order the doctor's release to tend Mohamed, certainly drugged into sleep. And I heard finally his order to me, no less calm, to follow him. When I did not instantly obey, he drove me ahead like a sheep. The door was slammed behind my back, and there I stood once more face to face with him. But not alone.

The hall inside was larger than any I had seen, having the same tiled floors and fretted pillars and curved archways, but on a bigger scale, a noble room, suitable for a lord's entranceway. It was crowded with people like a circus tent. Companions, councillors, clansmen with their bodyguards, allies with their own retinues, all stood and stared. Their cloaks of different colors swirled as they drew back out of their leader's way and he pushed through them, suddenly impatient. Here were all the hangers-on, the supplicants, the learned men and fools, the leaders and their rivals, who make up a tribal court, all of them edging forward, edging away, looking for advancement, fearing defeat, savoring gossip as men do food. One look at their leader's face, one look at mine, they broke off their whispering, hastened to take their departure without making their farewells. Now was not the time for talk. Outside the castle walls, or out of earshot at least, scandal would soon go flaring like the wind, a new story to relish and retell about the Lord of the High Tigran. Meanwhile, the guards looked perplexed and servants, in their red and white, scurried about, perspiring from indecision, seeming uncertain whether to proffer or withdraw the copper trays of food and drink. And standing apart, beside an inner door, I saw the older Vizier, waiting to speak when the confusion cooled. On foot, he was smaller than he had seemed, but there was no doubt what his look, his whole stance, meant: no retreat for him until he had argued his point, he was simply saving his arguments until the room was cleared and he sensed the best way to make his nephew listen to reason.

For the moment his lord ignored him, speaking instead to me, the first complete sentence since he had found me sitting on the floor. "In there," in French, not overpolite, soldier's French, "wash yourself, all your skin, to make sure there is no taint of poison. And"— as an afterthought—"wipe that stuff off your face." As if I were a child.

I was thrust into another chamber, a kind of bathroom that came as a surprise. It was large and had a source of running water. But before the door was closed I heard the Vizier's voice raised in question, "Why?" Another "why," but these were questions of his own. "Why have her here? Why display your folly openly to the world? Why do you allow her entry into your chambers? What do you mean to do with her?" I closed my ears to his angry tirade. It was not meant for me, I thought, nothing to do with me, what did I care for what he said? But as I dipped my face in a basin to rinse my dark-rimmed eyes, already smeared with fright, as I scrubbed at the rouge that mocked me with its pretense of experience, it seemed to me that of all the misfortunes I had endured, this was the nadir. Even on the ship, after its wreck, the future had not appeared more grim; this was worse than when Colonel Edwards had died. Death had marked him from the start; in death for him there was victory. But now, here, for me, there was nothing left, not even defeat. Better, I thought, to have died myself than be reduced to such helplessness. I tore at the golden silks as if they, too, were on fire. But I could not sit forever, staring into space. "Why, wherefore?" It took as much courage to come out of that room as it had taken to jump over the side of the ship. But in the end I did come, carefully wrapped in the shawl to cover myself from head to toe, to hide the pretense that was underneath, those harem clothes that turned me into a mockery.

A servant was waiting to guide me through the usual maze of rooms. Not a muscle stirred on his face, not a look, as if he were

used to such events, as if it were customary to have women screaming in corridors, setting the castle and its inhabitants on edge. Perhaps it was. He did not show in any way that he had noticed how I
had been pushed inside, or how I had been dressed, or how his
master had spoken to me as if I were a silly child caught out in some
stupidity. Step by hesitant step I followed him into a lord's domain,
with all the trappings of a man's life, where rugs, animal pelts, guns,
horns, were piled in heaps. The great ceremonial sword was propped
against a chest, innocent, shining, clean. I averted my eyes, refusing
to think how it might have looked had it been used. A soldier's room,
I thought, impersonal, remote, although there were books and papers
scattered everywhere. I should have known he could not have been
illiterate. I had to admit, almost shamefaced, that he was not as un-
lettered as I had hoped. Yet there was nothing soft or effeminate or
weak, even if he were "civilized." And in this room, an old man had
nursed his loneliness, waiting for his son, half-son, half-stranger, to
inherit.

The last room opened onto a terrace, like the one on the other
side of the locked door, obviously joined to it, part of one continuous
balcony. It was furnished with heavy leather couches and spread with
rugs, giving it an air of comfort rather than luxury. I thought, Here
is where the Master spends his time. He was leaning against the
balustrade looking out into space, down toward the valley below,
examining his kingdom, I assumed, and was playing with some object, tossing it back and forth. It was a key. I heard it clink as he put
it down. I groped my way toward him like a blind man, and as I
advanced slowly, I could see between the stone railings how the cliffs
stretched far beneath. Sensing my look, he said, "In spring you can
see the almond trees in flower. From here they appear like pink clouds."
When I did not respond, he spun around and gave me a quick look.
"The lock was jammed," he told me. "Here is the key, thrown behind
a bush. Tell me, who threw it there?"

I am not sure he hoped for an answer. I had none. Did he expect
me to admit having done so myself? When it became clear I did
not mean to reply, he beckoned to the servant who helped him
divest himself of belt and sword. The cloak was already gone, and
when the dark undertunic had been removed I saw him clearly in
his second guise, as the young officer in his European shirt, his
riding breeches, his army boots. But this time he was not half asleep,

not dozing a watch away, rather, he was the master of all that he surveyed.

I had only one thing to say, one question, and there was no need to ask it for he knew. "Why?" he echoed it for me. "Why, because you made it so."

"That first time," he said, "when you burst into my tent, like an avenging fury, what chance did you give me to speak—you were so sure of what I was. 'Where is your master?' as if I were a servant boy. And when we met a second time, 'a monster of depravity and lust,' was that your term for me? What hope could I have had to make myself known to you? Why should I have wanted to?"

I ached to say, You made a fool of me from the start. I told you things, asked things, in confidence. I did not expect you to turn them to your use; I did not mean to have you mock me with my own words.

"You told me things," he was continuing. "But not all the things you said were true. You called yourself a lady of rank, Lady Isobelle. Who is she, if she exists? You pretend to be someone different from what you are. You told the Vizier that I was a man without honor or faith? What promise did I make? You dreamt it up in your mind?"

You encouraged my mistake, I wanted to say. You pretended more than I did. You let me think you were someone different, when all along you had me at a disadvantage. Is that the way a gentleman behaves? Did it amuse you to hide yourself in disguise? You must have known that one day I should learn the truth. Did you find it easier to feign a new identity so I could begin to trust you?

He said, "Did you have to outtalk, outstare, outface me, as no woman does in this land, to show me what the 'civilized' world is? And now, today, what new disguise have you come in?" His raking gaze took in the hastily washed eyes, the hennaed hands; seeing the transparent silks beneath the decorous shawl and beneath them, I swear, the short bodice covering the red-tipped nipples. "Who are you trying to deceive? Me, or yourself?"

We stared at each other, with anger, impatience, and some other thing lying hidden beneath the surface; grief making me tremble; frustration marring his generous mouth; disillusion turning to hate in both of us.

After a while, "Come sit down," he said, in a more conciliatory tone. "I have not eaten all day. I have been hunting since dawn whilst you no doubt lay in bed. I am hungry. And you, you look as if you are hungry, too. You are as thin as a rake, about to slip through a crack in the floor."

I found my voice. "I forgot," I said, venom-sharp, "you like your women fat. Fat and stupid, so stupid," I went on, taut as a cord, "that they do not even recognize you."

And having said that, in truth there was nothing left to say.

After a while he shrugged and sat down opposite me. I had perched myself upon the edge of one of the couches. The position was painful, but the couch was too high and its back too far for me to sit. It was meant for lying on, and my leg was stretched on tiptoe to touch the ground. The muscles ached until I would have liked to cut the whole leg off. Between him and me spread a round table of polished wood, looking wide enough to make a barrier of its own, and when I refused to settle back in comfort, or join him in his meal, or talk, he had his servants bring him a dish of meat, which he began to eat, Arab style, crumbling the rice neatly between his fingers. But he sat like a European, not cross-legged, with his boots stretched out, as much at ease as he had been in his tent. For a thin man, I thought sourly, he eats a lot. I thought angrily, He does all things well. If he were alone, his feet would be on the table and his shirt cuffs undone. And in a moment he would lean back, take a cheroot from his pocket, light it, let the smoke drift, and clap his hands for some dancing girl. Of course he has women, all he needs. No wonder my questions seemed naïve to him; no wonder he laughed to himself afterward. And I thought, anger as quickly gone as it had come, a sadness overwhelming me, Apart from Colonel Edwards you were the second friend I had.

He had pushed his own food aside, and had taken a knife to peel an orange in long thin strips. I was fascinated by the curl of skin, by the careful strokes that his fine fingers made. All his movements seemed deft and quick. I thought, Yes, he can handle a gun, a sword, a horse. He can, no doubt, handle women with equal ease. I was wrong about his being too young. I was wrong about his being a monster of pride. I have been wrong about most things.

He said, not looking at me, intent upon the work in hand, "Suppose I tell you the truth. I began in jest, a joke that rapidly turned into a trap that caught us both. But you were so sure, so confident. Did not you see me in a certain way, and were blind to anything else? The tangible and intangible are never far apart. Beneath the outward and obvious are layers of differences. If I had told you to look at me again, that you were deceived, would that have pleased you? Did not you want to see what you saw? And then, remember how you heaped your misfortunes upon me in my Berber guise? You seemed to welcome finding in me a man to revile. I could say"— and now his hesitation was not to spare me but rather himself—"I could say I would have liked a chance to present myself in a better light." He gave a rueful smile. "Perhaps you would not have thought me completely despicable," he said. "Perhaps you would have found things to like in the Berber chief as well as in the fledgling officer. Or was it only as a young officer I seemed more familiar and therefore safe?"

I was surprised. Firstly that he felt I saw him only as he described (after all, I had had other thoughts about the Berber chief, and surely he was aware of them) and secondly, that he should tell me so. It made him seem more natural. But I hardened my heart. He had been willing to think the worst of me.

He pushed the plate of fruit across the table expanse. "Take it," he said. "It is quite safe." He kept hold of the knife, toying with it. "And now I will admit another truth. I misjudged. I misjudged the power of women on several counts." He was not smiling. "That poison comes from a plant; its name is *efelehel*. In the desert it is known, burning the flesh it destroys. I have seen it used there to pollute wells. Those who drink it foam like mad dogs before turning mad themselves. I have known men use it against an enemy, but never women against their own kind."

His admission gave me no pleasure. I remember thinking wearily, So I was right after all. But I did not believe they hated me that much. They might have had some pity for me. I closed my eyes to shut out memory, and when I opened them he was looking at me intently. "And I misjudged a second thing," he was continuing. "You told me I had an obligation to that Berber woman, although in her case, too, appearances deceive. Yet it is also true that I should have sent her back to her tribe long ago. If I had done so she would have used her shame as a weapon to destroy allegiance to our league. But that is a risk I should have taken, not left you to take it for me."

I had picked up the plate and was feeling round its rim, not to eat the fruit, merely to give my hands something to do. On an impulse I said, "Tell me, why did you want me to come here with you?"

He narrowed his eyes for a moment, lost in his own thoughts.

I expected him to say something else; his simple and direct reply startled me. "Because you wanted to." When I did not protest, taken off-guard and curious to know his reason, "If I had not saved you from those desert traders, what do you think would have become of you? There are real harems in this world. Shut up there you would be dead to everyone. And there, no half-European could have rescued you."

I sensed again that hint of bitterness. I said, "Is it true you dislike all Europeans, as your uncle claimed? With what cause? Just because your mother left you and your father behind?"

He said, "You are wrong. You seem to have a knack of putting things back to front. My mother certainly was French, daughter of a general in Algiers. She, too, came here of her own free will. I told you these rooms, the garden, the terrace, were my father's gift to her. But she came to hate them; perhaps she came to hate him. And when she left, she took me with her."

He said, "Do you think my father would have let her go if he had known she meant to take his son? Why do you think he sent my uncle to bring us back? In his time my father had many concubines, although he took only her as wife. He was a handsome man, strong and brave. For her sake he emptied his harem. To please her her sent away women, children, slaves, only Old Safyia was left, and she was old even then. And when his son was born, he took me up before him on his horse and rode down through the city streets to the castle gates. He carried me as a child, in his arms, to show the other chiefs. 'Here is my heir,' he cried. 'Know him.'"

He was silent then for a long while, as if forgetting me, and when he at last stirred it was as if he had still not done with memories. "She fled with me, and my uncle helped her. I was not so old that I could resist, nor yet so young that I did not remember. We went back to her own home. Where else would she go? Where else would I learn to speak as I do, or read, or write, or act the part of a gentleman?" And now there was no doubt at all of the bitterness and pain. "Where else should I have learned to ride or shoot or hunt except as the grandson of a French military officer? Yet never for a moment did I forget this place of my birth. And of all the men I have ever known my father was acclaimed the greatest horseman of his day. He had a horse, a dark bay, that he had nursed by hand. It would lie down when he ordered it. Four times it won the yearly race for speed. And once, they say, in defeat, it carried him across the desert flats, for three days and nights, without slackening pace. When it died he buried it like a friend."

He said, "I, too, have lived in an alien world. I know what it means to say things please when you count the hours to release. I know what it means to live a lie. I have served my apprenticeship a hard way that I would not wish on anyone. Not a day passed but I did not think of this place and of the father I had been forced to leave. And when my father died, my uncle made the long voyage to bring me back where I belonged."

He said, "Now you know me as I am, half of this world, half of a foreign one. I am not able to leach out the one nor wash the other off like a poison. Both are in my blood. Yet I admit I cannot give up this world. And what my father lost in his old age I have regained, and more. I have honored him. In the north, the Sultan reigns, a fool of a man, who does not see how the foreigners play with him. And when the time comes I shall fight them, the more because of what my father suffered from them. And in the end we shall win." He suddenly shot me a quick fierce look. "Not because they do not know how to fight, or because we are the greater, but because it is written in the stars. For it is also written that one day we shall be what once we were; what has been and will be, all one, part of a chain we call fate. Fate brought my mother here; fate caused my father to dote on her, to his great loss; the same fate brought me back. I came because I must. You asked me why I brought you? Fate, too, perhaps. Better that you tell me your reason." And he thrust out his hand, the hand with the red curling scar, as if pointing it at me.

I had no reply. My heart was thudding in my breast; that flood of words had drowned my reply. They had the same effect on me that I had known in the village square, or on the valley floor, as if I was in a vast and empty space, where, just out of sight, over the horizon rim, lay a mystery.

I think he guessed again what I thought; he had that power. His gaze held mine, as intent as the sharp look of a hunting bird. And again I thought a half smile formed, half formed, and drifted away. "Speechless," he said. "That at least is an advantage. I misjudged you, too, you know. I knew you were brave and capable of endurance as few women are. But I did not know your power with words. Had your tongue been a whip you would have torn my shirt off. God knows you lashed me hard enough. They say, in the Berber speech, to know a woman's mind you must take her answer and follow its opposite. So tell me, Miss Isobelle, sitting there on edge, as if you expect me to throw you over the cliff (as my uncle already has advised), what is in your mind?"

Flustered out of thought, I said the first thing that came into my head, sounding more stupid than the simplest village idiot. "I'll not return to that empty room; I'll not sleep there by myself again."

It is said that there are doctors who see into our brains and read our thoughts. They claim that what we utter is the opposite of what we feel; that we say what we think we should because convention forces us to. But sometimes, when we can no longer hold these two conflicting forces apart, then finally we say what we mean. His laugh made me realize both my stupidity and my desire. The more I tried to explain the more he laughed. "You see," he said, "I told you how it would be. It never was my intent to leave you alone. But let that pass. I know no other woman who blushes with your charm. You shall not return, although I had hoped to make you happy there. Well, we have broken convention enough for one day." And now he did grin, that young grin that I had always sensed in him. "Even my father did not bring his mistresses here but went to them. Let us hope my reputation will not be too much jeopardized. However, my quarters, such as they are, are at your command."

He stood up, abruptly. "I shall be pleased if you make yourself at home," he said. "Meanwhile, I have a duty to perform."

He bowed with his almost military grace and began to stride away. He had not gone more than three steps when my own self-control collapsed. I ran after him, clasping his sleeve, his arm, any part of him I could reach. "Do not leave me," I cried. "I thought you were my friend. I trusted you."

And I spoke to him as the young officer, as the young guard whom I had wanted to believe.

With one swift move he closed the space between us, his arms wound about me. Against his heart I felt the thudding of mine, as he smoothed my hair and gentled along the spine. He said in my ear, since my face was buried against him, and my loneliness was spilling out, such as I had not felt since the death of that other man whose friendship I had valued, "Did you think I meant to? When you asked for help three days ago did you think I did not long to comfort you? From the start I had planned my mother's rooms for you, close to mine. I thought you, too, would feel at home. I should then have had time to get to know you and let you know me. You are a strange prim thing, sitting there in your governess shawl, never moving out of line, never willing to be moved by force. Since first I saw you, so courageous and so afraid, I have longed to know who you are. I have longed to show you who I am."

I had only kissed one man, and that was the hour he died. Until he kissed me I had never been kissed before, except chastely upon the cheek under mistletoe by older men at Christmastime. I had never felt a man's breath, hot upon my cheek, as now, nor his hot full look, nor his attention full and hard. "Ask me again," he was whispering, "ask why I brought you here. You must know."

His kisses were soft, like moths' wings, brushing along the skin. Close to him I could not avoid the intensity of those large dark eyes, with their unexpected gleams, nor the long eyelashes, fanned against the cheekbones, as he looked down from a height that seemed taller than I remembered. I could not avoid noticing the difference between his soft mouth and the rasp of skin where his beard would grow. Of course, I tried to push him off, unable to breathe, unable to take in meaning to words that made more sense than any I had ever heard. Of course, I should not have listened to him, nor let him hold me, nor taken any of these liberties. But I did.

He did not give way, nor could I have moved him in any case. His hands were like bands across my shoulders and around my waist; his voice was saying things I already knew by heart, as if they came from my own mouth, as if these were thoughts that, coming from some innermost place, had already been long known and expected. "Do not fight me. Let be. Let me show you what I wanted for you. Let me show you why you came."

I thought he smiled. "You wanted to come," he was whispering, "for the same reason that I wanted you to."

Then I did begin to struggle. My arms and shoulders were entwined in the soft pleats of the shawl, and I was painfully aware that if I moved too fast the flimsy folds of silk would fall apart, held together as they were by those slight golden bands. And I was equally aware he knew so, too. I wanted to throw back my head and cry out some reproof, some contradiction, that would protect my honor, and would save me from this slur. I knew my struggle was as false as if that Isobelle upon the ship had not struggled against her cousin's drunkenness. On shipboard all had been false, unclean, wrong; here all was right; here, now, was as it was meant. And the more I struggled, the more he seemed to smile, holding me both loosely and tightly, until, I know not how, I found myself seated again, upon the couch, the shawl tangled beneath my feet, and I on his lap.

I was a country girl. I knew what life's facts were as far as husbandry goes, but I did not know how to translate them into human terms. I had seen breedings on a farm; I had never discussed, nor thought about, what happened between women and men. Mohamed had told me how stallions mate and how the mares are tied with cords. I had not thought girls would fight as fiercely as mares, nor men breathe so hard, their hands hard, seeming as unyielding as steel bands, that held and gentled at the same time. All the training of my youth, my feelings of delicacy, my sense of right and wrong, seemed to be swaying; I felt myself waver, bend, soften, as if my bones were melting, as if the flesh were disintegrating from the inside out; as if the more I fought, the less I accomplished, as if in the end I were not fighting at all.

"See," he was telling me, his soft French mixed with the softer Arabic, until I could not tell what language he spoke, nor even what words he used, his thoughts, my thoughts; both already joined, reflecting each other even before they were put into speech. "Your little breasts are beginning to rise. They strain against the cloth, like pomegranate seeds, ripe to the touch. I can see the nipples' outline, like red fruit. Did not you paint them red for me?"

The golden bodice was unfastened; the hooks undone; the shoulder straps somehow were hanging down on each arm like golden threads. "That is a sign," he was telling me, not touching my breasts, but encircling them beneath the rib cage. "And so your breath. Do you know how sweet it tastes, how warm. It runs between your lips, moist and hot. That, too, is a sign to a man." And he kissed me, for the first time covering my mouth. "What sign?" I wanted to ask, but I knew, even before his kiss put all thought out of mind.

"You are virgin," he was saying. "No need to lie. No need to have offered yourself as you did, three days ago. Nothing would have changed; not then, not now. One touch here, one there, would have proved the truth." And he stroked beneath the bodice curve, along the ribs, tracing down my body's length, not a touch, a feather's breath, to where the silk was still closed across my legs. "Lie still," he said, I thought he said. "You are not used to men, nor making love. But if it pleases you, we can change that."

He said, "Does it so please you, my dove?" And I felt myself sink back against him as if I had moved without my knowing how.

"There are many ways to love," he was saying, "and so I will show you, one by one, if you wish. Four orifices are in your body, for your delight, and mine. First I shall touch your mouth, so, run my finger across the lower lip, outside, and in, until you see how it opens of its own accord, waiting to be fed. And then I shall touch your ear, press against it, so, so; blow inside it to arouse you. And there, inside, do you not hear, as within a shell, a soft sound, the sound of waves upon a distant shore? But the others," he said, I thought he said, "are kept secret from men's eyes; better so, in secrecy there is a mystery. One in front," he was whispering, "one behind." And again he stretched with his hand, not exactly touching the folds of cloth, caught between my loins. I felt myself shift and stir (and in my mind I seemed to see that great open space, that horizon's rim, that distance, far and wide). And as I moved, I sensed his other hand, already there to slip between, placed so that as I moved it moved as well. "Hidden from all men," he was saying against my ear, "save me. And one day you will bare them to me of your own desire, one day you will ask of me."

I tried to break the spell. Never, I wanted to say. I tried to remember something, what? Prudery, reserve, shame? My last attempt was lost in his half smile. "That, too," I thought he said, I thought he thought. "I promise you. Lie still now; I shall show you how."

His mouth had gone from earlobe to neck, sliding down the bare collarbone. One hand, that strong, thin hand, was riding up the layers of silk, baring my leg as he had done once beneath the tunic. I could feel the stir of air as the two trouser halves divided easily on either side, opening easily upon the bare flesh. I tried to tug the material down, holding it together; nothing kept it firm but the band of gold, and he took my hand in his as he smoothed on the inside of my leg, up and back to the jagged scar. "Let be," he said, I thought he said, "I am meant to look; and you, you are meant to let me. You know I must."

But he did not look at first; rather, he was watching me, a little smile, part amused, part something else, as he made me watch him trace one fingertip between those painted breasts, between their deep pink cores, down the bare skin to the golden waist. "Why else," he said, "wore you these clothes, except to have me part them thus, to have them open thus, to have me touch you here."

I felt myself shudder with each move, as he watched as if he could see the ripples running beneath the skin; sometimes he let his hand run idly; sometimes lingeringly. Sometimes he watched me watch myself, until his hand slipped beneath the gold waistband. And underneath, as I lay against him openly, the feel of the other hand caused me to shift and stir until I felt myself spread, and all those private places, the secret ones, where no one had been, were bare.

I was gone past shame, past care, past thought, as his hand closed there, running past folds I never knew I had; fingering along the inner lips, widening a gap that seemed to widen of its own. "I know," he was whispering, I thought he said, "no man has touched you here, the woman's path to love. But now you have me there I will touch you like this night and day, until you cry, 'Enough.' "

"And now," he said, "my hands are clasped about, behind in front; I have covered both your secret parts. I have encircled you. Open so," he said, "come up, come down." And up and down and round and round, until the sea came falling into my ears, surging upon a lonely shore.

When it had ceased to fall and I with it, he was still watching me with the same intent look, part that, part something else. "That is one mystery," he said. "Presently I shall show you another one. Do not be afraid; it is meant to be. Lie still." And he drew me against him, legs still spread, his hand still touching me, soft and slow. Pressed to his own body, I felt, down low, how it started up, as if my heat had spread to him. "There am I," he said, I thought he said, moving me gently to and fro, against that hard and living thing. "That is the part of me, unlike you, made to fit into you and spill my seed into your womb. God made us so, you soft to open like a flower, I hard to thrust within." And he took my hand and had it unbutton his shirt and unbuckle his belt, and slide beneath, so that my own palm was caught against that warm and swollen thing.

"You see," he whispered, I thought he whispered, "it is not so bad after all. It belongs to me; it has a name, as do all our parts, although I think you English women are ashamed to use their names. You are so badly taught, so ignorant, that you know nothing of the important things of life." And he had me pronounce the names, touching me or having me touch him so there should be no mistake, the *feurdji*, the *ʒambur*, the *subb*, words whose English equivalent I had never heard except perhaps as curses shouted by country lads, and then I had not known what they meant. But in his language they seemed to assume a delicacy and become what they truly are, marvels of science and intricacy. And all the while he held me until, as he had promised, I felt pressure build, not only without but within, until I almost cried for release.

And afterward we still lay together, he holding me, I holding him, until we slept. Or at least I did, a falling into sleep as absolute and pure as that strange other heavy falling. And when I awoke I was alone.

Our passion had sated me. My eyes were drowsy, my body drugged with pleasure. I lay upon a wide soft couch, anonymous, without a name or past, without place, without having a part in time. Beyond the balustrade the eye-level clouds were touched with the red of a setting sun, and small birds, like swifts or swallows, darted among the trailing vines. From head to foot I felt myself unwind; my toes stretching, my back arched. The very hairs upon my head seemed alive. And for a little while I felt as confident as an explorer who has almost reached that distant horizon. For a little while, that is.

Then other sounds began to assail my ears, all the hum of the castle in whose inner sanctum I now was installed. I could hear the servants moving quietly, their heelless slippers flapping over the tiled floors, and, as if from a distance, I heard a great shout, a sigh, carried on the wind, dying fitfully away. Gradually, I cannot tell you why or how, an uneasiness began to take hold of me, a coldness, tunneling up from whatever depths wherein I had buried thought. I began to wonder what all these sounds meant and how I should react to them. I began to wonder where the lord of the castle had gone and what he was about. Memory of his hand tightening on that great sword hilt came back to frighten me. Not for the first time, nor the last, the weight of the difference between us, between myself and this man I had let make love to me, these differences of custom, religion, and habit, all rose up to confront me, stark and uncompromising. In my country no man would talk or behave as he had done. But how could such a man be both so gentle and so cruel? I thought of Old Safyia and her harem lewdness; what had happened to her? What was the "duty" that he had spoken of? *A just lord, not merciful.* I thought, How can he act executioner? How can an executioner turn so quickly back into lover again? How can I allow him to touch me?

I wound the shawl about my shoulders and began to pace up

and down. The balcony was separated from the inner rooms only by wooden folding doors that I could not lock. I began to feel sure that on the other side I would find slaves crouched down, as Safyia might have done, listening, watching, with little smiles still on their lips. I thought, How am I different from a street whore, one of those my cousin enjoyed when he could escape from his wife? Why did not I submit to my cousin on board the ship if all that matters is the enjoyment, not the man who gives it? And I thought, winding the shawl in knots, How can I face him again; I cannot make love with a murderer. How shall I resist?

To another world, another age, I suppose my maiden scruples might seem absurd. After all, England is not the most moral country in the world, and who was I to set standards. But certainly I think its women are among the most repressed. My little gestures of self-preservation and remorse came too late and must appear feeble if not hypocritical. But this was my last effort, one last try, to hold on to the ways I knew; one last attempt to save myself from what I knew my fate must be. And I thought—for now there was no holding back my thoughts, they ran unchecked—Suppose that cry came from the crowd, witnessing justice being done; suppose when he tires of me, they will shout out in the same way. Harlots are stoned to death in this land. And such was the confusion in my mind, that when at last I pulled apart the folding doors, the only thing that stood out clearly was a space, an emptiness, where that great sword of his had stood.

The servants obviously did not know what to do with me. They bowed so low that their turbans reached their knees, and I could not see their faces. I suppose I hoped that they might escort me out. Instead they took me to the one place I should have avoided most, their master's bedroom. I sat down on the bed and let panic sweep over me. If even servants knew what I was to be used for, what chance had I of salvaging anything of a ruined reputation? Had there been anyone to talk to, even Dr. Legros with his fussy practicality, I might not have acted so foolishly. But having let myself be led like a lamb to a slaughtering, I did not mean to act the part of a lamb again. Nor did I mean to give in to a man who now seemed everything that the doctor had meant by "barbarian."

The bedroom was large, a man's room, comfortable, with many rooms opening off it, sitting rooms, dressing rooms, even bathrooms (luxurious these, not at all like the outhouses that the ladies on the ship were always whispering about, the "thunderboxes" of India).

All formed the private quarters of the lord of the citadel. There were windows in every room, but they were high, barred with thick iron grilles, and although I tried to look through them they were obviously built into the outer walls and were useless as means of escape. One glance through the bedroom-door keyhole showed me two Berber guards already installed and the slave who had brought the message the first night hunkered down patiently. There was no way out, but I had not really expected one. I do not ask anyone to understand what I did next. I do not really understand it myself. I can only tell what I did, which was to shift all the furniture that could be moved to make a barricade against the door. I think now I imagined to myself if I could not get out he should not get in. But perhaps I was not thinking rationally at all, to believe that small tables, chairs, a cushion or so to fill the gaps, a rug dragged along the tiled floor, would prevent a man from taking possession of what was, after all, his room. Most of the furniture in any case was too heavy to move, massive chests and tables, carved out of tree boles. But when I heard the noise outside the door, the gasp of slaves who, I presumed, had been peering through the same keyhole, I took it as a gasp of dismay at my resourcefulness. Well, such is the effect of morality that folly, pride, and complacency are known as the main results. But since human inconsistency is also well known, I need not apologize for my subsequent actions. I sat down again, out of breath, exhausted by my efforts and satisfied. Like a martyr thrown to the lions in ancient times, I had done my best to preserve my Christian innocence and was willing to leave the rest to God. And so, I stripped myself, tore off those golden silks, and, having washed in that running water, crept naked into bed, a Daniel asleep in a lion's den. And if you think, with justification, after all this discussion of right and wrong, that I should have tossed and turned, you would be mistaken. I slept as peacefully as a child and dreamt of nothing at all. And I awoke only when the door came crashing wide, as, of course, in my heart, I always knew it would.

The servants, certainly scandalized, were bent scooping up the remnants of my blockade, whilst behind them in the dark, their master leaned upon his sword. I started up, then slid calmly down, conscious of my undressed state, conscious of his dressed one. He looked as I had seen him often before, in black cloak, black head-dress, black robes, as menacing as he had ever seemed on horseback, as threatening as one of those black scavenging birds. And when, with remarkable calm himself, he skewered the cushions apart and strode across the wreckage of my barricade as if across a fallen bastion, I thought, with the sudden clarity that comes only from deep instinct, He will never understand the subtleties of what horrifies me; and he will never try.

He sat down, pushing forward one of the discarded stools for a footrest; his slave crept in to give him a bottle and glass; he leaned back in the heavy oak chair, boots crossed. He might have been my cousin home from parade, sipping whiskey in a drawing room. He said, calm-voiced, as my cousin could not have done, "They are dead. Those who plotted your death have confessed and have themselves been executed."

I looked at the naked sword. It gleamed faintly in the candlelight, for he had not ordered lamps. We were still half concealed by the dark as we often had been. I felt my stomach heave. But I fought the sickness down. He was continuing, the man who but hours ago had talked and held me as gently as a child—what Englishman speaks with such gentleness, what Englishwoman knows such kindness even in her husband? "Old Safyia took her own life. Better so. The black eunuch she controlled, the halfwit slave, blubbering with fear, the guardsman, fool enough to let them in, those we captured. But the Berber woman escaped. She left her accomplices to bear the blame and got through the gates before they were closed." *A just man, not merciful.* I shut my eyes, praying that I would not be ill. He said, soft-voiced, "It was admitted, and justice has been done. So. It is finished with. You may return to your own room; now I should like to return to mine."

There he lounged, that is the word. I looked at his hands, looked away. I looked at the sword, hard and sheer. I looked at his face, impenetrable, hard, the eyes' glint the only thing I recognized. I thought, suddenly frozen with fear, Where is the younger, gentle man gone? I thought of myself, naked beneath the coverlets.

He shifted to stretch his long legs. "Modesty does not become you today," he said, with the touch of irony I had come to appreciate. "You forget I have seen you naked before. Once when you came into the square; once when the doctor worked over you." He let a hint of mockery creep into his voice. "Would you have preferred I let you bleed to death? Or did you think I would purchase something I had not seen?"

He said, still in the same even way, "I did purchase you, you know. A considerable sum, to soothe my conscience and keep those traders quiet. I thought you would be worth the price. I did not think you were a coward to shrink from facts."

He poured himself more liquid in the glass, held it up to the light as if to test its contents. I thought, He dares me to fight with him; he provokes me into anger myself, whilst he hides his own. But if he could guess my thoughts once, he could again. I tried to hide them away, but they came crowding to the fore, so strong, so loud, he must have heard them. "What am I, a thing, to be bought and sold, a thing to have no feelings left? What have you done to those other women today?"

He interrupted me. "Do you think," he said, "I have tortured them or loaded them with iron to drown in the river gorge as my father would have done? Those who were instruments I spared. Those who were culpable I killed. Do you think I would give an order that I could not myself perform? Do you think I like to kill?"

The hand that held the glass suddenly tightened, so that the goblet shattered on the tiles. "Do I need a hangman to act as slave for me," he cried, "as your country's rulers do? Damn your bigotry. And had my father's concubine tried to keep him from his bed, he would have had her flogged. As I may you."

He stood up abruptly, boots crashing to the ground. "Get up," he said, hauling at my wrist. "I owe you no explanation. Get you gone, before I take a strap to you as you deserve. Keep your judgments to yourself. This is not your land; these are not your laws."

He loomed over me, anger making those eyes, those large beautiful eyes, spark. He was fumbling with his belt; I think he was angry enough to strike. But however much I might feel fear when he was not there, before him, somehow, I dredged courage back. I said what perhaps had always been in my mind: "What will become of me when you are tired of me. Suppose there is a child . . . ?"

He stood stock still, hands on his belt. He said, in the same hard voice, "You stupid little fool. I have not done anything to you either, anything, that is, that would cause that possibility. Nor would I abandon you if there were a child; not probable, since at this moment you are locked a thousand miles away, safe in your stiff English righteousness, and may it choke you, if you do not die of dullness first. And I am here, a weary man, glad to sleep alone. I knew Englishwomen were kept in ignorance, but, dear God, do not you know that to have a child there are still some steps in the process of procreation which so far I have left out? And since it is unlikely I should want to have a son for you to steal away when you please, I shall take all precautions that there be none. Not all pleasure leads to fruits of sin, my foolish moralist. I have had women before and none I think unwillingly, nor none I think that have borne my bastards. You may consider yourself a virgin still. I have not deflowered you yet, and your English husband will have no reason to suspect your honesty."

I had never met a man who talked as he did, who talked himself into and out of rage; who spoke of sexual things with such a mixture of seriousness and joke. Even my cousin, who had wanted sex, would never have admitted it so openly. Only Colonel Edwards had been as blunt, and perhaps he had learned how from his little Eastern wife, perhaps that was what she had taught him.

He said, lazily, all anger gone, not looking at me but stirring the pieces of shattered glass with his foot, "I told you no one blushes as daintily as you do; your skin glows pink to the collarbone, and no doubt beneath although I do not mean to look. But if you are leaving, do so soon. After all, it is you who tries to block my door."

He said, "My father's power was broken by a foreign woman. They say mine will be, too. You do well to remove yourself from such a possibility. But, out of politeness, you could have consulted with me first. I did not think you would run away. What do you have to fear that you need to make me look a fool?"

I could not resist him anymore. I looked up at him, as one by one he stripped off his cloak, his scarfs, his belts, all his dark ceremonial dress, until gradually he was revealed again as the man he also was. The white shirt collar, beneath the tunic, stood up like a priest's, the wide sleeves came down to the wrists, and as he bent to blow out the light, his face was outlined for a moment, like the profile on an old coin. He stared at me, and I at him. He said, huskily, as I had not heard him speak before, his French and Arabic quite gone, only his own language left (and so I must guess at what he said; I reconstruct from other times), "In my mind's eye I have seen you naked since we met. One day, I thought, she will let go her sexual fears as she has braved all other dangers. One day I will find the fire beneath that English calm." He took a step toward me, his eyes predatory, his step smooth, as if stalking his prey. "How else could I have kept you," he was whispering, "unless I purchased you? I needed a reason to show the world. But the real reason lies here, beneath those coverlets." He said, "There are many ways to make love, and if you remain I shall show you them. But you must tell me to. I have not yet begun to make love to you. Do you want to remain ignorant all your life?"

And without a word I held out my arms to him.

I could write many things about that night, about myself, about him. In time I shall. Perhaps what we did was not new to him, but he found newness in my response. And when I saw that half smile, half something else, cross his face I knew that, at least for now, he also found pleasure in me. One by one he took those covers off until my body gleamed like lustered pearl. I shivered, but he held my hands apart so I could not shield myself and let his gaze wander at will, from mouth, to breast, to thigh. Down came his hand, down came his mouth, a pressure where I needed it. I had not the words to say what I wanted, not even the body signs, but I felt myself flatten, stiffen, arch up, as he held me.

He smiled again. "See," he told me, holding my hand across my own rib cage, my own muscles. "I told you you would beg. Look how your body asks of its own. In a little while I shall give you what it wants. Lie still. You tremble like a colt new-foaled, and that will make you stiff and sore. First let me gentle you so, so. In a little while I shall penetrate you. It will hurt at first but not much, and afterward you will know great happiness. Settle down. Put your legs against my own. Let my body warm yours. First I shall gentle you, and when you grow warm and moist, so, so, when you are ready, then you shall let me in yourself."

I lay upon my back supported by cushions soft as down; his body was half-covering mine; his legs were between my own, so that each time he moved he shifted my foot with his; one hand still spread along the backbone feeling out each knob and joint, down to a dark place, where all was lush and wild.

"When I pleasure you," he was whispering, intent himself, his voice hoarse, "your little body runs like honey, molten and thick. It laves me, it laves you. In a little while I shall enter you."

His two hands were joined, clasped about a hard ridge. I felt his thumb glide against a center core. "Here is the third orifice," he was whispering, "here the fourth, the secret ones, hidden from the world." He kept his hand between them, upon an inner lip, like a saw edge to cut between. "And here is the passage that I shall enter by."

His own sex was stiff and hard. He showed me how to hold it, close to the root of that live and pulsating flesh, so that without any need for thought I knew how to steer it toward the body entrance where all my life suddenly seemed centered. The tip was larger than a fingertip, round and warm. Its heat startled, then pleased me, seeming to match my own heat, like a furnace running molten. "In," I said, trying to come closer, his hand showing me how, my body knowing already. I felt the panting start; my breath came in waves matching his. I was covered with sweat, drenched with it, his sweat and mine. Half in, half out, he showed me the way he went, his hair dark against my white skin caught inside the little vent. "Now," he said. With both hands he lifted me and plunged. I felt myself scream, but not with pain. This was what I had wanted from the start.

"So, so," he was muttering in my ear, "come up, come down, so, little one." His hands were about my waist, my body arched to meet his thrust, a great surging thrust that reached into me, washing me away upon a primeval wave. And I cried out a second time.

After a long while, "That," he said, "is why I wanted you, and why you came."

And shameless, like any street whore, I begged for it again.

CHAPTER 8

Caught in his bed, I stayed there. Why not? Why not admit the truth? Once having admitted it to myself, what should I care for the world, or its censorship? Without boasting, I think I may claim that no mistress ever spent so much time in a bedroom as I did. For one thing, there was nowhere else to go. I had refused to return to the quarters that had been set apart for the ladies of the household; I had refused to leave my lord's side. Therefore I stayed where I was. I remember now how I used to daydream the hours away when I was alone, on a bed not much used for sleeping in when he was there. I did not find escape in dreams, as Mohamed had, or as those harem women had done; no, in dreams I relived moments of content, or anticipated new pleasures to come. When the Master was absent on state affairs, when local conferences or council meetings were held (almost daily, it seemed), when messengers filled the reception rooms with strangers, discreetly I stayed out of sight, although not always out of earshot. In this way I came to hear those secrets that it had once been said no European could resist. I do not think I behave as a spy, if I say now that although those discussions were frequently prolonged and furious, they usually ended in friendly accord. The disputes and complaints of his own tribe, for example, were often settled amicably, without delay, albeit the claims and counterclaims of grazing rights, the attacks and counterattacks centering on water holes might have taxed the wisdom of a Solomon. Listening to the pros and cons of things that could only interest a Berber world I had to admit that the Lord of the High Tigran made a good judge, in these matters at least. He was fair and dispassionate, and when events moved outside his knowledge he listened carefully to his advisers, especially his Grand Vizier, whose judgment, I also must confess, seemed equally rational. Except in one thing. For when that Vizier was present I always took special care not to be seen, sensing that the most acrimonious arguments revolved around my continuing presence. Like some large desert bird, the ostrich, which fables say buries its head in the sands, I buried mine, pretending that I did not know what was wrong, although I knew very well that one day there must be a reckoning between the Vizier and myself.

There was one other thing I heard about, which was to be of importance in later times, the significance of the Sultan who ruled in the north. When his envoys arrived they brought imperious demands from His Most Exalted Majesty that were preposterous. How could he expect any tribal leader to hand over all his wealth, and then himself, to a ruler who declared that the reward for such surrender would be impalement alive? I remember another story about that Sultan, too, which circulated gleefully throughout the citadel. It appears that the Sultan's army, which had never been well controlled, had been ordered to attack a village in the foothills. After the soldiers' victory, when the command was given to pursue the enemy, the Sultan's men decided to remain in the village instead. In full view of the Sultan and his officers, ignoring his impotent rage, the regiment had removed their baggy blue pantaloons, tied the trouser legs into improvised sacks with twine, and stuffed each one with loot. I came to doubt the ability of the Sultan as much as the Berber council did, and certainly had little faith in his military skill. I began to sense, more than ever, the real importance of the Berber league, even if the Sultan considered it a hostile force and its leader a rebel who should be hunted down like a mad dog. And I could appreciate the task that leader had set himself. And although I am sure he never underestimated the cunning of the Sultan's court, I did.

•   •   •

When my lord returned from wherever his duties had taken him, I willingly unfastened his cloaks myself and struggled with the buckles and belts, untying the lacing of his tunic and removing his spurs and sword. Under all those outward trappings I found the man I had first come to like. I undressed my lover to discover the body that pleasured mine. That body was as familiar as my own, with its scars of old wounds, showing blue across the skin, even those that I had caused. I could have recognized it by touch, even blindfolded. I learned to watch his lean muscles' grace, quite different from my halting limp; I liked to measure the length of his legs with mine; even on tiptoe I scarcely reached his chin. Most of all I liked to rouse his virility that always took me by surprise and never ceased to satisfy. *I did not think you would know what lust means.* I came to know it very well. And, like the desert wind, it burns as it consumes.

One day my lord opened up the inner garden door and showed me again the connecting terrace walk, with its marble pillars and its tiles. He had ordered the servants to drag out the old tables and chairs and made me sit there as if I were on the balcony of some Mediterranean country house, while he walked up and down, looking at me. He never said why, but I guessed he was trying to imagine his mother in my place, and like a child again, was wondering what had caused her to run away. And once when I had put on a straw hat I had found, large brimmed, covered with faded silk flowers, he untied the bows and threw it aside. "No," he told me abruptly, just as Colonel Edwards had done, "I like you better without a hat." I did not challenge him, realizing too late that perhaps that hat had been hers, but I felt again that rush of pity for him, as I had before —for her.

Another time he took me into the garden that his father had created for her. I went reluctantly at first, but when he showed me how the door and windows to the corridor had been newly bricked shut, so that truly the garden had become enclosed on all sides by high blank walls, I felt more at ease. I stood beside the little pool, dressed in the courtesan clothes that he preferred, and, like a courtesan, undid the silken bands myself, letting the garments ripple to my knees, like sunbeams reflecting in the pool. I slid first one leg, then the next, from those delicate folds, standing there at the water's edge, so that from below my reflection looked up at me. I had strung the golden locket around my neck. Its gold caught the sun until my lover, curiously, opened it. There was the Eastern girl, her eyes downcast, hands turned out to show their reddened palms, feet turned out to reveal the little slit between her legs. And there I stood, like her, in the same pose, my cleft showing its dusty pink, coiled like the inside of a shell. My lover reached up to touch me there, held me low about the hips, drew me down upon the grass verge, entered me, as her lover had done those years ago. And as he moved in me and I on him, it seemed there was no difference left between her and me. We had become indistinguishable, just as my lover and I were one, all reserve between us, all secrets, gone. But I never spent another night there willingly, even with him, and would never stay there alone, nor swim in the pool although he asked me to, conscious of some old watchful presence like a snake's eye, unshuttered and venomous.

By now the cold had begun to depart from the sheltered slopes of the valley where this fortress hung, suspended like a wasp's nest, fitted into the cliff side with cunning intricacy. I could sense the arrival of the spring, its prospect revealing itself daily in the feeling of growing, blossoming, uncurling heat, like a sun just beginning to wake up. I do not know how other lovers behave, but, as each day passed, it seemed to me, too, our absorption grew, like that heat. Sometimes my lover carried me upon the terrace in the noonday sun, and there he would undress me, watching the play of light and shade upon my skin. Its whiteness, turning again to brown, seemed to fascinate him, as did the color of my hair, which, now having begun to grow, he would spread as a cloak across my back. Most of all my desire aroused him. He had only to look at me in a certain way, or put one fingertip between my breasts or let his hand brush along my loins, and I would know I was ready for him. And I had only to move in a certain way, or turn my hips, or begin to speak (he said my voice was more provocative than any harlot's) and he was equally ready for me. My awareness of his erection was as exciting to me as to him. Sometimes he took me by surprise; sometimes without a word, lying naked on those leather cushions. Sometimes he feigned indifference to tease me into making the first move. At other times he played with me, trying those different positions that Safyia had wanted me to learn, himself showing me how to lie or move, arranging my limbs to fit with his. As taught by him, this knowledge became joyful, as natural as the air we breathed, desire burning away all inhibition or awkwardness. Sometimes I tried to run from him but always let him catch me before I could go too far. He bore down on me, covered me. And if in the night he held my body against his own, turning it, opening it, penetrating all those secrets places, I let him have his way with me, not only because I knew he must but because I wanted him to. And so we allowed the nights and days to pass, absorbed by our own absorption in each other's happiness. Until the real world returned.

It was the little doctor who brought back reality, like a cold shower. I had not seen either of my two companions for a while although I had had news of them. I knew Mohamed at least had recovered from the drugs (which had been given rather to keep him out of the way than kill). And I knew a place had been found for him and he had been given work to do as a stable boy. Since he did not have to ride, but merely look after the finest horses in the world, at last it seemed he was completely content. And I knew the doctor had been set free, first to look after Mohamed, then to do or go as he pleased, within the confines of the citadel. His imprisonment had been more tedious than severe, and soon I learned he had become a familiar figure, trotting up and down the castle halls. Ever busy with advice and still full of thoughts of reform, he had earned the name of "gadfly" among the servant girls, they claiming his incessant curiosity was as irritating as a fly's bite. But they accepted him as a harmless fool, either one of God's unfortunates or a magician, whose salves and pills had the power to charm sickness away. They were no longer suspicious of him and although I do not suppose he found their interpretation of his methods flattering, yet no one these days accused him of being a spy.

When he was brought into my presence, I was both pleased and distressed. It had been a long time since I had sat to speak with a man in a regular sort of way; I was afraid I might have lost the knack. And I will confess that I was disturbed by what he might think or say about my new life. Afterward I decided that it showed how much confidence was placed in him and in me that, although he came in the guise of medical adviser, as he quickly revealed, his visit was not simply a professional one, and his purpose (as ever, he made it sound complex and obscure) was both to advise and warn.

He seemed unchanged himself, his clothes somewhat the worse for wear, the black a little rustier, the shine a little more pronounced. When he sank down with a sigh into one of those French-style chairs (for I had been sitting on the balcony), his feet let the heelless slippers dangle from the toes, for his own boots had fallen to bits, and he had not yet learned the knack of keeping the slippers on and either left them behind when he walked or kicked them ahead, much to the amusement of the castle inhabitants. I looked at him affectionately. It began to dawn on me that despite all these outward trappings that made him look the same, there was a difference in him. I could not put my finger to it, but I knew it was there. And perhaps he found me changed. For when I had answered all his medical questions readily, a novelty that he must have appreciated, he leaned back again and eyed me speculatively, as if seeing me amid these relics of a French past was somewhat disturbing. Perhaps he would have preferred to have found me penitent, squatting on an earthen floor, pouring water from a pottery jug. But I do him wrong. He had not come to censure.

"Well, Miss Isobelle," he said, accepting the glass of tea thankfully, although once he would have turned up his nose, "you have made a good recovery, and so I shall tell your lord. You may be bothered with a limp; at least you still have a leg to limp upon. I think you need fresh air and exercise. But"—and now he began to speak rapidly—"I have come to tell you something else."

I looked at him, for there was a note in his voice that sounded alarming. He said, "Soon the passes will open again and the route back to the coast will be clear. The Vizier, whom I have come to respect, has promised to arrange for me to leave. I trust his word. And when I go he wants me to take you with me, *nous deux, ensemble, comme autrefois.*"

"Think of it," he said after a while. He put his hand persuasively on my arm. "We could reach the coast within the month and there are plenty of ships at this time of year. We easily could get passage home." He tried a smile. "I have not kept any written notes," he said, *"mais, ils sont là."* And he tapped his domed forehead significantly.

I did not know what to say. At last I told him the truth. "But I do not want to come." I smiled at his crestfallen expression. "I am not a prisoner," I told him. "I suppose I am as free to leave as you are. But"—I did not know how to phrase it delicately—"but what should I do anywhere else, if my happiness is here?"

He set the glass down so hastily that the tea spilled, and he began to fumble in his pockets for his handkerchief to polish the sweat off his spectacles as if we were sitting in the full desert sun and not on that shaded balcony. "I did not know," he began, "I half thought ..." He let the words trail off, and sat, musing to himself. After a while he roused up, to begin afresh. Suddenly earnest in a way that was new to him, he spoke passionately in French, as I try to translate here. "Miss Isobelle, since I have been in prison I have had time to think. It was a good place for thought, although a guardroom is full of noise. *Je voudrai vous dire quelque chose.* I should like to tell you something." He paused again, sweat pouring out of him in the effort to make himself understood, in the effort to reveal secrets from his past. "Life has not been good to me," he told me, "or rather, I have abused what good there was. I became a revolutionary in my youth; well, that fitted my student days. There was no more ardent exponent of reform and rebellion than my bourgeois self. It frightened the young woman whom I loved and so she married another man." His voice had deepened; I sensed that he, too, was lost in memories that had left their mark on him. "In a fit of rage, not so much of jealousy but pride, for I could not believe she would jilt me, I went to visit her one day. I meant only to stand at the door and talk to her; I do not think that I even loved her then, but seeing her I could not prevent myself. Any more"—he hesitated again—"than I could in that mosque, although I knew what I did was wrong. She refused all my advances, and the more she rejected me, the harder I tried, although part of me watched myself, as if I were another man. When her husband returned and found me there, it was as if I had wanted that to happen all the time. He was obliged to fight to defend her honor, and in the duel that followed, I shot and killed him." He smiled mournfully. "I told you I knew military ways," he said. "I was forced to flee. I came to North Africa to forget, and joined the Foreign Legion, as you once suspected. But one does not forget how three lives were ruined because of angry willfulness. Just as I do not forget those six men who were killed." And now he was silent for a long time. The rest of his story was soon told. Sickened by army life, full of self-disgust and despair, he had deserted his post and come into the foothills. And there he had settled in a native village, to practice a little of his medical skills and drink himself to death.

"I have been a fugitive," he said, "a deserter, an exile, and a drunkard. Nothing mattered in my life until you came. Nothing changed my way of thought, *rien*, until that day in the canyon when I saw what loyalty could mean. I have come to know what the Vizier felt. And I have come to know his nephew very well."

He said simply, "I admire him. I admire the way he has subdued and led a people whose very instincts drive them to faction and discord. In my old age I have come to see what true revolution is and to support the men who inspire it. But there are many rumors running riot here these days; you may have heard them yourself. There are those who see the disloyalty of his men as proof of a power that has begun to crumble. I speak, you understand, of what I hear and what the Vizier thinks, not of how things truly are. I know the guard, for example, the one who was executed (as he deserved), was not one of the Master's own companions but simply part of the regular castle troops, a stupid, greedy fellow tempted by a handful of gold and a woman's smile. But rumor whispers that if the Master cannot control his womenfolk how can he hope to control his men? Rashmana's very escape has become an excuse for more rumor, for they say he should have gone after her, not let her return to her father's tribe to stir up dissension and unrest. He has many enemies who will try to use these rumors against him, as they have before. That Sultan in the north would not be sending envoys without thinking he had some chance of rallying these enemies against their lord. And there are those who claim that you have unmanned him."

I did not want to hear these last things; they chilled my blood. I wanted to cry that they were not true; I wanted to insist that rumor lied, to pretend that I forced him to do what he did not want to do.

Dr. Legros had one more argument, the strongest yet. "*Excusez-moi*. Forgive me," he said, "but remember how he was brought up, and where. I do not speak against my own country, *vous comprenez*, but since his return here, he has had to behave more carefully than other men, to prove himself. Because he has not lived here all his life he feels forced to excel. Over and over again he has to show his strength, either because he strives to quell his inner doubts or because, like the leader of a pack of animals, he must defend his leadership. Weakness is a luxury he cannot permit himself, and he has become a better Berber than the Berbers he leads. But the strain upon him is great. His enemies play upon that, too. I have lived in the north and know that the Sultan is a fool, foolish enough to try to destroy the one man who might save his throne when the time comes. But you see how things might seem to those northern courtiers who tell the Sultan what to do. Dissatisfaction among the tribes, disloyalty among his men, subservience to a foreign woman; these are things to make even a fool think."

He looked at me where I sat facing him, my own head bent under the weight of all these arguments. "The same people who shouted out in the square that day against a traitor when he was beheaded," he said, "will be the same who will shout against you if these rumors become facts. And just as the Vizier does not want his nephew to suffer a fate like his own, I do not want you to."

That simple statement moved me most. I knew Antoine Legros

and I were old friends; we had already shared more hardships than most people do in a lifetime. There could be no secrets between us. That he cared for me touched me deeply, and I felt for him, and for the tragedy that had ruined his life. But I could not do what he wanted; not because anyone would prevent me, but because I could not make myself. Over the doctor's warnings I seemed to hear Colonel Edwards's voice; it was the first time I had thought of him in many days. "If you want an English life, marry an English gentleman and go home," he had said. "Do not try to change a foreign world to your own." But I thought, This *is* my home. This is where I want to be.

The doctor understood my silence, I think. He sighed again and rose to leave. "I will tell you when the plans are made," he said, still speaking with his same intense eloquence. "But also think of this. The Master is young. The abstinence that until now he has shown is unusual and might make him suspect to his councillors, who have been urging him to take a wife. Even if he were to marry you, which God forbid he should try to do, he could not do so without incurring the anger and resentment of his tribe. By Muslim law he could take four wives, and heaven knows how many concubines. Suppose you married him; would you want to share him with other women? And suppose you should have a child." He frowned for a moment, then broke out in his old impulsive way. "Whatever the consequence would be in our own world—and you yourself know as well as I what treatment is given, what stigma is attached, to an unmarried woman with a child—how could you have a child here? Even if you survived the pregnancy, the favor of your lord could not support you through the agonies of primitive childbirth in a primitive land. And would you want to bear a son only to have him taken from you and put to death because he might be a threat to some legitimate inheritance?"

In one way he said no more than what I had sometimes thought myself. In another, he presented arguments I would not have dared contemplate. His words came against me like bullets. I felt them pierce and tear. Again I had to stop myself from crying out, That is not true; He is not like that; He would never abandon me. I wanted to say, To bear his child would be the best thing that I could imagine, but I stopped myself, not out of fear of what would happen to me, but out of a sudden instinctive fear of what might happen to the child. I wanted to shout, Stop, stop. I will not listen to you! I said instead what perhaps he guessed I would have to say, what he had long hoped that I would say, "But if you remained here with me, I could rely on you."

Did I say it? Did I make that appeal to his sympathy? Or did I only think it so clearly that it seemed to have been said? The little doctor cleared his throat and wiped his glasses again. "I make no secret, Miss Isobelle, of how I have longed to have the chance to return home. Sometimes I think I can even smell the good French soil and taste the new wine and hear the wind in the larch trees. But perhaps I am too old to change. For I will admit to you that this place, these people, have done me good. I said prison was a time for thought. I have offered to take you back; I could perhaps find something worthwhile to do here; I leave the choice up to you." He suddenly shrugged, as was his way, but the shrug was not French, it had become a symbol of that Eastern belief in fate that he had once scorned. If God wills, it said, if Allah will have it so.

But before he left he made one more appeal. "It would be hard to leave you, Miss Isobelle; I am not sure I could. But be careful. And remember all the things I have said, *n'oubliez pas.*"

How could I forget! Yet it was true, since my arrival here I had ceased to think of a future. Lust has no future, no past, only the vivid present. The doctor's warnings rang in my ears like the clamor of an alarm bell. Once more I felt responsible for him, as he did for me. For his arguments had caught at me. They showed me a change in him; they showed me a change in myself. Despite our Victorian morality, it is not lust that is difficult. Taking a lover, pleasing him, letting him please us, those things are not difficult, and are easily learned. It is love that tests us. Marriage, husband, children, household, those are the outward trappings of a much more intricate emotion than lust. Underneath those outward layers are nuances making up a complexity that we call love, and that love imposes upon all those caught by it. Danger, sacrifice, death, can be part of love's demands, as Colonel Edwards had found out through his own experience. It might well be that I, too, would find them out, as all must do who let love into their lives. For the first time the thought occurred to me that perhaps my turn to accept those consequences had come. Except that I was not ready for them.

I did not speak to my lord of what the doctor had said, although he knew of course of the visit. Perhaps he knew also of the Vizier's hope to be rid of me. I do not think the Vizier would plot in secret, although his suggestions were not always ones his lord approved. But I also knew that their affection, their love, was strange and intricate, full of many complexities, in which guilt and gratitude played their part, often inhibiting open accord. And certainly my lord sensed my mood—indecisive, troubled, full of forebodings, half real, half imaginary.

I lay on his lap while he smoothed my hair. He said, with his mocking smile, "They say I keep you penned too tight. Tomorrow I have planned a surprise for you."

He laughed at me. "You will never succeed as a courtesan," he teased. "You are not greedy enough. But I have thought of something that will give you pleasure. Tomorrow when I go hawking with my men, you shall come with me. And I have found a horse for you."

He said softly, "Do not be afraid. On its back your lameness will not bother you and I shall have someone ride beside you to lead the way. Would that please you, my dove? Would you rather I scatter rubies at your feet? Is there nothing else that you would like?" I was unwise enough to say, "Only you. Only your promise not to send me away; only your word that I do not have to leave." I lay on his lap and felt his body tempting mine. "We shall not go far," he was whispering, "do not be afraid. I shall not let you run from me." And after that there was no time for talking of anything.

•　　•　　•

He came bursting into the room next day at dawn, a falcon on his wrist, gesticulating to me to get up, up, up, like a boy let out of school. I had heard him go out earlier and pretended to be asleep. I told myself, He is merely going to the stable yards, as he does, to prepare. He will return. But I could not sleep again, tossing and turning in the bed where the imprint of his body beside mine was still visible. Today he will take me with him, I thought. But suppose what Dr. Legros says is true? Suppose he will be obliged to leave me or I leave him? Suppose some force, some power we cannot prevent makes our parting inevitable? What then should I do? Where should I go? What would become of me? When he came back I had worked myself into a panic, ready to cling to him as I had before. But I made myself lie still. I thought, I must show more restraint. I am a woman not a child, I argued with myself, as I might have done with Antoine Legros. Enjoy what you have, enjoy what is now, do not look for anything else. Whoever in your former life, for example, has had a man appear like this, armed and equipped as if for a medieval hunt, while she lies on a couch and waits for him? Is not this "now" enough for you? What more could you want that he has not given you? It was love, not lust, that answered: A future.

He put his hawk down on its perch and threw me a cloak. It was long and dark, but not as thick or long as his own, which was almost too heavy for me to pick up. He told me to tie up my hair, and gave me his old riding boots. "There," he said, standing back, "you will look like a boy of my household. When they see how I fondle you they will accuse me of unnatural vice, which, by the by, in our world is not considered unnatural at all. Perhaps I should practice fondling you in advance." And he almost spoiled his plan by touching me beneath the cloak, beginning to embrace me and play with my breasts until the nipples rose. He stood over me, in his black robes, booted legs apart, looking down at me hawklike. That look made me tremble almost like a hare waiting to be caught. Without a word he thrust me down upon the bed, opening me, boring within, filling me. I sank back, welcoming him. I knew I should never fear him again although he stood there in all his black disguise. All I could think of then was to be covered by him, to be drowned by him, to drown, to fill and be filled. And when we had done, "That is to remember me by," he whispered, "that is to set my seal all day long." That, too, was to be a prophesy.

After a while he took me down into the courtyard, through several secret corridors, one arm across my shoulders to give me confidence. I felt his strength and energy flow out to me. "I cannot ride with you," he told me as he hurried me along, "but the captain of your watch will." He shot me a look that I knew. It said, as strong as words, You had me spare his life so now he shall take care of yours. But be merciful. Let him see you know something of horsemanship. Show him some sport. That look gave me courage. Beneath the black cloak I straightened my shoulders as I tried to keep up with him. I had ridden before, I told myself, I knew what to do, I did not need a groom to ride with me. By now, all thoughts of what the doctor had said had been laid aside, in the novel excitement of the day. Warnings are like church bells; one should listen to them. But when I saw the stallions being saddled I confess I forgot everything except how not to disgrace myself by falling off. Those stallions were

big-boned, long-legged, powerful, typical of the Barbary horse that
the northern world was just beginning to appreciate. My lord planned
to ride his black horse and had prepared a small gray one for me.
Gray horses are noted for their speed and sure footedness, but to me
it seemed gigantic, compared with that old white mare I used to rock
upon. Mohamed held it for me to mount. I am not sure he recognized
me at first, but when he did he gave his wide and flashing smile, and
drew me to one side so that we could talk. I am not sure I would
have known him either. He had grown and filled out so he no longer
looked cowed or furtive. "This is a beauty, Miss Isobelle," he told
me, smoothing the horse's flanks. "I groomed it for your use. It will
bear you easily. But where have you been? I have heard ..." He
broke off and almost blushed. I let his indiscretions go unchecked. I
could imagine what he had heard. Yet for the first time I suddenly
felt older than he was as I complimented him upon his advancement,
asked him questions about his life, let him lecture me on what to do.
I wanted to grip his hands, as once those slave traders had done, not
to test his strength but truly to show my affection. I wanted to tell
him, Be happy for me. I wanted to say, Mohamed, after all you are
right; I have found paradise.

"Hold tight," he kept telling me. "Loop the reins about your
thumbs, and grip the mane. If you begin to jump do not try to pull
up." His running string of instructions showed he had not lost the
knack of becoming an expert in everything, though had he been in
my place, he would have already been trembling with fear. Only the
presence of the Master himself, cantering close by, caused him to
remember what I now was, and he let go the reins with an awkward
bow. I wanted to scold him for this show of servility; after all, we
were old friends, but it was time to depart.

Although the lord himself did not ride beside me, his captain
did, as he had promised. Like a groom, he never left my side, taking
me out of the press and, when the gates were opened, guiding me
to higher ground where I could watch without being in the way. I
cannot suppose that young man much enjoyed himself, although by
the day's end I had regained enough confidence to feel that another
time I might take part myself. He was good-natured, tolerating my
chatter with good grace. And for my part, I thought I had never seen
anything so wild or beautiful, or so effortless as those horses, those
horsemen, those hunters.

The falcons were carried by falconers, riding one pace behind their lord. They were down-feathered, yellow-eyed, wide-winged. They shifted on the falconers' leather wrist bands, spreading their talons, despite the jesses that held them. "They are female hawks," the captain told me later, in his terse style. "They do not like to be disturbed. As they are faithful to their mates, so they are loyal to their masters. So should be all female things."

I was not sure if he meant that as a warning or a compliment but I think the latter. For although he was an expert horseman, like every Berber I have known, and rode his own horse as if he had been riding since birth, he was not very skilled at small talk. Yet by the day's end even he had forgotten my presence.

The air was clear that morning, like glass. The dun-colored earth shifted beneath the horses' hooves as if thrown up by them in a fine dust. Against the folds of the hills our shadows seemed to float and the black-cloaked guards were outlined like a frieze upon a clay wall. There was a cry. The falconer threw up his arm. The hawks soared like arrows shot into the pale sky. Then they turned, hovered, and swept down in thunderbolts. As if at a given signal the black line of horsemen began to move, flowing as easily along the ground as the birds had in the air. The clods of earth fell behind them, the earth shook, the drumming sound of horses galloping swept through the hills. And I watched them all day long.

At the sport's end, when for the last time the falconers had whistled in their hawks and settled them again upon their arms, their master came back for me. Most of the hunt had now turned to ride home, but he lifted me up in front of him, and with just a few of his men spurred on toward the edge of the wooded slopes we had threaded our way through the night of our arrival. When we reached the first scatterings of trees, he turned and smiled and took my face between his hands to smooth my hair that had blown loose. "That is how a good Berber rides," he said in my ear, "a horse beneath him and a girl between his knees," and as he had promised he held me tight beneath the cloak.

The trees were strange to me, unknown, but on these northern slopes they made a great mat of cover with spindly bushes growing underneath and yellow grass spotted now with spring flowers. We stopped in an open space, among a scattering of rock, and there his men built a fire. They crouched about it, laughing and joking among themselves whilst they cooked some of the game they had caught.

We sat on a blanket spread upon the ground, he and I, and he fed me pieces of meat from a spit, smiled at his men's jokes, smiled at me. Wrapped in the cloak I hugged my knees, looking up at the cloudless sky, tracing out the thin branches of the trees, just beginning to come into leaf. I thought, This is a day for remembering. And here I remember it, the last day of my happiness. I should have had it end then. Remembering shows me only what I have lost.

By now we were all stretched upon the ground, singing some of those Berber songs that I caught only snatches of, some I think more raucous than the rest, for my lover gave me the sort of nod that said, Not now my love, later. Later I will explain, later I will show. A wave of content crested over me. If he had beckoned to me then, I would have gone to him without a qualm. But by now the air was growing chill. "Mount up," he said. "Sit behind me." He swung me up onto the broad saddle. "I am not sure I can have you sit in front," and he gave his boyish grin. I knew what he meant. Sit behind me, was what he was saying, so I do not have my arms about your waist, so I cannot press you close. Sit behind me, with your arms upon my belt, like a staid housewife. I laughed myself. I should never be a staid housewife, I thought, and I told him so. That was the last exchange we made that day, but I remember it. And had I not ridden behind him my story would have ended here.

We did not hurry in the evening cool, but picked our way along a track that skirted the edge of the hills, just below the tree line, winding in and out of the rocky slopes. It was pleasant under the ridges of the cliff, and I felt my eyelids droop as I sometimes let my head nod against his back. The talk of the men came in fitful snatches caught upon gusts of air, and the horses' manes and tails seemed to be blown by a wind. Sometimes the trail widened to give us a view of the valley floor, and the outline of the castle at its head; sometimes it narrowed underneath the lee of cliffs, below outcrops of rock, which arched above to form a tunnel; sometimes it wound between big, free standing boulders, poised like sentinels. We were in front and had just rounded a last stand of stones, turning west, so that the sun was in our eyes. A sudden low mass of rock seemed to loom overhead, sending a thick shadow on the ground that made his horse half rear. I clutched at him, hindering him, I suppose, as he kicked it forward beneath the darkness of that natural bridge. And as we passed I heard a sound I had never heard before, a low throaty sound, half purr, half snarl. It made me look up even as the mass on the keystone seemed to separate itself, seemed to widen and spread into teeth and claws; seemed to cut off the sun with its golden weight.

There was no room to turn aside, no time to do anything. My lover threw his free arm up to bear that weight upon his own back. He fell sideways in a jangle of reins. There were snarls, shouts, the clatter of stirrups. I heard my own voice scream. I clung to the pommel of the saddle as the horse plunged ahead. I saw a tawny body, a long tail; I felt a gush of fetid breath. The catlike shape seemed without form or style, seemed to pour itself through the air, seemed to fill and block my sight. The men behind me cried out sharply, flung themselves off their horses, and tried to take aim. In front of them, their lord struggled to throw off that animal shape that had pinned him to the ground. The rolling figures defied the guns; no one could tell who was on top, who underneath, until, with a violent thrust, their lord was able to free one hand. A dagger point glittered and fell once, twice, three times. With a final heave the huge body collapsed, its belly showing rose and white against the gold. And my lord half rose to his feet, clutched his shoulder, lurched, and collapsed again, a stream of blood already gushing beneath his robes, beading his hair.

The violence had been so sudden, like that other time, I had no chance to take it in; one moment peace, the next blood, darkness, and death. I felt sickness rise into my throat as I tried to scramble off his horse. His men had already gathered around his unconscious form and were stripping off the cloak. I closed my eyes at the sight of those dreadful gashes ripping through the cloth to bone. They tied him up with rough but practiced care. The head wound they left alone, it was nothing; it was the claw marks along the shoulder and arm that were more serious, these and the effects of the fall. They hoisted him onto his horse with a man to support him in place; they took me up somehow, no time for explanation or formality, and they took up the corpse of that mountain cat, wrapped in blankets so the horses would not shy. We rode forward soberly at a steady pace; a messenger was sent ahead to sound the alarm, and it was only after we had clattered through the castle gates and they were bolted tight that any of us seemed to breathe again. But not until we reached the main square, where the castle household were rounded up and the doctor waited anxiously, did reason began to revive in me, reason and consequence.

It was Mohamed who, in his usual direct way, clarified things for me. My rider had set me down like a bag of grain, consternation on his face more poignant than speech. Mohamed helped me limp aside, pulling at the cloak to cover me, although I think no one had time to notice me just then. His eyes were almost starting out on stalks, but he would not let me go, although I strained to break his hold so that I could run to my lord's side. But there was nothing that I could do for him, only hinder what was already being done. Mohamed had begun to mutter prayers beneath his breath, both Muslim and Christian. "Allah be merciful," he intoned, "how came that lion there?"

When I tried to explain an accident that had seemed to me as stupid as to make no sense, as random as a summer storm, "That was no accident," he cried, "that is not an animal from these parts. I know it; it is a species only found in the mountains of the Rif, far north from here. It was brought and set and released. God spare us, who did such a dreadful deed?"

If a stable boy, a camel slave, had recognized at once a fact that had escaped me, how quickly the men who were there must have known, how quickly the lord himself, who had been its victim. And had I ridden in front, the beast would have leapt at me. Even before we had returned, the obvious clues must already have been assessed, word running ahead of us like a gorse fire. To begin with, the choice of place was an ideal one for an ambush, the rocks forming a natural hiding ground and the trail narrowing where the sun was in our eyes. Then, too, the way the animal had been poised, as if expecting us, suggested that it had been left there deliberately, carried perhaps in some sort of cage and kept until the appropriate time, by someone who must have waited for us to pass. I thought stupidly, Why not have used a marksman with a gun? A rifle shot from a hidden assailant would have been simpler and certainly more efficient. But I knew the answer. Efficiency and simplicity are European virtues, not Eastern ones. This was a Berber way, planned by mountain men used to deviousness as well as treachery. Two things alone had flawed the plan, and saved our lord's life. Since the arrangements had to have been made in haste, and of course, in secrecy, a larger animal (which would have surely achieved its aim) would have been more difficult to transport or hide. This wildcat (and afterward when I saw its hide I could not look at it, and turned away in loathing, yet it is the cat's nature to attack), this mountain cat was too small, a female, to have killed at the first leap, although it certainly almost had. The second thing was the very place that had been so well chosen. Since it lay in the heart of the lord's own lands, whoever had set the trap had been so desperate to make good his own escape that he had not had time to destroy the evidence left behind. There was no need to have brought back the dead animal with the marks of the rope to bind it; a later search soon revealed even more damaging proofs: the scuffed-over tracks of men's feet; the wooden sledges upon which the cage had been rolled; the cage itself, with its door thrust apart and the wooden stick that had been used to pry the beast out toward the overhang. And on the other side of the rocks were the trails of horses riding north, back into the forested hills where it would be difficult to hunt men down. But there was one other thing, and that the most disturbing of all. Mohamed pointed it out, his eyes round. "Someone waited for you to leave," he said. "Someone saw the way you went; someone spied on you." And that, too, was a fact that could not be ignored.

All these points were causes of intense discussion afterward. They were to have a profound effect upon my future life, as upon the lives of everyone. But then I could only wait, as we all did, anxious and silent in the square, while they carried the body of their wounded lord, still wrapped in his bloodstained cloak, to the nearest anteroom, where Dr. Legros tended him.

(I should pause here to comment that had the doctor selected this set piece to prove his skill, he could not have chosen a better subject nor a better time. I have no doubt myself that even if my lord's people had given all the care they were capable of, he would not have survived; he would have died, if not of his wounds themselves, most certainly from the infection that followed them. In the desert, it is true, wounds seldom putrify, the heat drying out infection perhaps, but this is not the case with a wild animal's attack. Although not anticipating such an accident, Dr. Legros was more than prepared to cope with it. Since cleanliness had long been his prime concern he did what later would be considered the most ordinary thing in the world; he kept the cuts clean and disinfected, and his patient warm and quiet. And whatever my lord's men would have done, such was their respect for him that when he recovered consciousness enough to order them to let the doctor attend him, they obeyed.)

I did not go to him at first, I repeat. I learnt afterward from the doctor how the wounds were washed and stitched, the broken bones set, the drugs administered that kept the fever in check. I sat there with the other members of his household, wrapped in my cloak, like them dazed, anonymous, waiting for the word to come of his progress, for good or ill. But once suspicions had been put into my mind I could not obliterate them; I merely pushed them aside until I had time to reconsider them. And I knew if my reasoning went the way it did, so must others'. I began to sense a crisis brewing. I felt it in the air, forming over my lord's inert body, hanging like a sword overhead; a challenge issued to him, and in response, an anger, a slow burning rage that was to consume us all.

The only question worth debating was, Who?, the who being more important than the why. Everyone knew why, took for granted the why, except perhaps myself, who was the main, if not the only, cause. But who had planned to kill him in such a cruel way? There were factions in his own tribe, but just how divided they were or how prepared to make such an open attempt upon his life I could not judge. Perhaps no one could. Yet surely since he had made that unexpected raid on the night of his return, his detractors had been quiet, and it seemed to me unlikely that they would risk murdering him. As for sedition in his own household, that, too, seemed unlikely; the last traitor had been dealt with so summarily that no one would dare again. Besides, only his own guard had ridden with him today, and they were like his second self. So if not among the household of the Lord of the High Tigran, nor among his clansmen, then the attackers must have come from beyond his tribal borders, where he had many enemies it is true—part enemies, part friends, waiting to see how the wind blew. And there, among these distant tribes (who, it must be pointed out, were members of his confederation and as such owed him loyalty of sorts), the use of a mountain lion rather than a gun to kill took on special significance that only made sense when it was explained to me. For the lion was the emblem of several of those tribes, their symbol that they held in veneration and awe in their primitive way. It would have appealed to them as a means of vengeance, a fitting choice, suiting their mood and style, since a mountain lion is both shy and vicious. And since, when it is goaded into rage, it will attack whatever crosses its path, man or beast, it is often kept for such a purpose (and whoever had caged this one had certainly goaded it thoroughly). But there were other clues, too, equally convincing: the fact that this particular species came from the north where the Sultan's power held sway, the fact that it was a gift he often presented to a southern tribe whom he hoped to bribe into loyalty, and finally, the legend, as revealed in old stories and fables, that an attack by a lion as a weapon of revenge was favored by disgruntled women who perhaps found it easy to identify with its fury and its claws. These were ideas that needed to be considered, and considered they were, mulled over endlessly during the next days. And in time it came to be accepted that only one tribe fitted all these theories, and that was the tribe of the Berber woman of the harem who had tried to murder me. But at the moment I had no thoughts to spare for her or for her tribe; all my hopes and fears were concentrated upon the well-being of the man who had now suffered for her revenge. However, there was one thing I knew, and will repeat again, for it seems to me of the highest significance. Tribal unity, tribal loyalty, flared and subsided like a fever, one moment running high, one moment running low. Since my capture unrest had been smoldering fitfully. There had been no bond among the Berbers since the fifteenth century; perhaps it was useless to expect a miracle. But if they did not unite soon, the chance would be lost to them. And if their lord died they would never find someone to replace him, and their hopes would die with him.

When I had been hurt I had retreated into some inner private world, and so did he. Like a wounded animal he lay for three days and nights without moving, scarcely seeming to breathe. He had been brought up now to his own rooms, and was placed in the great bed where we had made love, where his father had died, whilst at the door and sometimes even inside the room his councillors and friends hovered, as if, should there be something to record, some order given, some sign made, they would all be there as witnesses. The first time I saw him lying like that, the energy drained out of him as the blood had been drained, I thought he would never move again. His face had not been touched, except for that gash beneath the hairline, and his right side was unharmed. Perhaps the thick folds of his cloak had served as some protection. I laid my hand over his where it lay outside the blankets and sensed, rather than felt or saw, how somewhere deep inside him the nerves responded, like a thread of light, like a stir of a current in a stagnant pool, like a sudden surge of blood. I could not be sure if it came from him or me, but it gave me hope. He did not open his eyes or speak; and watching him then, with his hair cut back to reveal the stitches beneath the scalp, I saw how his profile had tightened and purified, more than ever giving him a look like the effigy on some gold coin, minted when the world was young. And after three days, when he opened his eyes, it was as if he had kept them shut because he willed them to. *Three days I give you.* That is what he gave himself.

Dr. Legros was not exactly hopeful, not exactly resigned. Without his being there I might not have been able to enter the room at all. The guards would have let me in but the councillors turned their backs on me as if I did not exist. It did not occur to me until much later that had he died my life, too, would have hung by a thread. I never thought of that then, only of him. And when I sat beside him it seemed to me that just as on the ship I had felt myself journey with that dying man, so now I did with him, wherever his spirit had gone. So that, when I came back to myself, it was as if I returned from some long and lonely trail in which I had not only passively accompanied him but was constantly making an effort to draw him back. And when I returned, if I may use that word, it seemed to me sometimes that the pressure of his hand in mine strengthened, as if he were assuring me that one day he would return as well.

Dr. Legros tried to assure me too. "I told you," he said, sitting beside the bed, ever watchful himself (I do not think he slept or ate those days), "if he were wounded he would dig out the bullet with his own teeth and fight on." He smiled in mournful complacency. "I could show you a score of such men I have known whose ability to endure pain is something they have trained themselves to do. *Moi-même*, I have seen a man with his arm torn off kill his enemy before he let himself collapse. I have seen a woman with half-blind eyes allow flies to walk across the swollen lids, without bothering to brush away an annoyance so great we could not endure it for an instant. There are stories of injured men who have crawled across the desert flats in heat that would have killed most men on their feet. I cannot tell you why or how it is," the little man said with a shrug, "nor why they should want to endure such hardship. But they do not consider it as courage, as we might, rather as a virtue that all men should emulate. That a man who is half-European could learn the skill is almost a miracle. Had we part of their ability to control our minds and had they but part of our ability to work with practical things, what a race we would engender. Except, I think, the day that they acquire our technicalities, all their delicacies and subtleties will be destroyed." He flushed, surprising himself with this sudden outpouring of praise, quite at variance with his scientific detachment. I knew he spoke to give me heart as much as to give heart to himself; but his enthusiasm was new, and had these been less trying times, I would have commented upon it. It became him and revealed a generosity of spirit. And his words were ones to carry with me when I took my leave and went to wait alone.

When I was not physically in my lord's presence, I stayed nearby, on that outer terrace, where men always stood on guard, watching me as carefully as they ever had, or more so. Sometimes it was the young captain who had ridden with me on the hunt; sometimes his comrades, the three men whom I had pleaded for. They never spoke to me, but their constant presence was a comfort as well, something solid and enduring to hold on to. I lost track of time, and would suddenly realize with a start that day had dawned again or that the moon had come up like a beacon above the sleeping valley. I do not remember eating or drinking, as I suppose I must have done. I do not even remember thinking. And when I came there on the third night and took my usual place I suppose I must have fallen asleep myself.

It was late when I awoke. The lamps in their sconces against the wall had guttered into molten wax, and the stars were gone. It was the time of night, or morning, when shadows flicker like bats' wings and when the sick rally or slip more deeply into oblivion. I got to my feet clumsily, legs numb, back stiff, having slept in a position that had set all my bones out of joint. And for a moment I felt my heart lurch as a figure came toward me from the doorway where he had been watching me. It was the Vizier. I felt myself cringe as he approached, in his black cloak looking more than ever like one of those birds of prey that hover over the dead and dying. But it was not news of death that he brought this time, not yet.

CHAPTER 9

I had not met with the Vizier nor exchanged words nor looks with him since the day in the Berber camp, and that was so long ago already it seemed to belong to another life. I have explained how I had always tried to avoid him, sensing in him a festering dislike, and I certainly had no wish now to be accosted by him or be forced to defend myself. I knew at once that he would only appear before me like this, unannounced, watchful, malevolent, because some special circumstance forced him to; even acknowledging my presence seemed distasteful to him, and just as I had tried to pretend he did not exist so he had behaved toward me. I could imagine the mixture of scorn and displeasure with which he now made himself approach, eying me unwaveringly, his face an indistinct blur, his dark robes blending in with the black of night, his hatred gusting out unrelentingly. But as he began to move, slowly, his step heavy, almost weighted, in turn I began to make out details of that face, belonging to a man caught between youth and age, caught between awareness of his youthful folly and his older self-contempt for the weakness that had betrayed him then. In the wan light I could see the lines that spread downward from the corners of his mouth, stern, unrelenting lines, which even his beard could not disguise. Disappointment, harsh resolve, and bitterness were written there. And one other thing that I saw, a flicker, before his eyes dropped their lids like a hood: an uncertainty, a nervousness, new to him. I sensed suddenly the almost imperceptible tic beneath those hooded eyes and noted the smudges of fatigue, as if he also had become used to sleepness nights. When he stood opposite me, bulky, silent, menacing, I thought, suddenly aware, He stands like that because he does not know how else to stand; he hooks his thumbs on the inside of his broad belt like that because he cannot bear that his hands be seen; he looks through me because he does not see me at all. All he sees is that other woman who was here; all he thinks of is what he must do to counteract her influence; I am only a symbol of a past he regrets and wishes he could forget. And I thought, with an insight that surprised me, He does not hate me as much as he hates himself. So we eyed each other, two strangers who had little in common except out mutual love for the same man. And that, he would not allow me to share.

He spoke to me in French. The heavily accented voice sounded strange, gave him a wooden formality that contrasted oddly with what I remembered. Afterward it occurred to me that he spoke in French merely to ensure I understood; he could not afford to have a misunderstanding at this stage. Yet of all languages it must have been the one he abhorred. And he spoke to me because he believed that I could help. But what he said astounded me.

"Mademoiselle, go to him. He has said he will ride with his men at dawn to lead his *harla* out. He must not, yet. You can stop him, you alone."

Afterward I could understand what deep affection for his nephew brought him to make such a request; afterward I could appreciate how it must have galled him to ask for any favor, especially of the person he blamed for the present predicament. In one sense I suppose he flattered me, at least he paid me a compliment by suggesting that I had any influence over his nephew (although at the time the implication I would use my influence in such a way, had I any to use, that is, seemed more of an insult than flattery). But these were all thoughts for afterward. At the time, it was the realization of what his nephew was about to do that made the room sway and dip, and caused my heart to miss a beat. *You do not know what* harla *means.* Now, alas, I knew the meaning of that word well. And if he were to lead his men, that could only mean one thing; a *harla* rides to fight, and he would fight with it.

I stared at the Vizier as if he did not make sense, until he felt constrained to repeat his message, impatient now, pronouncing each word distinctly as for a deaf-mute or a fool. All I could think of was how I had last seen his nephew, motionless, stretched out, like a man crucified. His eyes had been closed and he had seemed gone, far off, into that halfway land between sleep and unconsciousness. I could

not believe that in so short a while he could have summoned up
sufficient energy to open his eyes, to say nothing of dragging himself
out of bed. But it must be true. And I thought, Of course, why else
should he have lain so still, except to harbor his strength, to will it
to obey him? What else should he prepare himself for, except for a
cause? In the silence that followed the Vizier's second request I heard
a hum, a steady drone, as if a door had been thrown wide open,
causing the sound to crest through the citadel. It was the noise of
men and animals, vibrating deep down, as in a hive, when bees are
preparing to swarm. And I thought, I cannot stop him any more than
his uncle can. Of course, he means to lead out a war party to revenge
the insult done to him; of course, he will make himself go, wounded
or not; he must, before his enemies take advantage of him, before
they try to brand him a coward. He has no choice. And I cannot
prevent him.

Hearing that noise, that hum, the Vizier's eyes unexpectedly
blinked as if in silent prayer. I felt a great surge of pity for him,
almost as great as for the Frenchwoman who had destroyed him. For
the first time I saw him not as a threat, not as an enemy, but as he
truly was, a man torn by unexpected conflicts whose genuine concern
for his nephew was at sharpest odds with his own fighting instincts.
As much as any Berber in the fort he would be burning for vengeance too. Only fear for his nephew's safety held him back; only
that fear forced him to turn to me.

Hardly knowing what I did, I held out my hand to him. "Come,
Lord," I said to him softly and smiled at him. "We can try."

But I knew we would not succeed.

Maybe I thought I knew what the Vizier meant when he spoke
of his lord's riding out to war, but I am not sure I really did. What
did I know of war? Yet I must have appreciated the danger involved;
war is always dangerous, how much more so for a wounded man,
who scarcely could bear the weight of his clothes, who would need
all his strength just to survive the campaign, to say nothing of planning and leading it. But when I look back to that time, as I followed
the Vizier along the terrace with its guttering lamps, as I hurried
behind him past the guards through the crowded anterooms, it was
not so much actual danger that obsessed me as a sense of inevitability. I felt that something overwhelming was just about to begin,
something that could not be stopped, something that had been destined long ago. It reminded me of one of those mountain torrents

which, in full flood, is capable of sweeping under everything in its path. So for us; I saw how contentment, happiness, peace would be washed away and lost. And we would become minor victims in a greater catastrophe. Like the Vizier himself, I would be faceless, nameless, inconsequential in the ruin of years. I do not want anyone to think I openly spoke of disaster, ill-wished it, foretold it. The army of the Lord of the High Tigran had always been victorious before and might well be again. I can only tell what I sensed. And I knew the Vizier sensed it, too. Both of us were powerless before that knowing. But I also knew that I would not have prevented my lord's departure even if I could. And that, the Vizier did not expect of me.

The inner room was crowded with men as it had been the first day I had come there. But now they were not gathered for a hunt or a feast. They clustered together, not talking, not laughing; waiting. The servants bustled about making a show of importance, but they could not hide the apprehension and fear that made them start at any unexpected sound. Louder than ever, through the open doors, the tramp of feet, the clash of weapons, the shouts came gusting along the corridors. And above everything, like a shrill whistle, rose the keening cry that women give when they mourn. Hearing it, I closed my eyes. And when I opened them I saw the Vizier's hooded gaze fixed upon me once more, as he stood aside to let me in. *War is no place for women.* Even so, his look said, you shall try to stop it; you must.

At my approach the doctor turned, as if he, too, were hoping for a reprieve. His face had aged these past hours and had crumpled into weary lines. On seeing me, he let it tighten for a moment into a set mask. I almost felt the shrug of his shoulders, as if to say, I have done my best; now do yours. But his former patient did not turn, did not hesitate, and went on with what he had been doing, testing each cartridge as he slid it with one hand into the bandolier, carefully, methodically, as I had often seen him do. He was on his feet, and his feet were already stamped down firmly into his European riding boots, the one concession he allowed from his European upbringing, the only outward difference between him and the men he led. Except for his left hand held stiffly across his chest where, in a while, someone would strap the broken bones in place, except for the long scarf wrapped about his waist to take the weight of belt and sword from his ribs, he seemed as he always had been. His black cloak was spread across the bed, the sword and gun were propped

against the wall. He did not turn around I say, and his back was to
the door, but I think he knew I had come in. More than anything I
wanted to go to him. I ached to press my head against those broad
shoulders and hear the heart beat steadily and strong; I longed to
feel the shift of his blood and flesh. I wanted to run my hands through
that shock of soft young hair, barely hiding the bandages. Stay, stay,
I wanted to plead. Wait until your wounds are healed. There is danger enough without running headlong into it before your full strength
returns. Wait. I did not move to touch him, did not say anything.

Nor did he look around, not yet. Some of his bodyguards were
helping him, bending to strap on his spurs, easing him into the shirt,
drawing it over those long raking scars, adjusting his sword so that
he could pull it out easily. From time to time he spoke to his men,
sending one of them swift-footedly away. I knew what was in his
mind as clearly as if he had given the order aloud. I could almost
hear his thoughts flying past: the number of men he could muster
within the walls, how many horses stabled here, the rest to be com-
mandeered in the valley outside; the names of allies who could be
trusted to feed and shelter him; the others, whose neutrality would
mask indecision until his arrival would stampede them into ardent
support; and, in one sense less dangerous, those who had openly
declared their hostility. And these last would be already up in arms
themselves, would be waiting for him. Allies, enemies, provisions,
arms, he marshaled them one by one, ordering them in his mind
before giving voice to command; one thing settled, he moved swiftly
on to the next, no time for hesitation or regret, no turning back. I
thought, I have known this man as lover and as friend. I have feared
him as a judge, quick and implacable. Now I am seeing him also as
he is, a soldier, grandson of a general. Now I can understand the full
power of a mind that cannot be diverted once its course is set. There
is no point even in trying to stop or change him. He has already
gone beyond me. And I felt his thoughts overleap the castle walls,
beyond the mountain pass, flaring out from this secret citadel, searching out his opponents, assessing them, testing them before they came
to search for him. I thought, All that men have said or feared of him
is true. I have not always believed it before. But that is because he
did not choose to show me all. He has always kept some part of
himself inviolate. I know him gracious, good-natured, generous, con-
siderate. These are qualities that the European world can appreciate
and these he has displayed liberally. Under them are harder facets

that I am not sure I know how to accept. Anger is there, and stubbornness, and that other thing for which we do not have a name, that sense of place, of destiny, of self that will not let itself be diminished. To dishonor it would be to destroy the man. I thought, Nothing I can say or do will sway that part of him unless, like that other woman intruder here, I bring destruction down. He will leave at dawn because he said he will. *Three days.* At daybreak, on the fourth day, he will go. All I can ask is to share these few remaining hours.

He said quietly, over his shoulder, "Leave us now, all of you." They made their way out in a group: the young guards; Dr. Legros, nervously tugging at his beard, his eyes blinking behind his spectacles; the Vizier, still rigid-faced. But I caught the expression in his eyes again, before he lowered them. Resignation was written there, and surprise. I thought, He came to me, asked me, because I was the last chance he had. He knows as well as I that I would never succeed; he never did have great hopes of me. What he did not expect was that I would not try. He had not thought me capable of restraint. But then the door was closed, and my lord and I were left alone.

Some of what we spoke of, did, whispered in that fast-spinning night, is perhaps better left untold. There are some things that I cannot write, not even here. Not because of modesty but because of love. If in the act of procreation all men sense their own mortality, how much more poignant are those feelings between lovers now forced to part? In parting, who has not felt the warmth of love more overwhelming than the pangs of desire? But I will share what I can. What I keep is to sustain my own loneliness. And that is branded in my mind like flame.

He said, "Do not be sad. There is no danger except that which my enemies think they prepare for me. But they do not expect me yet." He smiled. "You see how weakness will become a strength if I use it to trick them."

He said, "I could wait, a month, two, three. I could wait out my life, as my father did. I could become a prisoner here as he was, hostage to their enmity, despised by all men. One day they would make me face them on their terms. Better now, on mine, than then."

He said, "I shall leave my uncle to defend the castle. But I leave my household to you. Take care of it. Anything you need, you have only to ask and my uncle will advise you and tell you what to do. Until my return he will barricade the gates so no one can come in or out. Trust each other, as I trust you."

He said, "Do not leave me, my dove. Wait here for me. I give you all my memories. There is no place for memory where I am going, so you must remember for both of us." He took my hands, held them close together, palm to palm. "Like that," he said softly. "Do not let one drop spill, so that when I return I shall find it all intact."

He said, "But first tell me good-bye, so that you will have one last thing of your own to hold me with." He cupped my face with his good hand, stroked my hair, and ran his thin fingers down my throat. Oh, God, I do not want to remember the parting that we made. Memory is all I have left. I do not wish to share it with anyone. Except this. That virile body that had pleasured mine might now be hurt, its strength perhaps impaired; that does not mean that I could not still pleasure him. In love, as in lust, all things are possible, and the giving of love is as good as the receiving of it. And at the end I gave him the little gold locket that I had worn so long, so that its luck might be passed on to him.

In the anterooms messengers waited. He sent the same message by each. "Ride with me." In the courtyard horses were being saddled in haste, bridled, tied with provisions, ammunition, water bags. Grooms tested each strap and girth; the short curved swords flashed in the predawn light; anvils clanged. From time to time a rifle shot echoed above the battlements, and voices wailed afresh. At the top of the flight of stairs I waited, apart from the other women, hidden like a dim shadow. And when at last the day began to grow, so that, as if a lamp had been lit, out of the semidark what had seemed shapeless re-formed itself into the familiar, I thought, That is how God made the world, out of chaos, out of darkness turned to light. Except what here is light will turn to darkness for me when he is gone.

There was a sharp cry, like the cry to prayer. Perhaps it was to whatever gods of war one should pray to. There was an answering cry. The men swung themselves onto their saddles; the horses began to fret, and from the stable undercrofts the Lord of the High Tigran came out, already mounted, dressed in all his black robes. But today his face was bare and the sun, coming up now in a rush behind the topmost tower, caught at him, caught at the flag floating behind him, caught at his accoutrements, outlining them in gold. He raised his right hand. From a hundred throats the cry went up, "Go forth with God." The cavalcade began to unwind in its leisurely way, each horse in its turn separating itself from the mass and prancing down the narrow road. Their lord rode at their head as he had said he would. I could see his face clearly although he already seemed a long way off, and he never looked in my direction or turned to me. But his men saw him and acknowledged him. He greeted them as casually as if he rode with them to hunt. Then he fastened his scarfs in place, hiding everything that I held dear. Nothing was left of the man I knew, only a dark stranger who urged his black stallion into a trot, a canter, a gallop. They swept down the path, through the gates, toward the valley beyond. In my mind's eye I rode with them. And when the last man had cleared the gates the Vizier gave the order to swing them shut and ram home the heavy bolts.

•   •   •

I had never lived in an embattled place; what part had war in my quiet little home? Yet in my village there were middle-aged men who had willingly gone out to fight in far-off places in the Crimea and some of the older gentlemen remembered the time of Napoleon and still spoke of Waterloo. One doddering colonel had ridden with Wellington. It would have been hard to match his faltering steps and half-blindness with those eager young men who had left today. But all those wars had been fought far off, on foreign soil. I had never lived where the doors were locked to keep back an enemy, where lookouts were posted day and night, watching for an unexpected raid or for the return of our victorious army. Awed by such a display of might, Mohamed tried to explain its importance: how many men were engaged, how many horses, their attributes, and the qualities of the men who rode them, just as he had on the march here. It seemed to me that the numbers were fewer than I recalled, but I kept that worry to myself and let Mohamed boast of names and accomplishments, incidentally displaying his own expertise. His enthusiasm at least was undiminished and his confidence served to shore up my hopes. "One swift advance," he was fond of repeating, "that is all it will take, to make the opposition crumble to dust. That is our master's style. I told you he was a leader without equal. When he first returned from foreign parts his tribe was not overeager to receive him as their lord, but the Vizier forced them to. 'You want a victory,' he told us then," (the poor lad's enthusiasm caused him almost to imagine that he had been there at the time) " 'Watch me; I shall give you one.' He did not command many men then, you understand, only those who, out of respect for the Vizier, came reluctantly to serve him, and certainly none were as devoted to him as all are now. He was young, untried, seeming a foreigner himself, used to foreign ways. We could not believe he could even ride, dressed as he was, and secretly we scoffed at him. The other tribes did so openly. 'Send out your little heir,' they used to shout. 'Or is it an heiress?' with many other obscene remarks and gestures of contempt. But he curbed his anger and showed his soldiers what he wanted them to do, taught them how to attack and then, at the last moment, retreat, as if in fear. Lured by this apparent show of cowardice the hostile tribes would be tempted to throw all caution to the winds. Thinking to have him in a trap, they would pursue in wild expectation of victory. Hidden in the hills his reserves would sweep down behind them, encircling them. But he always gave them one last chance before he struck. 'Choose,' he used to say. 'Join with me and go in peace. Or fight, and accept death or imprisonment.' Myself," he added with gory relish, "I would never have been so lenient. I would have cut off their right hands to ensure they never fought again, as his father is said to have done. That would certainly make them keep their word. Perhaps now he will. But if he could persuade men to fight like that then, imagine what victories he will win now."

I thought, Strategy can serve once, it cannot be used a second time. Men who are fierce as wolves will not hesitate to destroy him if they have the chance; they will not show his tolerance. When he fought before, he was young and untried. Many things conspired to give him confidence. Moreover, he fought for his inheritance and that is a concept all men can understand. Now he fights for an abstract dream, burdened with a label of traitor that his enemies can turn to their use. He is older, wounded. Perhaps he senses that his own stubbornness has been part to blame, perhaps he, too, fears defeat. But these were thoughts to keep to myself.

Dr. Legros was equally dour. "I expected something like this," he said, torn between satisfaction that he had been proved right and distress that common sense had failed. "*Moi,* I knew he would never lie calmly in bed. *Bien sûr,* of course it is madness. The wounds are healing well, unless he jars them open again, as no doubt he will. And broken bones do not knit because you tell them to." He must have seen the expression on my face for he suddenly put a stop to his complaints although the silence into which they dwindled was almost as revealing. "*Mais, qui suis-je,* who am I," he muttered after a while, "to tell a soldier when, or when not, to go to war. They used to claim he was invincible, his body encased in steel, so strong it would deflect any bullet aimed at it. Perhaps that is true. At least I vouch that the will is steel. And if a man thinks himself invincible, sometimes he is. But since you and I are of more human stuff, admitting our weaknesses, we might as well make use of what poor gifts we have, rather than worry over someone who does not even know how he abuses his strength. And while the passes are as closed by war as they have been by winter storms, let me show you instead what I have done here." And in his fussy precise way, beaming with pride, he began to tempt my interest in his various little projects, about which, hitherto, I had only heard whispered jokes. Seizing me firmly by the wrist he led me down into the town to show me the school he had set up where he tried to teach children to read, not very successfully, since the more he ranted and raved at their ignorance, the more his little pupils wriggled and smirked, their shaven heads and plastered scalps suggesting he had had more luck with his struggle against lice and ticks than against their illiteracy. His showplace was the room where he had set up his surgery. "Imagine," he said briskly, setting his instruments out, and arranging his remaining bottles of quinine and Seidlitz powders, "they have no more idea of cleanliness than flies. When their time is come the women squat in the fields to bear their child and rely upon a friend, as ignorant as themselves, to bury the afterbirth." He did not add, as I knew was true, "And when I give them salves to rub into their cuts they eat the paper that I write my instructions on, and save the ointment." I let him talk, not always suitable topics for an unmarried female, but useful perhaps if I should ever have a child myself. I knew he wished me well and found women's ignorance of their own bodies and bodily functions exasperating, whether they were Berber tribeswomen or European ladies collapsing into vapors over indelicacies. And I thought suddenly, clearly, as clearly as if he had spoken aloud, Why, he is as happy here as Mohamed is; he is as happy as I am.

But when I returned to those inner rooms, I found the Vizier waiting for me. He never let drop a word of reproach at where I had been, a breach of etiquette on my part almost unheard of, to move freely, without pretense, among the ordinary people; nor did he show approval or disapproval of his nephew's last order to me. He never mentioned it. But acting on it ever after, he came each day to report to me on the state of the citadel that he had been left to guard and to ask me what my needs were. (And perhaps I should state here that, henceforth, I went openly into that citadel, little by little gaining confidence, little by little becoming accepted, so that I think, in the end, I may claim that I was tolerated, perhaps liked, as much as the doctor himself. And this slow winning of the people's trust, although I never had that aim in mind, was to have a consequence for me, too, when I least expected it.) This first time, however, the Vizier spoke abruptly, without preamble: "I misjudged you. I thought your hold upon him was complete. I thought he had become besotted by you."

As an explanation it was not polite; as an apology worse, but I decided to accept his words in the spirit he had given them. "The past never quite repeats itself," I told him, trying not to show any resentment, trying to keep my voice as emotionless as his had been. "I think you have misjudged your nephew more than me."

Unexpectedly he smiled. For a moment that smile softened his face, giving it a family resemblance that I had been searching for. "Just so," he said. "That is something upon which we can both agree. And I shall tell him so when I see him next. As for the past repeating itself, that remains to be proved. Although I will admit this: Such a woman as his mother was is known but once in a man's life, for good or evil, only once. Since you do not seem to covet her power, nor yet to possess it, let me say one more thing. When the campaign is done and the routes north secured, why not depart before he returns? Call an end, for him, for you. You know it can lead to nothing but grief for you. And you have seen now, all too clearly, what it has brought on him. He will not go back to Europe with you. You could not last here long. If you care for him as you claim, and as I have seen for myself today, you will show you care again."

Well, the doctor had warned me of the Vizier's plan, and there was a certain charm to him that made it easy to agree. I said stiffly, the words stiff, my eyes too bright, my whole body trembling with effort, "You thought you could trick me into doing what you could not do yourself or were perhaps unwilling to try. Do you think I liked seeing him leave? Do you think any woman would send the man she loved into danger willingly? But I promised I would remain here. He asked me to keep his household and, as long as I can, I shall. We can work together or not as you please. But I mean to keep that promise to him."

He eyed me again for a moment, stroking his beard. I felt his will strike out against mine, reminiscent of his nephew's; felt it meet, lock, prepare to struggle to overthrow my own, and subside. He opened his mouth to speak, closed it, and left without another word. But from that day on a truce was declared between us, albeit an uneasy one. He ordered a new set of guards to accompany me (for my captain and his companions had gone with the other men). These new guards were boys, too young to fight, and I have no doubt they were more in the Vizier's power than mine, but they took their duties seriously, and wherever I went they trailed close to my heels. He left me in sole occupation of the lord's quarters (which I suspect, by right of Regency, he could have claimed for his own), and punctually, every day at noon, he visited me to give me the news—a ritual visit, with one of his men to announce him and call out his titles, almost as impressive a list as his nephew's. Not that he ever had much to tell: a dull list of accounts, of storage supplies, occasionally a report of some foraging party sent out as from Noah's ark to test the state of the surrounding land, sometimes details of some petty crime, the sort that occurs among women and old men shut up without much to do. And when I had offered him the ritual cup of mint tea, which he, as ritually, set to his lips, he saluted me as formally as when he had come in, scrupulous in his leave-taking. Meanwhile with Mohamed and the doctor in tow, I took advantage of the Master's absence to explore the world over which I had been given domestic control and which, until now, I had never really seen. I took that word *household* literally, meaning the care of house and family. Now I had the chance to go behind those heavy wooden doors, those iron grilles, to wander down those twisting lanes where the ordinary life of the fort went on. The citadel was crowded these days, people from the surrounding valley seeking shelter during the troubles whilst their menfolk were gone. In many ways it reminded me of a medieval world, a resemblance that the presence of those high battlements and towers enhanced. But it was not only the environment that encouraged that feeling; everywhere it was implicit in the way people moved and thought and behaved. Despite the absence of modern conveniences (if I may term them so, equally lacking, I should add, in the cottages at home), I was constantly struck by the general feeling of content. These are happy people, I thought, not because they do not know what they miss but because they are satisfied with what they have. I learned now to admire the women's fortitude, as strong as their men's. I learned how to duck beneath the low lintels of their doors and accept their cups of tea or honey cakes; I learnt to praise their little bits of garden tucked away between the walls, soon to brighten into flowers and herbs; I learnt to smile at their sharp-eyed children who stared at me openly as their mothers were too shy to do; I came to envy the grace with which they carried their copper water jugs, the way they endured the wait for news of their men, the way they steadfastly put anxiety aside and went on with the daily business of their lives. I listened to them talk until sometimes I think they almost forgot I was there. And in all these things I found much of beauty and simple goodness.

One day I went with Mohamed into those lower cellars where was kept the armory, consisting of old swords, hide-covered shields, lances—years old. Beyond them were the great storage pits, dug into the stone floors to serve as granaries, with iron gratings bolted across the top. "That is where the Vizier spent five years of his life," Mohamed told me in a hushed whisper, "before his brother could decide what to do with him. And when his cellmate died, such was the jailor's fear of him that he was left there, bound to the corpse, side by side, for fear of loosening the chains." I bent down to look into that dreadful depth and could not repress a shudder at the gust of cold and noisome air. *They can endure pain.* What pain he must have suffered, I thought; how could anyone spend five years there and remain alive, or emerge sane? My grudging respect for the Vizier increased. But except for those daily visits, as I have recounted, he never spoke to me, person to person, I mean, and the gap of misunderstanding between us was as great as it had ever been. Until the day news arrived. And then it was too late.

Mohamed and I were in the courtyard when we heard a trumpet's snarl, a sign of someone fast approaching the castle. I suppressed my longing to run and look over the walls as the other women did. I was not an ordinary woman looking for an ordinary man. Wait for me, my lord said. I would wait for him where he had asked me to. But when I regained the security of the terraced walk I cannot say I sat in patience. A mixture of yearning and fear drove me up and down, wearing out a fresh track across the stones with my own fevered fretting, as once, long ago, that other woman had done. Except I longed for someone's return, not for my own escape. But it was not my lord who came back, that bright day when the sun turned dark.

I am not sure I would have recognized my captain of the guard although they had already tied up the worst of his wounds and wiped off some of the blood. Supported by Dr. Legros, trailing one shattered wrist, he might even have tried to go down on his knees to touch the hem of my dress as he always did, had not his legs buckled under him. They say that to expect the worst, to anticipate it, is nature's way of staving it off. Anticipation of evil becomes an offering to the gods in place of reality. The sight of the captain's face told me all I needed to know, that reality suddenly, brutally, revealing itself worse than all the imaginings. Nor would he have returned like this, alone, unless he had had no choice. I knelt beside him where he had slumped, trying to help the doctor rip off the tunic, whilst, behind us, the Vizier stood like death's messenger himself, arms crossed on his breast, head jutting out for a blow, watching a man whose news was self-evident. By now that news had gone winging through the castle; I heard it in the rising wails, like the ghost of a wind moaning through the cracks in the stones; how he, half-conscious on one horse, had led the second one, a black horse, lather-streaked, its saddlecloth torn and soaked. And how, behind him, beating slowly out of the hills, one by one the stragglers already had been seen filtering through the pass, the remnants of that proud mustering. Those images were to appear and reappear before my eyes in a sequence that I could not break; two horses, one rider leading them, followed by a succession of shadows, as shapeless as the morning they had left, as if, in reverse, we were moving backward into chaos. And yes, one last thing, the captain's muttered whisper before he again slid into unconsciousness. "Mistress, they wanted only him. They let the rest of us go deliberately."

I stood on legs that did not know they supported me; I walked on feet that did not touch ground; I heard with ears that did not register noise. But gradually, when realization came thrusting back, I think it was the Vizier's voice that made me accept what was being spoken about. "Not dead then," he was saying, "captured, to make an example of." I had expected death. The captain and other men would never have left their lord if he were still alive. Why speak of capture? I looked at the Vizier as if I thought he would change his mind; as if, in a little while, he would relent and apologize for tormenting me and would tell me what I hoped to hear, that my lord was free, unharmed, and would soon arrive. But, "Captured," the Vizier was repeating. "And to show contempt for us, letting the rest go free. But imprisonment is not death. Men can survive imprisonment." So he spoke, a man whose life had been wasted in such a prison. I felt my own hopes die, even as the Vizier was continuing, "Be patient; Rasheed will explain as soon as he can." Yet as I accepted the older man's patience (patience is the last resort of men in extremity), as I registered the captain's name, which I had not known before, as I registered there would be an explanation, all I could see was that word *imprisonment*. I knew now what they did to prisoners. *We killed our men so they would not be taken alive. I will string you up by your thumbs. I shall torture and impale.* I could only see the gratings across that dark pit; *five years they buried him.* That bottomless hole seemed to widen, deepen, creating a void into which I fell. For the second time in my life I suppose I must have fainted. And when I recovered, it was as if time in between had not moved. Not dead, captured; not dead, thrust into a pit to rot. I found myself almost praying beneath my breath, "Better death than that."

But life does not give up hope easily. Although I did not yet know it, with every breath I took, new courage was beginning to stir. I think even as I sat back in the chair where I had been placed and waited for the captain to be revived, I was already beginning to think how to turn this news to some advantage. It is to the Vizier's credit that he had had the captain brought before me so I could hear his tale, as well as the councillors. They now came crowding in, anxious, silent, grim. It must have gone against custom to have had a woman present, but I think it was the way the Vizier showed some respect for me. And no one in any case had time for custom; all were intent to learn how that chaos had been let loose.

Rasheed spoke at last. (I give him his real name. I do not know if learning it made him seem more real, made him less so; that, too, was a thing of no consequence. For all his suffering, he seemed to me then only a messenger of defeat, as impersonal and remote as the Chorus in an ancient tragedy.) He talked in short fragments, croaking out phrases like a cracked bell that rings out of tune. I fill in the details here as we learned them afterward, piecemeal, from those stragglers, riding in by ones and twos, then in their half dozens, wearily, by stealth, furtively, revealing in the very act of secrecy the classical symptoms of defeat. Most of them let their horses stumble through the gates and fell off, willpower alone having kept them upright this far. Some carried injured companions in front of them, cradled in their arms, the wounded showing signs of dreadful hurts that no sword or gun could have caused; others, bowed with disgrace that they had survived, crept, lackluster, into the courtyard, no cheering crowds to welcome them, no heroes' return. In defeat itself there was no dishonor; dishonor came from living to speak of it. It soon became obvious that, like Rasheed himself, they had been ordered home. To men who take defeat as personal insult, to have obeyed an order that went against their deepest instincts was the greatest compliment they could have paid their lord. And although half of them were lost, in time the rest returned to form the nucleus of a new army as their lord had intended they should. But let that wait. First to his story, as his captain told it, fleshed out by all these later accounts.

In the beginning it seemed the campaign had gone well, much better than the men had hoped, for few shared Mohamed's optimism. It was clear, although Rasheed did not say so, that the constant criss-crossing back and forth from hill to plain, the night attacks, the sudden raids on hostile villages, the forced marches to catch recalcitrant tribes by surprise had taken their toll. The Master's recovery had been slow; his wounds had stiffened and fever had set in that taxed even him and sapped his strength. Often he was too weak to ride, and once he had ordered his men to tie him in the saddle so that even if he lost consciousness he would not be seen to fall. But this night, the night before calamity had struck, five nights ago, for the first time he and his army had begun to sense a turning in their favor, as if a cold wind had shifted from its course. They had all felt the difference, a slackening, a sense of relief. That night they had had time to rest and to assess their gains. There had been some success. Although in places the passes were still snow-blocked, twice they had swept down from the Tinzi Gap to drive the enemy into the desert sands. Without real engagement they had stopped a large troop from joining its main band, and, on presenting it with the familiar choice of surrender or imprisonment, had had the satisfaction of seeing most of its tribesmen lay down their weapons, give up their horses to be branded with the Tigran mark, and prepare to hike back home after again swearing an oath to keep the treaty they themselves had broken. That night then, when our men had bivouacked at the head of the Tinzi Gap, they had reason to be satisfied. Their lord had seemed almost like his old self. Flexibility was returning to his arm. Soon, he had jested, he would be able to slice off heads both left and right. And soon the last force still remaining defiant would be cut off from their home base and destroyed. "And that," Rasheed whispered, "was the tribe of the Sejilmi."

The name meant nothing to me, but on hearing it the other men scowled and spat, and with one voice cried out their horror and shame. Afterward the Vizier explained, still calm-voiced, not excusing nor expecting excuses. "The Sejilmi," he said, "are a Berber group, a large and powerful conglomeration of tribes whose Sheikh was once our lord's friend. He controls those men with an iron hand, and, although aging, he is still a cunning warrior, a suspicious foe. He is the father of the Berber woman, Rashmana, who escaped from here."

The councillors muttered and scowled. I thought, The Sejilmi, that is another name to remember, another cause to blame me for, to list upon the Vizier's reckoning sheet. But Rasheed was continuing. "Our scouts had warned us of their presence, but until this time we had avoided them. Now we felt strong enough to make a direct confrontation. We were camped between them and the head of the pass, so that there was no easy retreat for them except into one of the many blind canyons running off the main valley floor where they would be trapped. South of them lay the open desert where they would not dare go far. If we could come upon them in a rush, harass them, before long they would be obliged to make a stand. And in a standing fight, although they outnumbered us, we felt confident of victory." He hawked and spat himself, trying to wipe away the beads of sweat that soaked into him, until the doctor soothed him with some calming drink. "We did not know," he cried, "how should anyone—that their Sheikh had made a bargain with the Sultan's court."

There was a groan. There were many men the Berber tribes abhorred, but the Sultan was an anathema to them, trying to impose his rule, and his taxes, from afar, trying to encroach upon their freedom. However much they might dispute among themselves, asking for help from the Sultan would be like making an alliance with a Barbary ape, as unnatural as to seem ridiculous. Yet the Sheikh of the Sejilmi had done so, it seemed; had gone against his own people's wishes and traditions, because the Sultan had tempted him with the one thing he coveted. The offer of the mountain lion had been but the start of a new attempt at influence in which bribery and greed had played their part. "We could have overrun them easily," Rasheed whispered again. "When they paused to water at the Tinzi wells we had them trapped. We were so close behind them we could have hurled a stone into their midst. They never would have escaped us there had not the Sultan given them guns. And had not the foreign gunners opened fire on us."

All Berbers use guns. Old muskets, hoarded as prized heirlooms, newer rifles, captured from whatever source, hand pistols, stolen, bargained for, exchanged, all were their weapons of choice. Even their curved swords ranked second to guns. But Rasheed did not mean that sort of gun. He meant cannon, artillery, such as the Berber world did not have, except perhaps for a few scattered pieces left over from Napoleon's day that, through the decades, had made their way south. The Sultan had somehow got his hands on modern guns after his last war with Spain. More valuable than their weight in gold, their worth was enhanced by the gunners who came with them. And now, somehow, he had allowed four of those precious guns to be detached from his northern residence, where he had had them mounted like the heads he nailed above his gates. The cannon must have been dragged south in secret by mules bred for such a task. And with the help of those foreign gunners, equally in secret, they had been installed in the cliffs above the wells to help the Sejilmi fight us. It was those four guns that had blown the Tigran cavalry to bits.

"There was only one thing to give the scent of alarm," Rasheed was continuing, and now the urge was upon him to speak; like some Ancient Mariner he seemed to be seeking absolution by confession, as if he wanted to drive into us the horror of that moment through which he had lived but during which so many of his companions had been killed. "At the last moment the Sejilmi had split in two. A smaller group had veered off into a narrow valley and disappeared. We assumed they were meant to act as decoy to draw our fire while the larger force went on toward the wells under their Sheikh's own command. We decided to pursue the larger company simply because they would not expect us to, presuming we would have followed the smaller one as bait. In a general sense our reasoning was sound. In fact, all the while they meant for us to continue after them. And it is true that when we saw them lounging around those wells, without a care in the world, taking their time, almost as if they were preparing for a feast, without guards, we thought we had them fast." He sighed and tried to wipe his forehead. "There were no guards," he cried. "They had those guns to guard them."

He had to pause for a while. The Vizier and the other councillors now began to pace up and down, refighting the battles of their youth when they had fought the Sejilmi tribe themselves, debating the motives, techniques, and strategies of a people they knew well. The Sejilmi clan were famed for their "trading interests" (a nice euphemism, that), meaning they were mountain men who took their living on the desert edge, raiding caravans coming inland from Timbuktu. They would seem the least likely of allies for the Sultan, whose merchants in those northern cities saw their profits disappear, swallowed up by robber raids. Nor were the Sejilmi noted for their finesse. Skillful deception was not within their power. But it seemed equally unlikely that the Sultan himself had been the originator of a plan that was calculated with such resourcefulness and skill. Then who?

But Rasheed had taken up his tale again. "We broke out of the gap at dawn," he was saying, his voice fainter now, as exhaustion and weakness took hold. "We had skirted west of the valley where the smaller group were camped, leaving a few scouts to watch over them, and had closed fast upon the cliffs beside the wells. Those of you who know the Tinzi Gap remember also how its water holes are placed, a line of them, scooped out under the eastern edge of an overhanging cliff, just where the sandy valley floor opens out like a river mouth into the desert sea. We could see the Sejilmi clearly, I repeat, clustered about the holes as if flaunting themselves to lure us on, their Sheikh even seeming to sleep there in the shade. Seeing such carelessness our master's suspicions grew. He deployed our troops so that only one squadron advanced at a time. God be praised he did. For when the first attack came within range, the cliffs spat fire." He turned his head as if to block out the sight. "The cannons were set inside the caves with which the cliffs are riddled," he whispered. "We could not even see them from below. The Sultan's foreign gunners had primed them right. Their shot exploded in a rain of steel so thick it stirred up the sand like a desert storm. And when the smoke cleared we saw a carnage indescribable." He said slowly, clearly, "I have been a fighter all my life. I took my first man when I was twelve. I have never seen men killed like that before. And had those gunners held their fire until our second line went in, we would all have been smashed like flies."

Afterward no one could explain how the cannon could have been brought to such a place, except it was clear no mountain tribe, no Sultan's court, could have arranged the transport nor set in motion an operation requiring such careful precision and delicacy. "They say," Rasheed told us, "that the foreign gunners shouted to each other in the flush of victory, claiming that their own masters would pay them well; they even began to anticipate how they would spend their reward. And the Sejilmi, puffed with satisfaction and pride, also praised those gunners, crying out that their mighty guns would open up the trading routes from south to north, believing, poor fools, that the foreigners who would open them would allow them free access for more plundering. But present gain is all they think of; they have not the sense to look ahead nor calculate how much the Sultan's help may cost them. And the Sultan himself, equally foolish, never sees that by accepting advice and help from foreign powers he, too, jeopardizes what little control he has left."

He lay back, drained of speech, this usually silent man whose horror had loosened his tongue. But his story was not yet finished. For although the Lord of the High Tigran had ordered an immediate withdrawal out of range, he could not retreat while the wounded still lay there. Although pinned down by intermittent fire, all day long volunteers from his camp had crawled forward to rescue their friends, but those who had survived were in such pitiful state it was clear that another day in the open would not be possible for them. That first night, then, it was determined that a group be sent to secure the cannons. They went on foot, as they had before, leaving their horses tethered behind the cliffs out of sight. The plan was simple, to scale the cliffs and destroy the guns. The cliffs were not so steep as those they had climbed when rescuing me. Using hempen ropes, made by plaiting horses' gear, they meant to swing down, ledge by ledge, toward the caves midway, where the guns were placed. Once having overrun the gunners, they would spike the cannon, enabling the rest of our men to mount a charge. As it was planned, so was it done, with initial success, a predawn attack that caught the Sejilmi asleep beside the wells, relying on the cannon above their heads. The cannons could not be turned to fire upward and before the gunners could cry alarm, they had been killed and their guns jammed with rocks. A flag was raised. Seeing it our lord prepared to give the signal to advance. It was then that scouts, riding furiously, brought the disturbing news that the second Sejilmi band had left the shelter of their valley and were bearing down hard.

"Like rats," Rasheed picked up the story, "like vultures, thinking to scavenge where the picking would be easiest. They must have heard the sound of cannon the day before and hoped for a share of loot from the battlefield. They had found the tethered horses we had left, and that, too, encouraged them. Whether they were meant to come, whether they disobeyed orders, is immaterial. Hearing them, the main Sejilmi troops by the wells took heart and began to resist more stoutly than before, preventing our men from climbing the rest of the way down the cliffs. And seeing us, the newcomers took advantage of our predicament, our divided state and impediment of dying men. They had had no intention of picking a fight with us, but such good luck could not be ignored. We did the best we could. We put the wounded in the center, made a human wall around them, and prepared to resist attack, giving up any idea of attacking ourselves. Our lord tried to comfort us. 'Stand firm,' he told us. 'They will have heart for only one attempt.' He knew if we could not drive them off, it would go ill for us and ill for our companions on the cliffs, still fighting on foot against the main force for control of the wells. We needed those wells," the captain added then. "We had no water left. Our guns were red hot, and our wounded, those who still were conscious, were crying out from thirst. I have seen wounded men before, but never like this, in agony. At nightfall of the second day the Sejilmi brought out a flag of truce. They had ample time by then to assess the nature of our plight, and those who could, including the Sheikh, had slipped off from the fight for those wells and came to swell the ranks of the newcomers. (For, lacking our support, our men were still perched fifty feet above the ground and, although safe as long as they stayed there, were too few to keep all the enemy penned in below. Without horses they had no means, of course, of pursuing those who got away and neither could they help us.) 'We will spare you,' the messenger sneered, 'in the way your master spares lives. Give up your weapons and horses and carry your wounded home. Leave us one man. We seek only one, but we shall keep him.' "

When the outrage had died down, "I tell you," Rasheed insisted, "that purpose lay behind their every move; that was the reason they had planned so cleverly. And our lord, who is capable of matching cunning with like cunning, recognized its origin. 'This is no Berber trick,' he said. 'And the Sultan has been used as much as the Sejilmi. I would swear a thousand crowns that my mother's people are behind this.' And so the Sejilmi Sheikh confirmed. 'Surrender, Lord of the High Tigran,' he shouted, well out of our reach I might point out, for he still was afraid of what we might do. 'You have had a long run and your hour is come. The French have prepared a welcome for you at the Sultan's court. After I have made you welcome first.' " Rasheed paused, almost bewilderedly. After a while: "Why

did he stoop to bargain with a Sultan he does not respect?" he wondered, a simple man caught up in complexity. "Why did he turn
traitor to his own kind? What did he want?"

I knew part of the answer although I did not speak. But the
Vizier did. "Revenge is what motivates him, to avenge his daughter's
humiliation. For a woman's whims he would destroy the only hope
our people have."

The end came quickly after that. But if revenge it was that the
Sejilmi sought, revenge in the end they got. "We knew," Rasheed
said, "there was no way we could break out ourselves without abandoning our friends, both those still on the cliffs and those lying there
among the casualties. The wounded men, those who could talk, begged
us to leave them and go on. But our lord refused. He sat with the
dying all night, held their hands, eased their passing. And in the
morning of the third day, when those who survived moaned at the
sight of the sun, he got up, straightened his sword belt, and told us
what he planned. 'Separate the dead from those who live,' he said.
'Tie the dead upon their steeds, as if they still had strength to ride.
They will forgive the misuse of their poor bodies, although what we
do offends the laws of God. I do not think either He or they will
deny us help one last time. We shall use them as a show of force, to
encourage our enemies to leave us alone. They want me; let us make
that a bargaining chip. But since we know they will never keep their
word, as soon ask a leaking bag to contain the water it lets out, we
shall turn that knowledge to our use.'

"He had us raise a flag of truce. We had never done so before
and some men wept openly. 'What security will you give?' he asked.
'Suppose I offer to surrender myself in return for the safety of my
men? Will you allow them to ride with the wounded toward the
wells?' At first the Sejilmi laughed, thinking he meant to joke, then,
beginning to realize perhaps he might be in earnest, argued loudly
among themselves. Some were for trying to squeeze out more demands, others were eager to take what they could, his capture bringing them a rich reward (which also smoothed the path of revenge).
Finally they agreed that we should bring the wounded toward the
water holes and that the Sejilmi there should withdraw, provided that
our lord remained where he was, in full view. We left them to their
arguments and hurried on with our own plans. First we selected
those soldiers who were family men, or who were young, or who
had been wounded slightly themselves. They were given charge of

the casualties. They hoisted the wounded up in front of them. To the remainder, the strongest, most reliable of old campaigners, the task was given of leading out the dead men. 'If God wills,' our lord said, 'the Sejilmi will keep faith and let you all go through. Once you reach the wells, you and our friends there will be safe. But if the Sejilmi attack you on the way, as I feel sure they will, as soon expect jackals to turn from fresh meat, those with the wounded must break through the enemy line and head for home, each man fending for himself. The rest continue to guide the dead toward the wells, so that, thinking you are twice as many as you are, the Sejilmi will hesitate to go on defending a lost cause. Your unexpected advance will ensure their speedy retreat. When they have gone, mount your companions there on the dead mens' horses and bury the dead with all respect, before making for home yourselves. One last thing. On no account begin to fight, or make a threatening move, or, once the fighting begins, linger to engage with the enemy. Surprise alone must win you through. Leave all the rest to my guards and me. I shall remain behind with them. And when I give the signal, do as I have said.'

"And that is what we did," Rasheed said. "He embraced us one by one. Then he rode apart, with six of his bodyguards. I stood with them. I swear we made no move nor broke our word as our men began their orderly ride, live men and dead. But from the start the Sejilmi began to crowd them round, harrying them, first with insults, then with stray rifle shots, then with flanking raids, until, like a dam of water held back too long, their whole line burst out in flood. Only then did my lord give the signal, only then did our men act, some firing as they broke north, the rest using their swords to hack their way toward the water holes, all intent on achieving what they had been ordered to. And waiting until this moment, our lord gave us, his guards, his last command. We swept down behind the Sejilmi ranks, taking them in the rear, almost overrunning their leader himself, who, flushed with victory, had been watching from a safety point, calculating his success. We could have taken him," Rasheed explained, "but seven cannot ride against a host. We rammed them through easily the first time, and could have made our own escape had we not tried to ram them through again, to force them to cut short their original charge upon our line, wanting to make them rally to their own defense rather than attack. When we saw the success of our initial plan, we tried to save ourselves. But it was too late. After our five companions had been slain, 'Quick,' my lord panted to me, 'take your sword and plunge it deep. They'll not have me alive.' But it was too late even for that. As I tried to turn on him they overwhelmed him, dragged him off his horse, and hurled him to the ground. 'Then ride,' he shouted at me before they silenced him. And since all their efforts were concentrated on him, I did, and they let me go. I worked my way north, and, after a while, heard the sound of galloping hooves. But it was only his stallion, which would never have left him either had he not ordered it. But he was alive when he fell, that I swear, and I think he must still live, otherwise his death would have been already proclaimed beneath these walls. As for the rest, I can only tell you what was done to try to save as many as we could, and if God wills, some of them will survive. But the Sejilmi have our lord as prisoner, as was planned from the start."

It was Dr. Legros who added what we others may have guessed but could not bear to put into words. "And they will sell him to the highest bidder at the Sultan's court, where the Europeans have long recognized him as their greatest threat. But only after the Sheikh of the Sejilmi and his daughter have had their way with him."

CHAPTER 10

I cannot pretend that I understood all these battle details; as you know, I had had little experience of war. But even I could smell the dust, feel the heat, hear the moans of men whose bodies had been so mangled that their friends did not want to recognize them. Even I was haunted by their screams. And as I sat there listening, in the quiet of that terraced walk, I could picture the pleasure the Sheikh of the Sejilmi felt as he and his men returned home with their prize. And, as clearly, I could envisage the silk-robed Sultan, farther north in his capital city, rubbing his hands at the news. And I could imagine those cold Europeans, equally smug, equally self-satisfied. It does not matter who they were. English, Spanish, French; secure in their cleverness, their contempt at the Sultan's childish glee would enhance their own sense of success. *One day they will remember our world.* Now they had. Why should they explain that the man they planned to kill was the best defense the country had? If the Lord of the High Tigran should fall a victim to their greed, so much the worse for him. Empire-builders do not remember victims, only victories, and once the Master was dead who would be left to prevent their full victory? They might not claim it yet; this was only a small triumph and the scramble for Africa had not begun. But it would. Here on the terrace of that medieval fort, built high above a valley that this tribe had owned since the world began, I felt a fierce resolve to resist those empire-builders with all my might. I cannot say that I put the thought into words, but I promised myself that my world, the world where I had been brought up, the world that once I had called "civilized," should not win. And as I forced myself to consider the plight of the people I had come to admire, I made myself think of the man I loved. I made myself envisage him, as I knew he was, wounded, alone, imprisoned by his enemies. You know very well what it is that they will do to him, I told myself; the screams you hear may soon be his. Strip off the last mask of illusion and face reality, although the concept sickens you. Send out your thoughts to him, across the miles, the loneliness, the defeat. Shout out to him, Do not despair. Wherever they have put you, we have not forgotten you. We will not leave you to die. And it seemed to me that across those miles I felt his thoughts stretch out for mine as they used to do. I grasped at them, held on to them, as in his sickness he had gripped my hand. *I have no time for memories.* Now in the darkness of that imprisonment he had all the time in the world. Hold on, I cried, remember me. If I am all that is left to you, I will not fail you.

Mohamed was the first to voice my feelings aloud. I found him in the stables, standing beside the black horse, grooming it. It raised its head and nickered softly as I came in. Perhaps it recognized me; perhaps it associated me with its master; had it not carried me upon its back? Perhaps it was simply living upon hope as we all did. No care of Mohamed's could conceal the cuts and hacks along its flanks, marks caused by sword and knife, wounds of war. Mohamed had thrown his arms about its neck, as its master used to do, was smoothing the thick mane between its ears and patting its nervous, intelligent head. The great eyes stared from him to me as if questioning us. "Look," Mohamed said. He reached behind him to pull at one of the saddlebags, stained and torn as if men had tried to tear it loose, and disentangled my gold locket from the shreds of cloth. It dangled in his hand, glittering, as it had in the desert when our paths had first crossed. I stared at it without touching it, a charm that had failed, a gift that had brought only bad luck. "Take it," Mohamed kept insisting. "He must have left it there for you. One day you can give it back, one day when he is free." His voice suddenly cracked. He fell to his knees to pluck at my gown, a gesture of respect he had never made. "He must be freed," he whispered, for once his fears showing nakedly. He gulped. "You know what a poor lame thing I am, with scarce the strength to mount a horse, with as little courage as a sheep. Yet if I can serve him, count on me." He gulped again. "I swear I shall never run from cowardice again; I swear my life, to rescue him."

I smiled to give him the courage he lacked and helped him to his feet. The word *rescue* seemed to hang in the air, like the sound of a drumbeat. Suddenly a fresh image flashed across my mind, as if it had been sent there deliberately, as if some god who listens to men's distress were answering me. I thought I stood again upon the ship, that fated ship that had been my loss and gain. I felt the heel and swell of it, heard the creak and groan of the spars, could almost feel the smooth-beveled edge of the doorway paneling. I was standing at the entrance to the main saloon, which the lady passengers had appropriated for their meeting place. As always, I was hesitating before joining them, drawing my fingers across the mahogany wood to give myself something to do, my hands seeming large and clumsy compared with their dainty ones. They were gathered around one of their group, their heads, under their large pale hats, resembling sun-bleached flowers, their bare necks, like stalks, pushed up from the frills and flounces of their gowns. Their voices floated toward me in gusts, rising and falling as their hats swayed together, swayed apart. "My dears, he married her. They had a son. He openly acknowledged her, lived with her in her home." There was only one man on board for whom they kept such a voice, envy-low, gossip-sharp; there was only one man about whom they spoke so often and so avidly, these memsahibs, who had appointed themselves guardians of respectability. "And when the Mutiny began, when the native soldiers, the sepoys, rose in revolt, and murdered all their English officers, only he escaped."

I remember staying where I was, rooted to the spot. I remember trying to imagine her, this native girl who had tempted him. Long before I saw her portrait I had thought of her. Half ashamed, I used to wonder what ways she had, what tricks, to turn an English gentleman against his own kind. How she had "caught" him, yes, that was the word they used; how had he let himself be "caught"? The whispers were continuing; they rose and fell with the waves as the ship glided on; there seemed no end of them; they grew and swelled to fill the room. "They say she heard rumors of the revolt and sent her father's servants to rescue him. When he ignored the warnings she had them capture him and bring him to her father's house. And there she kept him hidden, although at first he had tried to resist. When the sepoys came searching for him, they say she herself opened her father's door to them. 'If you are hunting for Englishmen,' she is supposed to have said, 'think of me, who was wronged by one of them. Come quickly, I will show you where they are.' She guided them across the *maidan*, away from her father's house, pretending to hunt for victims with them. Of course, by then, there were no English left alive and the cantonment had been looted and burnt. Of course she lied; of course she was trying to save him with her lies."

Into the pause that followed, the voice of my cousin's wife snapped like a sail. " 'Of course,' fiddlesticks. It was never proved. And she was killed for complicity."

The bobbing hats had grown still, grouped around her like flowers in a field. She basked in the effect her words caused. "There were too many witnesses; what she said and did were known. When the English returned, as they were bound to do, no one spoke in her defense. They dragged her out, and her son, before her father's house, and made an example of her. And they say . . . they say"—now her voice, too, had dropped, the nodding hats encircled her—"when he heard the sound of the shots, he burst out from the room where he had been confined and attacked his fellow-officers with his bare hands."

I remembered the gust of anger that had washed over me; I had turned to run away, doubly sickened by the story of that cruelty and by my cousin's wife's delight in it. So, now, I closed my hand about the locket as if to keep it safe. But nothing had saved her; nothing had saved the husband, forced to live with such wasted sacrifice. Suddenly Colonel Edwards's thin face with its blue eyes seemed to smile at me. "Nothing is wasted," he seemed to say. "We learn to survive. If we do not, then brutality wins. You are a survivor, Isobelle. Remember, no sacrifice is made in vain." His words seemed to echo in my mind, seemed almost to engrave themselves across the sky where, like faint smudges of cloud, the flowering almond trees reflected themselves, just as my lord had promised. My own resolution might have been a promise too, to him. Out of defeat shall come a victory. If all else is lost, then the Lord of the High Tigran deserves to have his love for triumph. I might have been that Eastern girl, crying her defiance to her murderers; what did it matter if they were white or black—she had tried to save the man she loved. As my own thoughts now hardened I felt her will become part of me. What she had done, I would do. I, too, could make sacrifices for the man I loved. And I forgot, as perhaps she had done, what those men who lived because of such sacrifice might feel.

My first concern, now there was time to think, was to try and guess what the Vizier would do. My perceptions suddenly became razor-sharp, all my energies concentrated upon this one thing. I had decided that the Vizier would not let his nephew die. Perhaps he already had a plan; perhaps, before the nephew left, a plan had secretly been drawn up: if this happens, or this, do thus and thus. But I soon rejected that idea. Although it would be like the nephew to have dealt with such contingencies, I was convinced that in this instance he had not. He would be the last man to beg for help, and he had given himself up willingly. If asked, he would have said, "I may die but the cause lives on." He would not admit that without him there could be no cause. But the Vizier thought so. The Vizier was not likely to value the cause more than the man. Mutilated or not, the Vizier would force his crippled hands around his sword; he would himself mount his war-horse, would himself lead out the men to win his nephew back. He would offer his life to spare the man he loved as a son. And he would act without delay.

I began to reconsider what I knew as fact. As far as I could tell from what our men had said, the Sejilmi had wasted no time in continuing to defend the wells. Their Sheikh had ordered their retreat, together with their prisoner, to their winter quarters, leaving the cannons they had prized to rust away in the desert sun. Usually they spent the winter months housed in a fortress rather like that of the High Tigran, built at the end of one of the valleys with which the Middle Mountains were laced. Although the spring season was approaching now, when normally they would take to their tents, moving their flocks into the high pasture lands, although an attack at this time would strain their winter supplies, they had obviously decided it was better to sit out a siege than run for their lives in the open. But even if they did not stay in their winter quarters long, once on the move they would be hard to catch. I thought, Suppose the Vizier surrounds them, suppose he threatens them and hems them in, they still have one last advantage left. They still have their prisoner. The Vizier may be brave and resolute, willing to risk his life to save the nephew he has made High Lord. The Vizier, too, acts because he must, else all his old sacrifices are in vain. But even if he charges alone, even if he tears down the walls with his own maimed hands, he still cannot release the prisoner unless he knows where the prisoner is. And the Sheikh of the Sejilmi will not hesitate to use that prisoner for barter if he must.

I had a second vision, clear as the first. I saw the red-mud battlements, the laughing enemy, the besieging horsemen outside the walls. I saw the Lord of the High Tigran, blinking in the sudden light, manacled, stumbling upon the uneven stones, his long legs cramped from the cage where he had been thrust. "One step closer, he hangs," the Sheikh would cry to the Vizier as the Sejilmi soldiers brandished their swords menacingly. The Vizier, immobile on his horse, his crippled hands folded on the saddle bow, what would be his response to that threat?

I tried to think myself into his mind, that quick hard mind that old grief had turned to prejudice. "The Lord of the High Tigran is but a boy," he would reply after a while—would lie. "He is not worth the price you hope to get when you sell him to the Sultan. But I could offer you something more lucrative, someone in exchange, someone you could really want, to please the ladies of your household." And he would smile, his cunning smile that gave nothing away, and flick his fingers as gamblers do, when they play their highest card. "My nephew for a foreigner," he would make his bid, "a Christian worth what you want to give for her, long sought after too at the Sultan's court, twice the value they have offered for him. And the cause of your daughter's disgrace."

I thought, still calm, still logical, making my mind move in time with his, If I were the Vizier that is what I would do, giving a twist that would please the enemy, a Berber joke, to exchange a man for his mistress. But the Vizier's plan will not succeed. Not because the Sheikh of the Sejilmi may not be interested in what he offers, not because I am not worth that much, but because his nephew would never permit it. And that was something, too, the Vizier would not understand.

I suppose at one time the possibility of being used in such a way would have horrified me, would have reduced me to blind fear. But I held panic down. I made myself assess the Vizier's ideas rationally, weighing the strengths, noting the weaknesses, as coolly as he might himself. I was expendable; I could not resist, and the Sejilmi might, just might, be tempted. Suddenly stubborn myself, I thought, The Vizier may use me to bargain with, he still does not trust me at all. He does not accept that I can be as steadfast, as true, as once he was, although in time he will come to honor me.

For there might be other ways to achieve the same result, and I made myself consider them. First, I had friends. I knew whatever we planned would come better from them than from me. The Vizier would never listen to me, would suspect all I said; he might listen to them. Mohamed had already offered all that his friendship could, and

I knew I could count on Dr. Legros, although I hesitated to put too great a burden on him. *I will not go if you do not; I let you choose.* I was still not certain how strong his feelings were about returning to his own home; I did not want to jeopardize that chance. In any case, the man I needed most was the captain of the guard. Although I knew he was wounded, weak from loss of blood, deliberately I went to him. "Will you repay an old kindness?" I asked him simply, not wanting to prevaricate. Still as white faced as on that day when he had waited for the sword to fall, Rasheed answered me as simply. "Lady, my life is yours. Ask; what I can do I will." When he had heard me out, as patiently as when we had been on the hunt, he explained what he thought best, discussing and arguing various ideas with his two companions when he had summoned them. And like huntsmen they began to plan the trail, although the game we hunted was dangerous.

I must admit though, it was not his support that counted in the end, although as a soldier his suggestions carried weight. No, it was the little doctor who surprised everyone. Perhaps he surprised himself. I think it fair to say that without him the rescue of the Lord of the High Tigran might not have been planned the way it was and certainly would not have succeeded. I have often spoken of the comradeship between the doctor and me, although not often of the affection, no, that is too weak a word, of the love. At least I think there was love on his part, although he never mentioned the word aloud. Now he showed his devotion. I have said that I had hesitated to ask him anything, not wanting to presume too much. Looking back I can see how blind I had been to the way he cared for me, although all the clues were there. I think, too, I had blinded myself to the realization of what the High Tigran had come to mean to him, perhaps not the least a symbol of his own revolutionary youth. Then again, perhaps I had not understood fully just what he felt it offered him; what hopes he had, after a life so full of sadness and mistakes. Had he himself not said that here, there were things that mattered more? When he spoke up I was reminded suddenly, almost comically, of the way he had offered to face the Master in the square, a courageous act although he himself did not seem made for heroic deeds. But most of all it was his loyalty to me that shone clearly, as well as his affection for the people here. And so, although there was no need for him to have become involved, he did.

First, I should explain that the Vizier had summoned us all to council, again unusual, but in these unusual times not so out-of-place as it sounds. I tell no secret when I admit that the sight of the Vizier advancing with his councillors, like black crows, made my courage sink. Yet they say that at the center of a hurricane there is a strange, pervasive calm, almost as overwhelming as the surrounding storm. I felt a similar stillness in myself, as if here, at last, another mystery would be resolved. I think the Vizier sensed it, too. For a moment his stride faltered, as if he felt that calm reach out to him; then he snapped his fingers to his men and continued his approach, those of the household guard who were left fanning out on either side. I knew why they were there, of course. And why I was. For when he had told me what he meant to do and what my part was to be, if I resisted, if I gave way to tears, to cries for pity or sympathy, he would merely smile and gesture to his men to take me away. But he knew I would not resist. He thought he knew me well enough that he could rely on me; he had seen how strong my devotion was and now he planned to make use of it.

The smile he gave me was a genuine one, not of affection or approval, but almost of complicity, the sort of recognition a man might give a gallant enemy when he sees him fall. Well tried, that smile seemed to say, but today the end is come. I told you that it would; you have only yourself to blame. But when he had outlined the details of his plan (very much what I had already guessed, in effect that when he left I was to go with him), my response startled him. I repeat, his plan seemed sensible; there were no surprises in it for me, and he certainly made no appeals to sentiment, no attempts to play upon my sympathies; he was too sure of me. I had even guessed the time of his departure, although that was not difficult. One quick glance through the citadel would have revealed to anyone the same state of alert as before. Could not the women's keening be heard again? And the armory doors were open wide, although now it was young boys who came eagerly to pick their guns. And were not old men seen reaching for weapons they had hung long ago above their doors; were not horses brought out and saddled? The Vizier meant to lead the remnants of the *harla* out, to save their lord, and he would take me as the means to release him.

Beneath my cloak I was dressed, Berber style, for traveling. In the stable Mohamed had saddled the gray horse; I thanked God for the chance I had had to ride it before. I noticed Rasheed standing with the other guards, prepared too, although he still looked more like a ghost than a man. We were all ready then, ready to leave when the Vizier did, but in our own way, not his. I turned to him with a smile of my own. Once, having to confront this group of dark-robed men would have terrified me. Swarthy-visaged, stern-browed, bristling with weapons like porcupines, they overwhelmed me. What hope had I, a mere woman, to withstand them, far less persuade them to do as I wished? But I had to try.

I spoke as calmly as if I had been used to tribal councils all my life. "Lord Vizier, lords all," I said, a general myself, assessing my own battle plans, "we have heard what you propose, now hear us." And like a general I held up my hand.

If I had shot at him point-blank the Vizier could not have been more startled, and the councillors, already muttering at irregularities, stepped back, avoiding that most unnatural thing, a woman with a mind of her own. The Vizier began to scowl; his mouth opened upon words that, once spoken, he would regret and would never be able to recall. It was upon this threatening scene that Dr. Legros's offer burst like flame.

"Lord Vizier," he said, speaking rapidly without restraint, proof, if proof were needed, of the rapport that had grown between the two men, however unlikely that might seem. "*Allez, departez*, go, tomorrow at dawn, as you intend. But let me leave first. Lend me men and mules. *Je vous jure*, I promise you, that I will fetch you back those guns." If he had said, "Give me the right to leave as you promised," that might have made some sense, but not this offer of military help. The Vizier gaped at him, as he continued briskly, "If those cannon could be dragged all the way from the Sultan's court, surely we can haul them one-fifth, one-sixth, as far to the Sejilmi fort. Just allow me the chance to clean and reset the firing pins." He added, as an afterthought, "Then in your own good time you can use those guns to knock a hole in the castle walls. And, if need be, I will fire them for you myself."

He looked about him almost belligerently, and shrugged. I knew what that shrug meant. I am a fool it said, but forget all that. I have lived so long in this land, what matter if I waste a few more days? And, more surprising still, he winked at me. If you can trust a camel slave, he had already told me dourly, I suppose you can trust me, giving me to understand that he and Mohamed had already had discussions of their own. And so that wink implied.

After this, Rasheed's offer came as an anticlimax, yet he, too, spoke well. Upon cue, he broke in, and perhaps it is true he had asked the doctor what to say, for I recognized many of the arguments. Yet such was his determined air, such was his will, strong as his lord's, that he, too, persuaded the councillors. And if the Vizier still hesitated, perhaps fearing some trick, Rasheed's honesty alone must have decided him. "Lord Vizier," Rasheed cried, "I offer myself and my two men. Our lord once spared our lives; by law they belong to him. Against my will I left him on the battlefield; he ordered and I obeyed. By custom, that gives me the right to return for him. We believe he lives; we believe him held within the Sejilmi fort, but we do not know exactly where that prison is within the walls. We must know that. You, Lord Vizier, appreciate the danger; more than any you know how difficult it is to pry a prisoner loose, even if one holds the keys to his cell. Under attack, a prison is no safer than any other place. What good would it do us if the castle falls but the prisoner is killed? Unless we are there to protect him when you approach, the Sejilmi may decide to murder him." He let these ideas sink in. "This lady has offered to be used as bait; but rather than bring her there openly, let us disguise ourselves to deceive the enemy. You and the army march as planned. Let the doctor go ahead to retrieve the guns. Let her leave with her slave boy, pretending to escape, which in your absence would seem reasonable. Disguised as Arab guides, my men and I will wait for her. As Arabs, looking to make a profit on the sly, we will lead her to the Sejilmi, pretending to betray her to them. Once inside the fort—for they will never resist such an easy prize—we shall find the means to reach our lord and will release him when you make your charge." He ended on a passionate note of his own. "I stake my honor we shall not fail. But I swear before all of you in council here, that I would rather kill myself, and her, than live again with the taint of defeat." And to prove the sincerity of his words he raised his right, unwounded arm, fixing his gaze upon me earnestly so that I should know he spoke the truth and should follow his example in swearing it. And when the Vizier still appeared to hesitate, chewing his lip, as if caught between suspicion and hope, "Pardon me, Lord," he added cunningly, "but on her own this lady could never find out where our lord is kept. Nor could she rescue him as we fighting men can. And, pardon me again, but if we do not rescue him, what will the world say of us? Are we sunk so low that we must let a woman do our work? I trust the lady

with my life," he ended in his simple way, "I go with her willingly."
And he looked at the Vizier hard, as if to say, So should you.

I repeat: I recognized many of the doctor's arguments but the
words came freely, from loyalty. They so cheered the councillors that
the Vizier scarcely could refuse. I cannot pretend to judge what served
our cause best (although clearly I think my decision to remain silent
and let the others speak was wise). Yet the plan was agreed to, more
easily than I would have thought. And it may well be that, having
realized himself how slender his chances were, the Vizier was willing
to grasp at straws. In any case, with Rasheed and his men accom-
panying me he had little to fear that I was planning some trick of
my own. As for myself, I will only say that nature did not intend me
for an Amazon. I am not brave by choice; bravery has been forced
on me. It is only doggedness, an obstinacy which my cousin's wife
had likened to that of a Welsh terrier, a stubborn tenacity which will
not let go, that serves me in place of courage. I can only tell you
that, although I was aware of danger everywhere, I felt the rightness
of our cause so strongly that I could not turn back. And if that is
courage then I think that all men must be considered brave.

The doctor left first. I still cannot speak easily of our parting
after so long, we three friends who were to start on our travels again.
When we embraced each other I sensed the little man's ready tears,
although he tried to hide them and turned his head, wiping his glasses
furiously. "Some good, at last, *enfin*," was all that he would say. I
think he meant some good at last after the lack of it in his life. I
think for him, just as for the Vizier, this rescue had assumed an
importance of its own, and had become a symbol of the way he could
rectify a wrong that had marred his life. Now he welcomed an opportunity, a chance, to make amends. I only guess at this. There was
no chance to talk, to say all the things we might have, or tell him
what I felt. And when I tried to express my gratitude, he turned my
thanks aside, beginning instead to fuss in his usual way at the slow-
ness of the start. And so I watched him trot off into the dark, as he
had come trotting in; resolute, determined to make a success of this,
his last gift to me. (And to keep the records straight, this is perhaps
the place to add that he and his little company arrived in good time
at the Tinzi Gap, following a route known to the Tigran men. Once
there, they had no difficulty in scaling the cliffs above the wells. They
found the wrecked guns where our men had left them, still in place,

anchored to the ground at the entrance to the caves, their gunners' equipment scattered but intact. Only one of the guns could be pieced together again, the others having been so destroyed as to be virtually useless, but with his surgeon's skill the doctor achieved a second kind of miracle, his sensitive fingers fixing a new set of firing pins. Similarly, having repaired the gun carriage that the Sejilmi had also abandoned, he had the single gun bolted on, and in other ways prepared for the long haul out of the gap through the hills. To make sure secrecy was maintained, he even had the carriage loaded with goat and sheep skins, to make it appear like part of a wagon train, and, despite the smell, had all his men wrap their horses in the same way to enhance the effect. All this was done with remarkable precision and speed, so that when the Vizier and his men arrived at the Sejilmi fort he was waiting there for them. In this way his soldiering ability was put to good use, too; the gun was trained upon the fort, the signal to attack was given, and the gun fired.)

As for the rest of us, a short while before dawn the Vizier and his men rode out, not with quite the open flourish as before but quietly, determinedly, doggedly, that quality which my cousin's wife had decried, yet, as I have often seen, is one that can move the earth. The army was to wait for us, keep time with us, and parallel our own line of march, when, again, later by a few hours, we left upon the same quest. We rode alone, Mohamed and I, through a side gate. We did not follow in the army's trail, but stopping once or twice as if to mark the way it went, turned quickly on a different track, as if avoiding it. The path we took went westward and brought us under the shelter of the trees. We left at early morning, ourselves, furtively and in haste, so that if anyone was there to spy, as perhaps there was, he would see nothing to suggest that we were other than what we were: prisoners, taking advantage of confusion and unrest to make good our own escape. To enhance that impression we rode horses from the stables, which we might have stolen, and rode hard, as if to avoid pursuit. I should explain that this part of the journey seemed at first the most dangerous, and, if in truth we had been prisoners, trying to make a break, we could not have seemed or been more nervous. While we traveled on our own we were at the mercy of any passing enemy, and it was not until well after noon that we met up with Rasheed and his men. They had departed with the Vizier's army and, one by one, had slipped away, each making his own way to our rendezvous. Together now, we five in company, Mohamed and I led by "Arab" guides, would make our way as fast as we could toward the Sejilmi fort. And whatever doubts the Vizier might have had, once we five had met (and a prearranged signal had told him so) the rescue was set in motion and could not be stopped.

On rereading what I have written, I suppose I make our plans seem more simple and haphazard than they were. At least I have simplified my part. I did so deliberately at first, partly to convince the Vizier, partly to convince myself. For as Mohamed and I toiled up the slopes in the midday sun, I suddenly had time to realize the many dangers that lay ahead. Until then, time, or the lack of it, had seemed the enemy. Every moment's special preparation appeared to drag, every pause became labored and slow. Now I longed to race ahead, fearful that if we lingered, even for a moment, we would arrive too late. Either my lord would be dead, or the Sejilmi, growing impatient themselves, would try to smuggle him north, or, fearing some trickery, would conceal him where he never could be found. Rasheed had tried to warn me of the many hazards, and haste was one of them. "All must be done in turn," he told me, "all must be seen to and well arranged." The magnitude of those details now became clear, as did the other aspects of our scheme, which hitherto I had ignored. Rasheed's vow, for example, had been made earnestly. It was a vow to be kept, and so he emphasized, even to the purpose of the little knife that he had ordered me to tuck beneath my robes. If all else failed, he had explained, I might have to use it on myself. Although I doubted if I would dare to draw it for whatever cause, its hilt pressed against my skin was a constant reminder of the nature of our enterprise. Then there was the complexity of the men's disguise. Even if it permitted them to gain access to the Sejilmi fort, there was no guarantee we would find our lord in time nor that we would deceive our opponents long. The Sheikh of the Sejilmi was no fool and his daughter's shrewdness was notorious. Nor was it even certain that we should be allowed to go inside the fort. Arab guides might seem easy game for a mountain tribe; there was a distinct possibility we might be attacked ourselves and killed before we got that far. Nor was it clear what the daughter, Rashmana, might do. I remembered how she had enjoyed tormenting me. If she had me in her power things might go hard for me. As for my first fear that I was not worth much . . . but I have told enough to prove how my thoughts spun round and round, and to show how I tried to think of every possibility, every likelihood of danger, so we could be on our guard.

At least Rasheed reassured me about one thing, although his assurances suggested as many new difficulties as solved old ones. "Not one of the Sejilmi," he told me cheerfully, "could resist a chance to cheat a trader or make him look a fool. When they learn that we are Arabs, hired as guides to foreigners; when they realize that, like petty thieves, we plan betrayal, they will take delight in defrauding us while we are busy defrauding you. Such twofold duplicity will appeal to them. The more we seem to bargain with them to give you up, the more they will promise and agree, all the while ensuring that we end with nothing for our pains."

I supposed he was right. But that brought me to the real weakness of our plan: how Berber horsemen could disguise themselves sufficiently to deceive other Berber men, trained to trickery, on watch for it. I will confess when I saw Rasheed and his men waiting for us where they had said they would, I felt relief, not that they were there, but because I did not even recognize them. Now their slow and careful planning made sense; now their methodical style began to seem convincing. Every precaution they could take had perfected their disguise. Their clothes were travel-stained and worn, the sort of faded *jellaba* or grimy woolen robes that small-town traders wear. Their weapons, of course, were concealed beneath these robes; their sandals were scuffed as if they had been walking far; their horses were old, broken-down, poor nags, captured in some previous raid, and all distinguishing marks had been removed. Even the horseshoes had been ripped off so the workmanship could not be traced, and the saddles, saddle cloths, and other gear were equally old and dilapidated. Nevertheless, I still worried that they rode those horses too easily, hands on hips, and their very ease, their carriage, their air, was too free, too arrogant, too much at odds with what they were supposed to be. I thought that they would never learn how to shuffle along, nor keep their heads bent in mock servility, nor peer furtively as they should; not with those hawk-keen eyes. If there was some sort of scuffle, some insult, they would never remember to keep their weapons hidden but would instinctively reach for them as soldiers do. Even Rasheed's wounds, although healing fast, might betray him as a fighting man, strange wounds indeed for a trader, whose rank and class were well known for cowardice.

But these, too, became concerns to be laughed away. Rasheed himself ripped off the doctor's bandaging and replaced it with a dirty rag, smelling of garlic and sweat. I had to laugh myself, the thought of the little doctor's anger suddenly seeming familiar and safe. But there was little time for amusement as we wound along just below the mountain ridge, keeping within the cover of the trees on its northern side. The forests here were dense, made up of large oaks that kept their leaves all year long, interspersed with stands of junipers and cedars. In sheltered spots, already, spring flowers and herbs had begun to carpet the ground. When we rode over them they released their scents about us in a cloud, and small colored birds rose up from their breeding nests like butterflies. But apart from them and the herds of goats feeding on the wild argan trees, we saw no one. Yet we knew that in the valley below, the Vizier and his army were following us, and that was strangely comforting.

They kept in line with us, for since it was deemed imperative that we should not arrive before they did, they had to match their advance with ours. (And how that was done I cannot tell, some system of leaving signs I think, of making marks that would be visible to distant watchmen who would know where to look, perhaps a way of tying tree branches in place, or laying stones upon the open screes.) "We do not want to startle the Sejilmi from their lair," Rasheed said, "nor frighten them too soon. Gently, gently, we approach, like catching a desert snake out of its hole. If they should make a break we would never catch up with them." I accepted his reasoning without argument; it seemed to me that he and his companions were so well schooled in military strategy that I must rely on them. But everything still made me long to hurry ahead, and it took all the will I had to obey them.

I do not recall much of that ride; the thick-foliaged trees, the scented flowers, the darting birds. I remember once, as we followed our guides down a grassy slope, thinking how our lives, Mohamed's and mine, had come full circle; after all that had passed nothing had changed, we still seemed to journey on to a destination as illusive as it had ever been. And when we finally crossed the mountain divide heading now south and west, we returned to the world I had first known, of barren hills, of rocks, of arid plateaus overhanging the desert flats. Those open stretches of rock made our journey more difficult. There was no way of hiding there; like birds in the air, our passage could be marked from far off. And when we rested in the heat of the day it seemed to me that the hot air surged toward us from the plains, as if it had come to find us out, searching for us again, across a thousand miles of sand.

I have a memory of one night. The moon hung low, so close to hand it seemed we might stretch out and touch it where it swung in the velvet sky. Rasheed had told us that the next day would bring us to the border of the Sejilmi lands, and that news had set us all on edge, although we tried to hide our nervousness. We had camped about a small wood fire, upon which we were cooking the remnants of some animal that we had trapped. Although I for one had no appetite, the roasting meat smelt good, and to cheer himself and perhaps cheer us, one of the younger Berber guards had been amusing himself with mimicry, first of birds, then animals, which he did with easy skill, then, as he grew more daring, of people whom he knew, even ourselves. I had been lying with my back against some rocks, idly pecking at the moss, digging into it with a stick, until the surface flaked away. Beneath the crumbling roots the moonlight picked out a line of thin shapes, scratched or carved into the stone, figures of people and animals, surrounded by simple wheel shapes. Seeing it, Mohamed tried to draw me away. "They are evil signs," he cried, hoarse-voiced with fatigue. "Evil people put them there to bring bad luck." But I was not afraid of them. To my eyes they simply appeared as marks, as drawings made by men who had vanished long ago. Yet I felt the poignancy of them. If people like us, with their own hopes and fears, had lived here once, where were they now? Where had they gone; what had happened to their homes and herds; were these drawings all that were left of them? When our time comes, I thought, shall we, too, fade away, disappear forever, be forgotten like them? A cold wave flowed over me although the night was warm. The hot wind blew, the blank cliffs shimmered in the moonlight; we tossed and turned, sleepless under the stars. They glinted overhead, distant, remote, mocking our little lives. That was the night I resolved that I, too, should make a record of ourselves. If we survive this night, this day, I thought, if we are all united again, I will take my journal with its pitiful entries, and fill it with detail. As the doctor used to do, I will crisscross the page, capturing upon the blank sheets all the thoughts that surge through my brain. And even if those writings are lost like these primitive drawings, even if they are buried in the sand, I shall hope someone will discover them and learn who we truly were. The wind blew the desert heat; the thorn trees rustled their scaly leaves; *nothing is what it seems*, the past is gone. And now the present lay in wait for us; now reality took the place of dreams.

The next morning, before daybreak, we began our swift descent, following the course of a mountain stream. It fell in long leaps, running through the undergrowth with a cheerful sound. We made no attempt to hide ourselves but we saw no one, heard no one, until we reached the valley floor, although there were huts along the banks, and on the lower ridges of the hills small outposts reared up, outlined upon the morning sky. These little forts seemed to resemble dark watchful birds, hunched against the sun, yet no one appeared upon their walls; everyone had run away or been shut up with the rest of the Sejilmi garrison. We might still have been traveling through a deserted land. But by now, news of our approach must have spread. As we straggled along, Mohamed and I in the rear, as we had planned, our "guides," hastening ahead, chattering eagerly, fierce horsemen came galloping up, to take a closer look at us, surrounding us, questioning us, peering at us, especially at Mohamed and me. There was little for us two to do, except try to act as we might if we had begun to suspect treachery. And if in truth we had been what we claimed, that is, prisoners trying to excape from the High Tigran, putting our faith in unscrupulous men, those men could not have acted more in part.

All their skills came into play. Rasheed, too, had retired to the rear with us, partly to allow his younger companions full rein, partly to ensure a careful watch was still kept. Even he was startled, I think, at the zeal his young friends showed. Had they been on a London stage the critics would have applauded them.

The youngest man, the mimic of last night, turned himself into a caricature of the man he was supposed to be. He let his long legs dangle, turned up his toes, hung on to the saddle desperately while trying to beckon the Sejilmi outguards to approach. A more mean-spirited ruffian never inhabited this earth, with wringing hands and fawning ways, and sidelong glances, full of deceit and greed. And the Sejilmi, recognizing all these signs, reacted to him as he meant they should. (And had I in reality "hired" him as guide I would indeed have been a fool!)

They slapped him contemptuously upon the back, almost toppling him headlong; tried to prod his horse into a trot so they could laugh at his lack of horsemanship. To every hint he let drop of having something "special," something "worth their while," they mocked him with its uselessness, tormenting him into revealing more than he meant. And when, at a secret sign he gave, Mohamed now joined in the act, asking what he was doing, questioning where we were, threatening him that we would take our money back, excitement grew. More and more riders came galloping up the track, dust rising from the hooves in clouds. Messengers were sent ahead to the fort, which began to throb with life. And presently, whether we would or not, we found ourselves being edged down a track that led to its gates. Soon we were herded inside while our new captors surrounded us.

Until then I had kept myself hidden as Rasheed had said I should. Now I rode forward, too, to confront him and his men. He had told me exactly what I should do. "Protest," he said. "Shout, try to make your horse rear, show all the signs of outrage. Scream, although perhaps not quite so loudly as you did before our lord's door." And he had permitted himself a secret grin, which shows how close our friendship had become. So now, on cue, that is what I did. A more outraged symbol of English womanhood had never proclaimed so much injured innocence. As for the "Arab guides," I berated them; I berated the Sejilmi, who had "encouraged" them; I demanded immediate withdrawal; I demanded immediate explanation and apology; I demanded, demanded, until my throat was sore. I spoke in a mixture of Berber and Arabic so that there was no mistake, and the more I protested the closer we came to the main courtyard, until, as if by chance, as if most naturally, we were all crowded inside. And then I felt triumph swell, even as I went on with my pretense, even as I made my "Arabs" cringe, even as I tried to shake Mohamed hard for making a mistake in choosing them.

The Sejilmi guards had come pouring out in full force; the messengers who had escorted us, the castle folk, their children, hens and goats, went scuttling before my self-righteous wrath. Men, women, children, animals, all were agog to see how a foreign woman threatened men with a riding crop. At first glance the inside of the Casbah, or fort, was not impressive. It hardly merited the name of fort, seeming more a ragged mass of walls, piled together like a sand castle. But those red-mud walls were surprisingly thick, fired to stone by sun and wind. Steps ran up from the entranceway to the ramparts where a watch was kept, and beside the gates a massive tower housed the remainder of the guard. The courtyard itself was aswim in perspiring humanity. We seemed to ride above a sea of unwashed bodies, stinking of sweat and urine, and underfoot we floundered through a forecourt littered with refuse piled in unsavory heaps, where half-starved dogs scavenged at will. Mohamed had already slid off his mount as if the violence of my shaking had unseated him. This was his chance. Quick as a flash he was already slithering among the crowds; no one would notice him as he disappeared, all eyes still intent upon the rest of us, urging us on, as at a play, with repeated taunts. For this was Mohamed's chance to go where no one else could, to penetrate the castle's secrets, to find, if possible, where the prisons were, and to prepare the way for Rasheed's men to release the prisoner.

Meanwhile, they played their part enthusiastically. They argued back at me, protesting their innocence, all the while making open signs to the Sejilmi to fetch out their Sheikh. "Quick, quick," they shouted, "before this she-wolf claws us to death," and other absurdities of this kind, calculated to rouse interest. The disturbance had a secondary aim, other than gaining admittance to the fort that is, and when a sudden hush, a sudden falling back, alerted us, we felt we had achieved it.

I had often heard Rashmana speak of her father, not always to his credit and seldom in complimentary terms. I knew him to be ruthless, implacable—all Berber traits—a veteran of many wars, and, as these past weeks had shown, treacherous. Most of all I knew him to be cautious, careful even in battle's heat, as Rasheed had warned. And cruel. I had not expected such an active man, believing him physically long past his prime. The body beneath the crumpled robes was still strong; the face beneath the broad white turban was chiseled, stark, like those crags we had been riding past, and his eyes were bright and suspicious, like a bird's. He had his daughter's height and quick gait, stiff-backed, proud-chinned, displaying all her arrogance, and the way he flashed his golden rings, snapping his fingers at his guards, showed the fear he inspired in them. But the mouth was hard, vicious; it had a cruelty that the small grizzled beard could not hide, and the heavy red lips were full-fleshed and sensuous.

Rasheed, who knew him best, began to scramble from his horse, a parody of mock servility. He looked ungainly as he was meant to, a city man, of trading stock, set down uneasily amid these warriors, like a pigeon among cats. "Allah be praised," he whined. "We have been looking for you. We have something for you, Lord; we have . . ." His companions jerked him into silence, trying angrily to hush him up, protesting they did not know what he was speaking about although every word, every move, enhanced the impression that, of course, they did. They, too, acted with great subtlety, pretending to vie with each other to be heard, pushing and elbowing the Sejilmi men aside, as if trying to attract the Sheikh's eye, meanwhile surreptitiously edging me to the rear, where, since my part was done, I was meant to remain out of the way.

Up to this point our plan, or improvisation of a plan is perhaps a better term, had worked perfectly. We were inside the fort; Mohamed was already making his preliminary search; the Sheikh had appeared, as we had hoped. Rasheed and I were to be left in the courtyard: I, to give the alarm when our lord's prison was found; Rasheed, with Mohamed's help, to release or guard him when the attack was made. Meanwhile our two companions were intended to play out the farce by engaging the Sejilmi leader in "negotiations" for a transfer of "goods" (myself), distracting him when he should have been most on the alert. Although I cannot pretend that our part in the courtyard below was not without some dangers, these paled in comparison with the risks our two friends would now face, under the scrutiny of those cautious eyes. Such maneuverings (which I have heard likened to an art), such discussion, would, of course, be made doubly delicate by the skill needed to deceive a man hard-bent on deceiving them. But in the normal course of events these intricate formalities would take place in private, far from the ordinary world of barracks and courtyard. In the Sheikh's inner apartments, no less, our men would sit, gossip, eat, drink, discuss everything under the sun except the real reason for their being there. Such discussions take time. And time is what we needed now. Time, which before had seemed to drag, which I had wanted to compress, must now be stretched to its uttermost, to enable Mohamed to find our lord, to warn the Vizier to advance his troops, to enable the doctor to aim his gun. And if for a moment it seemed, it really seemed, that we could achieve all of these things, even as we hoped for success, almost tasted it, already our plan was threatened with failure.

I have said before that this is a violent land, a land of change, sudden and unexpected. If the future looks promising, that is when to beware. Out of a clear sky, like a sandstorm, out of nowhere, violence will erupt when you least look for it, destroying people, their hopes, their dreams. We had relied on Mohamed. If anyone could have slipped furtively, skillfully, unseen, into the inner places of the fort, he could. I had seen him do so a hundred times. But for all the Sejilmi lounged and mocked, for all they appeared indolent, they were not so stupid as they seemed. They had not forgotten him and they had sent someone to hunt for him. Now there was a sudden disturbance, shouts, angry shouts, at first in the distance, then drawing near. Two guards appeared, like giants compared with our poor friend, a thing of rags and bones, whom they held by the feet, dragging his head unmercifully through the filth. As they passed I caught a glimpse of his face. His eyes were closed and tears of frustration mixed with the dirt. From his expression I knew at once that his search had failed and that he had been caught too soon. And unless we could find where our lord was imprisoned our mission could not proceed. But you see how it is in this land: Never think that its gods favor you. One moment fate seems to smile, the next it turns its back. Twice before I had seen violence erupt out of nothing; twice before I had measured the destruction it brought. Now it seemed I was about to witness the third time.

Meanwhile the Sheikh of the Sejilmi had not been idle. First, Berber style, he had noticed my horse, picking on the thing he knew most about. "Whose brand?" he cried, but he must have known; the mark of the High Tigran would have been familiar. He snapped his fingers at his men, ordering them to bring the gray horse close; suddenly eager, like a hunter, hot on a trail. He had taken a step upon the stairs, trying to straighten his rumpled robes, trying to straighten his belt, his feet surprisingly small for one so large, his eyes greedy for confirmation of what he guessed. And as his men tried to grab the reins, almost unseating me, "A woman," he cried a second time. "Whose?" and he took another eager step.

It was at this moment that his guards appeared with their catch, whom they dropped contemptuously in our midst. They clamored for attention, too, shouting out their accusations, some close to the truth, some obviously absurd: that Mohamed was a thief, a rapist, a spy, whom they had found loitering near a well; had he come to poison them? He lay there, in a heap, not having the breath to contradict, while his companions, as confounded as I was, drew back as if to avoid contact with him but in reality trying to find a place where they could resist if the Sheikh should grow suspicious of them. I felt their sudden fear, rank like sweat; any moment now, one threatening move, and they would reach for their guns, desperation forcing them to reveal themselves.

Although I was afraid myself, dear God, I would not like to

admit how afraid, I knew a confrontation would spell our ruin, and must be avoided at any cost. I do not try to explain what made me do and say what I did, nor do I regret it, although it was to cost me dear. If I say it was as if some voice were prompting me, I may seem mad. Perhaps I was. Perhaps fear struggling for so long with hope had proved too much for me. But madness gave me strength.

Shaking off the Sejilmi guards, who were still trying to rein back my horse, I kicked it forward to the foot of the steps. I spoke in a voice that sounded used to giving commands, that precise English voice belonging to a parade ground; and although I spoke once more in Berber, simple phrases that I knew, they sounded as English as if I were giving orders to Englishmen.

"Leave him alone," I cried, hoping Mohamed would forgive my description of him. "A poor lame fool. He is my slave. Treat him carefully as I expect you to treat me. Could such a one spy; could such a one take women by force? Just look at him! We have come to throw ourselves at your mercy, Lord of the Sejilmi; is this the way to treat your guests? As for those Arab guides," I pointed to them impatiently, praying all the while they would understand the double meaning I gave the words, "as for them, I shall do their work for them. Let them stay here and cool their heels whilst you and I discuss."

And for the first time I looked at the Sheikh, holding his hard gaze with one as steadfast.

CHAPTER 11

If I were to close my eyes I could reconstruct that moment from memory: the smells, the heat, the flies, the sudden absence of noise, even Mohamed's moans lessening and fading into silence. I could see how we were all fixed into place, poised like statues about to start into life: the Sheikh on the stairs looking at me with his hard knowing stare; Rasheed and his men, hesitant, fingering their belts as if searching for the weapons that should have hung there; Mohamed, covering his head with both hands, weeping to himself for failure; the Sejilmi guards, their indolence vanished in a flash, suddenly professional, watchful, and alert. And myself, the epitome of all English womanhood, the memsahib, in full voice. Then one of the Sejilmi sniggered and whispered to his neighbor behind his hand. "Mercy," he said, "I know what sort of mercy she'll get," and he sniggered again. His attempt at a joke eased the tension at once. Other men began to grin, to make their own comments, pointing at me, distracting attention from my companions, laughing at what they thought I should expect. But the point of their joke was unnecessary. I had already grasped its meaning in that one exchanged look.

Well, I had accepted the possibility from the start. I had realized what my part might involve and had offered myself of my own free will. I knew its dangers. *Shall we send women to do men's work?* If so, then, like a woman, I would do it, women's style, and abide the consequence. But as I dismounted from my horse, the trembling in my knees belying the confidence of my voice, as I began to climb the stairs, leaving my friends behind, I began to be aware, however dimly, just what those consequences might entail. A few months ago I would never have known them for what they were. Now, one hard look had told me enough to send my senses flaring ahead.

It may be that the Vizier was more cunning than I knew; perhaps he was familiar with the vices of the leader of the Sejilmi and meant to play on them, although if that were so, he intended a cruel fate for me. It may be that Rasheed had known of those vices as well and planned to use them to a lesser extent. And perhaps I had always known of them myself, although I had beat that knowledge down. For why speak of "bait" if there was not someone to tempt? But Rasheed certainly had not appreciated the true nature of this man. Nor had I. As I followed him meekly enough, I found myself already searching frantically for a way to break free of a new trap.

I have said that the Sheikh of the Sejilmi was cautious and that was true. He was. ("Any man who thinks of safety in battle's heat," Rasheed had warned, "any leader who remembers to keep clear of danger, has caution inbred in him. Imagine then how cautious he will be, shut up in his own fort, and suspicious of everything that moves.") I myself knew him as treacherous and cruel. I did not know how he used passion to enhance himself. I had met men engorged with rage, men burning with self-righteous zeal, even men who, like animals, were intent on satisfying their lusts at any cost, but never a man who used his desires to gain power. This Sheikh's intentions were revealed not only by his look, but by his very stance, his walk, his strut. His half smile of contempt, at odds with his half smile of complacency, had showed me immediately the way his mind ran. So did his use of words. "Whose woman?" he had asked. He meant, "Whom does she belong to, who owns her?" not "Who is she?" (And in any case, that was a question he need not have asked; there could not have been many Englishwomen running loose in these hills; he had only wanted confirmation to please himself.) I know now there are some men who cannot bear to see a woman without wanting to possess her; for them, such wanting is not true desire but a sign of ownership, of greed. Men of this breed feel their masculinity threatened by all things female; women for them are objects lacking in all humanity; a woman whom another man has used becomes a thing to be had at any price; how much more true of a woman who had belonged to a younger enemy. Such a man was the Sheikh of the Sejilmi. I write the words *used* and *belonged* deliberately, since these are the expressions he would have employed, and that is how he felt about women. I do not want to exaggerate the importance of that look he had given me; it was only gradually I learned what it meant in full. But I sensed its meaning from the start and events were to prove me right. This was the man that I was now forced to outwit, alone, as best I could. No wonder I followed him despairingly! And as I moved, one step at a time, I remembered the little knife tied at my waist.

Yet as we went into those dank and airless inner rooms, reeking of smoke, heavy with unsatiated lust as indifferent as it was cruel, I felt, I cannot explain how, that I was not alone. Those voices, of which I have spoken, seemed to be surrounding me. Hold on, they said, much as I had sent a message to my lord. Do not give up. Watch, improvise, turn knowledge to your own use. Was it Colonel Edwards, ordering me on the ship, or his ghost? Was it his little wife, confronting her enemies and his? I know only that when my hope was gone they gave me hope; when my courage failed they gave me courage afresh. And at every step, the handle of my little knife caught against my ribs.

I have said the Sheikh must have known who I was, but he still was careful enough to make sure. He must have decided that the "Arab guides" were harmless, as long as they were kept outside. And as long as they were under guard I suppose that was true. Dismissing them, he concentrated his attention fully on me. There was only one person in the fort (other than my lord, I mean) who could identify me for certain, and so he summoned her. From a personal point of view the appearance of his daughter, Rashmana, was most disquieting to me. But if I had to endure her presence, I must; anything to keep my part of the bargain and gain time. As for my companions, under close scrutiny, it would be increasingly difficult for them to help. But somewhere out in the hills, the Vizier and his army would be moving forward by stealth, relying on us, waiting for a sign. And since the burden now had fallen on me I had a duty to perform. And when some opportunity, some chance, presented itself, I must be prepared to take advantage of it. But I promise you that at that moment, when I heard Rashmana's name again, I did not think God would grant me any chance at all.

The Sheikh had dropped down upon his couch, as if exhausted

by his exertions, stretching himself upon the thick cushions with a self-satisfied air. The couch was wide, carved like a ledge into the thickness of the walls, and from the way the coverlets were scattered on the floor, as if thrown aside in haste, from the feel, the look, the sense of heaviness that seemed concentrated there, I began to suspect he had been lying there before, engaged perhaps in his favorite pastime, when he had been disturbed. Now he kicked off his slippers, revealing dainty feet, made for riding not for walking, and beckoned to his slaves to rub his ankles and legs while he refreshed himself with a pipe. The pipe, with its scrolls and curves, reminded me of the one the watchman in the High Tigran had used, and sure enough I smelled the familiar sweet smoke of *kief* curling through the air. I noticed how the Sheikh's eyes had closed, like those of a cat lying in the sun, but I knew, like that old watchman, that he was not asleep but was merely waiting for me to make some mistake, to make some move that would give myself and my companions away. I forced myself therefore to stand still, keeping my face expressionless, not even flinching when maliciously he threw a sudden handful of nuts at my feet, causing a monkey on a chain to run up and down, gibbering in delight.

It was difficult to focus in the semidark but I strained my eyes, trying to make out where we were. I noted how the outer door opened onto the stairs we had just climbed, how the many archways and grilles led to the usual warren of inner chambers. Apart from two windows placed high on the outer walls, there was no other source of light, and the guards who remained on duty sat on the topmost step to enjoy the sun, leaning back against the walls and cracking nuts themselves, as secure and self-satisfied as their lord. Like the courtyard below, the inside of the Casbah showed the same mixture of strength and decadence, the same proportion of squalor and magnificence. There were the same thick mud walls, the same half-crumbled pillars propping up the central beams, the same litter on the broken tiles where hunting hounds scratched for fleas. A distant sound, which I could not at first identify, revealed itself as the noise of sheep and goats, these presumably tethered somewhere in some lower vault. The presence of these herds compounded the overwhelming sense of indifference and decay and enhanced my impression that this was a place where men just came, not lived. Their real life was in the open, in their tents. This was simply a shelter for dangerous times, but not where they felt at home. Yet once, like the fortress of the High Tigran, this fort must have been built and occupied by men who understood beauty as well as defense.

I determined not to lose the initiative. I did not mean to sink into panic and let opportunity slip away while the Sheikh smoked himself into a calm mood, waiting for his daughter to appear. I told myself if I were going to negotiate, like a man, I should start in proper style, greetings first, then business (although I plunged from one to the other too abruptly). "Salutations, Sheikh of the Sejilmi," I said in my most formal tones. "My guides were insistent that we come here, but as you know I was reluctant to accept their advice. Now I see their wisdom. We are escaping from our enemies, who, I think, are your enemies too. I am sure you recognize horses belonging to the stable of the High Tigran. I have been made a prisoner by its lord, who tried to hold me against my will. Now I am asking you for help and am willing to pay you well."

Such blunt speech contrasting strangely with my formality disturbed the Sheikh's musings. He jerked upright, looking at me with narrowed eyes. Good, I thought. I did not want him to lie there and ruminate; better he paid attention to me. "And now, Lord," I said equally brisk, although it went against the grain to call him so, "now, Sheikh of the Sejilmi, I am weary. I would wash and eat. My servant and I had wandered many miles before we met these Arab guides. I promise to make haste to refresh myself, unlike your Eastern ladies." And I gave him a smile. It is not easy to smile, in that way, at a man who is your enemy, and I did not know I had the skill. It made him sit up again and fidget restlessly, while a snap of his fingers sent his men scurrying for a water bucket. And while I waited for their return, and a miserable receptacle they brought, muddied and foul, more suitable for a horse, I used the opportunity to arrange my hair, loosening it. I pretended the little golden locket was a looking glass, so I could turn it this way and that to let the light from the door catch its golden chain, and, provocatively, to let the light catch at my skin as I bared my arms and legs, rolling up the sleeves and straightening the tunic hem above my knees.

It was as well I did so while I had the chance. For behind us now there came a flutter of movement, a stir like a draft of air, and a waft of perfumed oil, steeped in some thick-scented flowers, wafted out from one of the latticed archways. I heard the little clink of bracelets as their wearer clasped the iron bars of the grille, and I felt the full force of a dark and venomous stare.

I would have recognized Rashmana's voice anywhere. "She lies," she hissed, a snake defending its own territory, spilling out her hatred in a familiar flood. "She is a thief who stole my jewels; she is a no-body, worse than a slave in her own land. She is this, she is that, she is not...." All the familiar complaints came tumbling out. I let her clack on without argument, her insults no longer having the power to hurt and sounding to my ears almost commonplace: idle women's talk to which the Sheikh of the Sejilmi might well be in-ured. I remembered how I had used the name of the Lord of the High Tigran for protection in his harem and resolved to make use of this lord in a similar way. It was clear at once that the intervening weeks had not diminished Rashmana's jealousy, even though it had caused the defeat of the man she had professed to love. And she still hated me although I had not wronged her as she had me. I noted she did not boast, at least not then, of having tried to murder me. I thought, If it is not guilt that silences her, and I am sure it is not, then it must be fear. But not fear of me, since in her eyes I am still a fool, almost not worth murdering. Fear then of her father perhaps. It dawned on me that she might not have told him all the truth nor all the reasons for her leaving the High Tigran; after all, if he were avenging her wrongs, attempted murder on her part was not exactly a wrong done to her; and if she had not schemed to murder, she would still be living peacefully. I stored that information away. But it was her anger that was to be her undoing.

Since I had left the harem of the High Tigran where she had known me last, I had learned many things, other than the obvious, that is. Understanding of the Berber mind was one. Little of what Rashmana said that day escaped me. I knew what all her nuances meant, although she spoke rapidly, using words in dialect, talking about me in the coarsest terms to slander me. In the past I had always tried to humor her and, as you know, had wanted to keep the peace. Now, I was ready to challenge her. And it seemed to me that she was not as clever as I had once thought her. For one thing, she had always spoken of me as a naïve simpleton and perhaps, once, by her terms, I had been. Not now. She could not credit me with sufficient intelligence to change since she had not changed herself. Let her rage on, I thought, my new awareness giving me confidence. In her anger she will be unguarded, and her carelessness may give me some advantage. Ignoring her, a tactic she had used against me so effectively, I spoke to her father again. "I am no thief," I told him quietly. "And if I were, this should be more than enough as compensation." And, just as he had teased the monkey, I dropped the little gold locket, as if by chance, upon his couch, except I made sure it fell face up, open, within his reach.

"Nor am I a whore," I went on, trying to pick my words carefully, the more careful since she, Rashmana, was not. "In my country women do not sleep with men unless they choose." I turned to Rashmana, still hanging on to the bars behind the lattice grilles. "Tell your father, did not you see me attack the Master of the High Tigran when he came to force me? Did not you see me stab at him?"

There were many things with which I could have challenged her. But I chose the one thing that was hard to dispute, having the merit of being true, in her eyes, that is. It took her by surprise as I meant it should and as her unexpected silence showed. That silence spoke more than words. It also showed that the memory of that day was calculated to refuel her deepest feelings.

"She is a conniving slut," she howled, "a stupid fool. She was red-hot for him." And when the Sheikh did not respond, being too much taken with the contents of the locket to listen to her (for, as you can see, her anger made her incoherent; no one can both be a fool and a conniving slut, not both a slut and an innocent), she suddenly cried, "Haul him out; ask him yourself. Have him up here to tell you what she did."

This was the chance I had been looking for, and I seized it. The Sheikh was distracted. He looked at the locket, looked at me, back and forth like a man entranced. The locket dangled between his thick fingers, its delicacy overwhelmed by them. It was as if he had taken a beautiful, fragile thing and, unknowingly, crushed it. I raised my arms as hers were raised, bent to dip them in that vile brown scum, pretending to lave my throat and neck, pretending to toss aside my hair as if the heat were oppressive, pretending to loosen the lacing of the tunic so that the skin showed bare. And against my ribs, at every move, the knife hilt pressed.

"If the Master of the High Tigran is here"—my voice was so

nonchalant I might have been speaking of anyone; so disinterested, I might have been talking of a casual visitor, not of a possibility that made my heart pound so that I had to close my hands over my breast—"if you have him prisoner, so much the worse for him. He tried to hold me against my will. Let him know what it feels like."

And I gave another smile.

I knew by now what idea I was trying to plant in the Sheikh's mind; I sensed immediately when he thought of it, and how the idea grew, to make him smile in turn, not a pleasing smile but a calculating one of cause and effect. Rashmana could not see me but she could see that smile. "No, no," she begged, rattling at the lattice as if she would claw her way out. "Be careful, Father, I beg." The Sheikh ignored her, snapped his fingers for his guards, ordered her away. He was a careful, cautious man, but greed meant more. "And if he were to see me here," I said, letting the words drop carefully, letting the thought drop carefully, letting the tunic drop to bare my breast; just a second's glimpse of skin, just the barest hint, "what a lesson that would teach; how that would humble him!" Stealthily, gradually, I encouraged the Sheikh, played with him, led him on. Until he swallowed the bait. (And even now I admit I might not have succeeded had not he been smoking that drug which dulled his wits and had not his daughter tried to prevent him.)

I could see the idea growing in the Sheikh's mind; it warmed him, like a glass of wine; he savored it, allowed himself to dwell on it, let himself revel in its delicious possibilities. The humiliation that the Lord of the High Tigran would face, coupled with the thought of his own prowess, stirred his blood. His Berber cunning reveled in it and took it to his heart. The double appeal to lust and revenge became more than caution could endure. His daughter's warnings were ignored, no more to him than a thousand women's whims. When he ordered her to unclasp her hands and pull together the heavy shutters that closed the grille, when I heard her protests die away, when he gestured to his guards, suddenly decisive, I knew I had won. An hour ago I had been admiring my companions' skill; it paled beside my own. An hour ago I had despaired of taking their place; now I believed that however skilled they might have been they would have failed. Something, some flaw, would have given them away, would have roused that suspicious mind. But a woman, a silly foreign woman, what danger could there be from her? With a smile that was more than ever self-satisfied he lay back, dangled the locket on its chain, waited impatiently. And I, I waited, too. *Shall we send a woman to do men's work?* Now I must show what sort of woman I was, when the guards had dragged my lover from his cell.

I said, lifting my hair as if the heat oppressed, as if excitement had begun to mount, fanning myself gently with the edge of my wide sleeves, as long as I talked and he listened, in control, "Now you must show me hospitality, Sheikh of the Sejilmi, as is fitting and correct. First water for washing, then something to eat."

My impudence made him smile again, and, to give him his due, he was not insensitive to my charms, only obsessed with his own overwhelming of them. He called to his slaves to bring trays of food and fruit that I did not want although I pretended I did. And when he heard his guards approach he motioned also to the slaves to leave, so that we could be alone, alone, that is, with the man he held as prisoner.

I could hear him stumbling through the inner rooms; there was a clanking sound of chains, the drag of heavy weights, the slow and laborious lifting of each foot, so unlike his usual step I thought pity would overwhelm me. They brought him along those crisscrossing corridors, up from some dungeon where he had been buried, somewhere beneath the milling animals; perhaps that was why Mohamed had failed in his search, unable to find that iron-barred pit under the trampled dung and straw. His arms were still chained tight but his legs had been partially loosened so that he could walk; they had flung the heavy end of the chain about his neck so that it bowed his shoulders like a yoke. His eyes had been covered but when the blindfold was torn off I think he still could not see, for he blinked painfully, as if this dimness were brighter than sunlight.

I thought, They have kept him underground in the dark; he does not even remember what light is. I could see how pale he was, unshaved, his face bruised and cut, his clothes in rags, his tunic stiff with dried blood. I set my own expression in a mask as they forced him against a central pillar and tied him there. I refused to let myself be moved by the way he stretched his neck painfully and flexed each knee as if his legs had been cramped too long under him in a narrow space, as if he had not been able to sit or stand, or touch or see, with only darkness solid about him and above him, a darkness without end or shape. I made myself count the advantages instead: he had not been so tortured as to be helpless; they had neither blinded nor maimed him. His legs were still in one piece, and best of all, in their haste now to leave, the guards had taken off the chains and used ropes of hemp to tie him with. I made myself notice all these things to bolster my courage and to plan what next to do. And when the guards were gone, I did not hesitate, afraid that even now our chance might slip away.

The Sheikh was already fumbling for me, trying to pull me down; his eyes were moist with lasciviousness, his lips wet where he licked them. He threw back his head like one of his hounds scenting the air, and he swung the golden locket like a talisman, invoking, anticipating pleasure. He might have been a monkey, gibbering to himself with delight. I willed myself not to flinch as his hand crept closer to my leg where I stood by his couch, still pretending to comb my hair. "Wait," I said. "One moment more." And I turned and walked toward the man tied in the center of the room.

I walked fast, although, as in a dream, I scarcely seemed to move at all, gauging the distance from couch to pillar, from pillar to door, measuring every step. And at every step I felt the little knife slide into my waiting hand. My lord turned his head at my approach, as if he recognized a woman's walk. Perhaps he had expected Rashmana; perhaps she had already come to taunt and torment him previously. Perhaps he expected some new torture from her. I could not risk giving him time to recognize me, nor yet say anything for fear it would spoil what I had in mind. I came so close to him that my body shielded his. Yet I knew I was so carefully watched, I did not dare hesitate or make a false move or do anything that would rouse suspicion again. Instead, I steeled myself as for a blow, but the blow was one I gave, hitting my lover across the cheek as hard as I could. "That for my honor, monster," I cried as his head snapped back against the stone, starting open one of his many wounds. I seized the shock of soft dark hair with my left hand as if to force his head up again. "Look at me," I cried, and with the right hand, my unseen hand, I slashed hard at the cords that bound his arms. I did not dare glance down to judge my aim and the knife edge was razor sharp. But I felt one of the strands give, enough at least for his hand to reach and grasp convulsively at mine as I closed his fingers over the knife hilt. Then his head sank forward, slack-eyed, and his chest heaved and I stepped back as if satisfied.

One of the hardest things I have ever done was to leave him tied like that and walk away. Bloodstained, foul-clothed, the smell of earth and darkness on him like the grave, he still seemed the most vital thing I had ever known. I felt his spirit like a coil, like a current, as fresh and sharp between us as if it were visible. I longed to wrap my arms about him and shield him from harm. I wanted to keep him safe as once he had saved me. But I had to fight those feelings down. There was still one last thing I had to do, before the end of the game was reached, I mean. I walked toward the open door, at the same steady pace, still unhurried, still calm. I paused at the opening where the guards before had sat in the sun and threw up my arms again, as if invoking the heavens as witness. "Victory," I cried, "Hurrah," and other such absurdities, waving my arms above my head like a triumphant athlete. No matter that I shouted in English, no matter what I shouted. My companions in the square heard, that was the only important thing; they would know I had achieved my aim, and they would decide how to proceed.

As a cry I admit it was awkward, lacking in finesse, and had the Sheikh of the Sejilmi had one ounce left of his usual caution it would have immediately roused his suspicions. My enthusiasm certainly puzzled him; perhaps it disturbed his sense of decorum. He expected his women to be subdued, subservient to his every mood, not invoking moods of their own. He made as if to follow me and perhaps he would have done so; and perhaps on seeing my companions, heads up, staring at me, he would have remembered them. Midway to the door a sound arrested him, a sound between cry and groan, a sound I think that no torture could have forced from his prisoner. The captor noted the captive's drooping head, and frowned. But I think it was only the prisoner's condition that bothered him; unconsciousness could not be permitted to spoil the fun. He picked up the bucket with its brown scum and threw, so the water cascaded over the bent head, drenching the prisoner to the bone, washing away the dirt and blood. As the dark eyes flared, "Good," cried the Sheikh of the Sejilmi in his turn. "You are meant to watch."

And deliberately, sensually, he clasped me hard about the waist and drew me down with him.

Flesh is as subtle as a sounding board. It can reveal changes, nuances, shifts of tension and feeling that to the uninitiated are meaningless. I could not bear the proximity of those fleshy hands, nor the closeness of those fleshy lips. I was sickened by the smell, feel, touch, of those crumpled robes, by the nearness of that old tough body beneath. Once, long ago, when I was innocent, I had tried to imagine such a scene. How would it be, I had thought, to be brought to such a Bluebeard's castle; what were such men like? Visions of dancing girls had flashed through my mind, as now they flashed through the mind of the man who held me, inflaming him. To be forced into the act of love is bad enough: to submit to it at knifepoint in rape is obscene, degrading, unjust. To allow it deliberately, to welcome it, with a man you hate, with an enemy—to use him as he uses you— is something I had never imagined and do not know how to describe, except to say that it takes nerves of steel and determination almost as strong as the man who forces you. It is a dreadful thing to turn grace into a parody of itself, to befoul beauty, to perpetuate an ug- liness, and yet that is what I did.

The Sheikh of the Sejilmi knew no such qualms. Why should he? He had what he desired. Sex and power, power and sex used to gratify and humiliate, what more did he want? Like a man half starved, he ran his fingers over me, too greedy to hold still at any place, too frightened of missing something new if he let himself linger. He tore at my clothes, tore at his own, almost stifling me with his weight. I let him look. I told myself that prostitutes submit to acts like this every day; London is full of prostitutes they say, who live by satis- fying men's desires. I closed my ears to the sounds he made and the things he said. But I could not close my ears to the second cry my lover made, a cry between groan and shout, forced out of him as no torturer could.

The body is a strange thing. It has a will of its own. The familiar gestures came to me easily; I could not unlearn what I had learnt. There are clever men, scientific men, who claim that women should not know passion or be exposed to it, since they are either too weak to withstand its excesses, or knowing it are unable to restrain them- selves. Perhaps they are right; perhaps we are all whores beneath the sheets. But all I could think of as my body moved with the moves I had been taught, as my limbs spread, was to move in such a way, to turn, to smile, in such a way that the Sheikh of the Sejilmi, moving in time with me, would keep his back toward his prisoner. And while we surged together in pale imitation of the beauty I had known, I gave my true lover the time to free himself.

The Sheikh was an older man. For all his desire he could not last. He did not want me as much as he wanted to display his virility. The more he tried to pin me under him, fumbling with himself, fumbling with me, the more of his own clothes he threw off to press his matted chest and groin against me, the less of a man he became. He grunted and perspired, rolled, heaved; he might have been a bag of flesh that I watched from a distance dispassionately. And like many men, who believe that they are omnipotent, his greed rendered him insignificant. And before he could try again, the signal I had been expecting rang out.

Simultaneously then, several things happened. They still reverberate in my head so confusedly that I feel my senses reel even in trying to remember them. I shall try to sort them out. Start with the signal; remember, it was to have been made when our lord was found. It was meant to have been three pistol shots fired in succession to alert our army outside. Rasheed and his men had understood my strange cry of victory and had responded as I had hoped they would. A sudden quarrel between them had broken out and a sudden scuffle. This was the simple excuse they had used to enable them to draw their guns without interference from the guards. And before the Sejilmi could react they had fired into the air three times. The sounds, echoing and re-echoing along the valley floor, could be heard for miles. They were followed, in this case, by a regular flurry of shots, by shouts, screams, more shouts, the thud of feet upon the outside stairs as some of the Sejilmi guards returned the fire, as others burst into the chamber with stories of the disturbance among the "Arab guides" penned in a corner of the courtyard. But before this crisis had been thoroughly understood, the watchmen on the battlements came running with more alarming news: clouds of dust, sounds of horsemen, our army, I presumed, advancing in time (and how they had approached so closely without being seen was a tribute to the Vizier's leadership; the outer posts were already overrun, the undercover advance had been so stealthy that no sign had been glimpsed before). And now the army of the High Tigran came riding openly up to the very fortress walls to take them by storm. As they approached, amid the Sejilmi display of consternation and fright, the cannon went off with a thunderous roar.

The first shot whistled by harmlessly, too high; the second fell too wide; the third hit home, shearing off part of the battlement above our heads, as if someone had pared it away with a knife. Dr.

Legros had done his work well, and, stripped to the waist and sweating in the sun, he himself loaded and fired, like a regular gunner's mate. Inside the fort, clouds of dust showered down upon us, mud fragments, hard as rock, splintered, and a great gaping hole appeared in the ceiling. The Sheikh of the Sejilmi started up like an enraged bull. Caught off guard in bed with an Infidel, caught undressed, caught like a half-plucked chicken, he ran to and fro on his naked feet, trying to drag on his clothes, trying to round up his men, shouting orders, countermanding them before he had finished, screaming for his slaves to bring his sword, threatening to behead his guards for incompetence, ordering them to hold the gates. He never had time to complete a fraction of what he said; the last cannon shot ripped the gates apart so that they dangled on their heavy wooden frames as if on threads, their timbers splintered into matchwood. And into the gap they left streamed the first Tigran troops, some on foot to scale the walls, most of them horsed to occupy the first compound and seize the passage into the inner yard. I heard the ragged cheers my companions made, all of them still unharmed, although holed into a corner, all ready to break out to meet up with their friends. And in his inner private rooms the Sheikh of the Sejilmi caught the first whiff of defeat.

He stood still. He forced himself to consider. You could see the effort that it took, the muscles on his neck standing out like cords. He gave up shouting his ineffectual demands, waved away his guards, many of whom were now retreating fast; he ordered them to leave the inner courtyard and stairs, and to withdraw into that maze of under-passageways, where the best defense could be made. He gathered up his robes, thrust into his sleeves those thick, hairy arms that had just been trying to embrace me, and picked up his sword. He had lost his slippers, but not his dignity; that, he found somewhere, amid the ruin of his world.

"You die for this," he told me almost absentmindedly, "afterward." And taking up the great curved sword, the like of one my lord had used in his role of judge, he threw the scabbard to one side and advanced slowly toward the center of the room.

Afterward. He had not forgotten the prisoner then, still bound fast to the pillar by those hard stiff cords, made all the tighter by the water thrown over them. A mass of rubble surrounded him, although he had not been hurt by the cannon shot. But he was still tied, a prisoner, helpless, and there was nothing I could do to free him in time.

The rubble hindered the Sheikh for a moment, forcing him to pick his way carefully on his dainty feet. And calmly, the Master of the High Tigran watched him come. One strand of cord had been cut through, sufficient to give him a little leverage, but the rest still held, although he must have been sawing at them, back and forth, one by one. When the pistol shots, the cannon shots, had burst upon us, he must have realized that help was at hand. But his men would come too late. What they had feared, what we all had feared, what we had tried to prevent, was about to take place, before my eyes. As if Rasheed were speaking aloud I heard his voice, "What use to us if the castle falls, and the prisoner is killed?" What use, what use? And yet my lord faced his own death as he had lived, watching the lifted sword that was to end his life as if it were a toy, without the power to hurt. He was tied, no way to dodge the blow, unarmed except for that little knife held in one hand, unable to raise or lift it to defend himself.

The sword was in the air; the Sheikh hefted it with all his might, stumbling on the stones to come close enough. The sunlight from the open door glinted upon the jeweled hilt, casting a brilliant flash of blue across the shattered walls. I thought, I shall have to remember that flash, that blue glint, that brilliance. I shall remember them all my life, and the way the blue will turn to purple then to red, and the way the sword will fall, and the brilliance fade. I got up from the couch, ran across the floor, so many measured steps away, as I had measured them; my own bare feet made no sound, pressing down upon broken shards they did not feel. With all the strength I had, I caught the Sheikh about the back, took him unsteadily off stride so that he began to fall, bearing down upon him toward the bound and waiting prisoner, thrusting him down upon the Master's knife, so that its point slid in easily. The great sword fell harmlessly aside, the blue glint wavered into dust, and red was everywhere, upon the floor, upon the clothes, upon the knife point. Above it, my lord and I stared at each other, like strangers who had never met.

I was naked, sticky with blood, as once I had been with his when I had slashed at him. Now the blood was from another man, another man who had made love to me, who had just risen from the couch where he had lain with me, whose crumpled clothes soaked up the red like a sponge. I had seen men die because of me and caused men's deaths. I had never before been executioner. Kill or be killed, that is the jungle law, and now I had obeyed its command. I looked at my lord and he at me as if a distance had come between us, as if we were staring at each other across an open space, with no way to bridge the gap. I could not forget the sound he had made, something between a cry and a groan, witnessing what I had done for him. He could not forget what he had witnessed. And I could not forget what I had become for him, a harlot and a murderer. Sacrifice can come at too great a cost. I felt his horror of it branded on me like a second sword thrust. I felt my own horror branded on him.

Why did we not speak; why did we not say something? We were to regret our silence a hundredfold. There are moments so full of noise that they jar into a thousand bits and are lost. There are moments of stillness so long they reverberate unendingly down the years. And before we could make a fresh start, there was another rumble, and another falling shell. It sent a new cloud of plaster flaking through the rooms, shaking the fortress, cracking the mud walls, making the pillars tremble and the iron grilles break. There was a shout. A flood of people drove between us like a wedge, separating my lord and me. It was the women of the Sejilmi tribe. Like a stream of rats they came scurrying out of the nooks and crannies of the old fort, dragging their belongings with them, pulling along their little treasures wrapped in cloth or bundled in their arms. They did not know where they were going or what to do, but ran up and down the room, lacking even the purpose of rats, not noticing us but scampering into other holes or hurrying down blind corridors into the vaults where the fighting was still taking place, not having the sense to think of freedom now that their prison had been unlocked. "There are many harems in this land," the Lord of the High Tigran had told me. I saw now that harem women did not know how to escape even when freedom stared at them.

They ran back and forth in frightened packs, pushing, shoving, oblivious of my lord who was still tied to his pillar, oblivious of me and my nakedness. Except one, that is. She came last, slowly, head held high. Wrapped in a thick cloak such as men wear, she might have been a man; she was tall enough. She had never seemed as regal as she was then, gliding over the littered floor, scarcely pausing by her dead father's body but moving on, showing no sign of grief. When she saw me she stood still. I had been swept to one side in that frantic rush and, scarcely knowing what I did, had seated myself upon the couch, surrounded by the scattering of my clothes. Suddenly it had seemed important to put them on neatly, first the underskirt, over it the tunic, over it the blouse, piece by piece. I remember I did not even stop what I was doing when she looked at me, and then from me to my lord. "So," she said. And smiled. It was a strange smile, almost sad, almost satisfied. "So, Lord, you did not like what you saw." Her voice was subdued, unlike her own, as if she were being forced to talk, as if, like a sleepwalker, she had awakened in a place she did not know and was only gradually beginning to make sense. "So, Lord, you have been witness to my father's lust."

She turned back to me, and I felt the venom begin to rise. "And you, Christian, did you enjoy it, too?" She smiled again. "Old Safyia was right," she said, "she claimed you would win in the end. But not in the way she meant. I always knew you would do us harm. What harm have you still left to do?"

She plucked at the folds of her cloak, to pull it close about her, her head on one side as if lost in thought. When she went toward that central pillar where the man she had wanted was watching her helplessly, I remember crying out aloud, "Oh God, oh God!" but she did not try to touch him, merely stood and stared as she had at me. "So," she repeated for the third time in the same strange way. "Now you know what I felt. Now you feel the bite of jealousy."

She laughed. The laugh sent a shudder down my spine and it made my lover attempt again to break free, trying to wrestle himself out of the ropes, trying to force them apart, as if the sense of shock that had silenced him had passed, and he would shake the rafters down.

She said to him, "I never meant to kill her, only frighten her away. That was the fault of the servant girl, halfwit, with not the brains to measure the dosage right. I thought the fool would drink it all herself, believing she was missing some treat. I sent her back two times before, and not once did your paramour recognize her. As for your guard, he, too, was a fool, like all men taken in by a smile. But she, your paramour, she was cleverer than you thought. She knows how to use a man as well as I do."

She paused for breath. Her voice was lifeless, like her eyes, without fire, but there was venom burning underneath. "And what will you do with her now, Lord of the High Tigran?" she asked him. "What will become of her, who has left me fatherless, homeless, husbandless? Will you bring her back with you? Or shall she wander as I must, without hearth and home, without friends? I know why she came here and what she has done. But she has outwitted herself. No man, even you, would marry a woman who has been possessed by another man; no man, even you, could take back the lover of your enemy." She smiled again, a bitter sad smile. "And even if you were willing to, no one of your tribe would let you; a woman who has dishonored them and you."

There was no triumph in her, I say. She had never seemed so remote or distant, like the Vizier emerging from the depths of despair. The Lord of the High Tigran had grown quiet studying her. I thought, He hesitates to move or say anything now, for fear she will turn on me. And I, I cannot stop her if she tries to kill him. She has us both if she wants to. She said, "I shall not kill you, Lord of the High Tigran, although one day I may wish I had, and certainly in the past I have tried. But she, she is not worth the killing. I merely take her with me, your paramour. What was it," she spoke as if puzzled, "what was it you saw in her that you did not find in me? What made you choose her instead? What will she give you when she leaves?"

She suddenly took a step back and spread her arms above her head so that the two halves of the cloak fell on either side in straight lines, blocking the sunlight from the open door. "Only this," she cried, as if to show him the broken walls, the shattered pillars, the dead and dying.

With one sure movement she dropped the cloak over me; its thickness fell upon my head, blinding, suffocating. I tried to fight her, tried to cry out, but her hands were around my waist like steel bands, dragging me upright. Dimly, as if far away, I heard my lover shout at last, calling her by name, calling for his guards, struggling to free himself. His efforts died into silence, too, into darkness and nothingness. For as she pulled me through the open doors there was a final roar and one last flash. Blocks of coping stone fell in showers and lead rattled about us in a hail. One piece, I suppose, must have struck my head, for when I regained consciousness we were outside. She had managed somehow to pinion my legs and arms, and the cloak was still wrapped around me, like a shroud. A trickle of blood ran down my face. I could taste it on my lips but when I tried to open them, no sound came. We were in the courtyard, where the bodies of the Sejilmi guards were spread, lying almost languidly, as if still lounging in the sun. There was no sign of anyone else; my companions were gone, although somewhere in the distance I could hear their answering shouts. They were trying to break into those inner rooms to find their lord. I thought, They will rescue him; he will be saved; we have been successful, after all. But I shall not be there to share in the victory.

I had supposed for a moment that she and I were the only living things in the courtyard, but then I saw a shadow move. It was Mohamed, hidden in the corner where his friends had thrust him when the fighting had begun. He had been huddled there, dazed from his own rough handling, and seeing me started to scramble to his feet. I tried to shake my head at him to warn him to back away but she saw him first. She laughed her bitter laugh. "There," she told me contemptuously, "I have found a new man for you." And to Mohamed she cried imperiously, "You, boy, come here."

He came obediently, skirting the dead bodies, trying to shuffle along, his face a bewildered mask, wanting to catch hold of me, as if I were the only thing that made sense. "Lady, I tried," he began, simple as a child, but she seized him by the arm and twisted it with a cruel smile. "Fool," she said, "do as I say, or she dies."

Still half-dragging, half-carrying me, she made him follow us down through the open yard to where the horses were tied. She made him clamber onto one of the Sejilmi breed that were kept there, held its bridle in her hand while she mounted the gray horse of mine and dragged me in front of her. She tied the reins together and lashed at the gray with the loose strap so that it reared and bolted through the shattered gates, hauling Mohamed's horse after it, almost unseating him.

There was no one to see us go. The Sejilmi had retreated into the undercrofts and the Vizier and his men had followed them. We could hear how the continuing shots echoed and re-echoed under the castle walls. The fighting in the deep passageways would continue all night long; the Sejilmi had gone to earth down there like old foxes, needing to be dug out, one by one. But by the time they had been disarmed we would long be gone, and our tracks would be lost in the countless crossings and recrossings of all the other tracks that men had left on those hills today. And not until the battle's end would my lord be free to ask for us. And so we rode away, first down the path by which we had entered, then turning from it into the undergrowth, along secret ways that she knew, through the trees to the mountain ridge.

One other thing: I write another thing that you should know, something that is difficult for me to accept. The last shot from the cannon, which had cracked the coping and sent the lead flying, was the last shot of all. It, too, took its toll of sacrifice. After we had crossed the Sejilmi outposts where their scouts were lying dead, caught where they were supposed to be on guard, killed I think by the Vizier's men before we even had come into the valley, she paused to look at them. The kites had done their work, and a sweetness hung in the air so thick that even today the thought of it sickens me. Now she halted for the last time beside the Spanish gun. That cannon, which had been a Sultan's pride, lay on end, its carriage upturned, its brass fittings gleaming in the light where the shot had burst its seams. Among the scattered bodies there, I saw Dr. Legros. The Vizier's men had placed his spectacles carefully back upon his nose and for a moment he looked as he used to when asleep, his little feet in their slippers stuck up incongruously. She reined back then and looked at him, no expression on her face, while Mohamed and I were too grieved to weep.

"There," she said. "Another foreigner who thought to rob us of ourselves. What did he bring us? Only man-made things to destroy the work of centuries. And what has he gained? A small piece of ground to be his grave, if we grant him that much." And she leaned forward and spat.

I watched her, and it seemed to me her spittle was like the venom from a snake and that her words were poison that would leave their brand on us. Mohamed tried to cry out a better epitaph. "That was a good and holy man," he said, but she struck him viciously on the cheek where the bruises and cuts already showed, and ordered him to ride on.

So that is how we left the Sejilmi fort and wound our way back through the hills that we had crossed just hours before, not turning toward the High Tigran as once we hoped, but going southward, to the desert where I had started from. Presently the stars came out and the low full moon hung down, so that we could have reached up our hands to pluck it from the sky. We crossed the ridge and came again upon those barren slopes where not even footprints show. She never slowed her pace, but like a man drove us ahead; her skirts tucked up, she rode like a man, her feet thrust into the stirrups like a man, and her head high like a man, full of pride. And just as those ancient peoples long ago had disappeared into air, so we vanished into the vast distances.

CHAPTER 12

At first light we had reached the beginnings of the outcrops of rock that dominate this vast inland sea, like wave crests chiseled from stone. She called a halt to make her plans. She had regained some of her poise by now; her voice had reverted to its hard and calculating tone, and she pulled at the reins determinedly, pushing Mohamed out of the saddle as she did. "You, boy," she said, in the voice she used to intimidate, "you, what lies ahead? You are a camel-slave, you should know these desert wastes."

He was still trembling from the effect of the Sejilmi blows, and was dazed by all these unexpected events, his face purpled to a mass of weals, from which his one good eye stared out. But he had the grit to pretend not to understand her and his answer was so vague, so confused, that she leapt from the gray horse herself and began to advance upon him with a piece of shard clenched in her hand. "Draw," she told him, menacing him with the stone, as sharp-pointed as a dagger shaft. She cleared a space with her foot. Reluctantly he knelt down and began to make her a map, not one like Europeans use, but a time chart where she measured distances in days and weeks, and used the sites of water holes for landmarks. He dropped a line of small pebbles in place, one by one, to show how these oases were wound around the foot of the Sejilmi hills, like an anklet; and where they fanned out into the open desert, he scattered them at wider and wider intervals. She looked at them, measured the spaces between with her foot, eyed them reflectively. "And beyond here?" She pointed to the last stone, set apart from the others like a planet on the edge of a universe. "South of here, what then?"

"Nothing," he muttered, when she again threatened him. Nothing, I tell you, only more desert stretching to the end of the caravan trail, where few men go and I have never been myself."

"Liar," she said. "You have ridden with the caravans. Where they went, so did you. Do not pretend that you do not welcome the taste of desert dust; already it is clogging your nostrils, you lowland scum, who are not worthy of mountain air. Well then, how far is it to the end of this nothingness you speak of and to the end of this caravan trail?" And she stirred it with her foot, once more swirling the dust into clouds.

Piece by piece she drew the information out of him; there was no way he could withstand her. I had seen her use these methods scores of times in the harem when she wanted something her own way. "A hundred and thirty days of traveling," he told her finally. "Perhaps more. But it is a terrible land; ask anyone. The storms there are so fierce that in a single night whole caravans have been known to disappear, men and animals all gone, not even their bones left. The heat is so intense the skin shrivels up and the eyes grow blind. How do you think I lost my sight? No men dare live there, I swear, only the Tuareg, the Blue Men of the desert, as they are called, the slave traders, who prey on their fellow travelers. No one escapes from them."

She suddenly laughed, her harsh laugh without merriment. "I shall," she said. "Fool." She gave him a push that made his leg crumble under him. "You think to frighten me with your tales. But I have heard of the Tuareg; I have often thought of them. Take me there. I promise to free you when we reach their tents." And when he looked at her hard: "Well, then both of you. But if you do not do as I wish, both of you will die. The choice is yours."

He knew, and so did I, that her promise was a lie, but not so the threat to kill. And when Mohamed still remained obstinately silent, "Fool," she cried at him again, "what stops me from killing you now except that I need a guide? But be warned. Fail me and you shall watch her die before you do, and that I think will keep you tame." She rounded on him viciously. "Did you think I left the High Tigran only to become a prisoner in my father's house?" she cried. "I have had enough of harem life. My father avenged my shame it is true, but he did not pardon it. Did you think I would let him lock me up for the rest of my life?" She smiled. "The world is large, camel-slave, and I mean to take advantage of my freedom. The Tuareg are called the wildest men on this earth, but they honor women who are as free as themselves. Lead me to them and I will reward you well. They may be expecting me. I sent them messages long ago. What are you afraid of? I shall not harm you, nor her, as long as you do what I say."

Those, too, were lies, all lies, but Mohamed was forced to agree out of loyalty and love for me. And so she sat there for a while, hands on hips, legs apart like a man, studying the chart. Then, as if she had made up her mind, she dragged me forward, had Mohamed cut my hair and rub into it old ashes from some cooking fire to turn it gray and lifeless; she made me daub my face with a dye she had that burnt the skin as it darkened the color, and she retied the ends of the cloak so that they hid my head. "There," she said, standing back to observe the effect, and making him stand back to observe as well. "You once thought her a holy woman who would cure your infirmities, and there she is, an old hag, to answer all your prayers." She laughed once more, her hoarse, cruel laugh. "There were no secrets in the women's quarters of the High Tigran," she told him. "You should thank me for granting you your wish. She has become a holy woman to ride with us. But holy women disdain ordinary speech, so she shall remain dumb. And as holy women have no time for things of this world, not even the basic necessities of drink and food, she can live on air as they do. Unless you care to keep her alive." And when he looked at her, "Steal," she said. "That was what you were always best at; steal for her and for yourself, and me. And when we get to the first oasis sell this horse to buy the things we need." She pointed to the gray horse, against whose side I had leaned my own gray head, like the old woman she had made of me.

For the first time since leaving the fort Mohamed showed a flash of spirit. "That horse is not for sale," he told her, drawing himself up to his full height, and eying her. "It is not to be sold or traded. I hold it in trust for its rightful lord. And when he comes for us, as he will, I mean to return it to him. As I mean to keep my mistress safe." And when she laughed a third time, his little show of defiance amusing her: "We rescued him. So he will come to rescue us."

"As for his rescue," she said, her face darkening, "do not speak of it again. It brought me no gain. And do not count on his rescuing you; he will never come for you." She showed all her white teeth as I remembered she used to do. "He will never come," she repeated, almost gleefully. "Why? Ask her herself. Let her tell you why." She caught at my arm to force my head up. But I had no reply. Holy or not, I had become a woman to whom words had become unfamiliar, for whom words were drowned in the silence that I still felt surrounded me. I could not speak, could not think, could not feel, caught in a worse trap than any she could invent, a trap I had made for myself, however unintentionally.

"You see," she told him after a while. "She is already dumb. A holy woman then in word and looks. As long as she does not raise her head to reveal those pale eyes of hers, none suspect what she is or doubt her disguise. And if she is mute, her way of speaking cannot betray us. But if she breaks her silence to speak out of place, or if you do, first imagine how it might feel to be gagged with leather in this heat. No one will recognize that old woman, if she holds her tongue; no one will recognize you, nor me, if you do exactly as I say. Break that disguise, I will kill you both with my own hands. Now, mount and ride."

She wound a cord around my wrist and tied the other end to the saddle bow, then lashed us forward, driving Mohamed's horse beside her own. When we paused again she had him use the same dye upon the gray horse to darken its coat and with a knife she hacked at the hair around the Tigran brand so that from a distance, to a casual onlooker, it would seem completely changed. She did all this I presume to try to hide who and what we were; and although not as skillful as the captain of the guard had been, she concealed our traces sufficiently so that we seemed to sink from view, adrift upon an ocean that stretched to the world's end. (But nothing, or no one, could change the nature of that horse, nor change our natures I suppose, nor in the end destroy us as she hoped, although she came close to success. The horse certainly remained what it was, a Barbary stallion trained to loyalty. It had carried me because its master had ordered it, and I think it now carried her because I, too, sat on its back. *My father's horse bore him three days through the desert flats.* The gray horse was to carry us five times as far. And although a Barbary horse is not trained for desert use, it never hesitated, never spared itself, kept on, even when she forced the pace as hard as any man could.)

Now that she was free it was as if a devil drove her. She did not expect pursuit, yet she rode as if pursuit were hot behind. She flaunted herself, as willfully cruel with us as she had been with that little servant girl. Afraid of nothing, she preyed upon our fears. She kept me tied, like that monkey on a leash in her father's fort, and played with me, as with that monkey, mocking, tormenting me. She exacted from me the full penance that jealousy demands as payment for its wrongs. Tied close to her, kept close to her, I was more dominated by her in this open place than ever I had been in the harem of the High Tigran. And whatever guilt or remorse she meant me to feel, she made sure that I carried its full weight, feeding on it herself, thriving on it, a vengeance more cruel than the petty physical discomforts she delighted in. All those hateful characteristics I had noted in her before were now allowed full play, and there would have been no mercy in her had I asked for any. But although she kept me leashed with despair, and leashed Mohamed with fear (fear of what she would do to me, rather than fear for himself), her cruelty could not hurt me more than my own thoughts did. Why did she have such a hold on me; why did I listen to her taunts? How can I explain the desolation that was in me? Where there should have been feelings, emotions, hopes, there was nothing, a blank, deep as a pit. Like a traveler from some distant planet, as far off as those prehistoric times, I sensed I had become an exile from the one place where I longed to be, and never could return. I suppose anyone who has known great happiness and lost it must feel bereft. Was Adam happy when God closed the Gates of Paradise? Was Eve? But I felt neither happiness nor unhappiness; I felt nothing, I say. And everything that she told me, everything that she taunted me with, seemed only to reinforce what I had become. All that she said paled beside what my memories would be if I let myself remember. And if I knew that Mohamed spent every waking moment looking for, working for, hoping for his master to come, his hopes only accentuated my own lack of them.

I remember once when she slept (for she could not always stay awake, on guard, but she tied me then to her own waist, so that the slightest movement would rouse her), Mohamed and I had drawn close together, like two waifs, whom fate had brought together for old times' sake. We did not speak of the past nor dare to discuss the future, but to please me he had begun to tell me what lay at the end of those hundred and thirty days of traveling. I let him talk. His words were meant to be kind, yet even they sank like sour rain into the stony wastes where my feelings should have been. "They say," Mohamed had been whispering, his voice so low as to resemble the shifting of the embers of our little fire, "they say there is a palace made of pearl and jade. Beautiful women dwell there and gardens surround it, full of lemon trees. The women walk in the gardens beside a lake, singing songs to haunt us men so we will never want to leave. I do not say that such a place exists," he added, blinking his one good eye hard, a trick he had when deep in thought. "But it might. Yet of all the places I have seen, the valley of the High Tigran could best suit me. I could happily end my days there."

I could not remember that valley; instead made myself talk of those other gardens, of those other trees, and asked him the name of the lake, Lake of the Moon (a pleasant name for a place which no one had seen and from whence no one returns), until he interrupted me. "Lady," he said, bursting out, forgetting caution, "you never speak of the High Tigran, you never talk of our lord. Do you not believe he will be looking for us?" He did not dare add, Have you forgotten him?

Disturbed by his voice, Rashmana sat upright. "What are you plotting?" she cried, jerking at the cord around my wrist so that its knots bit into my flesh and I scarcely could suppress a cry. "Have you ignored my warnings?" She jerked again. "You think that the Lord of the High Tigran will find you in the end," she said to Mohamed. "You think he will send his scouts to track you down. I know that you try to help them," she pointed at him, contemptuously, "that you leave your stupid little signs for them to follow. Oh, do not deny it, I have seen so many times the bits of saddle cloth hung on a thorn bush, the bridle straps, the horse-prints that you place so cleverly at one side of the path. You can be sure they will rot or blow away before he comes looking for them. The Lord of the High Tigran has no need to track down whores. There are plenty of whores still left for him." I saw how her teeth flashed as she smiled. "He has returned to the High Tigran long ago," she cried. "You and your mistress are quite safe from him. He has forgotten her. She was only a little moment in his life, as she made me seem." And turning to me she cried again, "There is no place left there for you."

No place left, no place for you, a whore. These were the things she hammered into my brain; these were the things she tormented me with; these were the guilts she hung on me. And for all Mohamed's constant smiles, his winks, his attempts to leave some clues (for he never gave up trying), she sapped my belief in his efforts too. So, if I repeat that, in those early days, I tried to think of nothing, tried to remember nothing, felt nothing, I hope I shall be understood. Only in my dreams, where she could not go, was I able to think at all. And sometimes when I nodded as we hastened on beneath the mid-day heat, or dozed by seconds, jerking awake, or when I peered about me through the whispering darkness of night, if sometimes then the places and the people that were dear to me reappeared, these were the only times that seemed real in a world gone mad. And if sometimes in those dreams I felt that I rode with death, as if death were all around me with its sweet and sickly smell, so that its taint could never be washed off; if sometimes even in this dream world time stood still, as it had for me in that room, where I thought that forever I should be leaning into that foul embrace, forever be thrusting down toward that knife; if then I awoke, a scream soundless upon my lips, Rashmana's mocking watchfulness, her contempt, told me she had heard my scream and knew its cause. And then I feared that even in my dreams I could not be safe from her. Dream or reality, which was real, which false? There were times when I could not tell them apart.

Perhaps that was why I never dreamt of my lover, never dared to think of him. If he appeared at all it was as a dark figure on the far side of a closed door. I sensed his presence there, standing, lis-tening to me breathe. It seemed to me, as I stood on the other side, just as I had done in the garden of the High Tigran, that if I put my hand out I could touch him again. But when I did, there was nothing, nothing but silence, dark and deep. Sometimes since I have thought that because I knew him so well, I alone had the ability to wound him to the core. I had known him proud and arrogant, courageous to the point of folly, fearless when faced with death. But no one had seen him bowed until I had humbled him. Defeat had never shamed him as I had with his enemy. If that knowledge I had won so hard had been kept private between us, it could have been endured. It was her knowing, using, twisting it, that held the door shut. But afterward I sometimes thought it was not shame that I had surprised in him, but love, unexpected and painful. Love, not shame, had kept him silent. But that was long afterward. Now, these thoughts were too dark to dwell upon, and so I shut them away as well and never tried to revive them.

We rode night and day, as hard as we could, trying to avoid the other caravans that followed the same route, all of them seem-ingly, like us, setting off upon some distant quest. When we were obliged to ride in the same direction, we passed them quickly, heads bent, without stopping, although Rashmana, ever fearless, never hesitated to shout out greetings to them. At first it would seem that, of all the places she might have chosen to hide, the oasis world was the most unlikely one, yet in this land of constant surprise it served her purpose well. For when we reached the first village with its lake of peacock blue, its green strips of cultivated fields, its dense stands of palms, I was reminded oddly enough of a seaport, a harbor, much as one might find in the west country. There was the same air of expectancy, the same swell, like the movements of the tide, the same straining forward that ships exhibit when their sails are spread, and the same sense of relief when they return, their holds full and all dangers past. In these oasis villages travelers swarmed in the streets as sailors do on the docks, with a similar restless air, as if measuring distances or calculating returns. They were too busy with their own affairs, too wrapped up in themselves, to let their curiosity focus upon us long. Poised to leave, they saw other travelers as ephemeral as themselves. So it was easy for us to move through them unnoticed, forgotten, like flotsam, like driftwood. And the gray horse from the stables of the High Tigran carried us unfailingly, its broad hooves beating down the miles, its easy gait never faltering (although I could not say the same of the Sejilmi bay, which Mohamed had to nurse along). And so we came in time to that last water hole.

Most of the oases had been large and prosperous, with a life apart from the itinerant world of the caravans. Fed by mountain streams, themselves now running full with melting snow somewhere deep in the hinterland, the fields and lakes of each village had shone like a string of jewels. Yet as we had moved south, each settlement had become smaller than the last, as if the water were drying up too soon. This last one scarcely merited the name, was simply that, the last, beyond which there stretched a hundred and thirty days of nothingness, leading to that mythical Lake of the Moon. We reached this oasis after a long and wearisome ride under a sky as dull a yellow as a sulfur pool. Seeing that sky, Mohamed had reined up abruptly. His blind side was toward me and because he could not see me, he may have forgotten that I could see him. Lines of worry had creased his broad forehead and sharpened his fine profile, making him older, stern. He straightened his back where her whip had caught him painfully and raised his chin, for all the world like a horse scenting out the air. "This is where the southern route begins," he told her. "I have been no farther than here. But to go on would be madness. Can you not sense the storms that fill the air? It is a journey no man should attempt alone, and no woman could survive."

"I shall," she boasted in her confident way. "Look. There are my guides." She pointed with the butt end of her whip to the scrawny stand of trees where a few men were crouched, watching us. "There they are," she cried triumphantly. "I said that they would be there."

"And what of us?" Mohamed held his ground. "What of your promise to us?"

She did not bother to reply but urged the gray horse forward, forcing him to trot behind, winding my leash more tightly around the saddle strap. She smiled to herself; she might have sung. And overhead, the sun seemed to lower behind a thick and dense haze.

The Tuareg, the Blue Men, the Desert Men (these are some of the many names by which they are known) were different from any I had seen. Tall and slightly built, they may have been of Berber stock, for their language was similar, but they had a cruel and desperate look, like wolves trained to kill. Their skin had a bluish tinge, hence their second name, as if the indigo color of their clothes had become ingrained in their flesh; and their eyes had that same predatory stare that hungry, desperate men have everywhere. When we approached they stood up, holding their weapons lovingly, as if, given half a chance, they would have welcomed using them. Perhaps Rashmana had sent messages to them, as she had claimed (there would have been time and opportunity when she had first returned to her father's tribe). They did not seem surprised to see her, although they did not greet her, and their camels, lying on the sand behind them, stared at her as dispassionately. The Tuareg own the finest racing camels in the world, so Mohamed had said, and these were of that breed, even I could tell that, better groomed and fed than the men who rode them. Behind them though, there were other camels, tethered, with their goods still loaded on their backs, stolen goods, I suspect, and probably stolen animals as well. And beyond them, yet again, a little inner group, a cluster of women and children slaves, destined for the slave markets. And it was the sight of them that sent fear, heavy as lead, into us.

If the men made no sign of recognition Rashmana did not hesitate to approach them. She tapped her leg with her riding whip and tossed her hair, both signs of excitement in her. The days in the open had given her her spirits back, and since she always took the lion's share of the food and drink that Mohamed found, she did not have our drawn and exhausted look. She narrowed her eyes against the sun's glare. "Look at that blue skin," she marveled. "Old Safyia must have learned her tricks from them. Look at those camels, sleek as silk." And as the men began to circle us, like wolves in a pack, "I am glad to see them come. They do not always keep their word."

Once they had ascertained what we were, two women and an unbearded boy, the Tuareg behaved in a strangely easy way. They jested and laughed, which appealed to Rashmana's taste. She flushed and laughed herself and tossed her hair again, reminding me of how I used to think of her, how I used to hope one day she would be free. She jumped to the ground, lithe on her feet, and went up to them confidently as was her way. "I have come," she reminded them. "I told you I would. And see what I have brought for you—three things of great worth: a Barbary war stallion of such strength you could not buy him anywhere, a stable boy whose skill is known, and a holy woman who may be of use to you one day."

As the meaning of these words sank in, Mohamed suddenly stopped once more and shouted to her again, "What of your promise to us?"

She turned back to laugh at him. "Next time," she told him almost good-naturedly, in that voice she used when it suited her to be pleasant, "you will know better than to believe all you hear. Just as you will come to believe that your lord is not as loyal as you thought he was." And she turned her back on him, talking to the Tuareg chiefs, smiling at them, enticing them. "Come," I heard her repeat, "these two slaves will more than buy my right to journey with you." And she nodded at us as if we were animals to be bought or sold.

Now whatever Mohamed may have thought or believed, he certainly had not believed she meant to let us go. But neither had he thought that she would sell him back to slavery. As for myself, the threat of slavery had been present ever since I had first come here, but so much had happened in between that my first indignation almost seemed unreal. I think I could have endured slavery if I had to; I almost did not care. But for Mohamed it meant death, disintegration of the soul. The word *slave* fell on him like hot tar upon a field of wheat; it blackened his spirit; it withered him. All through this long and dreadful journey he had supported me, fed me, comforted me, and given me hope. I had come to rely on him. Seeing hope torn from him so brutally, I felt my own anger begin to rise in protest as it had not all through this hopeless while. I looked at him. He topped me by a head. Since that day in the courtyard of the High Tigran when I had first seen him happy and fulfilled, I had begun to think of him as a man. To see him now thrust down into the misery that he once had known was more than I could bear. I thought, It is the word itself that defeats him and sends him back to servitude. I thought, I called him a slave to the Sejilmi, to impress them, and Rashmana has never called him anything else; but he is no slave, and as far as I am concerned he never has been. I remembered suddenly how he had cried out that he had been born free; how he had knelt to kiss my hand; how he had overcome his own sense of fear. I remembered how he had stayed with me all this time, although he could easily have escaped or run away. It seemed to me that out of all this madness that had reshaped the world we now lived in, there was one thing left I could do for him.

Still tied on the horse, I suddenly raised my head as she had told me not to do, and threw back the cloak as she had expressly warned against. I made my voice high and imperious, as perhaps a holy woman would, if the spirit moved within her. And I used phrases that I thought would appeal to Mohamed although I meant for all those present to hear and take notice. "You are free," I told him, forcing him to look at me, stretching out my hands to him, although since I was still bound our fingers barely could reach. "You have served me faithfully and well and I release you from my service. I make no claim of you and never have. Henceforth no man or woman can enslave you. You are free, free, free, free."

I supposed there must be formal words for such a ceremony in a land where a woman can be divorced merely by her husband's saying so four times, hence my reiteration of the word *free*. But I chose to say it four times, shout it out, to impress it upon Mohamed himself. I had no right, nor wished for the right, to make or unmake anyone a slave. I thought slavery cruel, immoral, evil. But to make Mohamed free I had to make him feel so. When I heard the sudden howl he gave, throwing back his head, like an animal let out of a cage, I knew that I had won. She could not destroy him, I thought, as she had tried to destroy me. And for a moment I allowed myself to look at her, so she should know that the numbness, the apathy, that had enslaved me was broken too, and her power was done.

The effect upon our listeners was instantaneous. Rashmana herself was furious, more angry than I had ever seen; her anger lashed her like a goad. She turned upon me with her whip. I think she would have willingly thrashed me to death had not the Tuareg chiefs restrained her. Yet the stripes were worth the pain. I found I was no longer afraid of her. It was as if those simple sentences had also broken the chain of silence that she had wound about me and that somehow I had allowed her to wind. She had thrust forward at me, striking me twice before the men had caught the whip in midblow. But the gray horse, upon which I was sitting, had also felt the shock of her attack, if not its full force. It neighed, thrusting out with its forehooves, throwing back its head, its eyes wild. I clung to it, knowing that one more move from her, or from anyone, and it would show what it was: a stallion, bred to defend or attack.

Its response startled the Tuareg chiefs. Although some had drawn their swords, they stepped back hastily. On foot, no one likes to meddle with a battle horse. Only Mohamed dared. Scrambling in his ungainly way off the Sejilmi bay, he came limping to my side, snatching at my bridle and facing our opponents. Imagine us: myself, dark-skinned, gray-haired, high-voiced, tied like a monkey on a leash; himself, a crippled boy; and the gray horse, gaunt-eyed and proud, snorting defiance, pawing the ground.

Now, as to the motives Rashmana had had to put me in such a disguise, fear of discovery may have been one, but equally strong, I think, was the desire to make me seem ugly and old, so that no man would look at me. But in the days since our starting off, the sun and wind had had their effect, and my skin had lightened, and my hair had lost its gray tinge. There was nothing she could have done to change the color of my eyes, as she must have known, but it was the grayness of my soul that had lifted, and now she realized that. As for the horse, despite the heat and flies, the lack of food, it still looked well; its coat had grown and the roughness that the dye had caused had begun to wear off. Suddenly, I think, the Tuareg chiefs felt the need to look at us more carefully, as if what they had first seen was a mirage of a second presence: a beardless boy, a slave, who challenged his mistress, and an old woman who had become young, a holy woman, who had prophesied.

First they began to examine the horse, not coming too close in case it lashed out with its feet, but knowingly, discussing it among themselves. "Which brand?" they asked, just as the Sejilmi Sheikh had. Rashmana tried to laugh off their suspicions. "Forget the brand," she cried, "its former master has no use for it." Yet it was clear to

me her answer did not satisfy. For there is something about the
Tuareg that I was to understand later, and that helped us at this crisis
in our lives: their superstitious nature is stronger than their suspicions. Although many had drawn their weapons, others, equally vehemently, had begun to make open signs to ward off evil, just as
Mohamed had used to do. They did not dare come too close to look,
which also was an advantage for us, but they sensed something strange
and unusual in their midst that made them uneasy, on guard. And
although Rashmana attempted to woo them, smiled at them to lull
their fears, the Tuareg were not men to be easily led astray as had
been that poor guard in the High Tigran. The more she smiled, the
more they hesitated. "Whose brand?" they had asked, but they meant,
Who is the owner? What is he? As for me, their fears were such that
they did not question me at all, and whatever she told them later,
privately (all lies of course, for she would not tell the truth, either
because they would not believe her anyway, or believing, would be
more than ever curious; and the last thing she wanted was to make
them interested in me), they did not approach us nor attempt to harm
us. So that although we joined the slave train of the Tuareg, we were
not quite slaves ourselves; and although we shared their imprisonment and hardships, we still kept our horse. This state of affairs
would not have lasted long, I suppose, but it was to last long enough
to enable us to survive.

The Tuareg had established their main camp in the desert a few
days' ride away and had come to the oasis alone either to barter or
trade their goods, to collect or sell slaves, and to await our arrival, if
any trust were to be put in Rashmana's "messages." We left more
quickly than I think they normally would have, partly because of
these strange events (which were bound to attract attention even
though the few villagers usually kept out of their way, such was the
fear the "Blue Men" inspired), partly because they, too, had noticed
the color of the sky and sensed a weather change. When I saw where
they took us, when I realized the length of each day's march, the
height of the sand dunes we crossed, I wondered that men lived there
at all. For the hills of sand stretched as far as the eye could see, to
the horizon and beyond, mountains of sand eddying in gigantic ripples under that sullen sky. The Tuareg men were warriors; they left
their herds, their women, their vassals to fend for themselves while
they were gone, relying on slaves to do most of the work. Now they
hastened back, fearing a storm would break.

They themselves lived like feudal lords, summoning their followers to war by beating on large skin drums. They used only swords and spears in battle, considering firearms effeminate, and the killer lust was so strong in them that no boy was considered a man until he had killed—it mattered little how or when. But in other ways these great warriors resembled children, fond of simple jokes and tricks, and terrified of natural portents or strange events. They seemed remarkably tolerant of their womenfolk, whom, it was whispered, they allowed to take lovers and have congress with men as they chose. Perhaps this last was true; it would have appealed to Rashmana of course. And it is also true that when I saw her in the company of these blue-skinned, hard-eyed men, I felt that this was where she belonged. I could not wish her well after all the hurt she had done us, but neither could I wish her ill. I wished only that she could have begun this new life without dragging along the envy and malice of the old. But envy had driven her this far, envy choked her, stifled her; malice made her as much a prisoner as we were. And although she seemed almost afraid now herself that we might be followed, conversely, I felt sure that in the end we would be found.

We saw little of her or these desert warriors but much of the poor frightened people brought back to work for them. There was not a man among these slaves, only women and children; menfolk were for slaughtering. Added to the general grief, then, was mourning for dead husbands, brothers, friends. Our reputation had spread among them in the way the news has of spreading in this land, and they stared at us, round-eyed with fright, dragging the chains that tied them out of our way when first we joined them, for fear that we might curse them. I think they feared us as much as they did the Tuareg. Certainly none of them had seen fair complexions before, and at the first opportunity I had scraped off the remainder of the dye, preferring to scour my skin with sand than to live any longer in disguise. But when they found out there was no evil in us, and when we allowed the weakest of them to ride on the horse turn and turn about with us, they began to come crowding round. Still too timid to talk about what they had suffered, they soon felt free to question me about myself and my life. (Perhaps I should add that, except for the journey, which, for them, undoubtedly had been long and harsh and had seen the death of the weakest among them, they were not treated badly by their new masters, and when they reached the camp they were in fact made welcome by other slaves there who took care of them.) But although we were part of this slave train we were not *of* it. And when in time the women became emboldened enough to consult with me, then, strange as it may appear, I came to gain the reputation that Mohamed had always wanted for me. And equally strangely, I suppose, I accepted it. Not only the slave women. The Tuareg ladies as well came with one request, or perhaps variations of one theme is a better term; that is, how to have or not have or lose a child so that their husbands, lovers, masters, would not know. Once such talk would have horrified me. Not now. For like Dr. Legros I saw the sense of women knowing about themselves and how their own bodies functioned. And so, remembering what he used to say, I told them what could or could not be done, in the dispassionate way the good man would have told them, and I gave advice in his name, and so my reputation spread. And when, as came to happen, I learned that I myself should not bear the child of the Sheikh of the Sejilmi, I thanked God for his goodness. But I no longer accepted that we were doomed to an endless slavery, nor that one woman had the right to harm another, nor that God meant me to stay here without seeing my lover again.

Yet it is true that where we went with our new masters might have been likened to Dante's Inferno. Now we might be termed "wanderers," those whom the people of this land call "belonging to the night," or "inhabitants of the empty spaces," not humans, but wraiths who go where the wind blows. Our tracks were completely lost; along with our captors we seemed to disappear, sunk into a nothingness so huge that there was no known way to measure it. But I had regained my faith. Like Mohamed I had come to believe we would be rescued and that belief reached out to comfort us. We had reverted to our first life together, just he and I, a camel boy and the foreigner he led; and it seemed to me, sometimes, that just as then we had been waiting, expecting, something or someone, now we were again. It was that expectation, that hope, that kept us alive.

I have said the Tuareg ladies were curious, and less fearful of me than were their menfolk. In time I was to know them well, as well, that is, as a stranger could. They kept the camp in better condition, cleaner, more regulated, than those dirty warlords deserved. And although the women themselves were strident and outspoken, they were not unkind, the sort of woman Rashmana might have been had not envy marred her spirit. Once having noticed me, they became intrigued enough to insist I be brought to their tents, although they were careful to hide this fact from the men, who would have quickly driven us out again. They did not like Rashmana's presence, resenting no doubt her quick familiarity, and they may have enjoyed favoring us to spite her. But since they saw no threat in me, no sexual threat, that is, they were not afraid, and seemed not to care that I brought Mohamed with me. Although ignorant of most things that our modern world takes for granted, they were not stupid. When I told them that a woman ruled the land where I came from they thought that right and just, since in their tribe inheritance comes through the female line. But they thought it unnatural that she should also control her army since fighting was a man's prerogative with which they had no concern. Most of all they were determined that I should "prophesy" again, and whenever I opened my mouth they pressed around me in anticipation of some divine revelation. The revelation, when it came, was from God perhaps; at least it had the force of God behind it. And it was to help us to escape. Yet had the women's inquisitiveness not freed us from the slave quarters, we might not have had that chance.

We had been placed in one of the Tuareg tents. Since it was divided into male and female sides, Mohamed slept in one part and I in the other. When he shook me awake, I knew the reason before he spoke. He had but to say "Listen," and I heard that long singing sound, that constant moan that the sand makes when the wind blows it for a thousand miles, the singing of myriads of grains that Colonel Edwards had anticipated from far out upon the sea. "Listen," Mohamed said. No one could have failed to listen; the sound deafened, overwhelmed, like the cries of human souls in agony.

Mohamed had been expecting the storm; perhaps we all had, all of us who lived through those hot and stifling days before it broke. A rainstorm brings relief, a storm like this does not. This chokes and blankets down until there is a lack of air, a lack of smell, a lack of taste, and everything is concentrated on that noise. Soon ears, eyes, nose, throat, are blocked with sand until one cannot breathe or think. And where there might have been light, even at midday, there is only darkness, thick and tangible.

All around us we could hear the shouts and cries as the camp awoke from sleep and tried to prepare for the storm's approach. Women shrieked, children wept, men argued with one another as they struggled to secure the tents. Camels are used to sandstorms; they lie down, facing out of the wind, their backs making a kind of shelter for their owners to hide behind. The Tuareg now dragged them into a circle around the tents, using even their racing camels, tying strips of cloth about the animals' heads to try to filter out the dust.

Mohamed had been in storms like this before, although never one so fierce; this was the notorious desert storm of the southern route. "Quick," he said. He made me wrap cloth around my own mouth to form a mask and as swiftly made one for himself. He filled all the water bags that he could find and then backed out of the tent, beckoning for me to follow him. We crept silently through the camp, but we were the only silent people there. It was too dark for anyone to see us even if they had searched for us, and there was too much confusion for us to be missed. Those men outside were preoccupied with bedding down their herds and rescuing their goods before the sand buried them; those inside were trying to block all the vents and holes to prevent the dust from billowing in. Even the slaves had come clamoring for shelter and were let inside. No one but a madman would venture out at such a time. Yet with unerring skill Mohamed led us toward the place where the gray horse had been tied.

It was already straining at its ropes, its ears laid flat, its eyes gone wild with panic at the noise. We had brought spare strips of cloth to bind up its head and to blindfold it, although it reared, trying to throw off the bandages. We dared not linger to saddle it, but, slinging on as many of those water bags as we could, we scrambled up on its back. Mohamed cut the tethering cords and let it loose. Clinging desperately to its mane, clinging to each other, we heaved our way over the first dune beyond the camp, out into the gathering fullness of the wind.

A storm like that can blow for days, although this was but the harbinger, the worst yet to come. The sand can bury everyone, even those under shelter, even those within a hut, even those who are used to storms. We were in the open with nowhere to hide. But Mohamed was not stupid. He had been expecting such a storm; more than that, he had been hoping for it, waiting for it. He had seen those leaden skies before and experienced that heavy haze. As well as any Tuareg he knew what to do. Secretly he had been making his plans. He had marked out a place where we could hide, if we could reach it in time, one of those outcrops of rock with which this part of the desert is bestrewn. He relied upon the gray horse to carry us there before the storm burst upon us in full force. For although the violence of such a storm is known, funneling along at ground level in thick black folds, its path sometimes does not stretch so wide as long and a horse at least might have the speed to cut across it before it smothered us. That was a risk he took, but it was the only chance he had. He took it knowing what the result might be. And I followed him. So there we were, unprotected against the elements, plunging wildly, blindly, into the unknown where even the Tuareg would not dare follow us.

Mohamed's original plan had been to veer north, every step back one step gained, but the direction of the wind, its suddenness, drove us farther west than he had meant. But he had guessed accurately the speed of the wind's approach. Although the sand was bristle sharp, cutting against the flesh like knives, although the wind howled about us in great gusts, throwing up the dust in clouds, although at every moment its fury increased like a current racing toward land, the sand had not yet formed those drifts and gullies into which unwary travelers plunge, and we were cutting our way across one corner of it. The gray horse labored; its forefeet, with their wide hooves, could scarcely find leverage on the shifting surface, and its back was coated with sand. If a group of rocks had not appeared, either the ones we had been aiming for or another similar group, even a Barbary horse could not have saved us. As it was, we crawled beneath the rocks, gasping for breath while the horse sank to its knees, its eyes glazed beneath the bandages, its chest rattling with the efforts it had made.

We tore off the wrappings from its mouth and poured the contents of one of the water bags down its throat, massaging its neck to make it swallow. Mohamed put his arms around its neck, whispering encouragement. When it found the strength to move again, he found the strength of his own to drag it to its feet and pull it after us, out of the wind. The rocks were hollowed on one side to form a kind of overhang, common to many such places, eroded by the weather into a natural cave. Although the cave was too narrow for the horse, the overhang sheltered it, whilst further in we had space to lie down, huddled together for companionship. Perhaps we slept. All night long the volume of noise increased until it sounded as if it would split the rocks above our heads. All night and part of the next day the wind continued to blow, gusting the sand at intervals like rain showers, except this rain was hot and dry, sometimes falling sheer and sharp

as a scouring brush from black clouds, sometimes drifting and settling. When the sky at last blew clear and we crawled out, we looked
down upon a world that had utterly changed.

Where before there had been flat ground, now high ridges reared;
where before there had been hills, the sand was flat as a stream bed.
The wind had thrown up new dunes as easily as high tide scours the
shore, and as far as we looked, the surface of this new landscape
appeared unmarked, as unruffled as a beach. Nothing moved or stirred,
and the sand, the sky, and the sun seemed as new as if the universe
had just been formed.

We stared for a long time, overcome by the magnitude of what
we saw and our own insignificance. Then, sitting down, we made
ourselves face stark reality. We had water, not a great supply but
enough if we were to travel on. We had no food, but food we could
do without for a while. We had the horse. These were our advantages. On the debit side the list was longer and more involved.

First, the horse. It had run its great heart out. Even it could not
go on forever. Then there were the Tuareg, if they had survived the
storm. When they had sorted out their camp, assessed their losses,
dug out their animals, they would remember us. Finally there was
the terrain itself. Mohamed had no previous knowledge to rely upon,
and all the landmarks his quick desert brain had noted on the march
south would have been obliterated. He could only guess how far
back the last water hole was, and the general direction in which it
lay. He could not even be sure that it still existed. Villages, too, can
be buried by storms, and wells covered so deeply that no digging
can unblock them. We sat there while the sun burned overhead and
he patiently explained each choice we had, each difficulty. Listening
to him I thought suddenly how like a man he truly had become, how
now he was the one who planned and took charge. I thought, He,
too, has changed and has become what he wished to be—and I felt
joy for him.

He said, marking each of his thoughts with a stroke on the
ground to keep them straight in his head, "The Tuareg will hold a
meeting to plan what to do. They may decide to follow us; they do
not like to be cheated of what they think is theirs. But," he hesitated,
"they may also be glad to be rid of us." He did not elaborate, but I
knew what he meant. Rashmana might insist that they search for us,
not out of kindness but to ensure she was not deprived of her prey.
But they, never comfortable in our presence, wary of us, might as

easily tell her to do the hunting on her own. "Then there is the horse." He looked at it. It had stood patiently all night long, stamping when the weight of sand grew too heavy or when Mohamed crept out to brush it down. He said mournfully, "When it was foaled its master carried it upon the saddle, like a child, hand-fed it with milk and dates, and covered it with the finest blankets in his tent. It never will carry both of us; the sand is too deep, the drifts too high. The dunes will be carved out, hollowed out, by the wind into half-tunnels, thus." And he showed me how, scooping at the sand in front of him. I watched it trickle through his hands in a miniature landslide. "There is just a possibility," he began and then was silent. I knew so, too. We could not both hope to ride, only one could. And it must be the one who knew the desert best and could find the way. The other must stay until he returned with help.

"Go, then," I told him. "I would not even know how to begin." And when he was silent, I said more forcefully, "If we both remain we shall both die. You at least have more hope of finding a trail. Divide the water as you need. I shall wait here for you." The echo of those words, similar to the ones I had once said to my lord, sent a coldness beneath the heat like a shadow of warning. Death had already claimed one of our companionship. Upon which of us would it lay its finger next?

He did not say again how slim the chances were. He did not boast, as his old self would, that he would easily find the way there and back. He did not say he would be rescued by our friends before he went too far, although that at least he could hope for. He had no time to waste. With every moment the desert heat challenged us, rising gloatingly above the wreckage of the storm as if to demonstrate that even sand and wind were no match for it. He left me two of the water bags, the smallest ones, for he needed water not only for himself, but for the horse. He did not say good-bye nor utter any words of farewell but simply crouched for a moment staring out at the rolling waste of sand as if to try to impress its contours on his mind. Then he straightened himself up, bound the cloth about his face, and heaved himself upon the horse, like a man. As he slid down the first incline, he turned in the saddle to watch me until the shadow hid him from sight. At each crest he turned again, and so we watched, each of us growing smaller to the other, each of us appearing like a speck, until the distance swallowed us and each of us was left alone.

What did I think there, sitting in the shadow of those rocks, waiting for something that might never happen. At first I let my thoughts go with him, following him. Then I thought of old times, old friends. Sometimes I imagined Antoine Legros, his smiling face and mincing walk as clearly recognizable as when I had last seen him alive. "Are you happy?" I asked him. "Has good come from your sacrifice? Did it please you, knowing you had helped us? Do you feel lonely in this land; do you still long for your own home?" He wiped his glasses as if a mist obscured his view and walked on, in his black frock coat as enigmatic in death as he had been in life. Sometimes I saw the little Indian girl whose picture in the locket lay abandoned by the Sheikh's bed. "Are *you* happy now?" I asked her, trying to catch her hands, obsessed, I think, with happiness, tasting it, wanting to savor it again. The golden bracelets glittered as she moved out of my reach. "You have your lover with you," I cried. "Did your lies, your loving desperation, achieve all that you wished? What did you think when you saw those English rifles pointing at your breast?" Only once did she reply. "I have no regrets," she said. She smiled. "How could I, knowing what the choice was. But waiting, ah, the waiting may be long." She smiled then and leaned forward as if to reveal a secret; I sensed her presence, cool and soft, releasing the scent of jasmine flowers. "Do not despair," she said. "The space between the living and the dead is not so far that it cannot be crossed." Beside her, Colonel Edwards leaned forward as well, looking at me as he used to. "Things are not always as they seem," he told me. "Fight back."

And once I dreamt of the Vizier. Sometimes in the early days I had thought of him. I had imagined him permitting himself the luxury of a smile when the news of victory had been brought to him; I had seen him clasp his nephew in his arms. "Come, Lord," he had said. "It is done; it is finished and we can go home." I had seen him laugh in the triumphant parade in which I had once taken part; smiling up at the girls, already searching for a suitable one to take my place. "So, Lord Vizier," I had said to him, "you have won a greater triumph than you knew. Does it please you to find that I was all you said I was? Are you happy to have been proved right?" Now he leaned forward on his horse, his maimed hands clearly visible, and looked down at me. "Once I was sent to bring a foreign woman back," he said at last, "and grief it was to me and shame, and love. But most of all I helped her leave because of love. Must I now beg another woman to return?" His nephew came shouldering his way past. "Why, Uncle," he said, looking down at me in turn, "I do not think we need to beg." And he smiled at me. I felt my heart leap for happiness. Hold on, that smile said. Do not be frightened. I will come.

On the second day—or was it the third?—suddenly I saw things with startling clarity, as if everything before had been half obscured. I actually drew out the leather bag in which I had always kept my personal possessions, such as they were, and fumbled in it for the notebook that I had intended to use for a journal. I held it for a long time before opening it. It was small, water-stained from the sea, not half the size of Dr. Legros's notes, which I had made him burn. I smoothed the pages flat, those empty pages I had meant to fill. What if I should begin to write in them now; what would they say about what had occurred; what would they tell a reader about myself, my life, my friends? I turned each page, one by one, until I came to the beginning. *This has been the saddest day of my life.* Was that to be the prophesy that I would leave? I remembered how on the ride to the Sejilmi fort I had promised myself that if we lived, one day I would take those scanty comments and enlarge them; perhaps already it was too late. . . . Memory, which Rashmana had tried to destroy, rose up, beckoning to me, overwhelming me with the thoughts of former times. Do not give up, memory said. Do not let fate do to you as it will. You are like some swimmer drawn out of his depth; you can be content to let the waves wash over you, or you can struggle on. You do not want an epitaph that is found only in wind and sand. Like those prehistoric men, leave something of worth behind.

So I forced myself to sit there, Patience on a monument, while my thoughts crisscrossed back and forth. I felt I should never reach the end of them; they nourished me like food and drink. I lived off them. And it seemed to me that time stood still; the sun never moved, the heat grew no more, no less, and, as in the Sejilmi fort, I was poised forever in the same place. But it was a gentle, graceful place. Once I had thought that the way back to paradise was lost and I would never find it. Here in my memories it found life, and so I think I found my happiness again.

There are people who are torn out of place, who live and die in worlds that are not their own, and they are the unfortunates of this earth. There are others who, despite all odds, find themselves where they belong, even if they were not born there. They are the blessed of God. That should be my epitaph. The storm that blew me here had brought me home, had given me blessings and happiness, as well as sadness, and that, too, I wished to record.

But after a while I lay down again and let the hot sand drift over me. I listened to its shift and sigh, feeling neither heat nor thirst, nor fear. Simply, like a child, I pillowed my head upon the cloak that Mohamed had left. Presently in my dreams I heard again the breakers' roar, receding into the distance, then surging close again, a soft sifting of water running through sand, a shushing noise such as the tide makes moving inland. In my dream I told myself that the sound existed only in my mind, the sort of sound that exhaustion brings or that thirst causes, even in the sleeping brain. I knew there was no ocean, no water, but the sound of the moving sand, that shushing sound, could not be denied. In my dream I opened my eyes. I was lying beneath the overhang of rock and below me the sand dunes crested like a sea of waves. On the far side of the divide, across the crest, filtering against the darkening sky, a figure moved. And when, wide awake now, I opened my eyes in truth, I saw the figure move again. And there was a gap, a silence, between us, that must be bridged.

CHAPTER 13

I do not know how long we stood like that, poised with an abyss between us. Who can try to estimate when seconds drag like hours, when minutes seem decades? I know I closed my eyes, fearing he was some mirage of the sun, and when I looked again he was gone. He was moving, he and his horse, floating down the steep incline, as if they scorned to touch the ground. I thought, There is only one man who rides like that, who moves like that, effortlessly urging his horse down a precipice of sand, as if it were made of foam. The huge forefeet plunged, the haunches bunched and stretched, the tracks were scored like a giant scree. The wind had already blown away the ones that Mohamed had made. I thought, It will blow these away, too; these are the first tracks in the world; this is the first horse, and this the first horseman. I thought, There is only one man who rides as if he has been in the saddle since he was born, whose father carried him in his arms to show him to his men. And he has come to find me.

I could not have stood if I had wanted to, my legs as heavy as lead, so I remained where I was, on the ground beneath the shelter of the rock ledge, my tattered cloak spread over my feet, my spilled papers covered with sand. Horse and rider had disappeared again, under the shadow of the divide between the dunes, but I could still hear the shushing sound of sand as it moved, that slithering sound, and after a while, the snorting breaths as the horse began to breast the other side, froth flying from its bit. Up it came, heaving up, its sides curdled with sweat like cream, blocking the sun, silhouetted, a black shape suspended against the sky; black horse, black rider, black cloaks. I thought, He comes as the avenger; he comes as judge; he comes to cleanse away his shame. And I shut my eyes once more.

Water was trickling down my throat, across my face, wetting my clothes. It tasted of sulfur and goat, yet was fresher than any country stream. I swallowed, swallowed again, reached for more.

"Enough," he said. He was kneeling beside me to brush the sand out of my hair and to run his fingers across my cheeks. And having convinced himself, I suppose, that I still breathed, he leaned back as if satisfied, stretched out his long legs in their leather boots, settling himself against the rock face. He did not say anything for a while, and neither did I. Our silence was not exactly sad, not exactly thoughtful; it seemed waiting to be broken. Downhill from us the horse was tethered, tossing its head, stamping its feet, and farther off, on the other side of the ridge, I began to distinguish other sounds, bridles clinking, hooves clattering, men laughing. These were all companionable, familiar sounds that I knew well. But they created a sense of unease. I thought, He comes as warlord with his men to fight for what he believes is his, to avenge defeat. I thought, He must tell me first what he thinks and feels. It is his place to speak before I do.

He was staring out above my head, his profile hidden and his dark eyes expressionless. Yet I was conscious of him beside me as I had not been of anything since he left, the length of him, from the tips of those boots to the shock of thick hair. I could feel the warmth of him, the strength, although I was shivering as if with cold. I thought, Beneath those robes is a man I have lain with, slept with, made my lover. I thought, almost without thought, His wounds have healed; the Sejilmi have not harmed him; he can still ride and fight. I thought, He can still make love. And I felt the tension rise between us, like that current without a name.

Without looking at me he said, "So, here you are, horse thief, tucked away in your little niche, keeping a record of all your thoughts, I suppose, to impress your European world." He stirred at the notebook with his foot. "You have led us a merry chase. I have been following you," he cocked his head at the sun as if calculating, "more than twenty days." His tone of voice was one I recognized, distant, teasing, almost sardonic, hiding his thoughts, just as those black scarfs and robes hid the real man. "But I have wanted to return something to you." And he dropped the little golden locket into the leather bag, letting it dangle for a moment before he pulled the thongs tight. "There," he said, just as I had imagined his uncle would say, "that is finished with."

I did not try to answer. The effort was too great and there was nothing to tell. In any case there was a dryness in my throat that seemed to prevent speech. I remember thinking that what he said did not seem to need an answer, nor did he merit one. Keep silent, I remember telling myself. Wait. Soon he will say what he means.

Those strange-colored eyes were still staring over my head, analyzing all they saw, as if taking in the distances, the emptiness. I thought, Remember, too, the pain; it weighs most of all.

He said, "Your loyal shadow, your faithful stable boy, told us where you were. We found him crawling along to spare the horse." When I still did not answer, "So perhaps I shall spare him since he may make a horseman after all, although in our land horse thieves merit punishment more than reward." And when I did not smile, he spoke more thoughtfully, as if calculating: "So how long is it since you and he left the High Tigran; how long since you and I parted there?" Now came the thrust I had been waiting for, the rapier point. "How long since you promised to wait there for me?"

I croaked at him, "Then you should have returned, not let yourself be captured."

"Ah, yes." He was reaching beneath his cloak to unstopper a small flask; he poured the liquid onto his fingers and rubbed them over my lips, so that I was obliged to swallow. The liquid burned for a moment, then became strangely cool and soothing. I felt myself begin to shake, cold as if I were on the mountaintop in the ice, although the sun was so hot that the rocks behind our backs burned like coals. "Ah, yes," he was continuing, tucking the flask back into the wide belt, "when I was made a prisoner." He might have been talking of something else, as if he had already forgotten that time, as if what he had just been doing was of no consequence. I thought, Any moment now he will tell me he would do as much for his horse. As always he is in control. He is as effortless, as graceful, as he always was. It is only I who am like a puppet whose strings are cut. I wanted to cry out, "Suppose you had not been freed? Suppose you had been killed there? Is that what you would have preferred?" But

I did not say anything. Suddenly, to my amazement, I felt tears begin to roll down my cheeks. I made no effort to wipe them away, but let them fall. It was impossible to stop them, as if they meant to turn the desert into a sea of salt. I made no attempt to explain or apologize, but all the darkness of these past days (twenty days, they could have been twenty years!), the hopelessness, the fears were in those tears. And after a while when it became clear that I was crying more, not less, he touched my cheeks again, catching at the drops with the back of his hand. "Are those for me?" he asked. "I should be flattered." I sensed a smile, that half smile he sometimes gave. "Is that how you persuaded my friends and my uncle to follow you?" But I felt the other, if unasked, question hang like a sword above my head: "Is that how you persuaded my enemy?"

Now words came gushing out in floods, all those words I had kept pent up in the silence I had maintained on my side of the precipice. "I thought you would die. I did not care what happened to me if only you would not die. Is it so shameful to be helped? You have helped people in the past; you rescued me in the mountains. Did I turn that against you? You *should* be flattered; your men risked their lives many times for you."

He laid a finger on my lips again, and now I sensed he was smiling openly. "That is better," he said. "I prefer your tongue to your tears. Now hush, so we can begin in earnest." He smoothed back my hair. "When I first met you," he said, "you talked and talked. I could not get you to stop. Your silence is worse. Listen." He made me turn my head toward the dunes. "Those are my men," he said. "They have ridden farther than I have; for every mile I made they have gone three, searching for you. My best scouts have followed every caravan, questioning them, hunting through them for clues. We never thought you would go south. I never thought you would dare the hardest route."

He said, "My men and I have scoured the desert for you. Did you think they would let you go? Did you think courage was unnoticed in our tribe? Did you think we do not appreciate loyalty?"

He unfastened his cloak and laid it on the ground just as he had done once on that mountain pass. He folded it over me, for I was shaking now as if I had a fever fit that I could not control. "Did you think I would not trust my life to you? Did you think I was silent for myself? Did it not occur to you that I was afraid for you?"

He had begun to ease my tunic over my head, drawing out each arm. The sight of all those bruises that Rashmana had inflicted, the whip marks, seemed to affect him more than words, for he tried to rub them away, tipping out the rest of the water, spilling it in his haste. He sat back on his heels, looking down at his hands, as the water trickled into a furrow in the dust. "I only wanted to keep you safe," he said, almost helplessly. "I only wanted to cherish you. I cannot bear to see you hurt." And he buried his face in his arms as if to shut out the thought.

After a while he said, almost wonderingly, "Each time I see you it is as it was at first, when you walked toward me across the square, out of the shadows into the sun. I never expected to find such a one as you. I did not even know what to expect, this 'jewel' that they kept babbling about. I did not even want to find you. There, I confess that, my dove. I knew my father's weaknesses; I had sworn to avoid the same trap myself." He had slipped the clothes low over my breasts and was looking at me intently, running his fingers lightly across my shoulders and over the rib cage, not yet touching me, as if skimming the outline, like a man who does not trust sight, and does not yet dare use touch to ensure what he sees is real. "How long is it since I have held you like this?" he asked. "Each time I do, it is fresh and new. Each time it seems I cannot wait to begin. I will tell you a secret. When I was in the Sejilmi prison deep underground, the thought of you was like a light to keep me sane. I fixed you in my thoughts in the direction where I thought the sky must be, for, suspended in that cage within a pit, I could not tell in the darkness which was up or which was down, not even able to stretch out my feet, not even able to hold up my head. At first I admit I did not want to think of you, I tried to keep you away. But you returned, a presence to be reckoned with, a force that I could feel. Sometimes I thought I heard your voice. And then I realized that without you, without that presence, without that voice, I would not want to have endured. And when I saw you there in that hellhole, it was as if I were thrust back into an even deeper pit than any the Sejilmi could invent, and I was more helpless than before. I have never felt helpless until then," he whispered. "I have never known what loss was until I saw you there that day."

He turned to look at me. There was an expression in his eyes that I had never seen either. It both frightened and exhilarated me. "When I was a child," he was telling me, urgently, trying to make me understand, "when my mother stole me away from here, in my childish way I swore that one day I would return, that when I was grown nothing would prevent me. That hope colored all my childhood and youth. And when despite the improbability it was achieved, I felt that I had conquered the world. Call it hope, belief, confidence, call it luck, that sense of infallibility had never deserted me, until I saw you; until I knew what you had done to save me."

He said, "If I touch you now, if I hold you, I shall never let you go. You will be bound to me as I am to you. You have put a brand on me that cannot be removed unless you yourself cut it off."

He let his fingers follow the track that the spilt water had made, brushing my skin, tracing out the peaks and curves, marking an outline. "Will that please you, my dove?" he asked. "Will it please you to stay with me? The women of the High Tigran ask for you. 'Bring her home,' they say. 'Bring back your mistress and marry her.' My uncle has taken men to hunt through the mountain, believing that you would be taken there. When he left, 'Tell her,' he said, 'that whichever of us finds her first begs her to live with us. I myself will ask in my own name as well as yours.' There is not one of us who does not want you to return," he told me, "myself most of all." He suddenly let out a cry, near to a groan. I had heard him cry out like that before, a sound that is forced from strong men who pride themselves on their ability to withstand pain. "Without you," he cried, "there is no life in the High Tigran."

In answer I held out my arms to him.

He did not enter me until he had touched everywhere, until his gentleness had wiped away those fouler stains, until I felt clean and whole. And then I surged upon him like a wave, I felt his seed spring into me, I felt him drown in me.

After a while he brought me down to where his men had pitched their camp, on the other side of the sand dune. They seldom came this far into the desert, and the heat had tried them hard. But they stood up when we approached, as their master carried me upon his horse as if in triumph. They never said a word. It was not their way to utter praise or lavish compliments, but they saluted us gravely with respect. I saw Rasheed there, and Mohamed, and many other friends, and they brought us to the tent that they had set up for me. They had thrown rugs upon the ground and spread out food and drink, brought water for washing and other luxuries that a war band, a *harla*, would never bother with. They showed me the gray horse and it lifted its head to nicker as Mohamed led it past. And once assured of my comfort and safety, my lord left me there. "Wait for me here, my dove," he said. "I have a task to perform."

I watched him buckle on his belt, retie his cloak, unsheathe his sword. He gave his imperious signal for his guard to mount. Well, he was of soldier stock, bred a soldier on his father's, mother's side. He could no more prevent what he was about to do than a lion sheathe its claws. It was not in me to argue with him. *A woman's place is not on a battlefield.* I did not approve; it was not my way, but it was his. I could only try to accept.

So I did not ask, have never asked, what happened when he and his men burst into the Tuareg camp like a windstorm. Did they hear him coming, did they see him like that black cloud of sand and prepare to resist? Did he take them by surprise? I never asked and never knew how long the battle was, how fierce, how cruel. Nor did I ask what had become of the woman who had brought me here, nor what happened to the other women and their slaves. Sometimes I imagined Rashmana riding with the Tuareg men, for some Berber women know how to fight. Sometimes I thought she might have been left behind when the line broke, the Tuareg being such great warriors that they abandon their camp and all their dependents when hard pressed! In time I came to hope that perhaps she had forced a break through the Tigran encirclement, perhaps mounted on one of those racing camels she had admired, and had found her way south, to that mythical Lake of the Moon where women sing to ensnare men. Perhaps she deserved to go there. For what justice could be done to her who had suffered her share of wrong? *Did you think courage unnoticed?* And what is justice anyway, in a world that fate has made so unfairly just, where happiness and love are doled out in such unequal shares?

I never knew, I never asked. *It is over and done with.* But in the evening when the men returned, I waited until the night grew cold, until the little camp fires were dimmed, until by groups of threes and fours the companions left their lord and went back to their own bivouacs, until I was sure he was alone. And then I approached his tent, set in the central place, with its standard fixed in front.

There were no women to arrange my dress or tie the many layered underskirts I should have worn, or to braid my hair with colored bands jingling with silver coins. I had no silver necklaces, heavy with turquoise and pearl, such as Rashmana had begrudged me once, nor henna to paint my hands and feet. There were no girls to throw flowers on the ground so that the bride's path should be perfumed. But when the guards who ringed the tent saw me approach they fired their rifles in the air and made an archway with their curved swords. And they smiled among themselves as they drew back the flaps.

The tent was almost as dark inside as without; nothing stirred. There was no one there except a young man, sprawled out, booted feet propped up, his head leaning on a saddle. Behind him his weapons were piled in a heap and I saw how his eyes gleamed as he rose and came toward me.

"So you have come," he said. "I hoped you might. I wondered if you might come looking for the Lord of the High Tigran," and he, too, smiled down at me. I looked about me. All was the same, all different. The inner curtains of the tent were drawn; once I had stood in front of them and wondered what mystery they hid. Perhaps he guessed what I thought. He caught me to him in his cool and sure embrace. "Are you looking for a certain man?" he asked. "What sort of man would please you best? Shall I tell you another mystery that he has only found out? He does not know who he is, or where he is, nor what he wants unless you are part of him. He is not a jealous man as men are counted jealous, nor is he unkind or cruel. Many have called him obstinate and that perhaps is justly said. But if he chose a woman and she him, he would never let her go, even if he had to chain her to his side, like a hawk, so she could not fly from him. He would love her to the end, and love only her. If she felt the same way, that is."

I said, "Why should you think she would feel differently?" And I smiled at him.

I unbuttoned his high tunic front with its many elaborate fastenings. I undid the white linen shirt underneath to reveal the broad expanse of chest. With fingers that were both gentle and eager I explored the ridges of old scars, the raw edges of the newer ones, the unhealed welts where the Sejilmi whips had caught. I ran my fingers through the thick young hair springing from his head as if alive; I touched the long eyelashes that lay on the cheekbones like threads of black. I touched the lips that were soft beneath the unshaven beard, traced the chin and the strong neck. And I watched him watching me as he undid the sword belt with hands that trembled now themselves. He stood first on one foot, then the other, to kick off the boots, unbuttoned the trouser waistband with one hand whilst he held me with the other. He caught me low about the hips as I caught him; we fell together, rolled together, on the sand. It warmed our skin, soft as fine silk. For a moment he looked down at me, as I laughed up at him. "Where is my lord?" I asked. And he, thrusting, thrusting, cried, "Here."

Epilogue

In this harsh land where storytelling is still an art, as it should be, helping to soften the hardship of stark lives, giving a dimension to the desert wastes, there are many legends born from those times. One that has become a favorite tells how a lord, a prince of men, followed his lover for twenty days and nights, without stopping for food or rest, driving himself and his men to rescue her from the demon princess who had captured her. In the little firelight of a thornbush fire, its flames scarcely illuminating more than a foot or two, the storyteller pauses to spread his arms to take in all that waiting darkness beyond, to draw it in to encircle his listeners, to terrify them pleasantly with the thought of its immensity. Then depending upon the version he is following or upon the fertility of his own imagination, he will weave for them a tale full of delight and suspense, having all the ingredients that make a story of this kind: love, treachery, loyalty, self-sacrifice. One of the versions that became widespread revealed certain differences to the general theme that, as time went on, became more strange. Even at the height of the foreign invasions, which all thinking men knew must come, this version persisted in making the captured princess one of the Christians, and moreover changed the ending to suggest that she, not her prince, did the rescuing. And stranger still, this version of the story remained as popular as any of the rest, and in time gained its own following. It is even said that at those ritual gatherings of all the tribes, when for the moment hostilities are forgotten and only pleasure rules, the younger women especially like to hear this tale, and often act out its most exciting roles, sometimes embellishing them with dance and

song. To the sound of the simple stringed instruments and tambourines they sway under the clear desert skies, holding up their little
arms, their anklets clinking as they stamp their feet. Beneath them,
the warm sand grows scuffed, and underneath the palm trees, the
young men sit holding their knees and thinking of great deeds.

All this is legend, born from air, shaped and molded by the
storyteller's skill, fleshed out by dreams, not reality. This next is fact.
When the foreign armies invaded, seeking a route into that vast continent, trying to capture it, not for itself but so their rivals would not
get it first, when the Sultan of the north, another Sultan, equally
foolish, at last realized how he had been tricked, there was only one
people who had the will to resist. They came from the mountains.
High up in those inner hills from where the first Berber conquerors
had swept down to the sea, they manned their medieval fortresses
and endured. And when the time was ripe, when their alliance held
firm, they gathered their armies and swept down again. And at their
head rode brothers, sons of one lord, children of both East and West.
And they rode singing into battle as their father had.

The desert is a land of secrets, of surprises, of vastness that is
never still but, like an ocean, moves and spreads, drowning the past,
revealing the future. Men cross its surface briefly, are seen for a moment, and are gone. Somewhere in that vastness, somewhere in those
mountain ranges, the story of Isobelle lives on. As she had hoped, it
is not forgotten. Here in her journal, she tells the story in her own
way. And in the end, there is not so much difference between it and
the one to which the girls dance.